Nina Singh lives just outside Boston, USA, with her husband, children, and a very rumbustious Yorkie. After several years in the corporate world she finally followed the advice of family and friends to 'give the writing a go, already'. She's oh-so-happy she did. When not at her keyboard she likes to spend time on the tennis court or golf course. Or immersed in a good read.

Juliette Hyland believes in strong coffee, hot drinks and happily-ever-afters! She lives in Ohio, USA, with her Prince Charming, who has patiently listened to many rants regarding characters failing to follow their outline. When not working on fun and flirty happily-ever-afters, Juliette can be found spending time with her beautiful daughters and giant dogs, or sewing uneven stitches with her sewing machine.

THEIR ACCIDENTAL MARRIAGE DEAL

NINA SINGH

HOW TO TAME A KING

JULIETTE HYLAND

MILLS & BOON

First published in Great Britain 2024
by Mills & Boon, an imprint of HarperCollins*Publishers* Ltd,
1 London Bridge Street, London, SE1 9GF

www.harpercollins.co.uk

HarperCollins*Publishers*, Macken House, 39/40 Mayor Street Upper,
Dublin 1, D01 C9W8, Ireland

Their Accidental Marriage Deal © 2024 Nilay Nina Singh

How to Tame a King © 2024 Juliette Hyland

ISBN: 978-0-263-32131-9

05/24

This book contains FSC™ certified paper
and other controlled sources to ensure responsible forest management.

For more information visit www.harpercollins.co.uk/green.

Printed and Bound in the UK using 100% Renewable Electricity
at CPI Group (UK) Ltd, Croydon, CR0 4YY

THEIR ACCIDENTAL
MARRIAGE DEAL

NINA SINGH

MILLS & BOON

To my parents

CHAPTER ONE

HANNAH DEVINE WALKED into the pre-wedding celebration party, all the while cursing the life decisions that had brought her to this moment. This utterly, astoundingly, shatteringly humiliating moment. She had to be the only one attending these events solo. There was no doubt about it. No one else she'd gone to high school with would be pathetic enough to find themselves in such a predicament: attending the wedding of the most devoted couple in their class sans a plus-one.

The infuriating thing was she'd had a plus-one up until about a short seventy-two hours ago. Then she'd been unceremoniously dumped. By none other than the man she'd thought would be her own groom.

Ha! What a joke of an idea that was apparently.

The rooftop of the luxury Vegas resort was decorated like a tropical island. Complete with faux palm trees adorned with hanging plastic coconuts. Pictures of Max and Mandy decorated every flat surface.

She'd come this close to canceling, feigning illness or some kind of schedule conflict. But in the end, her pride had run out. After all, the reality of her broken relationship would reach the proverbial gossip vine soon enough. So she'd shown up to deliver the news herself to anyone who asked.

Hannah took a deep breath, summoned the will to pull herself out of the self-defeating thoughts. This week wasn't about her. She was here to watch Mandy and Max get married. M and M as they were called during their teen years. Reardon High's golden couple.

Honestly, it was rather surprising that the two of them waited this long before tying the knot. But maybe Hannah was naive about the realities of matrimony and love. After all, look at the state of her own romantic life.

Or lack thereof to be more accurate.

How could she have not even seen it coming? Justin had claimed she was oblivious to his moods and desires more than once. Turned out he was right. Because she'd really thought that this weekend would be her own step toward an official engagement. She'd actually thought Justin might propose given the romantic reason for this trip to Las Vegas. Instead, things had gone completely the opposite way than she'd anticipated. Rather than be swayed in any way, he'd said the idea of even attending a wedding made him realize just how unready he felt to take any such step himself.

He'd even tried to placate her with the "it's not you, it's me" garbage line. Except that wasn't very convincing. It had to be her to some degree, didn't it?

Hannah gave a brisk shake of her head and made her way toward the crowded open bar. Not as if any of those questions mattered. The simple fact was that she'd be attending this weekend's events solo. Starting with this outdoor reggae-themed party poolside at one of Las Vegas's most swanky hotel slash casinos.

She wasn't usually much of a drinker.

But she was going to need some liquid fortitude to get

through the next several hours as all the questions rained down about why she was here without her plus-one.

Though usually being a non-imbiber, she wasn't even sure where to start. What should she even order? Justin had insisted she join him as a devoted teetotaler. Alcohol was strictly off limits as far as her ex was concerned, even at special occasions. He was much too concerned about being in full control of himself at all times. Not acceptable to allow anything that would facilitate the lowering of inhibitions. Their nightly ritual consisted of Hannah brewing a small pot of tea, usually something herbal. The only times she'd allowed herself to indulge was when she'd been out with girlfriends. And then, if Justin got wind of her indulgence, he'd be sure to make his displeasure known. The following day would be spent in cold silence with hardly a word spoken between them until she'd made some kind of gesture to make amends.

Hannah gave herself a mental forehead thwack. This weekend was going to be utter torture if she insisted on rehashing the details of her now-defunct relationship.

But there was something else on her mind, or someone more accurately. Thoughts of him had been scrambling around in her brain ever since the invitation had arrived. She had no doubt that Alden would be invited to the wedding. The question was would he come?

The answer came soon enough.

She sensed him behind her before she even saw him.

Alden Hamid had a way of shifting the entire aura of an area as soon as he arrived in a space. Or maybe that was just the way she'd always reacted to him.

Funny how that hadn't changed after all these years. And now she was single… Hannah gave her head a brisk shake to knock that thought right out of her head. That line of thinking could lead nowhere good. She'd been down that road before when she was much younger and even more naive. No, where Alden Hamid was concerned, she'd do well to remember all the reasons she needed to stay clear of the man and protect her heart as far as men like him were concerned. And that man in particular.

Still, yet another wayward thought crept into her head. Had he noticed her?

Highly unlikely. Especially considering a swarm of their female former classmates had immediately rushed to his side as soon as he appeared, Hannah saw when she risked a side-eye glance his way. Not that she could blame said classmates. Even from this distance, she could see clearly that Alden hadn't lost any of his women-magnet, drop-dead gorgeous looks.

No, if anything, Alden was even better looking now. He'd grown into his features. His jaw was more chiseled. His cheekbones edgier. The man himself appeared edgier.

If she were bolder, she might have approached him as well. But she'd never been that bold.

A throaty feminine voice broke through her thoughts. "Here. You look like you could use this."

Hannah looked up to find a petite brunette holding a serving tray, offering her a frosty goblet of a sugar-rimmed drink. She took the offering with gratitude and downed a large gulp before thanking the server whose name tag said *Elise*.

"Is it that obvious?"

Elise nodded with a pleasant smile.

Hannah returned it with a sheepish one of her own. "Sorry, I haven't seen some of these people in several years. It's a bit overwhelming to be amongst all my old high school mates again."

Elise's gaze followed where Hannah's had been a moment ago.

"Friend of yours?" Elise asked, then quirked an eyebrow when Hannah didn't answer right away.

"It's…complicated," she finally offered. She wouldn't even begin to know how to explain her and Alden's relationship back when they'd both been teens. Sure, she supposed they'd been friends. But they would have never spent a moment in each other's company if Hannah's best friend hadn't been dating Alden's best buddy. The very bride and groom.

"I see. That's him then, is it?" Elise asked.

"I'm sorry?"

"He's clearly the one everyone's been curious to see again. I'd venture he was the big man on campus? The one all the cheerleaders and chess club geniuses alike swooned over?"

Hannah tapped her finger to her forehead in a mock salute. "Very perceptive of you, Elise. You are one hundred percent on the nose correct. How did you know?"

It was a rhetorical question.

He really shouldn't have come.

If the groom were anyone but Max, one of the very few people in this world who'd ever given a care for him, Alden would have steered clear of any wedding by miles and miles.

He'd only just gotten here and already the memories were swarming his brain. Memories involving one person in particular.

He'd spotted her just as she turned his way. There she

was. The girl that got away. Or, to be more accurate, the one he'd never actually had a chance with in the first place.

He and Hannah Devine had attended more than a few events with each other, had hung out together on several occasions during their teen years. But never just the two of them. And never alone. They'd simply been the couple tagging along to provide the second part of the double date. Alden had never been able to figure out if Max kept asking him to accompany him and Mandy out of a real desire to spend time in a group or because his friend had felt genuinely sorry for him. Most likely, it was the latter.

Now, here they all were. With one half of that foursome about to finally tie the knot. And the other half throwing awkward glances at each other across a rooftop bar.

Despite not having seen her as anything other than an online thumbnail on the Boston business sites, he had no trouble recognizing Hannah the instant his eyes landed on her. Not that there weren't subtle differences. Gone was the tight ponytail. She now wore her hair in loose curls that fell around her face and shoulders. Her facial features more angular and womanlike.

A feminine shriek of laughter sounded behind him, pulling him out of his thoughts. He turned to find the source of the noise approaching him, arms outstretched and flashing a wide smile.

The woman looked familiar in a distant way, enough to let him know they'd been in the same biology class back in high school. But damned if he could recall her name. Or anything else about her, for that matter.

Amy? Alison? Ariel?

Alden's mind scrambled to recall but it was no use.

Whoever she was, she embraced him in a tight bear hug as soon as she reached his side.

"How have you been?" she wanted to know once she finally let go.

Alden reflexively glanced in Hannah's direction before trying to come up with an answer. But Hannah was no longer in the same spot. Where had she gone? A sinking feeling hit in the center of his gut at the thought that she might have already left the party. Not that he'd had any intention of actually speaking with her aside from a quick hello. What would he possibly say?

Then again, he'd never really known what to say to Hannah. Some things never changed.

"Alden? You in there?" the woman in front of him asked in a light tone, yet he detected a slight hint of annoyance in her voice. He forced his attention back to her face and pulled a smile. Still had no clue who she was but he could hold a generic enough conversation without letting on. He was good at faking such things.

He'd had lots of practice.

What was this woman's name? For the life of him, the answer wasn't clicking in his brain. Plus, he had to admit, he didn't really care that much. Other than being polite, he had no interest in any of the people here. Well, aside from the bridal couple and one other.

"You don't remember me, do you?" the woman asked.

Alden was scrambling for a way to admit the truth of her words when his gaze was drawn to the person approaching from the opposite side. His brain instantly registered who it was. Hannah.

But it wasn't him she stepped up to when she reached his side.

"Alyssa Cambell. Is that you?" Hannah asked the other woman, a wide smile plastered on her face.

Huh. So that's who she was. The Reardon High Wildcats' lead cheerleader for most of their high school years. Lead cheerleader and head of the most exclusive clique. No wonder she'd been so perturbed that he hadn't remembered her. Back in school, everyone knew who Alyssa Cambell was.

Alyssa turned to face Hannah, blinking in clear confusion and irritation. She didn't seem to appreciate the intrusion.

"Hello," Alyssa answered. "And you are? I don't seem to remember you," she added without so much as a hint of apology.

"Hannah Devine. We were in the same calculus class. I tutored you before finals that year."

It was clear Alyssa wasn't listening. Her attention had moved to another focal point.

"Excuse me," she said dismissively after a few short beats. "I see someone I'd like to talk to." Without waiting for an answer, from either one of them, she turned and walked away. Leaving him and Hannah staring at each other in awkward silence.

Alden cleared his throat. "That was for my benefit, wasn't it? Did I look that uncomfortable?"

She smiled at him with a small shrug. "You did actually."

He gave her a small bow. "Well, thank you for coming so helpfully to my rescue. For the life of me, I couldn't remember who she was."

"You're probably the only one."

"I know exactly who you are, however," he blurted out without thinking. Now why had he gone and said that?

That sounded like he might have been thinking about her through the years. As if perhaps she'd been ingrained in his memory even after all this time. Like he'd scanned the business sections of websites and newspapers related to a city he hadn't even visited since moving out of Massachusetts. All to catch snippets of information without having to actually follow her on social media.

"I remember you too, Alden." she said simply. "I would ask you how you've been but there's really no need."

"Oh, yeah? Why's that?"

She ducked her head somewhat sheepishly. "I've been seeing your name here and there. One success after another. Taking the hospitality world by storm."

Huh. Maybe he hadn't been the only one mining for information. Did that mean she was impressed? Or was she just being polite? Probably the latter.

"The papers and websites often exaggerate."

"Funny, I don't recall you being particularly modest back in school."

He had to laugh at that. Little did she know, Alden's confidence back in school had all been a front. A disguise.

Hannah held her hands up in front of his face, forming a square bracket with her fingers.

"What are you doing?"

She shrugged. "Trying to measure your head. Making sure it hasn't grown too big given all your business successes the past year."

Her teasing elicited yet another chuckle. Wait. Was he actually beginning to enjoy himself? Very unexpected. Especially considering the last forty-eight hours and how much he'd been dreading this whole affair.

"So tell me what you've been up to. Still good at calculus?" he asked her.

Hannah didn't get a chance to answer as a noisy commotion drew their attention. A roar of cheers and whistles erupted in the air. It appeared the bride and groom had arrived and were being met with enthusiastic applause.

Hannah turned in the couple's direction and he took the opportunity to study her. Not much had changed. She was still drop-dead gorgeous in an understated way. Thick wavy dark hair that fell in waves around her shoulders. A slanted nose above full ruby red lips that she hadn't bothered to adorn with lipstick or gloss. And those eyes. The woman had the most striking eyes. Even more striking now that she'd grown into her features.

Those thumbnails hadn't done her justice.

Hannah was one of those women who didn't necessarily draw a lot of attention. Until one took the time to have a really good look at her.

Alden had no doubt she didn't know just how pretty she was, and never had. But Hannah Devine was one of the most attractive girls to graduate from Reardon High.

He'd always thought so, anyway. And still did.

What in the world had she been thinking? Breaking into Alden and Alyssa's conversation that way? The truth was she hadn't been thinking at all. The drink must have gone to her head. She really should have built up a tolerance before coming to a boozy wedding in a city that was considered to be one of the party capitals of the world.

Alden had just looked so uncomfortable, as if he were looking for a way out of the conversation. She'd simply been helping an old friend out of what was clearly an awkward situation. Only now the awkwardness had shifted to sit between the two of them instead.

Her mind reeled to various flashbacks of the two of them all those years ago, how awkward the air between them would feel during those short stints when they'd found themselves alone together. Yet another thing that hadn't changed much over the years. Alden and Hannah had never quite known how to fill the silence whenever it was just the two of them alone.

Hannah sighed and took another sip of her drink, much smaller this time. At the least, she had to slow it down a bit. If she were being honest with herself, she'd have to admit another truth. That something about seeing him with Alyssa had set off a squirmy sensation in her middle. The other woman was as beautiful as she'd been in high school.

But now, here Hannah was, standing there trying to come up with something to say.

Alden pointed to the glass in her hand. "You're running low. Can I get you another?" he asked.

That was the last thing she needed. But the little devilish Hannah that sometimes appeared on her shoulder popped up to whisper loudly in her ear. *What's the point? May as well enjoy yourself. If you can't let loose at a good friend's wedding, after being dumped by your almost-fiancé, what better time?*

Good question.

"Sure, why not," she answered, defiantly tossing back the remaining liquid in her glass.

Alden left her side and returned within minutes with a fresh drink for her and a sweaty bottle of beer for himself. He handed her the glass, then clinked his bottle to hers in a salute.

"To old friends."

"Here, here," Hannah answered taking another small sip. Was it her imagination, or was this cocktail even stronger than the last? Maybe she should have started out with beer like Alden. Or wine. She glanced at him as he drew a deep gulp from his bottle.

Upon closer inspection, she saw he hadn't really changed all that much. Except somehow he was even more handsome than the athletic muscular boy she'd sometimes hung out with before graduation. The years had added a ruggedness to his good looks. His hair appeared darker, curlier than it had been when they'd been younger. Alden Hamid was an intriguing combination of Middle Eastern dark features with tanned olive skin and dark hair, offset by bluish-gray eyes and nearly blond lashes. Features he'd inherited from his father and mother respectively.

Had he brought a date? Maybe he was here with a girlfriend who was powdering her nose at the moment. If the gossip sites were to be believed, he wasn't often lacking female companionship. The truth was she'd done more than her fair share of googling his name over the years. Not that she'd ever admit it to anyone, least of all to the man himself. Though it had been a while. She'd resisted the urge for the past few months. Now she wished she knew a bit more, particularly about his romantic life. Though it really was none of her business.

"Are you here with someone?" she shocked herself by blurting out and asking. Of all the things to say. Not to mention it was probably a stupid question. Even if he was here at the wedding alone, chances were good he was involved with someone. How could someone like him not be? Successful, handsome, well-known. A catch by any and all definitions.

If Alden were at all surprised by such a direct question, he didn't show it. Simply taking another swig from his bottle, he shook his head. "No. Here by myself."

Well, that hardly told her anything. Was he seeing someone but she couldn't make it here? Was he in between girlfriends? What was the story?

Why in the world was she entertaining such thoughts, anyway? She'd only had her heart broken a mere three days ago. She had no business wondering about her former crush's romantic life.

"What about you?" he asked a moment later.

To her shock, a well of hurt erupted within her chest. So overwhelming that she couldn't find her voice enough to answer. Damn Justin. She wasn't supposed to be here alone. She was to have arrived with the man she'd planned to spend the rest of her life with. She was supposed to have been part of a paired couple, like so many of the other attendees milling about this party.

Her silence was apparently answer enough.

"Wanna talk about it?" Alden asked.

She shrugged. "Not much to say. I find myself unexpectedly at a crossroads."

Alden blew out a breath, ending on a low whistle. "Wow. That's pretty heavy."

He gently took her by the elbow and turned in the direction of the elevator. "Here, follow me."

"But what about Max and Mandy?"

"We'll get a chance to say hello to them later. They're busy with other guests, anyway."

Two minutes later, they'd exited the elevator on the lobby level of the hotel.

"Where are we going?"

"Just away for a bit."

"Away?"

He nodded, leading her past a towering marble statue in the center of the lobby to the revolving glass doors at the entrance.

"I don't know about you, but I'm not exactly in a social mood. Sounded like you maybe could also use a break from being around all those people too."

His words gave her pause for their accuracy. How had he managed to read her so well after only seeing her for the briefest of moments? She must not have hidden her emotions that effectively. Just as well Alden had swept her away out of the party, then. The last thing she wanted to do was bring down what was supposed to be a festive celebration of two people getting married.

But now she was outside alone with him. Just the two of them.

Knowing full well it was a bad idea, she took a rather large gulp of her cocktail for some more liquid courage as she followed him toward the large fountain in the center of the courtyard. Only fountain wasn't quite an accurate way to describe the structure. Several torrents of water shot straight up into the sky, each one as tall as the building itself. A subtle mist kissed the surface of her face.

"So, you're at a crossroads, huh?" Alden asked after taking another swallow of his beer.

"It's a long story," she lied. It wasn't really. And a fairly classic one at that. She'd misread her romantic relationship in a colossal fashion. And now she was attending a wedding solo. A wedding that may as well have been a high school reunion.

"Your turn now. Tell me why you wanted to leave the party," she said, sitting down on the stone barrier around the artificial pond of water.

He rubbed his forehead, resting one foot on the concrete and taking another swig of beer.

"I'm beyond tired. Had to travel here all night from the Aegean coast—the jet lag is starting to catch up to me. And I haven't slept a wink for over forty-eight hours. Not to mention, I'm beyond frustrated."

"Why's that?"

"A business deal that's not exactly falling into place no matter how hard I try. If the couple getting married weren't Max and Mandy, I wouldn't have even bothered to show."

Hannah released an uncharacteristic giggle at his words. Funny, Alden was echoing her own exact thoughts about attending this wedding.

He leaned toward her, smiling. His aftershave mingled with the moisture in the air and tickled her nose, a more mature scent than the drugstore variety he used to wear back when they were kids. No doubt several times more expensive. "What's so funny?"

Another giggle escaped her lips before she answered. "I had the same exact thoughts on my way over here."

He lifted his bottle in another toast. "Well, now that we're both here, I say we make the most of it and have ourselves a good time. How are you at blackjack?"

Ninety minutes later, the answer to that question was abundantly clear. Hannah was absolutely lousy at blackjack. So much so that Alden made her leave the table before she lost any more money.

"So now what?" Hannah asked, as a server delivered yet another drink. Had she just slurred her words? She had to slow down on the cocktails. Even as she thought it, she took a large sip.

"Let's get some air," Alden said, gently leading her by the elbow out of the casino.

She had no idea what time it was. But Vegas was still completely awake and fully lit. If anything, the street appeared even more crowded than when they'd first entered the casino.

Alden led her to a nearby bench and sat her down, then rested his foot next to her thigh, draping his forearm over his bent knee.

"You are really bad at card games, Miss Devine," he teased.

Hannah shrugged. The world was slightly off-balance. She should probably find a way to get a cup of coffee. One thing was certain—she was absolutely done drinking for the night. Maybe for the entire month.

"I've never really played before," she explained in her defense. Actually, she'd never really gambled before, unless one counted the occasional lottery ticket. "And certainly not in a casino in Las Vegas," she added, then wondered aloud, "Why did Max and Mandy decide to get married here again?"

"Something about a central location convenient to most of the guests traveling for the wedding," Alden answered.

That made sense. "They're finally doing it, finally tying the knot. After all these years."

Alden nodded, an indulgent smile on his lips. "Looks like it."

A feminine shriek of laughter pierced the air as a giggling couple walked past. Before they'd gone more than a few feet past the bench, the man turned around with a wide grin. "Congratulate us," he yelled over to Hannah and Alden. "We just got married!"

Hannah watched as he picked the woman up and

twirled her around. "Huh. Looks like everyone's getting married."

Alden tilted his head. "Easy to do in this city."

"I thought I'd be getting married soon too," Hannah blurted out, then realized she didn't really want to talk about Justin at the moment. She didn't even want to think about him.

"Come again?"

She ignored the question as yet another high school memory surfaced in her head. "Hey, remember that silly secret ballot that was going around our senior year?"

Alden simply gave her a puzzled look. She went on, "You know, where you had to choose who you would marry if you found yourself single at the ripe old age of twenty-five? If the other person was single too, of course." The memory made her chuckle. "Can you believe we thought twenty-five was old, back then?"

Alden returned her laugh. "Yeah, now I remember. Trisha Sayton was asking everybody."

Hannah leaned closer to him, hardly believing what she was about to admit. "I have a confession to make," she said in a low voice.

"What's that?"

"I picked you."

Alden didn't so much as move, just stared deeply into her eyes. "What a coincidence," he said finally, his voice low and gravelly. For several moments, Hannah simply let the words sink in. He couldn't mean what she thought he might mean. Maybe she hadn't heard him right. She did feel rather off-center at the moment.

"Huh?" she said, by way of asking for clarification.

"I picked you."

Hannah felt her mouth drop. "You did?"

He tapped her nose playfully. "Is that so hard to believe?"

He had no idea. She might never believe it. But why would he lie?

"Wouldn't it be funny if…" Alden didn't finish his sentence. But she could guess what he'd been about to say. As ridiculous as it was.

"That *would* be pretty funny," she agreed.

"Hilarious."

"We're both way past the age of twenty-five," she declared.

"And we're both still single."

"True. And we did make a pledge. Trisha Sayton made us sign our names and everything."

"A binding contract, I'd say."

Hannah shook her head in agreement. "A contract is a contract."

CHAPTER TWO

ALDEN DID HIS best to try and open his eyes but his lids didn't seem to want to budge. An achy pounding drummed at the crown of his head. His tongue felt like he'd been dining on desert sand. The sound ringing in his ears could best be described as combination screech and jackhammer.

Something was clearly wrong. Terribly, horribly wrong.

Yet, somehow it also felt beautifully right.

Because in addition to all those unpleasant sensations assaulting his senses at the moment, there was also a much lovelier one. A warmth curling against his side, the scent of roses hovering delicately in the air.

Roses. Hannah always smelled like a fresh bouquet of summer blooms.

His eyes finally flew open as a bolt of alarm shot through his gut. He'd dreamed he and Hannah were lying on the king-sized bed in the suite he'd checked into earlier this afternoon. They were both clad in nothing but their undergarments. The curse he bit out might have caused his former football teammates to blush. Sure enough, the warm, soft, nearly naked body snuggled up next to him in bed was none other than Hannah Devine herself. He repeated the curse word more loudly before he could stop himself.

What in the world had they done?

What happened next appeared to be transpiring in slow motion. Hannah opened her eyes, then turned to face him. The she bolted upright, clocking his chin with her scalp in the process and adding a fresh new layer of agony to his suffering.

"Oh, my God!"

Alden rubbed his chin, tried to take a calming breath. The layer of new stubble along his skin told him it was indeed morning. So that would mean they'd spent the night together. One way or another.

Hannah gasped, scrambled to a sitting position as she looked about the room. "Where am I? And what—" She didn't finish, threw her hand against her mouth instead. "I'm going to be sick."

He could only watch as she fled to the bathroom.

Alden did his best to drown out the noises coming from behind the bathroom door. The ringing in his ears helped the effort. When she finally emerged, she looked about as green as he felt.

But his stomach sunk further when he caught sight of her expression. Beyond appearing physically unwell, Hannah looked shaken. Wide-eyed, mouth agape, she'd gone pale.

Alarm bells joined the screeching in his ears. Besides waking up next to him in his hotel suite, which, admittedly was rather unsettling given the circumstances, what could possibly have her so frenzied?

The answer to that question became clear when she lifted a shaky hand and approached him slowly from across the room. There, sparkling brightly in a ray of sun shining from the glass wall overlooking the Vegas skyline, sat a fat diamond on her ring finger.

"Alden?" Her voice came out in a shaky whisper so low he almost didn't hear her.

They were in Vegas, the elopement capital of the world. They'd spent the night together. And Hannah was sporting a diamond on her ring finger. One hell of a puzzle to piece together.

"All right. Let's not panic. I'm sure there's a logical and sensible explanation." He wasn't sure of any such thing but he was grasping at straws here.

"What happened last night?" Hannah wanted to know.

Then he remembered, the images flooding his mind. The two of them laughing as he kept adding game chips to her pile each time she lost at the blackjack table. The servers at the casino coming by time and time again with the complimentary drinks. He flinched at the last picture that popped into his mind. Him carrying her out of a brightly lit jewelry store and through the pastel-painted doorway of a small house next door. A house that looked suspiciously like it might be a twenty-four-hour chapel.

Hannah began to pace from one end of the bed to the other. Even now, with all that was happening, he couldn't help but appreciate the way she looked in her sensible tankini-style bra and matching silky boy shorts. The ensemble was more modest than many of the bathing suits he saw aboard a yacht or on the beach, but the way she filled it out had his mind traveling places it had no business going considering their current predicament.

Focus.

The pieces falling into place in his head were beginning to form a picture that had only one logical answer to Hannah's question. She had to be reaching the same conclusion. Hannah had always been a bright girl.

"Let's hope and pray we didn't actually go through

with it," he said, rising up off the mattress and onto legs that were less than steady.

Even as he spoke the words, his eye caught a piece of paper lying on the floor near his discarded shirt and pants. An official-looking document that looked suspiciously like a marriage certificate. Alden couldn't suppress his groan. Served him right for doing anything but getting some much-needed sleep after the week he'd had. Looked like jet lag, lack of sleep, and foolish quantities of alcohol made for a treacherous combination in the city of sin.

Hannah followed his gaze, dread flooding her features.

"We have to do something, Alden. This is a horrible mistake."

"Right. Of course," he answered. But all he wanted to do right now was swallow gallons of water and several anti-inflammatory tablets.

"We have to go back to that chapel. See if they can undo…" She lifted a shaky finger, pointing to the signed piece of paper on the ground that he could clearly read now that said *Certificate of Marriage*.

Hannah continued, "Or we have to find a legal office. See about some kind of annulment."

Before Alden could respond, the smartwatch on his wrist dinged with a notification. Absentmindedly, he glanced down at the message, then swore yet again.

"What is it?" Hannah demanded to know. "What else could there possibly be?"

Alden rubbed a palm down his face in frustration. Turned out there was indeed more.

She was married. To Alden Hamid, no less.

So not the way she'd anticipated her nuptials to go. She'd come to this wedding against her better judgment and had somehow gotten hitched before the actual bridal couple had.

How in the world could she have let this happen?

How could either of them not have had the good sense to stop it before the cataclysmic result that had resulted in them now becoming man and wife?

One theory was fairly obvious. She'd always been attracted to Alden. And the man he was now had sent all sorts of hormonal longings that she'd long thought dormant kicking into overdrive.

Stealing another glance at him, it was no wonder. Even under the dire circumstances, it was hard not to stare at the sheer image of male beauty that was Alden. Toned chest and arms. He wore his boxer briefs like the models on one of those billboards above the buildings in Boston's fashion district.

Enough of that. Those kinds of thoughts were the last thing she needed.

Or another theory might be more plausible. That her wounded feminine pride had been eager to make some kind of recovery after being so unceremoniously dumped.

Maybe all the above. Adding alcohol to that mix had been fuel on the proverbial fire.

Alden's watch pinged again before he'd been able to explain what the first message had been about.

She pointed at his wrist "What's going on?"

He gave her a steady stare, his eyes darkening with sympathy. "Hate to be the bearer of more bad news but we don't really have time to try and unravel this mess at the moment."

Hannah swallowed past the hard lump in her throat. "Why is that?"

"My calendar app and several messages from my best

friend, who happens to be the groom, are reminding me that I'm expected at a brunch for close friends and family of the bride and groom. Of course, you would be expected there too."

Hannah groaned out loud. She'd totally forgotten all about the brunch. Heck, she'd pretty much forgotten what day it was. Friday. The wedding was tomorrow. Which meant today was filled with events and get-togethers. Starting with an elaborate brunch for the bridal party and other special guests. "How much time do we have?"

His lips thinned. "Barely more than an hour."

Oh, no. This was a disaster. Every last part of it. "That hardly gives me enough time to shower and brush and throw a decent outfit on."

Hannah sucked in a deep breath. Where was her dress? She couldn't very well traipse through this hotel wearing nothing but her bra and panties.

Oh, God.

She was still cavorting around in her bra and panties. In front of Alden. She had to get dressed ASAP. Then she had to get back to her own room. Now that she was thinking about it, she wasn't even sure where her own room was. This hotel was a massive hotel/casino/convention center.

First things first. Where had she thrown her dress? Or maybe Alden had taken it off her. That thought had heat rushing to her cheeks. She had woken up in his suite, on his mattress, curled up against his side.

All that alluded to a possibility she'd been avoiding speculating on. Had they…?

Hannah gave her head a brisk shake. She couldn't deal with that question just now, as pressing as it was. She simply didn't have the time nor the mental bandwidth.

"I have to find my dress."

He finished throwing on a pair of gray sweatpants and glanced around the room. "It's gotta be here somewhere."

Hannah had to resist the urge to ask him to put a shirt on. Or the temptation to heed that shoulder devil again might be strong enough to have her pulling him back onto the bed.

Luckily, Alden distracted her from that train of thought by locating her dress. It had been hiding in plain sight below the glass coffee table. How had she missed it?

She thanked him and quickly threw it on.

"You're welcome," he answered.

Hannah rammed a hand through her curls, her heart hammering in her chest. Between her physical discomfort and the shock flooding her system, she was sorely tempted to just crawl back into bed and forget any of this was even happening. To be oblivious again to reality, as she'd been just a few minutes earlier. When she'd been snuggled close and warm in Alden's arms.

She bit out a curse under her breath.

"What's that?" Alden asked.

Hannah gave her head a shake. "Nothing. I was just thinking that we absolutely can't mention any of this to Max and Mandy. Or to anyone else, for that matter."

Alden nodded once. "Agreed. This weekend should be all about the two of them."

"Agreed," she repeated, with a nod of her own.

Several moments passed in awkward silence. Finally, Alden cleared his throat. "As far as getting ready goes, I don't have to do much. I'll help you. Whatever you need."

"I might need to take you up on that. Thank you," she said, and meant it with her whole heart. He could probably start with helping her uncover the mystery of exactly where her room was and how she might be able to get into it, considering there was no room key in sight.

He shrugged and smiled at her with a playful wink. For a split second, the sheer beauty that was Alden Hamid served to take her breath away and she could easily see why in an altered, uninhibited state of mind she would have pledged to marry him with eager enthusiasm.

"You're welcome," he answered. "It's what any decent husband would do."

Too soon. He really shouldn't have said what he had about being her husband. Alden cringed inwardly as he glanced about the banquet hall where the brunch was to be held. Not like the word meant anything in this case. They weren't really married. That certificate was nothing more than a piece of paper obtained during a drunken, reckless night when their nostalgia for the past had overcome their good sense. It never would have happened if he'd been his usual disciplined self. If he'd gotten any kind of sleep over the past two days.

No wonder Hannah's eyes had widened and she'd somehow gone a shade paler as the word had left his mouth.

He scanned the room once more. No sign of her still. Not surprising. By the time they'd located her purse— somehow it had ended up behind the heavy curtain in the main sitting room of his suite—and hence her key card, then made their way to her room on the other side of the hotel, she barely had half an hour to get ready.

Maybe he should go check on her. But before the thought had fully formed in his brain, he watched as she rushed in through the double doors of the main entrance.

His breath caught when he saw her. The woman sure

could clean up well. And she'd done so in an impressively short amount of time.

Even from where he stood at a distance across the hall, she was downright striking. She wore some kind of flowing, breezy, silky number in navy that brought out the amber highlights in her dark hair, which was done up atop her crown with a few tendrils escaping along the sides of her face. Her face looked fresh and flushed, and gone were the streaks of dark mascara from this morning. As if the messy morning they'd awoken to had never even happened.

His wife.

The word popped into his head without warning. He dismissed it with haste. He had no real right to call her that. There was no meaning behind it in their case. Again, he hadn't been himself last night. He was bitter and tired and angry about this damn deal that was causing him much more of a headache than anticipated. And Hannah had gotten caught up in his mess.

He really should apologize. He should do it now.

She was still scrambling around, trying to figure out where to sit. He began making his way over to her but didn't get very far. A noisy ruckus erupted from the settee area. The sound of a microphone being turned on rang through the air before a loud voice began speaking.

"If everyone could take their seats, the bride and groom have arrived."

Alden glanced down at the place card he'd picked up at the doorway with his name on it. Table number thirteen. Not his lucky number, it turned out. Because he happened to be standing next to table eleven. And he could see Hannah pulling out a chair across the room. Or rather, a tall gentleman with a wide smile wearing a tan shirt was pulling it out for her. A wave of frustration surged through him when the same man pulled out the chair next to her and sat down.

"Alden, it looks like you're sitting here next to me," a soft feminine voice sounded behind him.

He didn't have to turn around to recognize the owner. Alyssa Cambell. That confirmed it. Nope. Luck definitely was not on his side at the moment.

With a resigned sigh, he forced a smile on his face and turned toward his assigned table. Alyssa patted the seat of the chair next to her as he pulled it out.

"I'm glad it worked out this way," she said as soon as he sat down. "We didn't get a chance to chat at all yesterday before we were interrupted." The last word dripped with disdain.

Alyssa had no idea how grateful he'd been for that interruption at the time. Nor how much he wished for the same respite to come his way right at the moment. He stole a glance at the source of that interruption. Hannah had her head back, her hand to her throat in the middle of a hearty laugh. Whatever tall tan-shirt dude had just told her had apparently been hilarious.

Alden felt the muscles around his stomach clench tight. It should be him sitting there next to her. Alden should be the one making her laugh so delightfully with such abandon. He was her hus— He cut off the thought before he could complete it.

"Is everything all right?" he heard Alyssa ask next to him and forced his eyes back on her.

"Of course. Everything's great. Why do you ask?"

"Because you look like you just saw someone steal your car or something." She clasped at her chest with fingers spread. "I had that happen to me last year, you know. What. A. Nightmare."

What the devil was she talking about?

Alden listened with half an ear as she recounted the ordeal of the time she left the Lucky Lady boutique last year only to find her Mercedes gone. With her arms full of shopping bags, no less.

"I got divorced last year, you know," Alyssa suddenly declared. No longer skirting around the subject apparently.

Ironic. He'd just gotten married last night.

"What's so funny?" Alyssa asked.

Damn it. He hadn't realized he'd actually laughed out loud.

"Oh, nothing," he quickly told her. "Just wondering where the food is."

That was true enough. To add to his other mistakes last night, he couldn't recall taking the time to eat anything. Hannah had to be ravenous too.

Enough.

He had to stop thinking about her. Hannah Devine was out of his league. She always had been. That's why he'd never worked up the courage to ask her out back in high school. Hannah was furiously smart, raised by a single mother who would have done anything for her. Unlike Alden who'd grown up in a broken family that had eventually completely shattered. Hannah deserved the kind of loyalty and stability she'd grown up with. Alden knew he wasn't the kind of man who could give her those things in life.

The sooner they got this sham of a marriage dissolved, the better. His mind was just messing with him. Taunting him that the girl he'd gone to high school with, who'd accompanied him to various school events simply because they'd been friends with two other people who were a couple, had just happened to become his wife last night.

Well, he'd have to fix that. As soon as this brunch was over, he'd go get Hannah and they'd find the nearest legal office.

Then it would all be over.

CHAPTER THREE

THE MORE SHE sobered up, the more horrified Hannah felt.

To think, she was sitting here, trying to make small talk with this stranger when she'd gotten married to Alden last night.

She was doing her best to pay attention to what the man seated next to her was saying, he was certainly a talker. Hannah was making sure to laugh at all the appropriate times, nod when it seemed needed. But it wasn't easy. She couldn't seem to shake thoughts of Alden or what had happened between them last night.

In her haste to get ready and make it to brunch on time, she'd almost forgotten to take the wedding ring off. Now she was hyperaware of it sitting in a small pocket of her clutch purse. It had to have cost a pretty penny. What if she lost it? She had to remember to give it back to Alden at the soonest possible moment.

What lousy timing this brunch was. She and Alden desperately needed to talk. Even more importantly, they needed to see about fixing the mess they were both in. Instead, she was sitting here listening to one of Max's golf buddies droning on and on about the importance of investing in a high-quality putter.

Where was Alden, anyway?

Why hadn't he so much as tried to contact her since they'd left each other earlier? Granted, it hadn't been that long ago. But one would think... Actually, she didn't know what to think. What was the proper protocol when you woke up married to someone you hadn't even seen in person since high school?

She had no right to judge him.

That gracious feeling fled when she finally spotted him across the room. Next to Alyssa Cambell, who was sitting fully turned in his direction, her palm resting on his forearm. A spike of annoyance shot through her chest, one she refused to acknowledge as some sort of jealousy.

Because that would make no sense. It wasn't like Alden was really her husband. Well, on paper he was, but only legally. Which sounded ridiculous when one thought about it.

She stole another glance in his direction. He appeared to be hanging on Alyssa's every word. He had a dark suit jacket hung on the back of his chair. The deep burgundy-colored shirt he wore fit him like a glove, unbuttoned at the collar with the sleeves rolled down midway to his elbows. Even from here, she could see the toned, muscular definition of his shoulders and arms. Or maybe she was just remembering. After all, those arms had been around her all night. A muscle jumped somewhere in the vicinity of her chest.

And that was enough of that kind of thought.

Her irritation only grew with each course. By the time dessert was served Hannah had to remind herself to unclench her jaw. Every time she looked up, Alyssa's chair had somehow gotten even closer to Alden's. The woman was going to end up on his lap at this rate.

She stabbed at the chocolate cake that a server set in front of her and shoved a full forkful in her mouth.

"Like chocolate, huh?" the golfer asked. What was his name? Brett? Brad? She hadn't really been paying attention. How could Alden be enjoying himself? Had he forgotten their foolish circumstances? He should be stressing the same way she was.

Brett/Brad interrupted her thoughts. "Would you like mine?" he asked, pushing his plate of cake over to her on the table.

Hannah glanced down to realize with some surprise that she'd devoured her entire dessert. More the pity, she couldn't recall even tasting it. She could blame Alden for that too. He'd ruined her enjoyment of a perfectly good confection. It was at that moment she looked his way again only to find him staring right back at her. Was it her imagination or did he look equally as perturbed as she felt?

Brett/Brad began to speak again. "So, you went to school with Max and Mandy?"

"That's right," she answered absentmindedly, not tearing her gaze away from Alden's. He finally looked away first when Alyssa pulled her phone up to show him something on the screen.

With the meal finally over, Hannah pushed back her chair. "Guess it's time to mingle," she told Brett/Brad with a wide smile. "It was nice to meet you," she added, then stood and bolted before she learned any more about golf.

"Yeah, you too," he replied after a startled pause, but Hannah was already walking away. He'd seemed nice enough. But she had enough on her hands thanks to those of the male persuasion. Between the almost fiancé who'd dumped her, and the guy she'd ended up hitched to, her proverbial plate was full. The last thing she needed was to entertain some kind of flirtation with yet a third.

That little devil from before reappeared on her shoulder. The little cretin had the nerve to laugh at her! Right. *That's why you're rushing off to Alden's side.*

As annoying as it was, the words gave her pause. She couldn't very well interrupt Alyssa and Alden's conversation yet again. Once could be overlooked. If Hannah did it again, it might look like the start of a pattern. Alyssa was the type to call her on it too. How would she answer? It wasn't as if she could explain that she needed Alden to accompany her to their quickie divorce.

So now she was standing in the middle of the banquet hall just hovering. The ladies' room. She could go freshen up and buy herself some time. Hopefully, Alden would have extricated himself from Alyssa's possessive grip by the time she was done. And she could certainly use a little freshening.

When she stepped out of the ladies' lounge moments later, Alden was waiting for her in the hallway.

"Here." He extended a sweaty glass in her direction. "I brought you this."

Hannah immediately shook her head. "Did you really bring me a drink?"

"It's just mineral water. Figured you could still use the hydrating. I sure as hell do."

"In that case, thank you." She took the offering and indulged in several deep gulps. Alden was right. After their bingeing last night, Hannah didn't think she'd ever feel quenched again in her lifetime.

She wiped her mouth with the back of her hand. "Are

you ready to get out of here and take care of what we need to take care of?"

He stepped to the side and motioned for her to lead the way. "After you."

They didn't get far before they were stopped in their tracks.

"I've been looking everywhere for you!" Mandy seemed to appear out of nowhere in front of them to pull Hannah by the shoulders into a tight bear hug. When she finally let go, she poked Alden in the chest with a manicured finger. "And Max keeps asking where you might be."

Max materialized then as unexpectedly as his wife-to-be had a moment ago. What kind of couple's sorcery was this? His and Hannah's path out of the banquet hall had seemed clear only a moment ago. Or maybe they'd just been distracted.

"I sure have," Max agreed. "You've been AWOL, bro," he said, cuffing Alden on the shoulder.

Mandy's eyes narrowed as she looked from Alden to Hannah, then back and forth once more. "And now we find you here together. Imagine that," she added, suspicion laced in her voice.

Her groom nodded along in agreement.

"You left the party last night before we got a chance to talk. You both did."

Hannah clasped her hands in front of her chest. "I'm really sorry about that, Mandy. I was just so tired after flying out here. And besides, you looked pretty busy with the other guests. I didn't want to add to the frenzy."

"Hmm," was all Mandy replied with, before adding, "Well, here you both are finally. Together." She emphasized the last word again, another flash of suspicion behind her eyes.

She was onto them.

"We were catching up," Alden supplied. "I haven't seen Hannah in a while. And we were about to come find you."

That was a lie.

It dawned on Alden how remiss he and Hannah had been. Of course, Max and Mandy would miss them. Between the party last night and rushing out of the banquet today, that type of behavior would be certain to raise a fair amount of curiosity from their hosts. In Alden and Hannah's defense, they'd had some pressing matters to contend with and other things on their minds.

Mandy grasped Hannah by the hand. "Well, now that you two have caught up with each other, it's our turn."

Hannah's smile faltered. "Of course. I'd love that. I know I've said it before, but I'm so happy for the two of you."

"Thanks, Hannah," Mandy said, then punched her groom on the arm playfully. "Took long enough for this big lug to finally propose."

Max shrugged. "Just trying to preserve my bachelor days a little longer. We can't all be players with the ladies like my Alden here."

Was it his imagination or did Hannah let out an almost silent huff at those words? Wishful thinking, most likely. Though why he would wish such a thing made no sense.

Mandy stepped closer to Hannah, laid her hand on her arm. "I heard about your breakup. How are you doin', hon?"

Hannah's mouth tightened. "Fine. I'm just fine."

Mandy gave Hannah's arm a motherly pat. "Forget about that idiot. He doesn't know what he had and gave up."

Alden's thoughts echoed with a muffled memory of him uttering those very same words to Hannah sometime last night. Right before he proved them to her by proposing to her himself.

Mandy continued, "Your time to walk down the aisle is right around the corner too, Hannah. I just know it."

Alden could feel Hannah's slight cringe next to him while he groaned inwardly. If Max and Mandy only knew.

"Thanks, Mandy," Hannah replied with a gracious smile. "But I really am doing fine. And Justin and I are officially over. For good," she added with emphasis.

The rush of satisfaction Alden felt at those words shouldn't have been as strong as it was.

Mandy pulled Hannah closer. "What you need is a day of pampering. My sisters and I have full massages and facials scheduled in about half an hour."

Mandy's bridesmaids were her three sisters. As Max's groomsmen were his three brothers.

"You absolutely have to join us, Hannah," Mandy said.

Hannah immediately began to argue but she was promptly shut down. "I won't take no for an answer."

Hannah glanced at Alden, her eyes wild. If she was looking for a solution from his direction, he didn't have one for her. "Um—"

Mandy cut her off again. "Look, if you're worried about imposing, that makes no sense. You know I would have included you in the bridal party if Max and I hadn't decided to go with a small one with family only."

"Oh, that's not..." Hannah trailed off.

"Same goes for me, bro," Max added. "You'd have absolutely been one of the groomsmen. Without question."

Alden knew the truth of that without a doubt. He'd harbored no hard feelings about not being included in the bridal party. He understood. Not that he knew from personal experience, but he imagined weddings were hard enough to plan without worrying about offending friends. So many major and minor decisions to make. Unless, of course, the couple eloped in a drunken and sleepless stupor after gambling the night away.

"Their spa excursion works for us too, bud," Max was saying.

"Yeah?"

Max nodded. "My brothers and I have a full eighteen-hole round of golf scheduled. But Tom's gout is acting up. All these fancy buffets aren't helping. You can round out the fourth spot."

Alden cast what he hoped was an imperceptible glance at Hannah. Her eyes conveyed a clear message that said, *What choice do we have?*

She was right. They really didn't have a choice. Turning either offer down wasn't an option. They couldn't very well explain why they had alternate plans for the rest of the day. Not without admitting they'd gotten married. To each other.

"Sounds great," Alden answered the other man with resignation. "Give me a chance to change and I'll meet you in the lobby."

Looked like their divorce or annulment—he wasn't even sure what applied in their circumstance—whichever it was, was going to have to wait.

There was salad on her face.

Hannah twitched her nose and maneuvered her cheek muscles until the slices of cucumbers on her eyes fell back into place after slipping when she'd just sneezed.

The seaweed wrapped along her jawline up to her fore-head smelled of ocean and lime.

She, along with Mandy, had opted for the facial first while her friend's three sisters had gone with the massage as their first choice.

Now lying side by side in lounge chairs, Hannah was doing all she could to pay attention to the conversation at hand. She hoped her friend wasn't noticing just how distracted she was. In her defense, this was the first time she'd woken up as a married woman, then had to rush out to yet another wedding.

Mandy's next words pulled her right out of her distraction. "So, you and Alden seemed to be spending a lot of time together last night."

Hannah couldn't be sure how the other woman might have known that, so figured it was a lucky guess on her part.

"Just catching up," she answered, which was true enough.

"And you're both here solo," Mandy said, stating the obvious.

Hannah knew where her friend was going with this. She refused to take the bait. "I'm looking forward to the massage," she said, an attempt to change the subject. It didn't work.

"You know, we always thought you two would somehow end up together," Mandy said.

There it was. It hadn't taken her friend long at all to just come out and say it.

"Nothing in common," Hannah answered. "Not then. And not now."

"Hmm," was Mandy's only response.

Hannah sucked in a breath around her avocado face

mask. "Why would you ever think we might have ended up together? He never even so much as asked me out. While he'd asked out half the female student body by year three."

Hannah wanted to kick herself for the way her voice hitched as the words left her mouth. As if she were disappointed or somehow miserable about the truth of her statement. As if she'd been waiting all those years ago for Alden to ask her and he never had.

That was so not what she'd meant.

In an attempt to try and recover, she quickly added, "Which was just as well. Like I said, nothing in common."

Mandy was silent for several moments. When she finally replied, it was just with another, "Hmm."

Only this time, it sounded much more knowing.

Where was Alden?

Hannah dropped her gaze back down to her smart-watch without actually noticing the time. She already knew it couldn't be more than a minute or so past the last time she'd looked when it was after 10:00 p.m.

Much too late to try and amend their mistake of the previous night now. No legal offices were open this late. Not even in Vegas. No. The only establishments still open at this hour were the casinos, shows, and those cursed chapels like the one she and Alden had frequented last night. Or early this morning, to be more accurate. Chapels for the impulsive and reckless couples who wanted to get married without giving it too much thought.

Hannah sighed. She supposed most of those couples were genuinely in love when they made their vows in front of Elvis. Like the man and woman they'd encountered last night. Whereas she and Alden had just been drunk and foolish and swimming in memories.

Love had nothing to do with it in their case. Hannah gave herself a mental thwack. What was she even doing? Entertaining thoughts about love where Alden was concerned? Sure, she'd been attracted to him since they were kids. Had often thought about him over the years. In her more unguarded moments, she'd sometimes caught herself comparing the memories of him with the man she'd thought she'd end up legitimately marrying.

Thoughts of Justin only served to sour her mood further so she pushed them aside. Right now, the only thing she needed to focus on was getting ahold of Alden so that they could work on a plan B regarding rectifying their careless mistake of a marriage.

She texted him once more and received a response only moments later. Yet another version of the same replies he'd been sending all evening.

Can't break away just yet. Have tried. Will explain when I see you.

Hannah cursed and paced around her room. Compared to Alden's suite, her own lodgings would be considered postage-stamp-sized.

This was pointless. Surely, they weren't going to solve anything tonight. She may as well just go to bed. She'd already brushed her teeth and scrubbed her face, still tingling from the hour-long facial Mandy had so generously treated her to this afternoon before a ninety-minute massage. As inconvenient as the timing was, the pampering had indeed done her a world of good and wonders toward soothing her nerves. But now she felt tense and frazzled yet again.

She'd begun to pull the covers back to crawl under them when her phone tinged with a message. Alden.

On my way to hotel now. Can we talk? I think we need to.

Hannah grunted out a frustrated laugh. Oh, so now he wanted to talk finally, did he? Now that the time was so late. While she'd been here pacing for hours, trying to come up with a solution to their predicament. Well, damned if she was going to get dressed and rush to meet him somewhere.

She responded right away.

Already in my pj's. Please come up here to my room.

The least he could do was come to her. After all the waiting she'd been doing for him.

The response was immediate.

Will do. See you soon.

Hannah resumed her pacing. A frizzle of electricity ran over her skin. She didn't know the cause but was absolutely certain that it had nothing to do with the anticipation or excitement about seeing Alden in the next few minutes.

She had not been missing him all day. Absolutely not. And the way that Mandy had gushed throughout the afternoon about being so in love had most certainly not led to any kind of longing within her heart. Nor had all of

Mandy's words about how she'd thought that Alden and Hannah would eventually get together back in school.

No. None of it was material to her current mood. She was just hurting after the unexpected rejection by Justin she hadn't seen coming. Those feelings of longing had nothing to do with Alden himself.

The lady doth protest too much...

She pushed the silly quote away. In fact, she was more than annoyed with Alden at the moment. How could he have not found some way to get back to the resort earlier so that they could do something about this mess? And now that it was too late in the day, he was finally making his way back and asking to see her.

By the time she heard the knock on the door, her annoyance had grown to ire. She yanked the door open so fast and hard, the hinge made a swishing noise. He looked her up and down with an amused smile when she stepped aside to let him in.

"Nice sleepwear."

Hannah glanced down at the only set of pj's she'd packed—a loose tank and matching boy shorts adorned with penguins on a ski slope wearing long scarves and colorful hats. She'd been a bit preoccupied packing only her suitcase. Justin had often asked her to pack for him too whenever they traveled together, following a detailed list of all the items he required.

Her ire grew at the thought of all the ways she'd indulged the man only to end up here at a wedding, single. Except, technically, she wasn't.

Alden pointed toward the vicinity of her chest. "What's that particular penguin doing?"

She was in no mood. "Skiing. They're all skiing, Alden."

"Cute," he said, stepping farther into the room.

She followed close behind. "Never mind my attire, why in the world did you take so long to get back here?"

He raised an eyebrow. "I told you. I couldn't."

"Really? You've been gone for hours. Eighteen holes does not take that long."

He crossed his arms in front of his chest, and the amused grin had grown wider, which only served to grow her irritation even further. She couldn't even be sure who she was more sore with at the moment—Alden or Justin.

"What's so funny?"

He leaned over to tap her on the nose. "Are you really irate with me about golfing with the boys? It's like we really are married."

She gave him a useless shove. "Ha, ha. Very funny. You know very well it's not out of some kind of wifely concern."

But then his smile suddenly faded and his brows drew together. Hannah studied his face; far from appearing relaxed and recharged after a leisurely day of golf, Alden could be described as the complete opposite. He looked weary and haggard. His hair was matted in the outline of a sports cap, as if he'd just recently taken it off. Which made no sense. They couldn't have been on the course all this time. "There's a reason I didn't rush back," he said, his voice gravelly rough.

His serious expression tempered her annoyance. Something was not right.

"What's that? Is something wrong?"

He nodded. "In fact there is. Seriously wrong. We have a bit of a situation."

CHAPTER FOUR

HANNAH WASN'T QUITE ready to breathe a sigh of relief when she made her way to the pew and took a seat. Might be too early to celebrate just yet. In fact, she was still shaking inside, ever since hearing what Alden had told her last night—Max had been getting cold feet. After sending away the other men after golfing, he'd apparently confided to his friend what he hadn't been able to tell his brothers.

Max was inches close to calling the whole thing off. And he'd told Alden this with less than twelve hours before the wedding.

That would have been a catastrophe. Poor Mandy would have been devastated to say the least. So Alden had spent the rest of the evening talking him down, trying to reassure him that it was just pre-wedding jitters until he'd convinced him finally.

Hannah hadn't seen Alden at all today either. He was making sure to stick by Max's side to ensure the groom's feet stayed warm. Which meant they still hadn't done anything about ending their own marriage. Yet again. It was almost as if there was some strange force in the universe preventing her and Alden from undoing what they'd so carelessly done.

But Hannah couldn't worry about any of that now. All

that mattered at the moment was that Max went through with his nuptials. Surely, he wouldn't back out now, at ground zero? Most of the guests had assembled. The altar was all set up, the flowers arranged.

Though not quite a full breath, she breathed a sigh of relief when Alden appeared at the doorway, then made his way over to sit next to her. It had to be a good sign that he was here.

"Well?" she whispered, leaning slightly toward him. The smell of his new upscale aftershave tickled her nose and it occurred to her that she'd already grown familiar with its scent. With Alden's scent. She used that familiarity now to let it soothe her. As did Alden's mere presence. She hadn't realized just how on edge she'd been since hearing about Max's ambivalence last night.

Alden took her hand and gave it a reassuring squeeze. "Crisis averted."

Hannah finally released the remainder of the breath she'd been holding. "Phew. I mean, I thought you must have convinced him to see reason but I didn't want to assume."

Alden didn't let go of her hand. She made no attempt to remove it. "I admit, it was touch and go for much too long there for a while. Long enough to shave some years off my life."

"Thank heavens it's a go," she answered. Still, she wouldn't be able to totally relax until the vows were said and done. That was way too close. Damn Max for even considering walking away. And heaven help him if he left Mandy at the altar. Aside from an angry mob, which included Mandy's parents, sisters, and cousins, he would have Hannah herself to contend with.

"I just don't know what he was thinking," Hannah said,

still making sure to keep her voice down. "He and Mandy belong together. They've known each other for decades."

Alden's response was to merely squeeze her hand once more. After an eternity, which realistically could have only been a few minutes, the organ player finally appeared and began to play. Right on cue, a dark-haired little moppet of a toddler skipped down the aisle, dropping rose petals in her wake. Hannah recognized her as the youngest of Mandy's three nieces. She was followed by her soon-to-be uncles, Max's brothers. They lined up next to the altar.

The bridesmaids walked down next to take their place on the other side of the altar. After several seconds of delay that left everyone craning their necks toward the entrance, a very distracted little boy in a pint-sized tuxedo appeared, holding a satin pillow. He took his time walking down the aisle, eliciting chuckles from the attendees. Finally, Max appeared and Hannah's heart skipped in her chest at the sight of him. Pale and hesitant, he looked like he wanted to dash in the opposite direction.

"Don't you dare," she heard Alden utter under his breath. He looked for all purposes like a man ready to jump into action if needed, though for the life of her, Hannah wouldn't be able to guess what he might possibly do to avert such a disaster. Still, the fact that he was so ready to intervene had something quivering in the pit of her stomach. Alden cared for his friends. Deeply.

Too bad he'd never given any kind of indication that he cared for her the same way. He'd written her down as his backup option junior year. The thought had floored her the other night when he'd told her. She still found it hard to believe. Still. It meant nothing. It was a silly little exercise that no one had taken seriously. Except for her.

Finally, Max made his way down to stand next to his brothers.

The organ music changed to the traditional "Wedding March" and a collective intake of breath sounded throughout the chapel as Mandy appeared on her father's arm.

The look on Max's face as the pair made their way down the aisle toward him said it all—they'd really had nothing to worry about. Pure, intense love shone from every feature of the man's face. He really had been mistaking his pre-wedding jitters for second thoughts. Thank heavens he'd been made to come to his senses. Thanks to Alden.

Alden had been so right to make sure his friend hadn't made a mistake he might never have recovered from.

She felt the now familiar and reassuring tightness around her palm and looked down to find that not only was her hand still gripped tightly in Alden's, he'd tucked it into the crook of his arm. She hadn't noticed the movement because it had felt so natural.

Hannah couldn't help the direction her imagination took her in. How would it feel to be walked down the aisle as the man you wanted to spend the rest of your life with awaited you? Images formed in her mind's eye. In them, she wore a dress similar to the one Mandy wore now, but the tail was longer, the neckline more V-shaped. The bouquet she held was made up of red and pink roses rather than the lilies Mandy carried.

Her breath hitched as the pictures in her mind's eye rounded out. The man waiting at the altar for her wasn't Justin.

It was Alden.

* * *

His luck appeared to be better this time around. Alden reached for his name card for the dinner and reception, relieved to see that his and Hannah's both read the same table number, unlike at the brunch yesterday.

Hopefully, Alyssa would be sitting at an entirely different one. He had nothing against the woman; he just wanted to relax a bit now that the stress of the past twenty-four hours was finally behind him. Max and Mandy were safely married. He'd be able to enjoy this dinner and finally focus on Hannah and Hannah alone.

He knew very well she was eager to discuss how to end their marriage union officially once and for all. Maybe if they got some time alone, they'd be able to discuss how, at last.

Except…if he were being honest with himself, he had to admit to a bit of ambivalence about the whole thing. At some point, the idea of being married to Hannah had somehow become more and more feasible, not such a ridiculous notion. Less of an error in need of an urgent remedy.

Which made absolutely no sense. Of course, they couldn't just stay married.

Could they?

Alden gave his head a brisk shake and made his way to the assigned table. Hannah hadn't made it into the ballroom yet. Like so many other inexplicable things about the way he felt about her, he seemed to be able to instinctively tell when she was nearby.

He couldn't even be sure when the idea to maybe put off the divorce had wound its way into his head. At some point during yesterday and today, while with Max, he'd found some of the advice he was doling out to his friend about marriage was also resonating with himself as well. Advice such as what good fortune it was to be tied to someone you'd always cared for. How lucky he was to have found a woman like Mandy—talented, lovely both inside and out, accomplished.

All those traits could be attributed to Hannah. And many more.

The moment he'd laid eyes on her again at the rooftop cabana, he'd felt a jolt of an emotion he couldn't really place. Familiarity mixed with something else, something much more heated. All the ways he'd felt attracted to her when they were younger came flooding back to wash over him. He'd tried to tell himself that what he'd felt back then was nothing more than teenage hormonal longing. That argument held much less weight now that they were both adults.

Was it that ridiculous a notion that the two of them might end up together? The way they'd each written on that silly, adolescent questionnaire? Maybe his inebriated and sleep-deprived subconscious knew what it was doing when it helped him into that chapel the other night.

Maybe Hannah's had done the same.

Sure, their marriage had come about in a wholly untraditional and unplanned way, but some things happened for a reason. He knew that firsthand.

Look at where his life had led to after one impulsive decision to walk into the lobby of the Reardon hotel when he was sixteen to ask for a job. Fifteen years, a lot of hard work, blood and sweat later, he was a name to be reckoned with in the hospitality industry. That sixteen-year-old kid would have never guessed.

As far as he and Hannah were concerned, the timing was almost uncanny. They were both at a crossroads,

Hannah having just left a relationship while he was on the verge of a major business expansion in which it would only be beneficial and work in his favor to be a married man.

Just as he knew he would, he sensed the moment Hannah arrived. Spotting him, she made a beeline directly for him as she flashed him a wide smile, the sight of which did quirky things to his gut. He stood and pulled out a chair for her next to him.

"Looks like you saved the day," she said, taking her seat. "Well done, Mr. Hamid."

"Thank you, Mrs. Hamid." The words slipped out of his mouth before he'd had a chance to catch them. Now there was no taking them back.

Whoa.

Hadn't he sworn back in the hotel room that first morning that he'd be more careful with his words when it came to their fake slash real marriage?

"Uh…sorry," he said immediately, registering the instant look of shock on Hannah's face. Yeah, well, he'd shocked himself too. He could hardly blame her for her reaction at his slip. This was why he had to be so careful entertaining thoughts like the ones he'd had earlier. He was on a slippery slope that would only take Hannah down with him if he lost his footing.

Speaking of apologies. It was about time he made one for his real transgression.

"Look, what happened the other night, the way I got drunk and where we ended up. I hadn't slept in two days because of a complicated business meeting overseas. Then I flew straight here. It was irresponsible of me to have so many drinks given how tired and sleepless I was.

I know it's no excuse—" What a word salad. God. He was making a mess of this.

Hannah sat, blinking at him.

"I just wanted to say I'm sorry for all of it."

She nodded once, then reached for her water. Swallowed several gulps before turning back to him to answer. "I'm just as much to blame for what happened that night, Alden. I'm not some helpless nitwit who simply followed a man into a chapel."

"That's not what I'm implying."

She held a hand up. "I could give you a litany of reasons why I let my guard down so completely also. But those reasons would be excuses too. The fact remains that it happened. And there's nothing we can do about it tonight. Or tomorrow for that matter, given that it's Sunday. So we may as well enjoy this meal and this reception. And deal with our own mess at the first opportunity."

He held his own glass out to her in a mock salute. "Wise words. That works for me."

She suddenly looked away, as if unable to continue holding his gaze. "I do have one question, however." Her cheeks were growing redder by the moment. "We haven't really had a chance to discuss it. And I'm horrified that I have to ask."

He immediately knew what she was referring to. She wanted to know if they'd consummated the marriage.

He quickly shook his head, completely certain of the answer. *That* had not happened between them. He had no doubt. For he was certain that every cell in his body would be aware of having made love with Hannah. She wasn't the type of woman a man might forget touching, holding, being intimate with. The blood rushed away from his extremities and he had to rein himself in to focus on the conversation at hand.

"No, we fell asleep as soon as we hit the mattress and stayed that way."

Clasping a hand to her chest, Hannah blew out a loud breath in relief, then clinked her glass to his still upheld one. "To Max and Mandy."

"To Max and Mandy," he repeated.

He had to stop saying such things to her. Didn't he know what it did to her insides when he referred to her as his wife? Alden might be taking this whole marriage thing lightly, but in the couple short days they'd become man and wife—on paper—Hannah found her confused head often blurring the lines between what was real and what wasn't.

Max had called Alden a player and a ladies' man. He had such a reputation for a reason. It was hardly any wonder all of this meant so little to him.

Still, illogical though it may be, it was hard not to compare Alden to the other men in this room. Or to other men in general. Successful, handsome, driven, considerate. The way he filled out a tux could make a nun swoon. Alden would be considered any girl's dream catch. If he ever actually wanted to be caught. All indications said otherwise.

What might it be like to really be married to him? In all manner of ways?

Stop it.

The surroundings were just getting to her, that's all. Given how lovely Mandy and Max's ceremony had been, then the atmosphere in this ballroom, one could hardly blame a girl for entertaining fanciful thoughts about her own romantic future.

"Here they are," Alden said, pulling her out of her thoughts. Mandy and Max had entered the ballroom and were making their way over to the dance floor. A raucous round of applause followed by a standing ovation greeted them as they began their first dance together as man and wife. Mandy's smile had enough wattage to light up a large city. None the worse for wear. Thankfully, she seemed to have no knowledge of how close this magical moment had come to not even happening.

The evening could have been much less celebratory and bordering more on tragic.

"I'm so glad Max came to his senses," she said in Alden's ear, low enough that their fellow tablemates wouldn't be able to hear over the music. "They both look so happy."

"Thank goodness she has no idea."

"I hope she never finds out." Hannah didn't want to think about what that might do to their relationship or the start of their married life together. "She's radiant, isn't she?"

Alden nodded his agreement but his gaze was fixated on her rather than on the couple on the dance floor. "Absolutely beautiful."

Hannah's breath caught, her heart doing somersaults in her chest. His words were spoken directly at her, his eyes fixed on her face.

He finally looked away, not that it did anything to break the heavy tension between them. "I mean your dress," he said, gesturing toward her. "It's very original. I meant to compliment you on the one you wore yesterday also. Very unique designs."

Hannah glanced down at the jade-colored dress she wore, rimmed at the bottom with delicate black lace.

"Thank you. Both dresses are indeed one of a kind, in fact."

He released a low whistle. "Must have cost a good amount in that case. Not that I know much about ladies' fashion. Or anything at all about it really."

She chuckled. "They hardly cost anything."

He raised a surprised eyebrow. "They don't look second-hand."

The turn in conversation made her realize just how little they knew about each other. "The dresses were inexpensive because I made them both myself. I like to design and sew a lot of the clothes I wear."

His eyebrow lifted another millimeter. "Wow. That's really impressive. I would have never guessed."

Why would he? They hadn't exactly kept in touch through the years. She had no idea what Alden's hobbies or interests might be, or if he even had any.

It surprised her to realize that she'd be really interested to learn.

"A corporate accountant who makes her own wardrobe in her spare time."

"Some weeks, my hobby is the only thing that makes the accounting part bearable." Hannah couldn't even be sure why she'd admitted such a thing. She'd never spoken the words out loud before, not to anyone. Not even her mother. Well, especially not to her mother.

Alden's eyes narrowed on her. "You don't like what you do for a living?"

Such a complicated question, she couldn't guess how to begin to answer it. "It's my career. That's all. I don't exactly look forward to Monday mornings if that's any kind of answer."

She'd be looking even less forward to them now. Having to see Justin every weekday. Watching him go about his work, having to confer with him on mutual projects. So that's why everyone advised against becoming romantically involved with a coworker. She should have heeded the advice.

Alden's eyes narrowed on her face. "Maybe you should do something about that."

She shrugged. "A hobby doesn't pay a girl's bills."

"Maybe it could, under the right circumstances. And with the right kind of backing."

Before she could ask him what he might mean by that, the servers appeared with the first course. The food was delicious, and after a crisp and fresh Caesar salad, the main entrée arrived. She'd decided on the grilled salmon with citrus glaze and a side of root vegetables. Alden had gone with the braised beef with buttery mashed potatoes. He scooped a spoonful and deposited it on her side plate without asking.

A memory surfaced in her mind, the way he would share his French fries with her whenever the four of them stopped for fast food after their football games back in high school. He'd done that without so much as a word back then too.

She hadn't given the gesture much thought. Just assumed he wasn't much of a French fry aficionado. So why was she so touched right now that he'd done the same thing all these years later? She shouldn't be.

Most of the meal was spent making small talk with their table neighbors in between bites of food.

Soon the plates were cleared and the band fired up

the music once more. Max and Mandy appeared on the dance floor again, motioning for their guests to join them.

Alden gave her a wink and stood. He extended out his hand. "It's only polite to do as the bridal couple ask and dance with them. Shall we?"

Why not? She'd eaten her entire meal and could move around a bit. Plus, it might help release some of the strange tension she'd been feeling ever since her wayward imagination at the chapel earlier.

CHAPTER FIVE

IT DIDN'T SURPRISE her that Alden was a good dancer. The man seemed to be gifted at everything he did. He moved smoothly, not even a hint of awkward stiffness. And he stayed matched to the beat. When the band began playing a song for a group led dance, he knew all the moves and executed them perfectly. Unlike Hannah, who tripped up at least twice, laughing at her clumsiness, especially compared to Alden's dancing skills.

"I must have two left feet," she told him over the notes of the upbeat song. What a cliché.

In response, Alden crossed his own feet at the ankles and did a full circle, ending with a low bow in front of her. Hannah laughed at the perfectly executed move. "Show off."

"Who? Me?" Alden asked with mock outrage.

She was really enjoying herself. When was the last time she'd gone dancing? Not since she'd begun dating Justin. During her college days and years as a new adult professional, she'd gone clubbing with friends as often as she could, to some of Boston's hottest spots. Now, she wouldn't even be able to name one. Most of those friends had moved away in pursuit of their dreams. Justin had declared that dancing just wasn't his thing on one of their first dates when she'd suggested it as an option.

What were the odds she'd be having this much fun if Justin had accompanied her to this wedding? And what did that question say about the future she'd almost embarked on with him?

"Penny for your thoughts," Alden said, leaning closer and raising his voice above the loud music.

She chuckled before answering. "I was just thinking that you appear to be a man of many talents."

"Says the woman who designs and makes her own clothes."

As much as she appreciated the compliment, Hannah didn't really see her craft as any kind of talent. More so a labor of love. Sure, she'd thought about pursuing fashion arts all those years ago when she'd been a naive kid with a world of possibilities ahead of her. That was before her mother had convinced her pursuing a more practical field would make more sense. Her mother was nothing if not practical. And she'd always had very clear ideas about Hannah's pursuits in life.

She could hardly blame Mama. When they'd barely scraped by paycheck to paycheck with Mama's modest earnings as an aide in a care home, it was no wonder her mother had wanted her to pursue a job that provided a more guaranteed income. It wasn't as if her father was around to help. He'd abandoned them so long ago Hannah didn't remember his face any longer.

The last song wrapped up and the soloist tapped the microphone sending three booming echoes through the ballroom. "If the ladies would stay put on the dance floor or make their way over if not there already, it's time for the bride to toss the bouquet as per tradition."

Oh, no.

Hannah immediately turned on her heel to leave.

"That's both our cues to head back to the table," she said, not bothering to wait for him. She didn't get far. A feminine hand reached for her out of nowhere through the crowd and grabbed her by the forearm.

"Oh, no, you don't. Come back here." Hannah turned to find Mandy's maid of honor, who happened to also be her older sister, tugging her back onto the dance floor.

"Come on, Hannah," Lexie said on a trail of laughter. "We all know you're probably going to be next. May as well catch the bouquet and make it official."

Clearly, she hadn't heard about Hannah's broken relationship. But why would she? It wasn't the type of thing one announced while attending a celebration.

Hannah suppressed a groan. The last thing she wanted to do was stand here and explain to Mandy's sister exactly why it was such a horrifying thought that she try and catch the bouquet.

For one, her relationship was no more.

For another, she was already married!

How in the world would she even begin to explain any of that? She couldn't. Instead, she faked a smile and tightly followed Lexie back to the center of the dance floor. But not before catching an apologetic look from Alden who looked abashed on her behalf. Hannah could only shrug his way in resignation.

From the front of the crowd of ladies, Mandy let out a squeal of a laugh, then turned around and flung the bouquet behind her. Hannah watched in horror as it arched through the air in her direction. She could have sworn at one point it hung suspended in midair before it began to fall. It hit her square in the chest.

Hannah had no choice but to catch it.

* * *

Alden didn't know whether to laugh or groan out loud as he watched the bouquet head straight for Hannah and land in her hands. He knew the last thing she'd wanted was to be the one to catch those flowers.

Mandy had turned and was clapping with delight upon seeing where her aim had landed. Or was *target* a more appropriate word?

He began to pull Hannah's chair out, he'd already swung by the bar and procured two glasses of a bubbly cocktail for the two of them. But before Hannah could turn and make her way back, Max strode to his wife's side.

He had the microphone in his hands. "Now it's time for the gentlemen," he declared, then unclipped his boutonniere from his lapel. "It's only fair that one of the fellas gets a chance and then we can have a couples dance with the two winners."

Before Max had even gotten the last word out, close to a dozen men began making their way toward the dance floor. Hannah's jaw had dropped, a look of sheer horror plastered on her face. One of those men would get the chance to dance with Hannah.

Not if Alden could help it.

Setting the drinks down so abruptly they almost spilled, he shrugged off his jacket and strode toward the dance floor. Hannah caught his gaze and flashed him a smile he wouldn't be able to describe. Relief, mixed with gratitude. And something else.

Alden got there just in time as the boutonniere came flying out of Max's hand. Without much thought, he jumped into the air with both hands raised and a fervent prayer on his lips.

He'd never been much of a praying man but somehow

it worked. When he landed, the boutonniere was securely in his left hand.

Max actually winked at him once he turned back around. He motioned toward the band that began playing a slow jazzy number, which Alden assumed to be his cue. Walking over to Hannah with what he hoped was a reassuring smile, he stretched his arms out and waited until she stepped into them.

"I think we may have been set up," he said into her ear as she reached her hands around his shoulders.

"I'd say there's a good chance that's true."

"Looks like the next dance is ours, sweetheart." He pulled her close against him and they began to sway to the music.

He'd called her sweetheart. Why that endearment sent her heart thudding, Hannah couldn't guess. No doubt Alden had simply thrown it out carelessly. There wasn't any kind of real weight or affection behind the term.

He was a charmer. He always had been. She couldn't succumb to that charm now, of all times. She had a broken heart to mend, a life to get back to that was going to look significantly different than what she'd lived the past few months. Her confusing feelings for her high school crush had no part in trying to pull that life together.

She knew there were dozens of eyes trained on the pair of them. But somehow Hannah felt as if she and Alden were the only two people in the room. The scent of him wrapped around her like a warm comfortable blanket on a snowy day. She could feel his heartbeat through her skin at every point their bodies made contact. She couldn't have imagined why Max and Mandy might have planned this, if they even had. But for the life of her, she couldn't find any regret that this moment was happening.

Through her peripheral vision, she saw other couples join them on the dance floor. But they may as well not even exist. Right now, it was just the two of them and the music that surrounded them.

She knew she hadn't imagined it when he pulled her tighter against his length. Hannah wondered what might have happened if she and Alden were alone together and things between them were somehow different. Might Alden have kissed her?

Heaven help her, she would have let him. Maybe she might have even been the one to instigate the kiss. She couldn't be sure whether to be relieved they were surrounded by others or wish they would all disappear somehow.

How was this happening? How had her childhood crush on Alden grown into some kind of fantasy full of longing?

Was she just broken because she'd lost Justin?

The answer to that was almost embarrassingly clear. She'd dodged a bullet. If she could feel so much attraction to another man within days of their breakup, getting engaged to Justin clearly would have been a colossal mistake.

So what was she going to do about this inconvenient attraction to Alden? Further complicated by the fact that she was actually married to the man?

That telltale little devil popped up out of nowhere again.

Why don't you just enjoy yourself for just one night? Worry about all the rest later.

Hannah resisted the strong urge to literally brush an

imaginary piece of lint off her shoulder to remove the imaginary rascal who seemed to lead her straight into trouble so often.

The song came to an end all too soon. With great reluctance, she moved to step out of Alden's embrace, the bouquet of flowers still clutched in her hand.

Alden held onto her for just a beat longer than was necessary. The idea of it sent a jolt of electricity rushing through her system. Was he as affected by their dance as much as she was?

She wanted to know the answer so badly. But there was no way she could come out and ask.

Max appeared at their side, a mischievous grin spread over his bearded face. Hannah was torn between thanking the other man and attempting to throttle him. Her emotions were a jumbled mess.

The music turned bouncy fast with a song she recognized as a classic rock and roll tune. If memory served, the high school football team always played the song at home games. It was the one the team rushed out onto the field to while it sounded loudly from the gymnasium speakers.

One by one, Max's brothers materialized next to him and Alden. Hannah took the opportunity to rush away. She needed some air.

"Hannah," Alden's voice sounded softly behind her but she pretended not to hear. A glance back a moment later told her he'd been pulled in by the other men and was now performing some kind of complicated dance routine they all seemed to know.

She took a moment to watch, unable to tear her eyes off Alden.

What had just happened?

Why was her heart pounding, her pulse racing? Why had she been loath to leave Alden's embrace?

It was just a simple dance. She shouldn't have been so affected. Hannah stepped out into the sidewalk and took a deep breath. She had to get a grip. In less than forty-eight hours, they would be splitting paths and perhaps never see each other again.

First, they had to get that divorce.

When she returned to the ballroom a few minutes later, Alden was already back at the table. He immediately stood up as she approached.

"Hey, I was wondering where you'd run off to."

If he'd been as affected by their dance, he was doing a great job of not showing it. She could only hope her own demeanor appeared as carefree. She flashed him an exaggerated smile. "Just needed some fresh air."

The rest of the evening went by in a blur. Hannah made sure the only dancing they did from then on was fast and involved no touching.

By the time the bride and groom bid a cheerful goodbye to their guests to prepare for their honeymoon, the evening was swiftly coming to a close. Hannah's feet hurt and her emotions were no less chaotic.

"I think I might be ready to call it a night."

Alden nodded and retrieved his jacket from the back of the chair. "I'll walk you up to your room."

It was hard not to stare at him. All the dancing had lent a robust color to his cheeks; he'd undone the top several buttons of his collared shirt and rolled up his sleeves. The man really was a pleasure to look at. It was hard to get her fill.

She forced her gaze away and stood, following him out of the ballroom and into the elevator across the lobby.

When they reached her floor and made it to her door, she knew better than to invite him in. The temptation to ask him to stay might be too great to fight. As it was, the sheer magnitude of his allure was tempting her beyond comfort. But this was as good an opportunity as any to give him his ring back.

"Thanks, Alden. I had fun tonight," she began. "If you'll just wait here a moment, I've been meaning to give you the ring back."

He surprised her by arguing. "I'd like you to keep it."

"Alden, that's very generous, but I couldn't do that. It's worth too much. Let me go get it for you."

He reached for her, stopped her before she could open the door. "Look, there's something I want to run by you."

His eyes were focused on her face, his mouth tight. Whatever this something was that he wanted to discuss, it was weighing on his mind.

Hannah leaned her back against the doorframe. "All right. What is it."

He shook his head, crammed his hands into his pockets. "Not now. It's been a long couple of days."

She couldn't argue with that. Between her tumultuous emotions and the chaos of the past forty-eight hours, Hannah wasn't sure she had the wherewithal to consider anything Alden might want to discuss.

"Meet me for breakfast tomorrow," he continued. "We can talk about the ring then."

What was there to talk about? She'd assumed they'd get together at some point tomorrow to figure out what to do about a divorce.

But this sounded like something else. What in the world did he have in mind?

The curiosity alone was enough to help make her decision. "Sure, let's have breakfast."

Alden hoped he knew what he was doing. And he hoped Hannah would agree to his proposal. He just wasn't quite sure how he was going to go about asking her.

The time he'd spent with Hannah at the wedding last night had been one of the most memorable evenings of his life. He might describe it as magical. Not a feeling he'd had too often after spending time with a woman. If that made him a newly minted romantic of some sort, then he was more than ready to accept it. Dancing with her had sealed it. The idea vaguely roaming around in his head had taken full form after holding her in his arms while swaying to the music.

As preposterous as it might sound, he had to ask her. He'd never forgive himself if he didn't.

He could approach this as just another business proposal. Funny he couldn't recall ever being this nervous at a business presentation before, not even some of the more relevant ones. Somehow, the stakes here were even higher. Though he'd be hard pressed to say why.

The worse that could happen is that she would laugh and then say no. Leaving him no worse off, really. There was absolutely no reason to be as nervous as he was.

He'd suggested a diner rather than the elaborate buffet at their resort hotel. No doubt many of the wedding attendees would be there to eat and the last thing he needed were friends or acquaintances around to watch all this go down.

He led Hannah to an open booth and took a seat across from her. A server wearing a '50s-style uniform complete with a white lace apron and a cute bonnet appeared immediately with two personal-sized steaming carafes.

"Thank you, you're an angel," Hannah declared to the other woman, reaching for the coffee right away.

"Rough night?" Alden asked after the chuckling waitress had walked away.

Hannah took a sip of coffee without bothering with any cream or sugar. "I didn't get much sleep. How about you?"

He'd hardly gotten any himself, warring thoughts keeping him awake most of the night. Weighing the merits of his idea with the utter ridiculousness of how it was going to sound on the surface when he got it all out.

Hannah took another sip and reached for her purse. She pulled out a small velvet box he had no problem recognizing.

"Here, before I forget. Take the ring back."

He held up a hand when she reached it out to him. "Hannah, I really think you should keep it."

Her eyes grew wide. "Alden, we went over this last night. I can't keep something so valuable. I can't imagine a single reason why I should. Or why you would even suggest such a thing. Unless…"

Alden's pulse jumped, could she possibly have guessed what he wanted to do?

The next instant, Hannah's hand clenched tight on top of the table. "Is this another attempt at an apology? You don't have to try and buy me off for a mistake we both made together."

Whoa. Not only had she guessed wrong, now she was

offended and angry. It was not the way he'd intended this conversation to start. So he didn't give himself a chance to think or agonize any longer. Alden went ahead and blurted the real reason he didn't want to take the ring back.

"I'd like for us to stay married."

CHAPTER SIX

SHE COULDN'T HAVE possibly heard him right. "I beg your pardon." She laughed before being able to ask the next question. "I could have sworn you just said you wanted to stay married. I couldn't have really heard that, right?"

He didn't answer, simply continued to stare at her.

Holy heaven. She *had* heard right. And Alden had meant what he said.

Okay. This was a bit of a curve ball. One she clearly hadn't seen coming. She rubbed her fingers over her forehead to dispel some of the tension that had suddenly pooled there. She really didn't have time for this. A slew of decisions and to-dos awaited her back home. Her mother didn't even know about her breakup, for heaven's sake. That wasn't a conversation she was looking forward to. Oh, then there was the whole need to find another job because she couldn't stomach the thought of going to the office every day to work with her ex...

"Alden, if this is some kind of joke..."

He held his hands out, palms up. "Look, I didn't mean to blurt it out that way."

As if his delivery were the problem. "Why would you even think to say it at all?"

"I really have thought this through. If you'd just hear me out."

She didn't get a chance to respond as the waitress came back to take their order at that very moment. Her gaze shifted from the ring on the center of the table, then to the two of them. "Should I come back?"

"That would be great," Alden said while at the very same moment Hannah answered with, "No, I'm ready to order."

Their waitress pursed her lips before looking at him questioningly. He gestured toward Hannah. "Go ahead. And whatever she orders, make it two. I'll have the same."

"I'll have the tower of chocolate chip pancakes with extra whipped cream and chocolate syrup. And a side of candied walnuts."

Alden winced at her choice across the table.

"Coming right up with two," the waitress said, then pivoted away.

"I think I got a cavity in one of my molars just hearing you place that order."

Hannah wasn't about to admit that a small petty part of her had deliberately chosen a breakfast she knew he would have never picked for himself. Her mood had soured beyond reason. What exactly was he about to tease her with? The notion that they could stay married made absolutely no sense.

Didn't it?

She needed more coffee. Maybe a gallon more. "Alden, are you playing with me?" she asked him as she poured more into her mug. This time she doctored it with plenty of cream and a dollop of sugar.

"On the contrary."

"Then what exactly is happening here?"

He leaned over across the table, pulled the ring out of its box and studied it. "This is just a symbol. A talisman."

"And?"

"It doesn't necessarily have to represent a real union. Neither does a piece of paper signed by an official."

Hannah merely repeated the simple word yet again. "And?"

"It just so happens we got married the other night. And it also just so happens that I could really use a wife for my next business venture."

Hannah felt her jaw drop as Alden continued, "If you prefer, you can look at this as a simple job offer."

Business. Job. He was speaking in puzzles now. For the life of her, she couldn't seem to make any of the pieces fit.

"Let me explain," he said, pouring himself some coffee.

"I wish you would."

"I'm trying to form a partnership with a very traditional family in a rather conservative part of the world. The only other parties in consideration, my only competition, are stable family men."

"How can that possibly matter in this day and age?"

"I assure you, in many parts of the world, it still matters very much. I know for a fact I'm being viewed as a less viable option because of my status as a single man."

And also because of his reputation as a hard partying bachelor. Hannah didn't voice the thought out loud. Something told her Alden already knew that aspect about him was also playing a factor with the people he was trying to do business with overseas.

He continued to explain. "I fly out again in three days for more negotiations. I'm proposing you come with me. As my wife. Which, technically, you happen to be."

As his wife. Which she was. Three days.

No!

It was out of the question. Why was she even entertaining anything he was saying?

"Look, I have a life I have to get back to. I can't just drop everything and travel to the other end of the world with you. I'm supposed to fly back to Boston tomorrow night where my mom will be waiting for me, at which point I'll have to break the news to her that rather than getting engaged, I actually broke up with my almost-fiancé. The next day I have to go into a job where my ex will also be, and if you don't think that's going to be awkward, you're not thinking. And if you guessed that also means that I should start looking for another job, clap for yourself. Because that's absolutely correct."

She felt nearly out of breath by the time she finished. Alden actually had the nerve to chuckle. Hannah resisted the urge to toss a packet of sugar at him. "What exactly is funny about any of that?"

He leaned back, crossed his arms in front of his chest. "Because everything you're saying just helps to make my point that this is a good idea. For both of us." He began counting on his fingers. "One, you don't have to tell your mom your relationship fell apart, instead you can tell her you decided you're doing some traveling. Two, you don't have to go back to a job you don't enjoy, which happens to also employ a man you don't want to see."

Their food arrived, sparing Hannah the need to answer. She hated that he was actually making sense. And she had to admit, some of the points he made were actually worthy of consideration.

"There's something else you might want to consider," he added, pulling his plate closer and poking a fork into the bottom pancake.

"What's that?"

"We'd be traveling to one of the textile capitals of the world. Istanbul has the grand bazaar, which sells everything from silk to handmade rugs to fashion jewelry. Shopping in the Aegean boasts some of the most renowned boutiques and fashion houses. If you ever considered changing your career to one that involved designing and creating clothing, you'd find inspiration there like nowhere else."

Hannah paused.

Alden must have sensed the slowly forming cracks in her resolve. "Of course, I'll pay you for your time," he told her. "Consider it getting paid while you do some research about your next career move."

Hannah's head began to spin. Her life was about logic and numbers and order. Aside from when she designed her clothing. That was the only time she let her imagination and creativity take over.

There was nothing logical about the offer Alden just made her. Yet, somehow there was.

She had no clue how to decide. And she only had three days.

Maybe all the sugar had gone to his head. But he could swear Hannah was wavering. He had to balance on a very precarious high wire, like those stunt performers so well-known in this city. On the one hand, he wanted to press while he glimpsed a slight advantage. But this had to be wholly Hannah's decision. He couldn't push. He could only lay out all the ways this deal would benefit them both and hope she came around.

She suddenly set her fork down. "You know, I'm not much of a gambler."

Uh-oh. That statement didn't really bode well, now did it?

She continued, "But I was thinking of hitting the slots once more before we leave Las Vegas."

"The slots?" What did playing the slots have to do with anything? Was she deliberately changing the subject?

She took a slow sip of coffee. Then another.

Alden stayed silent, just waiting. She had to be going somewhere with this. Though for the life of him, he couldn't figure out where. She bit another forkful of pancake before answering and he lost his concentration for a moment as he gazed at her rich ruby lips.

Focus.

"I'm not sure how to respond to your offer just yet."

That lent him a small amount of hope. She was saying no outright.

"This would all be completely friendly," he told her. "We wouldn't actually..." He cleared his throat, there was no non-awkward way to say this. "That is, I mean, it would be completely platonic."

She lifted her shoulder in a gesture that said, *Duh*... "That goes without saying."

Yeah, maybe. He figured he should say it anyway. "What do you think? Up for an adventure?"

She chewed some more, left the question unanswered for so long that he thought she planned to completely ignore it. Finally, she set her fork down and blew out a long breath. "Let's leave it to chance, shall we?"

"How do you propose we do that?"

She shrugged. "We're in the city of games of chance. Let's let one of those games decide whether I accept your offer or not."

She reached for her purse, pulled out several bills and placed them on the table. "Breakfast is on me."

Then she stood and motioned for him to follow her out of the diner.

What choice did he have but to grab the ring, then follow her out?

Less than five minutes later, they were walking through the gaming hall of one of the larger casinos on the strip. Hannah hadn't said much on the way over here, but she certainly strode down the sidewalk with no small amount of determination.

"This one should work, plenty of empty slots," she said, looking around, the sounds of pings and bells and electronic ringing echoed through the air. He could only watch as she walked over to the window and exchanged several bills for two buckets of chips. She returned to his side and handed him one of the buckets with a smile. "Also on me."

Okay.

"Uh…thanks. But what are we really doing here?"

"Killing two birds with one stone."

"How, exactly?"

"We'll both play these slots. And we'll keep playing until one of us wins something. Anything. It could be less than a dollar. Still a win."

"What happens then?" he asked, though he figured he could guess.

"I win first, I go back to my formerly dull yet familiar life that's now suddenly tumultuous and uncertain."

She shook the bucket of chips before continuing. "You win, I come on this trip with you. And pretend to be your wife."

"You are my wife."

She poked him in the chest. "You need to stop saying that. Even though it's true."

"Can't we just flip a coin or something?"

"That wouldn't be terribly exciting now, would it? It's playing the slots to decide or my answer is no now."

He could merely stare at her in astonishment. "This is really how you want to make the decision?"

She shrugged. "As good a way as any. I'm just going to let fate decide for me."

Alden followed as she walked down the aisle and picked an empty machine. Joker's Wild said the neon sign flashing above it. He sat down at the one next to her. He was down to about half the bucket of chips when he pulled the arm and watched as three rows of bright red cherries lined up perfectly on the bright red line on the screen and the machine went wild.

Not quite the jackpot. But he'd hit a winning pull.

Next to him, Hannah jumped up and shook her head, disbelieving.

"I guess that settles it then, sweetheart."

She looked at him with acceptance and resignation. And if his mind wasn't deceiving him, maybe even a hint of excitement in her eyes.

"A deal is a deal," she said on a sigh.

Alden resisted the urge to pump his fist in the air, waited for the attendant to arrive to verify his winnings.

Hannah leaned over to study his machine. "It's still ringing and the lights are still flashing."

"That's because I just won several thousand dollars, sweetheart. All yours. Consider it a starting bonus."

CHAPTER SEVEN

Three days later

IF SOMEONE HAD told her a month ago that she'd be traveling via Alden's private jet to Istanbul as his pretend yet real wife, she would have asked them what romantic fantasy novel they'd been reading.

The sentence she'd just thought seemed straight out of a movie or book. Yet, here she was, walking up the steps to be greeted by a uniformed flight attendant and a dapper-looking pilot awaiting them in the main cabin.

"I can't say I've ever flown private before. This will be quite the experience."

When exactly had Alden become so successful? She knew he was a recognized name over in the hospitality industry. He'd manage to achieve a truly impressive level of success for someone so relatively young.

"I want to make sure you're comfortable," he said. "Anything you need, ask Sandra. We should touch down in a few short hours."

"Thank you. I will. I might just indulge in a nap, however." It wasn't until she'd sat down in the leather swivel bucket seat that she realized just how tired she was. The past couple of days, ever since the wedding, her life had been a whirlwind of activity and major changes.

She'd packed up her apartment and given notice at her job and finally took advantage of all the vacation days she'd let accumulate. It helped that she'd made sure to finish up her projects before the wedding.

And she'd turned Justin down flat each time he'd made noises about getting together to just "talk" about their undone relationship. As far as she was concerned, there was nothing to talk about.

"What did your mother think about you being away?" Alden asked, studying her.

She shrugged. "I might have been rather vague about my reasons for leaving."

Alden lifted an eyebrow in question. "Let's just say she made her own assumptions about what kind of business trip this was."

He tilted his head toward her. "And you let her make them."

"That's right." There would be time to explain to Mama later. And she'd certainly have quite a bit of explaining to do.

"After that, it was only a matter of moving out of the apartment, then finalizing things at work. Aside from Mama, there was no one else to even inform. No one else who might even miss me while I'm gone."

Womp-womp. That comment dangerously bordered on self-pity.

"No one?" Alden asked.

Hannah shook her head. "Not even a pet." She curled her legs under her lap. "Not that the lack of one was my choice."

"No?"

Hannah shook her head. "Justin was allergic to cats and had declared that he'd never been a dog person."

Now that they were over, it gave Hannah pause at just how incompatible she and Justin actually were—if one looked hard enough.

"That's too bad," Alden said. "Didn't you have a golden tabby back when we were in school?"

It surprised her that he remembered the small detail. "That's right. Tabeetha."

"Clever."

She chuckled. "I loved that furry little fluff ball. And I would have loved to come home to a tail-wagging puppy. Or a whiskered kitten. I love dogs. But I've always been partial to cats."

"Then you're going to love the time you're in Istanbul."

Before she could ask what he meant by that, Alden's phone rang on the wooden table between them.

"Excuse me, I need to take this if you don't mind."

She nodded and he rose to stride to the other end of the plane to take the call. Hannah took the opportunity to study him as he spoke. They'd communicated rather sporadically over the past few days, then this morning a limo had arrived at her apartment to drive her to the airport. In the meantime, he'd deposited a sizable amount into her bank account. Several times over the amount he'd procured at the casino slots that day.

What had she been thinking to leave such a major decision to such a fluky random act of chance? She'd never been so impulsive. But then, Alden sure seemed to bring out the impulsive side of her. She'd actually married him that way.

Now she watched as he shifted the phone from one ear to the other as he spoke. He'd come a long way from that cheery young teenage boy who'd pretty much had to raise himself after both his parents had left him to his own devices at the ripe old age of fifteen.

She couldn't imagine what that must have been like for him. Her own mother was overly vocal about her opinions and was definitely a meddler. She could be overbearing and opinionated. But Hannah had never felt lacking in parental love.

Unlike Alden who'd essentially been abandoned by both parents. First, his mom, then his father shortly after. Look how far Alden had come despite all the unfair cards he'd been dealt in life.

Her eyes began to droop and she could no longer fight her exhaustion. Alden was still speaking on the phone when she drifted off to sleep.

When her lids fluttered open again, she had no idea how long she'd been asleep. Alden was back in his chair across from her, hunched over the table between them, typing into a sleek black laptop.

He looked up before she could avert her gaze. Caught red-handed watching him. The corners of his lips lifted into a smile.

"What?"

She shook her head, uncurled her legs from underneath her. "Nothing. Just observing how driven you are. You're doing so much to ensure this deal goes through."

He shrugged. "I don't know how else to be. If you go hungry often enough as a kid, you work hard to avoid having it happen to you as an adult." His lips thinned as soon as he said the last word, as if he regretted what he'd just told her.

Hungry. Hannah would never have guessed. Everyone in town knew about Alden's situation. They knew his parents had left him alone in that house that they'd paid for outright when Alden was just born. But a teen-age boy needed so much more than a roof over his head.

"There was no one else to make sure the bills got paid so that the water ran and the lights stayed on," he said, not quite meeting her eyes.

"Why didn't you sell the house, Alden?"

He shrugged. "It wasn't mine to sell. And a fifteen-year-old walking into a real estate office to inquire about a sale might have raised a few eyebrows and a good amount of suspicion. I didn't need the authorities digging into my circumstances and then leading me straight into the foster system."

She'd had no idea. It was hard to know what to say. The whole town, except for Max's family, had pretty much left Alden Hamid alone. Including her and her mother. The fact that they'd had their own troubles at the time was no excuse.

And here she was complaining that she didn't have a pet to come home to.

His eyes darted around her face, then he leaned back and crossed his arms over his chest. His whole demeanor had suddenly shut down.

"No need to look at me that way, Hannah."

"What way?"

"With such sorrow. I don't need anyone's pity."

He couldn't have read her reaction more wrong. She hadn't meant to insult him. Just the opposite.

"I'm sorry. I didn't mean to."

"The Harpers made sure I got at least two or three square meals a week." He was referring to Max's family. "But they had their own several mouths to feed. As for the rest, I managed to scrape by."

He certainly had. No small accomplishment.

"I know you did," she told him. "And I absolutely didn't mean any offense. If anything, what you're seeing on my face is pure admiration."

His eyebrows shot up clear to his hairline. She'd shocked him.

Well, she'd shocked herself. But she wasn't sorry. She'd said what she'd said and she meant it.

The afternoon sun had begun to give way to evening by the time they touched down at Istanbul International Airport. The car his administrative assistant had arranged for them awaited outside by the curb. Within minutes, their driver was zigzagging through the busy streets on their way to the hotel.

Alden stole a glance at Hannah sitting next to him in the back seat. She couldn't seem to tear her gaze away from the view outside. He could hardly blame her. Istanbul was a bustling city, busy at all hours with both locals and tourists crowding its meandering sidewalks and hilly streets.

"I can't wait to explore this city," Hannah declared, turning away from the window to face him. Excitement was practically dripping from her features. "Please say we'll have time."

"We'll make certain of it," he reassured her. "What kind of hus—" He caught himself before he could finish the word. It was better to view each other as business partners more so than anything else. He began again, "What kind of business associate would I be if I brought you to Istanbul but then didn't take you to see the sights?"

Hannah actually clapped twice before turning back to stare out the window. Alden studied her profile with a smile. As cliché as it was, she appeared to be a kid viewing the glass case in a candy store.

Luckily, any awkwardness from the tense conversation during the flight over seemed to be past them. He knew he'd edged perilously close to snapping at her. He just wasn't used to discussing his past too often. Such talk brought to the surface all manner of painful memories he'd long ago buried and preferred to keep that way.

He'd known as a kid the way the townsfolk talked about him. He knew they referred to him as the poor Hamid kid who'd been abandoned by both parents. No one had been outwardly cruel. And the Harpers had made sure he'd had what he needed to graduate high school and then attend college on a scholarship and countless loans. But if he never returned to Reardon again in this lifetime, it would be too soon.

So he'd been short with Hannah, careless with his response. Then she'd said she admired his determination. No, she'd actually said she'd admired *him*. No one had ever said such words to him before. Darned if he'd been able to come up with a response. The whole conversation had thrown him off and he was happy it was behind them.

The driver finally turned onto a side street and stopped the car. Hannah looked at him questioningly. "A lot of these streets in the Sultanahmet area are pedestrian and trolley only. We'll have to walk the rest of the way to our hotel. Levin will make sure our bags make their way to our room."

The driver opened her door and tipped his hat to her. "I'll be sure you get your luggage right away, miss."

Alden took her by the elbow and they made their way into the throng of the crowd—shoppers, partiers, those out for an evening snack.

"I feel like I'm in a whole new world," Hannah said, her eyes darting from one area to another as they made their way through the square. The evening was balmy and warm, a myriad of scents in the air. How often had he walked through this square and not appreciated any of it the way Hannah so clearly was. The smile on her face appeared as if it might permanently be etched on her lips.

"We can come back down after getting settled in, if you'd like."

Funny, not less than twenty minutes ago, Alden was ready to crash in the hotel suite with a hot tea followed by a long shower, then sleep. He'd had no intention of heading back out. But the look on Hannah's face as she took in their surroundings somehow gave him a second wind. He wanted to see that look for as long as she held it.

"I'd love that! Yes. Without question."

"Somehow I knew that would be your answer."

"I was so afraid you wouldn't offer."

He chuckled, led her closer to their hotel. "Let's go get freshened up first. My regular suite happens to be on the south side of the resort. Prime viewing."

"Of what?" she asked, slowing to admire a vendor's rack of silk scarves and *örtüs*.

"The Hagia Sophia. You won't believe your eyes when you see it all lit up from the balcony."

"Our suite has a balcony overlooking the great Hagia Sophia?"

He nodded with another chuckle. "I mean, it might not compare to the fake Eiffel Tower we had a view of back in Vegas."

She punched him on the arm playfully. "Are you trying to compare a man-made tourist structure in the middle of a desert gambling town to one of the greatest architectural creations in the world?"

He laughed at her horrified expression. Vegas and the wedding already seemed like a lifetime ago. Images of the night they'd gotten married had gradually spotted his brain over the past few days. Though they hadn't been intimate in the physical sense, they'd spent the night in each other's arms. He may not have remembered much from that evening but he certainly remembered the way Hannah had felt in his embrace. The scent of her hair under his nose. Her warm breath against his bare chest.

They'd kissed. He couldn't even say if he remembered or was conjuring from his imagination, but he recollected the taste of strawberries and vanilla when he'd had his mouth on hers. Her hot breath intermingling with his as he explored her mouth with his tongue. A ball of heat curled in his middle.

Stop it.

He couldn't even allow himself to think such thoughts. He'd made it clear to her that this was nothing more than a business venture in which he needed her help. He couldn't let himself forget that.

Hannah's senses hummed on overload as she shut off the shower and stepped out of the stall. Wrapping a thick Turkish towel around her middle, she checked her reflection in the mirror. Despite the hours of traveling internationally—it was an entirely different experience to fly privately with access to exclusive lounges—she felt alert and full of energy. And excitement. It was just such a novel experience for her to be here in such a foreign-to-her place.

When was the last time she'd felt this excited about

anything? She couldn't recall. She could barely remember the last trip she'd taken. A weeklong trip to the Florida Keys with Justin and his family. Hannah had spent more time with his mother than she actually had with Justin. He and his father had boarded a boat daily, rain or shine, to deep-sea fish.

The Keys were fun in a subdued kind of way. But Istanbul was an entirely different vibe. She'd never been anywhere this exotic. The streets they'd driven through had seemed a cross between stylish Newbury Street in Boston and something out of a scene from an Aladdin or Sinbad movie. She couldn't wait to get back out there and explore as much as she could during the short time they had here.

One thing was certain, once all this was over and Alden had his deal in hand, she was going to find a way to come back here. Maybe she'd bring her mom. A pang of sorrow settled in the pit of her stomach. The next time she'd come here, Alden wouldn't be accompanying her.

Stepping out of the bathroom and into her private room, she headed over to the closet where she'd unpacked her clothing earlier. Alden's suite at this hotel appeared to be an entire floor complete with two separate bedrooms with their own bathroom and shower. Funny, she hadn't even thought to ask him about the accommodations to make sure she'd have her privacy. She'd assumed Alden would make sure she'd have it. And he had.

Picking out a pair of comfortable cotton capris and a fluid three-quarter-length colorful top, she quickly got dressed, then grabbed a sweater and her cross-body purse. When she made it out to the common sitting area between their rooms, Alden was already out there dressed and seated on the black leather L-shaped couch. The large screen television played an intense-looking soccer match with the announcer rambling loudly and quickly. Alden didn't really seem to be paying attention to it though, he had his laptop open on his lap with a look of focused concentration on his face.

A muscle fluttered in the vicinity of her chest as he stood and smiled at her. The man really knew how to wear his clothes well. Black pressed casual slacks that accented his hips with a short-sleeved Henley the color of an ocean sky that brought out the hue of his eyes and the tanned muscular skin of his arm. Lordy, she couldn't even remember noticing a man's arms before, let alone appreciating how muscular they might be.

He looked like he'd just stepped out of a men's cologne ad.

"Ready to go?" he asked, setting the laptop down on the coffee table and shutting the cover.

"Absolutely."

He looked her over. "You look nice." He turned away as soon as he said it, as if the words had slipped out unbidden. "I mean, what you're wearing is very appropriate given we'll be walking around a square of shops and vendors for a bit before dinner."

"Dinner?" Hannah had just assumed they'd grab a bite from one of the many food carts she'd noticed along the way. All of them had made her mouth water with the spicy, tangy aroma that wafted her way as she passed each one.

"I took the liberty of having a table reserved at one of my favorite spots nearby in a couple hours. The food is amazing. Hope that's okay?"

"Sounds great. Thank you for doing that."

"You're welcome."

"Shall we go, then?" Hannah wasn't going to bother hiding her eagerness.

"Just one thing." He stepped closer to her. The scent of his now-familiar aftershave did something to her insides whenever she smelled it.

Before she could guess what he was doing, he reached into his pocket and pulled out a very recognizable velvet box. Hannah's breath caught as he flipped open the box with one hand and took her arm with the other.

"You're going to need this again," he said, his breath warm against her cheek. "May as well start wearing it now." Her hand shook as he slipped it on her finger. There was no way he hadn't noticed. Hopefully, he would chalk it up to her excitement about being in this city rather than the truth. That the whole scenario was taking her mind and heart on a journey that would be perilous in all manner of ways.

Like imagining what it would feel like if this man were really slipping a ring on her finger because he'd just proposed to her, legitimately and soberly this time.

Somehow, she found her voice enough to answer. "Uh…yeah. I guess that makes sense." Incredibly, her voice was hardly shaky at all as she spoke.

When she looked up at Alden, he was staring at her with an intensity that had her knees wobbling. Hannah pulled her hand out of his with a bit too much speed.

Get a grip.

The ring on her finger may be a valuable diamond on a platinum band, but it might as well be costume jewelry. Because that's exactly what it was, just part of a costume for a role she was playing. It was like how those actresses walking the red carpet at all those events always wore those absurdly expensive baubles they had to return the day after. This wasn't any different.

Some day in the near future, she'd be returning this ring back to Alden yet again.

CHAPTER EIGHT

ALDEN WILLED THE elevator to somehow go faster down to the lobby because the silence between him and Hannah now was almost deafening.

He'd held her hand a little too long up there when he'd slipped the diamond ring back on Hannah's finger. Now as a result, there was a slight tinge of awkwardness between them.

Just like back in school. He used to get so tongue-tied near Hannah, always at a loss for what to say. Or he'd somehow managed to say or do the wrong thing. The same way he had upstairs when he'd lingered holding her hand.

It was no wonder she was standing there still and barely blinking as she watched the panel of numbers above the elevator doors.

In his defense there'd been a lot happening in his head during that moment. The action must have triggered some of the memories hidden from the night they'd eloped. Images of the first time he'd given her the ring. He'd simply handed it to her then, he finally remembered. The two of them both doubled over in laughter. Hannah telling him they would have done just as well with a plastic ring from the gumball machine at the arcade they'd passed on the way to the chapel.

Alden released a sigh of relief when they finally arrived at the first-floor lobby and the elevator doors slid open.

The crowd had grown thicker in Sultanahmet Square when they stepped outside. The chords of oud music could be heard coming from more than one direction. A myriad of spoken languages sounded all around them. Outdoor cafés were full with customers, both those lingering over their afternoon tea or those who'd just arrived for an early dinner.

"I'm not quite sure what I was expecting but this definitely exceeds my imagination," Hannah said over his shoulder, following him toward the first row of shops.

"Hope you feel the same about dinner," he answered, opening the door of a ceramic shop. Hannah was sure to get a kick out of this place. It boasted an elaborate display of ceramic handmade cats in all sizes and colors.

"What do you mean?" she asked. "What's so special about dinner tonight?"

"Everything in Istanbul is special. And rarely is any dinner simple. But you'll have to wait and see what I mean."

She looked like she wanted to press but was immediately distracted by the menagerie of cat ceramics. Her exclamation had him grinning.

"Oh, my, these are adorable." She fingered a small kitten figurine with long wire whiskers and a white spot over one eye. The thing looked so real, Alden half expected it to jump off the shelf and into Hannah's arms.

He couldn't help the grin that spread over his face at her reaction. It was just what he'd hoped for. "You said you've been wanting a kitten to come home to. Maybe you can start with a ceramic one for now."

Hannah actually squealed with delight. Delighting him

in return. "I wish I could buy them all. Just ship every single one back to the States."

He chuckled. "As much as the shopkeeper would love that, how about we just start with one or two for now?"

Said shopkeeper appeared from the back room at that very moment.

"*Merhaba*," she greeted them with a warm smile. "American?"

"*Merhaba*," Alden returned her greeting with what he hoped was a passable accent. "Yes, good guess. American by way of New England."

"Welcome," the woman beamed. "I'm Ayse. Which ones would you like?" she asked Hannah directly, motioning to the shelf Hannah was still eyeing with sheer adoration.

Not for the first time, Alden had to appreciate the savvy of these shop owners. Always assuming the sale.

"It's so hard to decide," Hannah answered. "I wish I could take them all."

Alden tried not to wince. That was the kind of statement that was music to a shopkeeper's ears.

"Take as many as you like," Ayse said, her voice dripping with temptation. "We can ship them for you."

Hannah tilted her head, as if actually considering buying several. "Hmm. My own litter of adorable ceramic kittens."

If there was anything Alden knew about this city, it's that the people loved their cats.

Ayse turned her smile in his direction. "Your wife will be so happy with these."

Alden almost corrected her before he caught himself. Hannah really was his wife. There was no misinformation to correct.

"I'll take these three for now," Hannah said, pointing to what appeared to be a tomcat, a momma cat, and a baby kitten. "How much?"

The shopkeeper named an exorbitant amount. Hannah appeared taken aback for a slight moment before she simply nodded, then reached for her purse.

Uh-oh. He hadn't told her about how customary it was to barter in this part of the world. From what little shopping he'd done last time he was here, Alden knew she was about to overpay more than twice what the items would normally sell for.

Ayse laughed and put a hand on Hannah's before she could pull her card out. "You're supposed to argue with me. Tell me that's too expensive. Make a show of leaving perhaps even."

Hannah blinked at the other woman before nodding slowly. "Gotcha. In that case, I think that's far too expensive. I refuse to pay so much."

The women play-argued for several more moments while Alden watched in amusement. So far, this trip was much more entertaining than his usual business trips. To add icing to the cake, he didn't have to order room service or grab a takeout box from the doner shop next door and bring it back to eat by himself as he appreciated the majestic sight of the Bosporus from his balcony alone.

The thought gave him pause.

Huh. He hadn't even realized doing things that way had been bothering him. Being alone in these cities was simply what he'd always done. But the thought of being here with anyone else wasn't meshing in his brain.

"I will not pay a penny more," Hannah said loudly with mock outrage, pulling him out of his thoughts.

The shopkeeper shook her head with a clearly exaggerated reaction. "Fine. Done. But you drive a hard bargain, Miss Hannah." The woman would have been much more convincing if her lips weren't trembling with unreleased laughter.

She turned her green kohl-lined eyes to Alden. "Your wife did good," she said. "You should be proud to have married her."

She would never get used to being referred to as Alden's wife. Not that there was any point in trying to get used to it. It wasn't as if the title was any kind of permanent, or even long-term, status.

"I could rush those back to the hotel room if you'd like." Alden pointed to the box she carried that held her precious newly prized possessions: a family of colorful ceramic cats. "So you don't have to carry that box around."

Hannah immediately shook her head to turn down his offer. Maybe it was silly of her, but she didn't want anything to break the momentum of this magical evening. She wanted it to continue unimpeded and uninterrupted with Alden by her side throughout.

"I think I'll be all right. I might need to buy one of those woven handbags over at that stall though to put them in."

"Looking to hone your bartering skills some more, are you?"

"I'm just getting started," she said with an exaggerated wave of her hand. Though the more reasonable, more logical part of her told her she should try and take it easy with the purchases. After all, money might be tight once she returned to the States. She was essentially unemployed, after all. Once this assignment, or whatever it could be called, with Alden was completed, she'd have to find another job.

Unless…she actually found enough inspiration during this trip to get started on sketching some designs. Enough to get started on a portfolio she might be able to shop around.

Could she really make it work? An entire career shift?

It seemed like such a pipe dream. Yet, Alden had made it sound quite achievable. Did she dare believe him?

Well, that's what she was here to find out. Already, her mind was spinning with ideas. Like maybe she'd draw a patterned dress the color of the Bosporus, intricately stitched with cat eyes along the hem and sleeves. Or maybe a pair of flowing wide pants that might work really well with the longer tunics hanging in some of the store windows.

"And where did you just drift off to?" Alden asked. "You walked right past the handbag store."

Huh. So she had.

"Sorry. There's just so much to see here," she said, backtracking her steps. Alden followed, shaking his head and smiling.

The handbag store was just as overwhelming. The colors and designs were so original and vibrant Hannah thought she might have stepped back into an animated movie again.

Two of the bags immediately caught her eye. One hand-stitched with ancient Ottoman lettering of intricate detail. The other a painted canvas of the Istanbul skyline accented with buttery soft leather. In the end, she just couldn't pick between the two. So she bought them both. Which of course just gave them yet more things to carry.

When they stepped out of the store, she turned to find

Alden flexing his arms and doing pretend arm curls, straining with imaginary weights. When he finally stopped that, he wiped his brow as if overexerted, then took several gasping breaths. He looked ridiculous. More than one passerby gave an amused chuckle at his antics.

"What in the world are you doing?"

He tilted his head. "Just trying to get ready for all the shopping bags I'm certain to be carrying before you're through."

"Ha, ha. Very funny."

"Maybe we should have brought a cart."

Now they were even fake bickering like some really married couple. Teasing each other the way an actual married couple might.

Just stop it.

Hannah was ready to resume walking when Alden's expression completely changed. His playful smile vanished, his eyes narrowing on a distant target in the crowd. Hannah could feel him stiffening. The muscles around his jaw grew tight. Whatever Alden was looking at, he was not pleased.

She turned in the direction of his stare. But all she could see was the same scene all around—shoppers, diners, people roaming about, enjoying their day.

"Alden? What's wrong?"

He continued to stare for a bit longer before giving his head a brisk shake. Finally, he turned back to her.

"Nothing. I just thought I saw someone I know. I must have been mistaken."

Whoever he'd thought he'd seen, he didn't appear to be a fan.

He motioned for her to proceed and they'd only gone a few steps when Hannah's curiosity got the better of her.

"Who was it?"

He shook his head. "No one. It's not important."

That statement certainly didn't ring true given his reaction back there.

Alden was a successful businessman. Anyone with that level of success had to have made a few enemies along the way, deservedly or not. But the expression on Alden's face moments ago had been intense. Fierce almost. Her gut told her it was no business-related matter. It appeared much more personal.

Was there a woman in his past who had wounded him? So deeply that the mere possibility of seeing her had elicited such a jarring reaction? A sinking feeling churned in her middle at the thought. A feeling she refused to consider might be jealousy. She had no claim to Alden Hamid. No right to feel any kind of possessiveness.

She just had to keep reminding herself of that fact.

The fun and jovial mood of just moments ago was gone now. Replaced by a tension in the air that only seemed to grow with each step they took. It didn't help that Alden seemed to be scanning that same area in the distance every time she glanced back at him.

Hannah wanted so badly to find another way to ask for details but there seemed no good way to do so.

She paused in front of a crowded café. "Maybe we should just go back to the hotel," she said, her earlier happy mood now gone for good.

Alden appeared not to have even heard her. He was still too distracted.

The view was doing wonders for her state of mind. Hannah stepped over to the balcony railing and scanned the horizon. The Bosphoros was alight, framing the Hagia

Sophia that stood majestically before it, the tall minarets shooting toward the sky above. She felt as if she might have stepped into a life-sized painting from the Byzantine era.

She'd made a beeline out here as soon as they'd arrived back at the suite after dropping her bags off on her bed.

Alden had immediately escaped himself and closed the door behind him after entering his own room with the explanation that he might as well get some work done until dinner. He'd encouraged Hannah to get some rest.

She wouldn't have imagined when they'd first stepped out earlier that this would be the way their evening might end. With both of them holed up in their own living quarters. Their excursion had started out so enjoyable and fun. But it was as if Alden's entire personality had changed after they'd left the handbag store.

So now, here she stood, admiring this wondrous view out here all by herself when she'd much rather be out there exploring it. With Alden by her side.

Wishful thinking. One would think she'd be over that penchant by now. Growing up without a father who'd abandoned them. Then being unceremoniously dumped by the man she'd wanted to marry.

Her limited experience with members of the opposite sex had been woefully less than ideal so far. What made her possibly think being with Alden would be any different?

He hadn't really wanted to marry her. If it weren't for this business prospect he was after, they'd be divorced already. The man hadn't even asked her out in high school, for heaven's sake. Despite having had countless opportunities to do so. He'd dated scores of other girls. But never her.

If it weren't for Max and Mandy's status as their respective best friends, the two of them wouldn't have spent any time together at all.

Things were no different now. Hannah was still the girl who was there because it was convenient. Nothing more.

She wasn't sure how much time had passed when she heard the sliding glass door of the common balcony entrance swish open behind her. Alden appeared beside her a moment later.

"Is it time already for dinner?" she asked.

He draped his forearms on the balcony railing, his head slightly bowed with his gaze focused on the horizon.

"No, we still have some time," he answered. "Just thought I'd come out here and enjoy the scenery as well."

Hannah simply nodded. Did that mean he might be ready to talk to her finally? About exactly what had gotten him so rattled back there at the shopping bazaar?

Alden answered the question with his next words. "I know you must be curious about exactly what went down earlier. Why I acted the way I did."

She lifted her shoulder to answer. "It was rather uncharacteristic and sudden on your part."

He nodded slowly, not taking his gaze off the horizon. "I get that. But I was hoping we could just enjoy the view for a few moments."

In silence was the implied remainder of that sentence.

"Of course," she answered. "It's not my place to pry, I know that. You don't owe me any kind of explanation." True enough. It wasn't as if she were really his wife. Why did she have to keep reminding herself of that so often?

If there was a woman out there who had broken his heart and left him so emotionally raw that the mere possibility of running into her changed his entire mood, it really was none of her business. Alden didn't really belong to her in any way. Not in heart. And not in body.

The fact that he didn't argue her last statement only proved her point.

A cover of clouds slowly moved over the night sky, darkening the balcony in shadows before either of them spoke again. Alden cleared his throat before he began. "There's been at least two occasions when I've traveled to this part of the world when I've run into my father."

Whatever Hannah had been expecting him to say, it certainly hadn't been that.

His father.

Her brain scrambled for a way to process what he'd just revealed. The last she'd heard, years ago, Alden's father had returned to his birthplace to a small village in Cyprus.

Alden continued, "I thought it might have happened again today," he added after several beats. "And I'm ashamed to admit that even after all these years, without any contact whatsoever, the possibility of seeing him again just throws me off." He sucked in a breath. "In any case, I'm sorry I let it ruin our first evening here."

For the life of her, Hannah couldn't think of a way to respond. Reflexively, she reached over to rest her hand on his forearm.

"You don't have to apologize to me. I'm the one who should tell you that I'm sorry."

He finally turned to her, blinking. "You? Whatever for?"

She struggled to find a way to answer. To put into words the jumble of thoughts scrambling through her brain. She should apologize for not giving him enough grace to explain it all in his own time. For jumping to a conclusion based solely on her own insecurities and the jealousy she had no business feeling. For selfishly worrying about her ruined evening rather than what Alden might be going through to have him react the way he had back there.

"Never mind," she answered. Maybe she'd be able to explain it to him at some point. But she couldn't summon the words right now. "Just want to say that you can talk to me if you want to. About anything." Hannah groaned inwardly. The words sounded so lame as she said them. So cliché. But it was the truth. Whatever this situation was between them, the whole fake marriage slash business arrangement. Beneath it all, they'd known each other for years. They'd both suffered the pain of abandonment by their fathers. On a deep-rooted level, they were friends. From where she was standing right now, that trumped all else.

"I appreciate that," Alden said, his voice thick. "But neither of my parents are topics I particularly enjoy discussing."

"Fair enough." She gave his arm a slight squeeze. "But I'm here if that ever changes." She meant that with her whole heart. Regardless of how this arrangement between them turned out in the end.

They stood silently, focused on the view for several more moments. How had it never occurred to her before just how much she and Alden had in common? The answer was simple. While both their fathers had abandoned them, at least Hannah had grown up with the benefit of having at least one devoted, committed parent, flawed as her mother may have been.

While Alden had been alone for years.

CHAPTER NINE

ALDEN FELT LIKE a fool. He'd only meant to go out there on the balcony to apologize to Hannah. Instead, she'd been compelled to try and comfort him, to assure him she'd be available to lend an ear if he ever needed one. As much as he appreciated her sympathy, he so didn't need to be viewed by anyone as some wounded soul who'd never gotten over past hurts.

Especially not by Hannah, of all people. After all, sympathy could all too easily turn to pity.

Because he *had* gotten over his past. He'd done quite well despite his past, in fact. That's what he preferred people to focus on. He was a successful businessman who'd grown from a hotel busboy to overall manager to hotelier to hospitality magnate, with an impressive cache of international resorts to his name. And he'd done it all before the age of thirty. That was the man he wanted to be perceived as. Not the confused, unwanted teenager who hadn't known where his next meal was coming from.

Now, as they walked to the other side of town to make their dinner reservations, he could only wish he'd handled the whole fiasco better.

The gentleman in the square most likely hadn't even been his old man. And so what if he had been? His father would have been just as much a stranger as some random tourist or local who may have looked like him.

Hannah pulled him out of his reverie by pausing all of a sudden in front of a bench. "That's the most interesting and unusual statue I've ever seen."

Alden looked up to realize they'd reached the famous landmark Istanbulians were particularly proud of. He'd been here so often the novelty had worn off.

"That's Tumbuli," he explained. "He was a beloved cat who roamed this part of the city. The shopkeepers made sure he was well fed and taken care of. He liked to hang out on that particular bench. He lived a long life for a cat. But when the time came, the locals were so sad when he passed they commissioned that statue in his honor to sit in his favorite spot."

Hannah clasped her hands together in delight. "It's fantastic. How right you were to say this city adores its felines. What does the name mean?"

Alden rubbed his jaw, trying his best to come up with a comparable term. He offered the only translation he could come up with. "I guess the best equivalent would be chunky. Like I said, he was well fed."

Hannah released a peal of laughter that had him grinning in response. "Chunky cat! And he has his own monument. How wonderful."

Alden shrugged. "I wasn't kidding about how much the Turks adore their cats."

Hannah stepped over and sat down next to the statue, reaching out her phone. "Please do me the honor of taking my photo with the infamous Tumbuli."

Alden stepped closer to oblige when a smiling couple interrupted mid snap.

"*Lutfen*," the man said, motioning to the phone. "We can take you both."

Alden glanced at Hannah to gauge her reaction. She nodded enthusiastically. Handing the gentleman the phone, he sat next to her, the bronze cat statue between them.

He'd never before even thought to get a photo here. The story when he'd first heard it had amused him, of course. But he hadn't given it much thought since. Hannah's reaction was completely different.

The sheer joy on her face as their photos were taken bolstered his mood severalfold. It was hard to remain morose when she was around. The tense events of earlier were growing more and more distant. He should have never let his emotions get the better of him the way they had. He should have focused on the woman he'd been with and made sure to show her a good time.

Well, he was determined to do just that the rest of the night. This was a good start. He couldn't believe he'd forgotten about Tumbuli. He offered a silent thanks to the lost cat for the way he'd served to further lighten the mood.

The man handed the phone back and Alden thanked the both of them.

Hannah scrolled through the scenes. "I can't wait to send these to my mom," she said, the smile on her face not having wilted the slightest. "She'll get a huge kick out of the story behind the statue."

She'd have many more photos to send before the trip was over. A few more probably from tonight, he had no doubt.

Alden led her to the door of the restaurant and they were shown to their table. A server immediately appeared to fill their water glasses. She introduced herself as Fatima. Hannah beamed at the other woman's remarks while telling her about the purchases she'd made.

Alden took a sip of his water and used the moment to study her. Dressed in a silky top with her hair falling about her shoulders, modest pearl earrings adorned her ears. The hazel green color of her eyes were accented by the soft lighting in the room. Her cheeks were blush with excitement, soft pink gloss glistened on her lips. Alden found his gaze hovering on her mouth. How had he not noticed when they were kids how lush and ruby red Hannah's lips were? Kissable.

The word came to his mind unbidden before he pushed it away. Thoughts like that could only lead to trouble. He had no business thinking about kissing Hannah. Once this trip was over, he couldn't even be sure of the next time he'd see her again.

"Alden?"

He looked up to find her staring at him inquisitively. The waitress had left their table without him even noticing. She'd clearly just asked him something and he hadn't even heard. Man, he had to stop drifting off.

"I'm not quite sure," he answered the question he hadn't even heard, hoping the response was general enough to cover his distracted state.

She blinked up at him in confusion. Clearly, he hadn't answered in a way that made sense.

"You're not sure what you usually order here?"

"Oh, the menu is preset. Unless you have a special request. I think you'll like it."

"I'm sure I will."

He was certain of it. Just as he was certain he had to make sure to avoid looking at her lips while she ate.

Easier said than done, a soft voice inside his head mocked.

* * *

The enticing aromas in the air as she stepped into the restaurant had Hannah realizing just how famished she was. Savory spices, grilled meats, and a sweet syrupy scent all mingled together under her nose and made her mouth water.

The room itself looked like it could be something out of a historical movie set in the Middle East. Thick velvet gold trimmed curtains in a deep burgundy red hung from the walls. The round tables were covered in ornate tablecloths. Brass genie lamps set in the center with glowing candles cast shadows about the room.

Her creative side immediately kicked into overdrive. She couldn't wait to get a chance to sketch out some ideas inspired by the rich colors and images around her.

Alden seemed much less affected by their surroundings. But then, he was used to such experiences, whereas all this was so new to her. And she had him to thank for exposing her to it. If she'd turned down his offer to be his pretend wife, she'd be back home in Boston right now polishing her résumé and updating all her professional profiles. Bored out of her mind.

She cast a glance at him now. His sky blue shirt combined with the soft lighting brought out the hints of steel gray in his eyes. He'd rolled his sleeves up again, making it hard not to focus on those arms she found so appealing.

Enough. Hadn't she decided earlier on the balcony that they worked better as friends? She had to keep that in mind for the remainder of this trip.

Fatima returned with a large bowl of salad and scooped out a hefty portion for each of them onto gold-colored plates. The fresh array of bite-sized cut vegetables along with the tangy scent of vinegar and zesty lemon set her stomach to grumbling. She dug right in as soon as Alden picked up his fork.

Before she knew it, a platter of assorted grilled meats arrived.

"You were so right," she told Alden between bites of food. "This meal is fantastic."

"There's more to this place than just the food," he answered.

Before she could ask what he meant by that, the lights dimmed drastically. A set of curtains she'd assumed were covering another wall drew open to reveal a low-level stage. Flame-lit towers stood on each corner. Fatima reappeared to clear the table with speedy efficiency just as a steady beat of drums sounded through the air. The beat was soon accompanied by a guitar melody. Hannah turned around to realize a three-man band had set up and were beginning to play.

She gasped in surprise and delight when she turned back as a figure appeared on the stage. A dark-haired woman with flowing curls wearing a long skirt and multiple scarves around her shoulders. She began moving her hips to the music and dancing about the stage in her bare feet. Small cymbals on her fingers followed the beat of the music as she danced.

"A belly dancer!"

Alden chuckled. "That's right. It's dinner and a show."

"This is so much more than I'd expected," she said, unable to tear her eyes off the talented woman who appeared to be double-jointed in all manner of limbs.

"What kind of hus—?" Alden stopped and cleared his throat before continuing, "What kind of host would I be if I brought you all the way to Istanbul and didn't treat you to a belly dancing performance?"

Husband. He'd originally been about to say husband.

For one insane moment, Hannah felt the urge to pretend. To make believe that what he'd been about to say was the reality. That she was here accompanying her husband on a business trip as she maneuvered a career crossroads. That they really were man and wife.

Stop. She had to stop. Friends, that's all they were.

The first song came to an end and the dancer jumped off the stage for the second one. Dancing about the room, she earned cheers and applause as she went to each table one by one. Hannah found herself bouncing and swaying to the catchy music right in her chair.

The dancer reached their table just as the third song began. At Hannah's chair dancing, she flashed her a wide smile and held out her hands. The woman was asking her to stand up and join her! In front of all these people. Hannah's heart surged to her throat, horrified at the mere thought. She didn't know the first thing about how to belly dance.

"Come on," Alden urged next to her at the table. "Give it a try."

The belly dancer nodded her head, reached for her hand.

She immediately shook her head, hoping she was doing so politely. "No, there's no way," she said, hoping the woman understood enough English, though her actions had to be clear enough about her response.

"I think you'd be good at it," Alden said with a laugh.

"No. I don't think so. There is not a chance in this lifetime you're going to catch me attempting to belly dance."

Yet somehow, she was on her feet a moment later, doing her best to move her hips the way the belly dancer was showing her. She had no idea if she was even close to getting it right. Doubling over in laughter every few beats didn't help.

The other diners began to clap but Hannah barely heard the applause.

She only heard Alden's amused laugher echoing above the music.

"Something tells me I'll be feeling a few aches in my hips and back tomorrow morning."

Alden led Hannah out the door of the restaurant and to the sidewalk. The stroll back to their hotel would take a while, but he figured they could use the air and the exercise.

"Nah, you're a natural. You may have been a belly dancer in a previous life."

Hannah laughed before replying. "Somehow, I highly doubt that. I'm lucky I didn't fall right over when she had me do that last move. I'm sure everyone thought I looked ridiculous."

That was decidedly not true. Alden didn't dare tell her the thoughts he'd been having while he'd watched her with the dancer. How he'd had to look away from the way her hips were moving to the beat and the effects those movements were having on him. As it was, he'd have to fight hard to keep from reimagining it all whenever he closed his eyes.

Man, he had it bad. It might be time to acknowledge that. So that he could make sure to fight it with all he had. This fake marriage set up was confusing enough without him blurring the lines even further simply because he'd been turned on by watching his faux wife dancing.

An image popped into his head of her dancing that

way yet again. Only this time, it was just the two of them. Alone in a dark room. Alden her only audience, Hannah moving that way just for him and no one else.

No. No. No.

There he went again. He had to get a hold of himself or the next leg of this journey was going to be a torture of temptation. He owed it to Hannah to remain professional until this arrangement was completed.

She suddenly paused and turned to him. The lights of the Bosphorus twinkled behind her, framing her face.

"I really enjoyed myself tonight," she said. "Thank you for setting up such a fun evening."

"You don't have to thank me, Hannah. I enjoyed myself too." She had no idea how much. The only time he'd been at that restaurant before, he'd been a guest of a potential business partner. He'd barely paid any attention to the entertainment then. Now, it would be all he'd associate the place with after tonight.

By the time they got back to the hotel, he'd managed to convince himself that if he tried hard enough, those images of Hannah dancing might somehow be erased from his mind.

Though a cold shower probably couldn't hurt.

She was much too hyped up to sleep. So far this day had been a kaleidoscope of new experiences. Hannah felt as if she'd lived an entire year in the few short hours since they'd arrived in Istanbul. It might have been nice to perhaps talk about it all with her companion slash fake husband, but Alden had excused himself and jumped in the shower as soon as they'd returned to the suite.

After freshening up herself, she just couldn't bring herself to crawl into bed knowing without a doubt that sleep would elude her. Wrapping the thick terry bathrobe around herself, she stepped back out into the suite and turned the television on.

A quick surf of the channels offered two different soccer games, a news show of some sort, and a movie. Despite not understanding the language, Hannah found herself sucked into what she could make out of the storyline, which seemed to feature some kind of love triangle where the heroine was torn between a penniless farmer and wealthy landowner.

Looked like some dramas were the same the world over.

Alden's thick baritone startled her from behind suddenly. "What are you watching?"

With a jump, she clasped her hand to her chest. So engrossed in the movie, she hadn't even heard him approach. Looked like she wasn't the only one unable to sleep. She hadn't even bothered to turn the volume up much, not like she'd be able to understand the words, after all.

"Sorry," Alden said. "I didn't mean to sneak up on you."

"Not your fault," she answered. "I'm just unexpectedly invested in this poor woman's saga. I can't even guess who she's going to end up choosing."

Alden narrowed his eyes on the screen. "Huh."

"I just wish I understood more of what they're saying."

To her surprise, he walked around the couch to sit next to her. He'd apparently showered with some type of minty soap that tickled her nostrils and had her resisting the urge to inhale deeply of his skin. The warmth of his body as he sat down next to her sent a shiver up her spine.

He wore loose-fitting gray sweatpants and a tight T-shirt that accented the contours of his chest and shoulders.

Hannah blinked and turned her focus back to the screen.

"I could try to translate," he said. "I've been here enough times that I might be able to catch a few phrases here and there."

Hannah wanted to jump at the offer. Aside from wanting to know the dialogue, it felt nice to have Alden here sitting next to her while they watched a movie together. "I don't want to keep you up," she said instead.

He shrugged, the motion making his upper arm rub against her shoulder and sending electricity through her core. It would be so easy to lean into him, then indulge in that urge to take in his minty scent. What would his reaction be?

Hannah squeezed her eyes shut to ward off the tempting thoughts. Alden had made absolutely no moves to indicate that any such action on her part might be warranted. He'd been completely aloof and unaffected. As far as she could tell, this inconvenient attraction she felt was completely one-sided.

"Whoa," he said suddenly next to her. "Did you see that?"

She had not. She hadn't even been paying attention to the movie since he'd sat down, despite being so fully engrossed before he'd entered the room.

The truth was it was getting harder and harder to notice much else when Alden was near her.

At some point, once the movie ended but before they'd had a chance to turn the television off, she drifted off to sleep. When she opened her eyes again, the television was playing a game show.

And she was wrapped around a sleeping Alden, sprawled in his lap on the couch.

She moved off before he could awaken and quietly made her way out of the room.

Alden appeared to have showered and dressed by the time Hannah made her way back out to the common area. She found him scribbling over printouts with a steaming cup of Turkish coffee. If he had any recollection of the way they'd fallen asleep together, he gave no sign. Except that he hadn't quite made eye contact since she'd entered the room.

"Can I order you a cup?" he asked as she approached, his gaze still focused on the paperwork in front of him.

"No, thanks. As good as it smells, I'm going to pass." The brew really did smell heavenly, rich and robust. But her heart was still beating rather rapidly as a result of the position she'd found herself in upon awakening earlier.

"I'll just wrap up and we can head out, then," he told her. "I have one more stop I'd like to make in the city before we leave for the island."

The stop he referred to turned out to be for her benefit, Hannah realized an hour later when she found herself in yet another shop that took her breath away.

She had to resist the urge to throw her arms around him as soon as they stepped inside. Yards of colorful fabric lined the walls and lay draped over fixtures throughout the store. Silks, satins, velvet, lace, and everything in between. The creative part of her mind slipped into overdrive. Already she could picture numerous dresses and outfits, her mind reeling with possibilities.

"I've booked us a private appointment," Alden informed her. "Take all the time you need to pick out what you'd like."

He had no idea how difficult that was going to be. Every inch of material in here called to her on an artistic level.

"They'll ship whatever you pick out back to Massachusetts," Alden added.

A flood of emotion rushed through her core. The gesture was so unexpected, so thoughtful of him, she couldn't find the words to express how much she appreciated it.

"I don't know what to say." Surprising her with an elaborate dinner complete with a belly dance show was one thing, but this was a whole other level of thoughtfulness.

Alden simply smiled at her. Hannah made herself turn around and made a show of studying the closest ream of fabric before she could do something foolish. Like throw her arms around Alden's neck and kiss him until they were both gasping for air. The way she so desperately wanted.

CHAPTER TEN

THEIR SHORT TIME in Istanbul had come to a close all too quickly. Hannah threw her bag over her shoulder and took one last longing look at the view of the grand Hagia Sophia outside her window. She'd have to make sure to make her way back to this city. Maybe with her mom, though her mother didn't really like to travel. She especially wouldn't relish the idea of traveling quite this far. Maybe Hannah would come back with a girlfriend.

A lump of sadness settled in her chest that the trip next time wouldn't be with Alden. Awakening in his arms wasn't a memory she would soon forget. On second thought, perhaps it would be a better idea if she didn't return to Istanbul at all. The memories might be too much, longing for a life she couldn't have too bittersweet.

As if thoughts of her mother had conjured it, her phone vibrated in her pocket and sounded her mom's ringtone. As inconvenient as the timing was—Alden was waiting for her to take her down to the boat that would transport them to the private island off the Greek coast—knowing her mother, if Hannah didn't answer now, she would just keep calling until Hannah finally picked up.

"Hi, Mama. I can't talk long, I'm afraid."

Her mother didn't answer right away. When she finally did, her voice sounded hesitant and more than a little irritated.

"I woke up early to call you, Han," she said, using the nickname she'd used since Hannah was a toddler.

Alarm suddenly raced through her. "Are you all right?"

"Yes, yes, I'm fine," her mother answered. "I called to ask you what exactly it is you're doing."

Hannah plopped down onto the mattress behind her. "What do you mean, Mama?"

Her mother sighed before answering. "You said you were traveling on business. But that picture you sent me with the statue. Han, it doesn't look like a business trip. And why are you out so late with Alden? I thought he was there helping you with a new international business client."

Hannah swallowed down a curse. She should have saved the picture for another time. She'd just been so enamored and excited to share her amusement with her mother that she'd emailed it as soon as they'd gotten back last night. Big mistake.

"We just grabbed a bite to eat together. That's all."

The truth was her mother had assumed quite a bit when Hannah had announced that she'd be traveling with her former schoolmate overseas on a business matter. Hannah had jumped at the convenience of not correcting Mama's assumptions. It was just easier that way. Just like it was easier not to go into too much detail about why Justin hadn't quite proposed yet. As far as her mother was concerned, Hannah was still gainfully employed and blissfully about to become engaged.

She didn't want to think of it as being dishonest with her mother. No, it was just a little fib to protect her parent from over-worrying, as she was so prone to doing.

But now one innocent picture had somehow thwarted her efforts at keeping her mother calm and unbothered.

"I see," her mother answered, her voice shaky and unconvinced.

Hannah sighed, noting silently to avoid sharing any more photos with Mama until she was back in the States to explain things fully.

"I just worry about you," her mother added completely unnecessarily. If there was anything Hannah knew down to her toes, it was just how much her only parent worried about her.

"There's nothing to worry about, Mama," she reassured, hoping she sounded convincing. "I'm just taking in a few sights while I'm here. I can't wait to tell you about it all."

"That would be lovely. I didn't even realize you were branching out internationally."

She was indeed. Just not in the way her mother thought. One more thing to explain once she had the chance. The two of them were going to have to spend a long day together upon her return. Not something Hannah was really looking forward to, as much as she loved her mother.

By the time she disconnected the call, Mama sounded only slightly less concerned. But it was progress and Hannah would have to take it.

Right now, she had a boat to catch.

Dropping the phone back in her pants pocket, she swung the door open to find Alden there mid-knock.

"Sorry, I'm ready to go. Didn't mean to hold you up."

He tilted his head, studying her. "Everything okay? You look flushed."

The time and effort it took to reassure her mother whenever she was riled up tended to have an exerting effect.

Oftentimes, it was exhausting and draining. But in Mama's defense, Hannah was all she had. Her mother had worked hard and put every penny she'd made toward ensuring Hannah had a secure future with a solid education and steady career to fall back on. Hannah was lucky to have such a devoted parent. Look how little support Alden had grown up with in comparison. Hannah really had no business complaining.

"Everything's fine. We were just catching up. She says to tell you hello."

He smiled. "I remember your mother," Alden said, wordlessly taking her tote bag and slinging it over his shoulder as they made their way out the door and toward the elevator.

"Nice lady," he added while they waited for the elevator doors to open.

"Nice and high-strung," Hannah replied. The words were out before she'd intended them. Hannah hadn't meant to say that part out loud. Alden merely lifted an eyebrow. He stood staring at her a moment longer, as if waiting for her to explain and tell him more.

Maybe someday she would.

Alden wasn't often at a loss for words. But he had been back at the suite before they'd left the hotel. It was obvious the phone conversation Hannah had been having with her mother that he'd walked in on was a heavy one. He'd wanted to make her the same offer that she'd made him. To tell her that he was there to lend an ear if she ever wanted to talk. That he could very well see how being the only child of a single mother might have had its share of challenges.

But the words hadn't come. Now it was too late.

It hadn't helped that he'd awoken on the couch and remembered they'd fallen asleep there together. Wrapped in each other's arms. He hadn't noticed when Hannah left his side before morning. But he'd felt her absence as soon as he'd opened his eyes. Then later, the way she'd looked at him back at the fabric store would be seared in his memory for a long time to come.

"Our bags should already be loaded onto the yacht," he told her as their town car pulled up to Ataköy Marina and the driver came to a stop.

Hannah blinked at him. "Yacht?"

He nodded. "That's right."

Their driver had reached her door and pulled it open, yet Hannah made no move to exit the vehicle. She continued to stare at him.

"Something wrong?"

With a shake of her head, she reached for her bag. "No, nothing. I was just expecting to take a ferry or something."

He had to chuckle at that. "Not too many ferries make stops at private islands."

"Right. Of course. Guess I didn't give it much thought."

She gave him a tight smile as he reached her side and they made their way to the vessel. When they reached their boat, the captain was on the deck, waiting for them. Alden recognized the man from the last time he'd taken this trip. Ali was a seasoned sailor with years of experience and a friendly smile. He helped them aboard and led them down to the cabin where a server greeted them with aromatic moist towels. Within minutes, they were sailing steadily through the Bosporus toward the Aegean Sea.

Hannah hadn't really said much since they'd arrived at the marina. Was she remembering how they'd fallen asleep in each other's arms last night while watching a movie? Was she as confused as he was about how things were growing increasingly complicated between them?

How so many lines were being blurred between pretense and reality? Between friendship and intimacy?

Or maybe she was just quiet because she was tired and he was overthinking things. Perhaps she was just hungry.

"Breakfast will be served fairly soon," he told her, in case that last theory was accurate.

"That sounds lovely," she answered, barely glancing away from her view of the water out the glass wall of the cabin.

Turned out he was right. Less than fifteen minutes later, the same server appeared with a cart bearing several trays and two steaming carafes. She rolled the cart between them and lifted the silver covers off several trays to reveal an array of dishes. Fresh fruit, feta cheese drizzled with golden oil, a colorful tray of olives, and crispy toasted pita bread the size of dinner plates.

"It's a traditional mezze," he explained to Hannah once the staffer had left, just for want of something to say. He reached for an olive and popped it into his mouth.

"I didn't think I'd be hungry for breakfast after all the food at dinner last night," Hannah said. "But this spread looks amazing."

She helped herself to a plate of cheese and pita bread, while he poured them both steaming hot black tea from one of the carafes.

Despite her appreciative words about the spread, Hannah seemed to merely be picking at her food.

"Is something on your mind?" he asked, setting his own plate aside.

Hannah put down her fork, took a sip of her tea before answering. "I guess I feel a bit unprepared. I don't really know much about this impending business deal you're after. Or anything about your potential partner who'll be hosting us. I'm worried about playing my part well enough if I'm going in cold."

Playing a part. Alden winced internally at her description. But the truth was she had a point. They hadn't had much of a chance to discuss the particulars. Now was as good a time as any.

"We'll be meeting Emir and his wife, Amal, upon arriving at their private island. Emir is looking to build an all-inclusive resort catering to families, hoping to draw clientele from all over the world. The idea is to develop a family-oriented version of a club med resort. With offerings that will include everything from excursions to water sports to a play park. The idea is to appeal to those with young children and teenagers alike."

"Sounds fun," Hannah said, sticking her fork in a piece of melon.

"That's the idea. Fun vacations with lots to do. And luxurious accommodations to rest up in afterward."

"That's where you're hoping to come in," she provided, taking a tiny nibble of the melon and distracting his train of thought before he could rein it back.

The key was to keep his eyes off those tempting lips.

"That's right," he answered, making sure to focus on her eyes. Though it was just as easy to get lost in their depths. "Emir's looking for an experienced investor to help him build luxury lodgings. I'm one of three currently in the running."

She nodded. "I see. And that's why you needed a wife. Because he's looking to appeal to a family-oriented market, so he'd prefer to do business with other family men."

Alden swallowed the bite of pita he'd taken. "Not that Emir has come out and said as such. Let's just say I needed all the advantages I could get on my side. And then you and I somehow ended up married anyway, so I figured it might be fate."

"Kismet," she said, without missing a beat. "As the folks back in Istanbul might say."

"Exactly," he answered, pouring more tea for both of them. "Kismet."

She'd never been on a yacht before. And to think, her first time aboard one, and it was taking her to an exclusive private island. For the first time since she'd agreed to this plan, Hannah was beginning to have some real trepidation about exactly what she'd gotten herself into.

What *had* she gotten herself into?

How in the world was she going to pull this off? She suddenly felt disoriented and out of place. The food in front of her looked heavenly delicious and smelled even better. But she could hardly summon any kind of appetite. She wasn't used to being served breakfast aboard fancy luxury vessels. Whereas Alden was so natural in such an environment that he'd actually forgotten to even mention how they'd be traveling.

The way Alden led his life could aptly be described as on a grand scale. Private appointments at exclusive shops, traveling by private jet and yacht, making business deals on private islands. Hannah had to wonder if a regular existence like hers seemed too mundane for someone like him. Like her father. After all, hadn't that been why her dad left? He'd wanted more than the quaint little family who lived in a small town on the outskirts of metro Boston. So one day, he just up and left. To look for something more than what her mother and Hannah could give. Something more grand.

She watched Alden now as he finished off the last of

his hot tea and poured himself another cup. He seemed so confident, so unbothered about what they were about to take on. While Hannah was a quivering mess inside. What if she couldn't pull this off? What if she made an error so bad that they were found out for the fraudsters that they were and he lost this deal?

To her surprise, she felt a set of strong hands wrap around hers and squeeze tight. She hadn't even noticed that Alden had moved over to sit next to her and taken both her hands in his.

"Hey, you're shaking. Are you a nervous sailor? Are you getting seasick."

She swallowed before she could say anything and Alden apparently took that as an answer.

"Jeez. I'm really sorry, Hannah. I should have thought to ask about that."

He looked uncertain and crestfallen, clearly beating himself up, thinking he'd been remiss about ensuring her comfort. Great, now she could add guilt to the mishmash of emotions churning through her center. There was an entire cornucopia to add that one to—anxiety, nervousness, among others. Oh, yeah, there was also that inconvenient attraction that she couldn't seem to squash no matter how hard she tried.

"I can go find one of the staffers, they might have something to help you with the motion sickness."

She was about to tell him not to bother when the world seemed to shift on its side. The whole yacht suddenly lurched sideways. One second she was sitting next to Alden on the sofa as he held her hands, the next she was sprawled over his lap.

Was it even possible to hit a wave while traveling along a strait? She wouldn't have thought so. And then she couldn't think at all. Alden's arms were suddenly around her, his face tilted close to hers. She felt his hot breath against her cheek, could smell the teasing scent of that now so familiar minty aftershave. The heat of his skin sent warmth over her own. Her breath caught as he leaned his face closer.

One thought echoed through her head, though she knew it was, oh, so wrong to be thinking it. Ever since they'd walked into the fabric store. No, even earlier when she'd awoken in his arms.

Kiss me.

She wanted it more than she wanted her next breath. She'd wanted to taste him since waking up in his arms all those days ago back in Vegas. Maybe even before then, when they'd been just kids in high school.

Alden had either read her mind or, heaven help her, maybe she'd actually voiced the words aloud. His eyes suddenly grew heavy and dark, his breath came out in gasps. Time stood still as his mouth finally found hers.

The taste of him sent a surge of pleasure through her body. His mouth was gentle yet firm, his breath hot. Now that he was finally kissing her, she realized just how much she'd craved his touch all this time. Untangling herself from his embrace in the early hours this morning had taken all the willpower she'd been able to pull from the depths of her soul. Now she wished she'd succumbed even then. For she'd only served to deny herself this inevitable pleasure. Why had she thought she could fight it?

The sound of footsteps reached her ears but she didn't care to try and determine where they might be coming from. All she cared about was the feel of Alden against her, the feel of his lips on hers.

Someone cleared their throat behind them.

She couldn't tell which one of them came to their senses first. The next instant she was off Alden's lap and he was standing to greet the man who'd entered the cabin. She felt his loss like a bucket of ice water. The taste of him still lingered on her lips.

If the captain had witnessed their entanglement, he was doing well to not show it.

"Ali, I was just about to come up and ask if everything was all right," Alden said, his back to her. Was it her imagination or was there the slightest tremble in the way he stood. Could he possibly have been as affected by their kiss as she was?

"We're fine up there. I came down to check on you two."

Alden spread his arms out. "We're fine. Just wondering what happened."

Ali shook his head in clear disgust. "Some fools in a speedboat not paying attention. We had to maneuver as fast as we could to avoid them."

"I see, I'm glad everyone above deck is all right." He motioned toward Hannah where she stood. "As you can see, we're okay down here as well."

"Glad to hear it," Ali said, his voice relieved.

"Thanks for checking on us," Alden added.

"It was a pretty close call."

She might say the same, Hannah thought, biting her lower lip as heat flooded over her skin. Who knew what that bone-melting kiss might have led to if Ali hadn't interrupted to check on them.

She had no doubt that if things had gone further, she would have been powerless to try and stop it. She wouldn't have even wanted to.

CHAPTER ELEVEN

HE'D BE HARD pressed to say what might have come over him. Hannah appeared shell-shocked. Well, he was a bit surprised himself. He'd kissed her. And she'd returned that kiss with wholehearted abandon.

Only, that had been so much more than a kiss. The world had tilted on its axis when he'd had his mouth on hers. He couldn't deny that he'd imagined what she might taste like, what she would feel like in his arms. But his imagination hadn't done justice to the reality.

The staffer who'd served them breakfast appeared as soon as the captain left the cabin. Now, as the woman went about clearing their plates, darned if he could come up with any remote possibility of what he might say once they were alone again. One thing was certain—he wasn't going to apologize. He didn't regret kissing her. It was practically inevitable. That didn't mean he could let it happen again. They were treading a thin line here between what was real and what wasn't. For both their sakes, he had to make sure they didn't fall on the wrong side of that line.

When the woman left a few moments later, Alden attempted what he hoped might be an acceptable way to broach the conversation.

"Hannah, listen. I didn't—"

Hannah held a hand up to stop him before he could go any further.

"Alden, that's not necessary. I think it's best if we just focus on what's ahead. Do our best to get through these next couple of days on the island and work to get you this deal."

Okay. Message received. Loud and clear. Hannah didn't want to talk about their kiss. Damned if he could come up with a counterpoint to argue about it.

"I'm going to go freshen up before we make landfall," she added a beat later.

Their conversation once she returned to the sitting area consisted of nothing more than small talk. But there was no denying the proverbial elephant in the room.

Finally, he felt the slowing of the ship and less than twenty minutes later they were within swimming distance of Emir and Amal's island home.

"It's much bigger than I imagined," Hannah said, her eyes focused out the window. "And so very green."

"It's a lush Mediterranean landscape. With lots of sandy beach in a prime location. Within a speedboat ride to both Greek and Turkish coastal land and tourist attractions. You can't ask for a better location for a resort," he told her.

She turned to look at him. "You really want this deal to go through, don't you? Even more than I might have guessed."

"It would be a tremendous advancement of my holdings. A once-in-a-lifetime opportunity."

She nodded, her lips tightening. "Then let's go make sure it happens."

Ali appeared a moment later to escort them to the speedboat that would transport them the rest of the way to land. Amal and Emir were there to greet them when they arrived at the beach.

Alden reached for Hannah's hand to help her out of the boat to find that she was trembling. The poor woman was beyond nervous. A stab of guilt hit his chest that he was the reason for her discomfort. He leaned over inconspicuously to whisper in her ear. "It's okay. I'll be with you every step of the way."

The wide-eyed expression she shot him in response was impossible to interpret. "They're warm, kindhearted, and genuinely friendly people," he added.

She simply nodded as he lifted her by the hips and onto land.

Amal approached Hannah immediately, her arms spread out wide. Hannah accepted the hug without hesitation.

"Welcome, dear," the older woman began while still embracing Hannah. "We're so happy you've come to visit us."

Emir meanwhile shook Alden's hand with enthusiasm. "Congratulations, my friend. Can't wait to meet your new bride. If my wife ever lets go of her," he added with an indulgent smile in Amal and Hannah's direction.

Aside from a fresh haircut, Emir didn't appear all that different from the last time Alden had seen him. Jet-black hair trimmed short and combed neatly, the man had a striking face with sharp features and dark soulful eyes. His wife could be described as a stunner by any parameter. With wavy dark hair that hung clear to her waist, thick gold bangles adorned both her arms. She wore a flowing yellow dress that reached her ankles.

"So lovely to meet you," she was telling Hannah now. "We were so thrilled to hear that Alden here had gone and gotten married since we'd seen him."

She flashed her wide smile Alden's way. "You certainly surprised us, I must say."

If she only knew. He and Hannah had been pretty surprised as well.

"You'll have to tell us how it came about," Amal added.

Hannah's eyes grew wide with panic. Alden could guess what she was thinking, that they hadn't even gone over together exactly what they would say to the Bashars about their unexpected nuptials. He tried to convey a reassuring message with his eyes. They'd be fine if she just let him do most of the talking and followed his lead.

"Thanks so much for your hospitality in having us," Hannah addressed Amal first, then turned her eyes to Emir.

"You're quite welcome," Amal answered. "We're so glad to have you both." She crooked her arm into Hannah's and the two began walking. Alden and Emir followed behind.

"So tell me about yourself. I understand you two have known each other for years."

Hannah glanced over her shoulder at Alden for some kind of guidance. But Emir intervened first.

"Give them a chance to catch their breath, *hanim*," he said, wagging a playful finger at his wife. "They only just got here."

Amal fake pouted. "Fine. We'll show you to your cabin to freshen up. Come find us at the main house whenever you're ready."

Alden's steps faltered at her words. It was his turn to feel apprehensive. Cabin? He usually stayed in a suite at the main house whenever he was here to visit.

He turned to Emir. "A cabin?"

Emir clasped him on the shoulder. "I wanted to surprise you, my friend. We've just had it built. A model cabin like those we'd like to build for the resort for guests who want a more private space apart from the central hotel. Right on the beach. You and your wife will be the first occupants."

"Uh… Alden?" Hannah looked about the freshly painted cabin that was to be her lodging for the next two days. Hers and Alden's. The quaint yet small cabin with only one bedroom. And only one bed.

"Hannah, I had no idea," Alden began immediately once Emir and Amal left after showing them the cabin. "Usually, I stay at the main house when I'm here. In a suite with two separate bedrooms like at the hotel."

"Well, now what? We can't very well tell them we refuse to stay in here. How would we ever explain why?"

He thrust his hands through the hair at his crown. "We'll make the best of it. I can sleep on the couch."

Right. Like that was even feasible. The couch was barely more than a love seat. Alden would either have to sleep sitting up or with his legs dangling off one end.

Hannah glanced about the room. Under other circumstances, the little house would be a delightful space to stay in. Nestled in a shaded brush area off the beach, the cabin was decorated with bright pastel walls and an elaborately designed woven rug on the highly polished floor. A large Palladian window offered a stunning view of the crystal blue water and the gray shadow of other islands in the distance.

A look at Alden's face told her he was thinking along the same lines. If it weren't for that kiss, they might even be joking about their predicament right now, teasing each other about who should get which side of the bed. But a boundary had been crossed back on the yacht. And there was no turning back.

But she had to try.

She crossed her arms in front of her chest. "Look, we can be adults about this."

Alden tilted his head. "I'm listening."

She nodded. "We've already fallen asleep together twice. Once in Vegas, albeit we were out cold. And once again in Istanbul. This will be no different."

He merely quirked an eyebrow. Alden was thinking of exactly how this time would in fact be different. The kiss on the yacht had been an acknowledgment that there was a clear mutual attraction between them. What if they were tempted to act on that attraction again? Their surroundings were certainly romantic enough to lend to temptation. The cabin practically hummed with honeymoon destination vibes.

They'd just have to ignore that. Hannah continued, "As far as what happened back at the yacht, it was a momentary lapse in judgment. I think we should both try and forget it happened. I, for one, have already begun to do just that."

The other eyebrow followed the first one. "Well, first of all, ouch. Also, what makes you think I'm concerned about that at all?"

Hannah bit the inside of her cheek. What was that supposed to mean? That he wasn't concerned because he was certain he wouldn't be tempted to kiss her again? Or that it wouldn't be any kind of big deal if he did? Both options stung. She wasn't even going to pursue the possible answer to either of those questions. There was no point.

"In the meantime, we have another issue to contend with."

Alden crossed his arms in front of his chest. "As much as I'd like to tackle one potential disaster at a time, I guess I'll bite. What issue would that be?"

"You heard Amal. They want to hear all about how we tied the knot. What exactly are we going to tell them? We have to be in sync."

"We stick as close to the truth as possible. I'll do most of the talking and you just follow my lead. That way, we won't even be lying to them."

Hannah felt her jaw drop. How could he even say that? This whole thing was one big lie. Alden leaned over and gave her a reassuring squeeze of the shoulder. "It'll be all right, Hannah. Trust me."

"Okay, it's just…"

"What?"

"I don't know. I just wish all this weren't necessary. That we didn't have to deceive such decent people."

"We aren't really, sweetheart. We've technically only told them the truth."

Technically. As far as the endearment went, she was going to ignore that for now. He'd clearly thrown it out absentmindedly, without any kind of meaning or intention behind the word. Just like the last time he'd said it.

"And what of later?"

"What do you mean?"

She shrugged, trying to put into words the anxiety that had been plaguing her since boarding that yacht hours ago. "Once the ruse is over. How are we going to explain what happened? Why we broke up?"

His eyes softened with sympathy. "You really care what they think, don't you? Despite having just met them."

"I care what they'll think of you."

He stepped closer to her. That minty scent she found so appealing now mixed with the smell of sun and sand and fresh sea air. "Don't worry about that. I'll think of a way to explain to Emir and Amal that things just didn't work out between us. That we wanted different things. As much as we care for each other, it just wasn't meant to be."

Yet more blurring of the lines. Were they still talking in hypotheticals?

She nodded slowly. "It's going to be like fiction imitating real life, isn't it? My pretend husband will break up with me just like my real boyfriend did."

Hannah wanted to clamp her hand to her mouth as soon as the words left her tongue. What an asinine thing to say. Her words made absolutely no sense. Alden wouldn't be leaving her. One couldn't leave someone they were never really with in the first place. They weren't even a genuine couple, for god's sake.

So why had she said it?

Alden reached for her then, took her hand gently in his, pulled her closer. A world of meaning swam in his eyes before he spoke. "Any man who would leave you is a fool, Hannah. One who never deserved you in the first place."

Alden's phone pinged in his pocket, breaking the heaviness in the air caused by what he'd just said to Hannah. Heavy or not, he'd spoken the absolute truth. He couldn't imagine being the man who'd had Hannah in his sights, had her committed enough to want to marry him, and then foolishly let her go.

Hannah released a deep breath before pulling her hand out of his. "Go ahead and check that," she told him.

He pulled his phone out of his pocket and wakened

the screen. "It's from Emir. He wants to know if we're up for some water sports. Says to change into swimwear and meet them on the beach if we are."

Hannah peered over to take a look at his screen. "Huh, I wonder what he means."

An emoji popped up in the next second on his phone. An image of an airplane. Followed by yet another, this time a set of skis.

"Looks like he's asking us to Jet Ski."

"I've never been on a Jet Ski before."

"What do you say? You up for it?"

Alden willed her to say yes. He could certainly use the distraction. Not to mention, being alone with Hannah in such close quarters, in this charming romantically decorated cabin, was distracting him in ways he had to stem.

She gave him a tight smile. "Sure. Why not?"

Less than fifteen minutes later, they were exiting the cabin dressed in swimsuits and lathered up in sunscreen. Alden made sure not to notice the toned strip of tanned skin exposed between Hannah's tankini top and her boy short swim bottoms. She'd wrapped a long sheer scarf around her waist. Her hair was clipped in a high pile above her head. Cat-eye sunglasses lent an exotic accent to the overall outfit.

The woman certainly looked good in beachwear. He gave his head a shake. So not the time to be thinking that way. Yeah, he could definitely immerse himself in some cold refreshing water.

Emir and Amal were waiting for them down on the beach. A pair of water scooter Jet Skis were anchored several feet in the water.

"Just bought these," Emir said as they approached.

"Plan on buying a fleet of them as an excursion option for guests. Thought the four of us could take them for a spin."

Alden didn't have to be asked twice. "Sounds fun. Let's do it."

Emir made his way to one of the machines, his wife trailing behind. Helping his wife onto the seat, he hopped on in front of her, Amal's legs cradling her husband's hips.

Alden turned to see Hannah swallowing, her lips tight. They'd be riding the same way.

"If you're not up for this, I can go for a spin by myself."

The other couple were waiting for them expectantly. Hannah shook her head. "No. I'd like to try. Looks like fun," she said, sounding much less enthusiastic than he'd felt when he said those same words moments ago.

He took her by the hand and led her to the empty Jet Ski. Helping her onto the seat, he took a deep breath before sitting down in front of her. The contact sent immediate jolts of electricity through his system. The seat wasn't very big. Hannah's legs wrapped securely around his thighs. Her arms curled around his waist.

Torture. Absolute torture.

Alden knew without a doubt that he'd be thinking about the feel of her inner thighs tight against him for the rest of today and well into the night.

And he'd be spending the night with her in a small secluded cabin. Heaven help him.

"Alden," he heard her say into his ear. "Emir's waiting for you to start the engine. Didn't you hear him?"

He'd be hard pressed to hear anything over the ringing in his ears. Alden turned to give Emir a thumbs-up, then turned the key and the Jet Ski came to life with a roar. The next instant, Emir had taken off and Alden followed suit. Hannah's arms tightened around his waist and another bolt of awareness speared through his chest.

Focus. He was operating a heavy machine for heaven's sake. Maneuvering it around water that was several feet deep. He had to get a grip and concentrate or they were both going to topple over.

In more ways than one.

In all her years on this earth, Hannah was pretty certain she'd never felt such a huge rush of adrenaline pour through her body. Alden was zigzagging around the water, the Jet Ski kicking up a spray that splashed all around them, thoroughly soaking her hair and skin.

It all felt tremendously exhilarating.

A flurry of sensations flooded her system. The cold of the water. The thrill of zipping through the waves. Hearing Amal's laughter over the loud roaring of the Jet Skis.

Oh, and there was also the exquisite feel of Alden's hard muscular waist and hips between her legs. That last sensation would have to be fought off with all her might.

"You still sitting securely back there?" Alden asked over his shoulder. "I can slow down if you want."

"Don't you dare. In fact, I think we should challenge those other two to a race."

Alden visibly did a double take at her answer. Well, she'd somewhat surprised herself. She was having fun! Pure and simple. Hannah couldn't recall the last time she'd enjoyed herself with such abandon.

Alden got Emir's attention and motioned for him to stop. When he did, he pulled up alongside the other couple and thrust his thumb back to motion to Hannah. "My lady here is challenging the two of you to a race."

Emir flashed a wide smile, his wife laughing and

nodding enthusiastically behind him. "Challenge accepted," he answered, pointing to the distance at a large rock structure jutting out of the water. "First to the ocean rock wins."

"Hold on, babe," Alden threw behind him. Then he floored the Jet Ski the same instant Emir did.

She held him as tight as she could as they flew across the water. By the time they reached the rock, it was hard to tell who won. It was also hard to tell which of the four was laughing the hardest.

"Rematch at another time," Emir yelled over the roar of the engines.

"Just name the time," Alden said, his voiced laced with mirth.

Hannah got the distinct impression this was the beginning of a playful new rivalry. Alden would be here a lot if he got this deal. Judging by how competitive the two men seemed, she was certain the Jet Ski race was about to become a regular tradition when Alden was here.

Too bad she wouldn't be accompanying him.

"I have sea salt in all manner of places on my person," Hannah declared when they got to the cabin two hours later.

Alden tried hard not imagine where those places might be, but his imagination was inconveniently way ahead of him. They didn't make it back to the cabin until the Jet Skis had begun to run out of fuel and each of them had taken a turn driving. He might have to invest in one of those machines to keep at one of his beachfront properties back in the States. Hannah had gotten the hang of it in no time, maneuvering the vehicle over the waves. He'd invite her over to use one when they were home. Maybe on a long holiday weekend when he happened to be in town. Nothing said they couldn't hang out together once all this was over.

Right. As if their situation wasn't complicated enough without further entanglement after.

"You should have warned me about how salty the Aegean is." She wagged a finger at him.

"You shouldn't have spent so much time in the water." He reached for her hand after shutting the cabin door behind them. "You're pruning all over."

It wasn't wise to keep touching her. Even a gesture as innocent as holding her hand only led to thoughts of touching her in other ways.

Not good.

"I'll be a gentleman and let you have the shower first," he told her, letting go of her hand but not before his skin brushed against the ring on her finger.

He certainly didn't feel like a gentleman a few minutes later when he heard the water come on. Immediately the images flooded his mind. Images of Hannah under the steamy spray, lathering her bare skin, the bubbles cascading down those crevices she'd mentioned having salt in earlier.

Alden bit out a silent curse. At this rate, he wasn't going to need any hot water once he got in there to shower. When she emerged from the bathroom ten minutes later wrapped in a thick Turkish towel with her wet hair twisted atop her head, Alden gave himself an imaginary pat on the back for looking away and not letting his gaze linger.

"It's all yours. I'm not sure how much hot water I left you though."

If she only knew how little he needed it. "You'll have to find a way to make it up to me, then."

Now why had he gone and said something like that of all things? Full of innuendo. Hardly appropriate. Hopefully, Hannah wouldn't take it that way. He quickly veered the conversation back to the more mundane. "You have some time to rest. We're not due to meet Emir and Amal for dinner for another three hours or so. They eat pretty late in this part of the world."

She gave him a tight smile. "Guess I'll go take advantage of some downtime before I get dressed, then." She shifted the towel higher above her chest. "I thought I saw a robe hanging off the wall in there."

Great. Now he would have the pleasure of picturing her lying down in the other room on the bed with nothing but a robe on. Well, he shouldn't be picturing her in anything. Wait…that wasn't quite right either.

Alden blew out a breath and made his way to the bathroom. One thing was certain, feeling Hannah's legs cradled around him on the water had kicked his libido into high gear. Which was absolutely unacceptable. He had to stay sharp while they were on the island. With his eye strictly on the prize they'd come here for. To get that contract signed and move forward with this deal. Whatever was happening between him and Hannah would have to be addressed at some point. But this was not the time. Marriage certificate or not, they weren't here on this island to play some pretend version of house. They were here on business. Meanwhile, he would have to learn to keep his inconvenient yearnings in check.

He repeated that mantra in his head as he made his way to the bathroom and stepped into the shower, and then several more times as he bathed. The cleansing water did wonders to clear his head. See, he could be a rational and sound man when it came to his quote/unquote wife. By the time he wrapped the large towel around his middle, he was convinced.

Hannah was still in the bedroom with the door closed when he finished. Which posed a small problem. All his clothes were in the closet in there.

Lifting his hand to knock, Alden stopped when he heard the sound of her voice behind the door. She was talking to someone. Had Amal shown up while he was showering? But that made no sense, the two of them would be sitting out here to chat. Not behind a closed door. Plus, Hannah's was the only voice he heard. She must be on the phone.

Alden waited outside the door, not wanting to interrupt. Hannah's voice sounded tight and strained. Maybe she was talking to Justin. A spike of emotion he didn't want to name speared his chest, a cross between irritation and anger. If her ex was upsetting her, he had half a mind to barge in there and grab the phone to give him a piece of his mind. That man was out of her life for good now. The sooner Justin realized it, the better.

Only, what if he wasn't? What if he was working to reconcile their relationship? What if he'd come to his senses and realized how asinine he'd been to let Hannah go?

The feeling in his chest expanded, turning into a gnawing ache he'd have been hard pressed to describe.

Deep in thought, he didn't even notice when Hannah stopped talking. An instant later, the door swung open and she barreled through it. Straight into his chest.

His towel wasn't going to hold.

CHAPTER TWELVE

SHE'D SOMEHOW JUST walked into a brick wall. Only the wall, though solid and hard, was made of flesh and muscle.

Alden was the wall.

And he was practically naked. Aside from a towel that he was hanging onto for dear life with one hand as he used the other to stay Hannah. To no avail, as she'd landed square against him.

"Oh, my God," Hannah blurted, covering her eyes in case the towel struggle didn't go Alden's way. But not before she got a glimpse of a set of hard toned abs glistening with moisture from his shower. "Could you please get dressed?"

"I'm sorry," Alden said, his voice reverberating around the cabin. "That's what I was going in there to do."

Okay. There was no need for panic. They weren't a couple of hormonal teenagers. Not anymore. Just because Alden's body was snug up against hers without any clothes, and the fact that she was also naked under this robe, wasn't cause for any hysteria. Squeezing her eyes even tighter and sucking in a breath, Hannah stepped to the side.

"By all means. The room is all yours. I'm sorry to have stayed in there so long."

Alden didn't move. What was he waiting for? "There's

no need to apologize. And you can open your eyes, Hannah. Towel crisis averted."

He was so wrong about that. Because her fingers itched to trail a path along those abs she'd caught a glimpse of. To rip the towel off him herself. Pity that he'd been able to catch it in time before gravity could have done it for her.

Just. Stop.

She lifted one eyelid and then the other. Alden cleared his throat. Still hesitating. Hannah took a small step back for some distance but still Alden made no move. The air around them grew charged and thick. The sound of heavy breathing echoed through the small space. She couldn't even tell if it was coming from her or Alden. Maybe it was both of them.

Finally, Alden cleared his throat. "I'll just go grab some clothing, then."

Stepping around her, he closed the door softly behind him. Hannah stared at the dark wood panel. What might have happened just then if she'd lowered her guard for even a split second? Would she be in his arms right now? No towel? No robe? Would his lips be on hers? Hannah lifted her fingers to her mouth, recalling the sensations from the way he'd kissed her back on the yacht.

She'd been so distracted after her phone call that it was a wonder she'd managed to keep her wits about her just now when they'd been skin to skin. For a moment, when Alden hadn't moved, she'd been certain he was about to kiss her again. Probably just wishful thinking on her part. He'd simply stepped around her to go get dressed while she'd stood there like a quivering mess at the contact.

As for the kiss before they'd landed on the island, she'd been the one to initiate it, hadn't she? The fact that he hadn't pushed her away meant absolutely nothing. He practically apologized for it afterward.

She had to get a grip. Alden was here for a business deal. Their marriage a simple convenience that would be rectified soon enough.

But it was hard not to imagine those hard sharp-cut abs under the waistline of the khaki shorts he wore when he emerged from the bedroom a few minutes later. A round rim collared blue-gray shirt matched the color of his eyes. He smiled at her. "Emir mentioned we'd be eating outside. Casual beach attire should work."

Was he hinting that she should get dressed? They still had at least two hours before they had to meet the other couple. In her defense, she'd pulled her dress out of the closet to throw it on before her mom's phone call had distracted her.

"I didn't mean to rush out and ram into you just now." She motioned in his general direction. "Impressive reflexes."

He nodded. "Yeah, that could have gone a whole other way."

He rammed his fingers through his hair, as if not quite content with the way he'd responded. For her part, Hannah wasn't sure how to respond in turn. Luckily, Alden changed the subject.

"You seemed pretty distracted. And I couldn't help but hear you talking to someone right before you came out."

So he'd heard her, then. Had he heard her try and stifle her sniffles? Could he guess that her throat was achy now from trying to hold back her emotions after talking to her mother?

Her expression must have given her away. "You wanna talk about it?" he asked. Alden was a pretty astute man.

Funny, she'd said very much the same thing to him back in Istanbul.

She sucked in a fast breath and made her way to the sofa before plopping herself down, rather ungracefully at that.

"My mom called again. She wasn't happy." *With me*, Hannah added silently. Mama made no secret of it when she was unhappy with Hannah.

Alden sat down on the other end of the sofa. "What happened? Is she all right? Didn't she have some kind of cardiac issue all those years ago?"

"Oh, she's fine. Her heart is monitored regularly at Mass General by one of the finest cardiologists in Boston. Physically, she's okay."

His eyes narrowed on her, listening intently. It surprised her that she did want to talk to him, to vent to someone willing to listen. She instinctively knew that Alden would do so without judgment or any attempt to advise. Unlike Justin. Who'd told her more than once that Hannah should simply declare her adulthood and brush it off whenever her mother was upset.

Justin had never understood just how much easier that was said than done, given the way she'd grown up.

"Justin stopped by the house to drop off some of my things," she told Alden. "Guess he wanted to get rid of what little I'd left at his place and didn't want to wait for me to return back to my apartment."

She thought she heard Alden utter a vicious curse before she continued. "I hadn't exactly given my mom all the details about what I'm doing here."

"Let me guess. Justin did the disservice of filling her in."

Hannah nodded in answer. "It's my fault really. I should have come clean before we left."

A flash of dark shuttered in his eyes before he spoke. "Why are you making excuses for him?"

She was doing no such thing. "I'm not," she said, more than slightly taken aback by the intensity in his voice. "I'm only saying that I shouldn't have put off the inevitable conversation I ended up having with my mom."

"What did you tell her?"

She sighed, recalling the long silences through her smartphone speaker as she waited, heart pounding for her mother to respond to each new revelation. "I said that we connected at Max and Mandy's wedding. And you mentioned a job opportunity that I'm here now exploring with you. But she pressed and pestered me with questions until I admitted that I'm considering a complete career change. Which she's not happy about." That was an understatement. "So she's now worried about not only my defunct relationship but also my stalled career. A career she worked about just as hard for as I did."

Alden reached for her hand, took it in his strong one. "I know she sacrificed a lot for you. It's only natural that you feel indebted."

Hannah bit the inside of her cheek. Not many people understood the bond between her and her mother. But Alden might understand better than most, given his background.

"All my life, I've only wanted her to be proud of me. Lately, all I've done is disappoint her."

He gave her hand a squeeze. "That can't be true. She has to be proud."

Hannah grunted a disbelieving response. "I don't know about that."

"How can she not be? You worked your way through school. Helped your mother out over the years. Look how accomplished and bright you are, with a head for numbers I could never hope for. And you have a creative side that you're not afraid to pursue. You're an amazing woman, Hannah."

Hannah swallowed; her mouth was having trouble working. Was that really how Alden saw her? The way he'd just described her had a lump forming in her throat. She couldn't seem to tear her gaze away from his.

"Thank you for that," she finally said when her tongue worked again.

"I'm only speaking the truth. Look how quickly Emir and Amal took a liking to you. They can see what a special person you are. And it took them no time at all."

She was perilously close to giddiness. "You should stop now, before my ego grows to the size of that massive rock out there."

He laughed, moved his hand to entangle his fingers around hers. "It must have been hard for you and your mother. Being each other's sole source of familial and financial support."

She shrugged, trying desperately not to be too distracted by the way their fingers were linked together. "I still considered myself very fortunate. We didn't have much materialistically, but my mom was devoted and loving. I never felt alone." She gasped as soon as the words left her mouth. How thoughtless of her to say such a thing, given what Alden had dealt with. "I'm sorry. I didn't mean—"

He cut her off. "That's okay. It's the truth, after all. I was often alone."

Her curiosity piqued once again about something she'd always wondered since they'd been kids, and she had to ask. "How did you manage, Alden?"

He lifted one shoulder. "You know how. Worked odd

jobs, ate at Max's often. Wore donated clothing." He said it all without a hint of embarrassment or self-pity in his tone, simply stating his truth.

"I don't mean financially. How did you manage without anyone there for you?"

The grip on her hand tightened for a second before loosening once more. "My dad wasn't really a warm father even before my mother left. I always felt like he was just going through the motions, you know? When it was just the two of us, he completely shut down. And then one day he just announced he was leaving to go back home to Cyprus. Wasn't sure when he'd be back." He grunted an ironic-sounding laugh. "I know now he had no intention of returning, was just playing me lip service."

Hannah's heart was shredding in her chest. Alden must have been so confused, felt so rejected. First his mother abandoning them, then his dad leaving. The two people who should have cared for and loved him more than anything else. Certainly more than themselves.

"He didn't ask you to go with him?"

Alden took a while to answer, staring at some vague spot between their legs on the sofa. "No. But I decided to try anyway."

"You did?"

A sad smile spread over his lips, without any hint of amusement whatsoever. "About a year and a half after he left. I scraped and saved, worked long hours on top of studying and football to save money for a plane ticket. Max's father helped, told me it was a loan but I don't think he would have ever asked for the money back. Finally, after several months, I had enough to fly to Cyprus to visit my father."

Whatever memory Alden was recalling, it wasn't a

happy one. He continued after a pause. "I told him I was coming, when I'd be there. Asked him to pick me up. I thought maybe I might even stay. Start a whole new life there with my dad."

She remembered hearing rumors during their sophomore year that Alden might move. Remembered how distraught she'd been that she wouldn't see his smiling face every day at school.

"What happened?" she asked.

The smile tightened. "Well, he hardly seemed thrilled to see me, first of all. Barely acknowledged me when I landed. Took me to his new house by the sea. By then he'd already begun a new family."

"Oh, Alden." He'd never spoken of it when he'd gotten back to the States. But everyone could tell there was something different about him back then. The ever-ready smile was just a little faded, the brightness of his personality slightly dimmed.

"New wife. New twins."

"So you decided to come back."

"There was no room for me there. I didn't fit in. Not in the country or village. And certainly not in my father's new house."

There were no words she could say, nothing to soothe the hurts he must be reliving. So she remained silent, letting him speak.

"However, like a fool, I still thought about maybe trying harder to fit in. Working around the house, helping with his acres of land."

She was afraid to ask what might have happened to change his mind. When he told her after a brief pause, the truth was so much worse than she might have imagined.

"One morning, I overheard his wife arguing with him,

demanding to know when I'd be leaving. She'd grown tired of having me around."

Hannah swallowed, itching to wrap her arms around him. "I remember freezing where I stood, listening. Willing my father to stand up for me. For once in his life to choose me."

She could guess how that turned out.

"He didn't," Alden confirmed. "His response was to tell her that he'd figure out how to get rid of me as soon as he could."

"Oh, Alden," she repeated, at a complete loss for anything else to say.

"It gets better. He went on to say that he'd never even felt any connection between us. The way he felt with his new children. Not when I was born and certainly not later."

Oh, no. She couldn't even begin to imagine the wounds that must have caused, overhearing something so callous and cruel. She pictured a shocked and saddened teen boy, barely more than a child really, hearing his own parent being so cold, so uncaring. And so soon after being abandoned by his mother. She couldn't imagine the devastation such words might have caused.

Somehow, when Alden continued, his story only got worse.

"But he wasn't done appeasing his new wife. Who clearly wasn't thrilled that he'd had a family before meeting her."

"What else did he say?" she asked, afraid to hear the answer.

"He added that given my light eyes, and how different we were in disposition and personality, he had his doubts about me."

Hannah's heart pounded as she asked the next question. "What kind of doubts?"

Alden rubbed a hand down his face. "He said he couldn't be sure I was even his son."

Hannah couldn't help her gasp. If Alden's father were standing before her now, she'd gladly throttle him until the man turned purple. How despicable to say such a thing about your own flesh and blood—apart from his mother's eyes, there was no doubt Alden was his son.

Her mind was scrambling for a way to tell him he hadn't deserved such cruelty. No teenage boy did. But she didn't get a chance. Alden suddenly dropped her hand and stood. A curtain seemed to drop between them. He was clearly done sharing and the conversation was over.

"Why don't you get dressed and we can make our way over to the dinner spot a little early?" he suggested.

Okay. If he needed to move on from all that they'd just confided in each other, she would have to honor his wishes. What other choice did she have?

"Right. I'll just go throw a dress on and put my hair up."

"I'll wait here."

Hannah stood, threw him a friendly smile. "On the way there, you can tell me more about how special I am."

He chuckled, taking her hand once more and turning her palm over. The ring on her finger sparkled like a bright star in the rays of sunshine pouring through the window.

"Trust me. One day, the man that puts a ring on your finger for real is going to realize just how lucky he is."

Just like that, her attempt at humor came to a sudden, halting crash. Alden might see her as accomplished, bright, and attractive.

But ultimately, not for him.

CHAPTER THIRTEEN

A GENTLE BREEZE drifted off the sea and ruffled the wisps of hair around her face, bringing with it the scent of salt water and fresh sea air. They'd walked along the beach mostly in silence. Hannah couldn't imagine what she could possibly say as a response to the things Alden had told her back at the cabin. To think, all those years ago back in high school, he'd been carrying such a burden and hardly anyone, except for Max's family, had even known. They'd just pegged him as the independent teen who lived alone in that big house.

"Sorry if the conversation got a bit heavy back there. I want you to know, I don't really talk about those last couple of years of high school with anyone."

"I'm glad you told me. I still can't believe we had no idea about any of it when we were kids."

He thrust his hands into his pockets. "Max knew the overall gist of what was happening. I just never told him the details. Actually, the part of the conversation I overhead, I haven't told anyone else but you about that."

That gave her pause. "Why not?"

Alden stopped walking, turned to face the direction of the water. Hannah followed suit and they both stared at the sun setting on the horizon in the distance. A kaleidoscope of bright oranges and shades of yellow layered the sky.

He'd been silent so long Hannah figured he wasn't going to bother answering her question. "It isn't exactly a fun story, right? The poor kid whose parents left him to head for greener pastures. Whose father didn't even want to claim him as his own son."

"Thank you," she said simply, meaning it with her whole heart. It meant more to her than Alden might have guessed that he'd trusted her enough to speak of such a private memory.

He humphed. "For what? Bringing down the mood after what was a fun, enjoyable afternoon Jet Skiing with new friends?"

She chose to ignore that. "Stunning view, isn't it?"

He turned to face her. "Absolutely beautiful." His eyes roamed her face as he stepped closer. The next moment, she felt his breath along her cheek as he leaned closer. With the barest of a touch, he brushed his lips softly to hers.

Hannah's breath caught, her heart hammered in her throat. Just the barest hint of a kiss. One might not even call it that. But she felt it clear to her toes, her skin tingling outward from her lips.

Until he leaned closer and whispered in her ear. "Hope that was okay. We have an audience."

Hannah turned to see Emir and Amal walking toward them in the distance. So the near-kiss was just for show, then. For the other couple's benefit. Alden may as well have doused her with a bucket of ice water. How horrifying.

Once again, she'd been ready to throw herself at him when Alden clearly had no such inclination. What in the world was wrong with her? Somehow, she managed to steady her pulse and paste a fake smile on her face in preparation for meeting the other two.

And if there was a subtle stinging behind her eyes… Well, no one needed to know that, did they?

Amal and Emir reached their side a moment later.

"We were just coming to get you," Amal said, putting her arm through Hannah's. "See if you were ready for dinner."

Another pang of guilt shot through her. Amal was so warm and friendly; she acted like they'd known each other for years as opposed to just a few hours. Hannah felt as if they were long-standing friends. It pained her that she wasn't being completely honest with such a genuinely decent person. Her husband too.

"I hope you're both hungry. Dinner's just been put out for us," Emir added. "We'll be eating outside by the water. This way."

The four of them started walking in the direction the other couple had come from. Soon, they approached a cabana tent with a round table in the center covered in a blue canvas cloth. Strings of tea lights hung along the rim of the top. Four place settings surrounded a round lazy Susan in the center. Alden guided her to one of the chairs and pulled it out for her. He took the seat immediately to her left while Emir did the same for his wife, then sat across Hannah.

Hannah lifted the silver cover in front of her to reveal a dish of grilled fish with a side of aromatic leeks dotted with gem-green scallions. A separate large bowl contained a generous helping of fresh vegetable salad with cucumbers, tomatoes, and herbs, and sprinkled with pomegranate seeds. A rounded circle of pita bread sat atop a quarter plate near the salad, steam drifting off the fresh dough.

"Today's catch," Amal remarked, lifting her own cover. "Fresh from the sea less than an hour ago. Just-caught fish tastes so different."

Hannah's mouth watered. Emir motioned for them to start and she did so with gusto. The food tasted even better than it looked. Amal hadn't been wrong about how fresh the fish was. The tender meat practically melted in her mouth. The vegetables and the salad tasted as if they'd just been picked off the vine. She suspected they must have been.

"Wow," Alden said next to her. "If this is the kind of food you plan on serving at the resort, I think we're going to have a very popular food destination here."

Right. She'd almost forgotten. This entire trip was all for ensuring Alden got his business deal. How silly of her to lose sight of that for even a moment. She felt for Alden, she really did. Her heart was still breaking over what he'd told her back at the cabin. He couldn't have had it easy, fending for himself after losing both parents. But this laser-sharp focus of his to achieve business success seemed almost excessive.

In many ways, that quality in him reminded her of the way she'd been brought up. No accomplishment on her part was ever enough. Mama was always focused on the next big achievement.

Apparently, so was Alden.

"So tell us," Emir said, pushing his now-empty plate away. "Last time Alden was here, he was an unattached bachelor. Then he shows up with a beautiful wife. How did that come about?"

Across the table, Hannah dropped her fork before Emir could even finish his question. It landed with a loud clanging onto her plate. She threw him a wide-eyed glance full of panic.

Alden shot her what he hoped was a reassuring smile. Did she honestly think he hadn't been prepared for such a question?

"Hannah and I have known each other for decades," he answered, dabbing his mouth with the cloth napkin, then setting it on the table in front of him. "We lost touch but as soon as we saw each other again at mutual friends' wedding, the sparks immediately began to fly. For me, anyway."

Now why had he admitted that last part? More importantly, was there any truth to it? He gave himself a mental head shake. Of course there wasn't. He just had a "type" he was attracted to, that's all.

Hannah sat staring at him with her mouth agape. He'd have to answer some questions later about that last statement, no doubt. But it wasn't as if he could pull the words back. "I guess I've always had a crush on her," he added, figuring that if he was in for a penny, he may as well be in for a pound.

Amal gave a delighted clap. "That's so romantic. Lost love that was found again. So many years later."

"Something like that," Hannah answered. Her cheeks were flaming red, her head ducked with eyes averted downward. He really owed her a world of gratitude, given how uncomfortable she was with the farce.

"So then I had to admit that I'd had a crush on her all through school. And apparently I never got over it."

Hannah lifted her head, her eyes found his. "I've had a crush on him too," she said softly. "All this time."

Whoa. For someone who'd felt so disquieted about playacting, she sounded pretty convincing. Unless...

Emir didn't give him a chance to ponder on it. He clapped Alden on the back. "I know I've said it before, but congratulations." He turned to Hannah. "To you both."

"Thank you," they said in unison.

Hannah added, "And we can't thank you enough for your hospitality. The island is paradise."

Emir removed his hand from Alden's shoulder and leaned his forearms on the table, addressing Hannah. Alden felt a momentary panic that he might be about to ask her something about their marriage she didn't have a clear answer for. He prepped himself to intervene. But Emir threw him a curve ball with the direction he took the conversation.

"I understand you're a corporate accountant."

Hannah swallowed. "That's right. Though I'm at a bit of a career impasse right now."

Emir rubbed his jaw. "Oh, that's too bad. I thought maybe you could help us with the books once the resort opens. Seeing as your husband will be a partner investor."

Wait. Had he heard the man right? Hannah did a double take, blinking across the table at Emir. So she'd heard it too.

Amal confirmed a moment later. She gave her husband a playful shove on his shoulder. "Emir, you're terrible to try and tease them so. Just tell them you've made your decision and will accept Alden's offer."

Emir winked at his wife playfully before turning to Alden and extending his hand. Alden shook it with enthusiasm, then gripped the table edge tight to refrain from pumping his fist in the air. Finally. After all this time, and all the effort, he'd achieved success. He could practically taste the victory.

He owed a large portion of that victory to Hannah. He might never have gotten this deal if she hadn't accompanied him on this trip as his wife. And the way she'd charmed both Amal and Emir had no doubt helped immensely.

"I'm so glad we'll be seeing more of you two," Amal said, directing the words to Hannah. "This island was a wonderful place to bring up our children, you know."

Emir laughed out loud, then wagged a finger at his wife. "What a sly way to ask them about having children."

Amal's expression was full of chagrin. "My husband's right. That was much too personal. I'm sorry."

"Don't be," Hannah immediately responded, patting the other woman's hand on the table. "It's quite all right."

"Thank you. It's just that I have four children, all adults now but they're still babes in my eyes. All at university in the States."

"You must be so proud of them." Hannah said.

"I am. Family means so much. I miss them terribly. The house is so empty without them. I miss all the noise that comes with having a large family about."

"I would love a large family," Hannah said, her voice low and tender. "Someday," she added on a sigh.

A small ache twinged in Alden's gut. If he needed any kind of sign that he and Hannah were on different life paths, there couldn't be a much clearer one. As far as he was concerned, family wasn't in his cards. Why would he even make an attempt at such a life, given the way his own childhood had gone? He didn't know the first thing about being a decent father. Or husband for that matter.

It wasn't as if he'd been given any kind of decent example by his own parents.

Hannah deserved so much better than him. She deserved the family she wanted. She deserved stability. She deserved someone who knew how to love and be loved. Who knew what it felt like to be part of a family.

None of which could describe Alden Hamid. He couldn't give her any of that. Not even if he wanted to.

He couldn't imagine a reality where he would.

CHAPTER FOURTEEN

FOR A MAN who'd just won what he'd referred to as a deal of a lifetime, Alden appeared pretty morose as they made their way back to the cabin. After enjoying a dessert of sticky baklava at the main house, Emir and Amal had bid them good-night with the latter promising to send Hannah her secret recipe for the traditional delicacy.

Alden didn't say much during the walk. And he was just as quiet when they reached the door and made their way in.

"I thought you'd be in more of a celebratory mood," Hannah remarked, grabbing a bottle of water from the refrigerator and taking a long swallow. "There appears to be a bottle of something bubbly in there if you want to toast to your victory."

"Not for me. I guess I'm just tired."

Huh. In all the years she'd known Alden and the amount of time she'd spent with him since Vegas, she'd never seen him exhibit any kind of exhaustion. On the contrary, he was high energy and constantly on the go unless he was asleep.

Her phone pinged in her pocket with an alert. For a second, she had a moment of dread at the thought that her mom might be calling or texting. Then a wave of guilt washed over her for having such thoughts about her own mother. She checked the screen to see it was just Amal.

"She's texted me a copy of her recipe card already for the baklava. I can't wait to try and make it back home."

Alden merely nodded, clearly feigning an interest he didn't feel. "I'm sure you'll do a great job," he said.

Maybe it was the scrumptious dinner, or maybe it was the fact that Alden's deal had finally gone through. Or perhaps it was all the talk about family back at dinner. But she decided to take a chance.

"Open invitation to come to Boston and have a piece when I try out the recipe. You have offices in the seaport district." She hated that her voice was shaky. Hell, her entire body was shaking. As casual as she was trying to make it sound, there was a lot riding on how Alden would answer.

He rubbed a hand down his face. That didn't seem like a positive sign. She was right. "I don't think that's a good idea, Hannah."

She knew she should drop it. Just let the matter go. Everything about Alden's demeanor and his voice flashed a bright yellow caution sign.

Too bad she didn't heed the warning. "What about around the holidays then in a couple of months? Christmas in Boston is always a spectacle to behold. The tree at the Common is enough to make the trip worthwhile."

He shook his head slowly, his eyes holding steady onto hers. "I won't be in New England over the holidays. In fact, I'll probably have to spend those months back here to get started with the resort grounds breaking."

Then invite me along.

Hannah wanted desperately to say the words out loud. That little devil was back on her shoulder and urging her to do just that. But the yellow warning had turned to bright red.

"I see. I hope it all goes well, then." She took another swig of water and set the sweaty bottle on the counter between them, none too gently. "I'll see you in the morning. I'm going to bed."

He was around the counter and had reached her in less than three strides. He took her gently by the arm and turned her to face him.

"It would make no sense for me to visit you in Boston, Hannah. Not for either of us."

She pulled her arm free and crossed them both over her chest. "Right. Now that you've gotten what you wanted. You're forgetting something though, aren't you?"

"What's that?"

"The fact that we're still legally married. Small detail."

Something flashed behind his eyes that had her heart splitting in two. She wanted to walk away with her ears covered to avoid hearing what came next.

"I emailed my attorneys earlier. Right before dessert. Directing them to draw up the paperwork required for dissolution of marriage in Nevada. We'll just sign our names and it will be like the marriage never happened."

Her mouth went dry. The coldness of his delivery shook her to her center. He hadn't even waited a full hour after he'd gotten Emir's acceptance to set the divorce in motion.

"So that's it, then? All loose threads will be neatly tied. You'll have your business milestone. And you'll be rid of the wife you never intended to have."

And where did that leave her? She had no job, no prospects unless she begged to reclaim a position she no longer felt fulfilled in. To top it off, now she'd be nursing a broken heart.

"Hannah, it's not like that."

"Then please explain exactly what it's like." She held her palms up, waiting for what he could possibly say to make any of this better in even the most minuscule way.

"I know I owe you a large debt of gratitude. I've already started the process of having extra funds delivered to your bank account. There should be enough there to give you ample time to decide how you want to proceed about your professional future. I hope you follow your passion. I wasn't kidding when I said you had the talent to really make something of it."

Hannah's mind recalled all those scenes from classic movies where the starlet swung her hand back to deliver a well-deserved slap on the face of the man she'd fallen for, her love neither appreciated nor reciprocated. Her fingers itched with the desire to do just that. But she was no starlet. And this wasn't some romantic foreign movie like the one they'd watched together back at the hotel. Plus, if she were being truthful, she would have to admit that it wasn't anger she felt clear through her cells.

It was hurt. She'd fallen for Alden. Hard and deep. Hell, she might have always been in love with him. Since they were both teens.

While he still only saw her as a means to an end that he'd now finally achieved. Despite the time they'd spent together and all they'd experienced since mistakenly tying the knot back in Vegas, it hadn't affected him in any way. Unlike for her.

And now he was sending her away with nothing but a payoff.

Alden watched the light go out under the doorway of the bedroom. Hannah had gone to bed. He wouldn't bother

her. He would stay out here on the sofa and let her get some rest. It wasn't as if he'd be getting any sleep anyway.

How had such a simple plan become so convoluted?

Hannah's invitation to visit her in Boston was so tempting on the surface. But he knew he'd be doing both of them a disservice if he took her up on it. He was too broken. Too damaged.

He had to disillusion her of any notion that he might be good for her. Hannah's future was too bright for him to dim it.

He stayed awake for hours, simply watching the sky outside grow darker until it finally began to lighten once more. The sun eventually appeared, flashing brilliant colors through the large window.

Eventually he must have closed his eyes. Because when he opened them again, the day had grown brighter. Thick puffy clouds dotted the sky above the water.

Someone had thrown a knit blanket over him at some point. Hannah. Even after the way he'd treated her, the thoughtless things he'd said, she'd cared enough to make sure he was warm during the night.

Glancing behind him, he realized the bed was made and the door was open. The room empty. Where was she?

Alden pulled his phone out of his pocket. It was already 11:00 a.m. Something else appeared on the screen. An email from Hannah.

He clicked it open and began to read.

Alden,

I've taken Amal up on her offer to travel to the mainland with her as she picks up supplies. I won't be returning when she comes back, giving her the excuse that I'd like

to do more sightseeing in Istanbul while waiting for you.
I've already said my goodbyes to both her and Emir.

I think it's best if I return home. Alone.

Congratulations. I'm glad things worked out the way
you hoped.

Alden read it again. And once more. He kept reading
until his eyes started to water, as if each pass through
would reveal some hidden message that he'd somehow
missed. Anything to make this awfulness feel better
somehow.

She hadn't bothered to say goodbye to him in person.
Not that he could blame her. It was no less than what he
deserved.

With a silent curse, he tossed his phone away in frustration. Only he used too much force and wasn't surprised when it bounced off the coffee table and landed
with a loud thud on the hardwood floor. A webbed array
of cracks appeared immediately on the screen.

Something else on the coffee table caught his attention. A flash of brilliance flashed in his eyes as the rays
of light from the sun landed onto the surface after a passing cloud. She'd left the ring behind.

Alden swore again and rubbed a hand down his face.
The way they'd left things between them didn't sit right.
A brick sat in the center of his stomach as he recalled the
way she'd walked away from him before going to bed,
the deep shadow of hurt behind her eyes.

He stood and reached for his phone. He had to at least
try and call her, to try and explain. But even though the
damaged device functioned enough to pull up the number and dial, the call went immediately to voice mail.

Hannah was gone. The only hint she'd ever even been

here was the ring she'd left behind and her last message still on the screen of his damaged phone.

It wasn't the only thing he'd broken so carelessly.

Maybe she'd taken the cowardly way out, leaving before Alden had awakened. But there really was nothing left to say to each other. He'd gotten what he'd brought her here for.

And if she were being truthful, she had to admit that he'd never misled her. Never pretended that this trip was anything more than a business venture.

It was her foolish heart that had betrayed her. Falling in love with a man who didn't feel for her the way she felt for him.

Hannah paced the boarding area at Istanbul International Airport, willing for her row to be called. The sooner she got on that plane and made it back to Boston, the sooner she could begin to put the pieces of her suddenly disordered life together.

All while nursing a broken heart.

"You look like you could use a cup of strong Turkish coffee, my friend."

Emir stood up from behind his desk, closing the cover of the tablet he'd been studying. They were supposed to go over initial plans and blueprints but Alden had no idea how he might begin to focus.

"I had something of a restless night."

Emir studied him with alarm. "Did you not sleep well? Is something wrong with the bed at the cabin?"

Alden shook his head. Not that he would really know. He hadn't spent so much as a minute on the mattress. He opened his mouth to assure Emir that the bed was more than adequate, that it was as comfortable as the beds he'd slept in at five-star hotels. He stopped short before the words left his tongue. In the overall scheme of things, it was a fairly small fib. But Alden just couldn't do it. Suddenly, it was all too much. The false premise under which he and Hannah had arrived, the small untruths that were nevertheless misleading—it all weighed like bricks strapped to his shoulders.

Even lying about a simple mattress seemed just one more step in a vicious cycle that no longer seemed worth it. Alden didn't even care anymore about signing the contract with Emir. He would be disappointed to have it fall through. But there would be other business opportunities.

There'd never be another woman like Hannah.

And he'd blown it with her. The way he'd acted, she likely wouldn't even consent to remaining his friend. She had every right to feel that way.

"Something on your mind?"

Alden looked up to find Emir staring at him, his head tilted in concern. There was no way he was going to continue with the ruse. Funny how much of a difference just a few short hours made with regard to what he'd thought were his top priorities. So many ill-thought-out decisions had brought him to this humbling moment.

Well, he'd just decided that he was going to stop lying to his friend. No matter what it cost him, he was ready to admit the truth. Without giving himself a chance to think and change his mind, he found himself blurting out the whole truth. Beginning with waking up married to Hannah in Vegas all the way to the horrible scene from last night and all the relevant details in between.

"I can only say I'm deeply, sincerely sorry," he finally finished, short of breath from all the talking.

Emir regarded him with eyebrows creased. Several moments passed without either one speaking a word. Finally, the other man cleared his throat.

"I thought my English was pretty good. But maybe not?"

Alden blinked at the comment. What did Emir's fluency have to do with anything? "Your English is excellent." He'd studied in the States, did business in Manhattan and Los Angeles regularly and several spots in between. So where was he going with such a statement?

"Then I'm wondering why I'm confused." He crossed his arms in front of his chest. "Let me ask you something. You and Hannah are married as of this moment. Correct?"

Alden could only nod.

"Hmm. I see."

"But we didn't plan—"

Emir held a hand up to stop him. "Please, just bear with me while I ask my questions."

Alden figured that was the least he could do. "Go ahead."

"It appears you and your wife had some type of argument last night. Is that correct?"

That would be putting it pretty mildly. And he really shouldn't refer to Hannah as his wife any longer but, on the surface, Emir was right, he supposed. "You could say that, yes."

"And you are an intelligent man. I know that or I would have never agreed to go into business with you."

Alden rubbed a palm down his face. "Uh…thanks, I guess."

"So please explain something to me then."

"What's that?"

"Why exactly are you here apologizing to me?"

Well, when he put it that way…

Alden blew out a breath. "Doesn't it bother you in the least that you were being lied to?"

Emir shook his head, gave him an expression that implied he might be second-guessing his estimation of Alden as a smart man. "My friend, I think you have been lying to no one but yourself."

His mangled mess of a phone began to ring just as Alden entered the cabin twenty minutes later. His heart leaped in his chest before he yanked it out of his pocket and glanced at the screen.

It was Max calling. Not Hannah.

Alden debated answering, his thoughts too jumbled to hold any kind of conversation at the moment. But then loyalty to his friend won out. What if there was some kind of emergency? He clicked on the call.

Max didn't wait for him to say hello. "And how is my only remaining bachelor friend?" he asked as soon as soon as Alden picked up.

Alden bit out a curse at the question. If Max only knew.

So, no emergency then. "Did you really call just to ask me that?" he asked, hoping he didn't sound short given the way he was feeling at the moment. "On your honeymoon, no less?"

Max's laughter rang through the tiny speaker. "Of course not. I called because—" He paused to clear his throat. Then he cleared it again. Several moments passed by in silence. Alden glanced at the screen to make sure the call hadn't dropped.

When Max spoke again, his voice was thick and rumbled. "I just had a quick moment and wanted to call because—" His friend paused yet again. Was he actually getting emotionally choked up for some reason?

"What is it, man?" Alden asked. Maybe he'd been wrong about the emergency, after all.

"I just wanted to thank you," Max finally spit out. "For talking me down back in Vegas. I would have never forgiven myself if I'd left Mandy at the altar."

Alden sighed and plopped himself on the couch, the phone still to his ear. So that's what this was about. As much as he appreciated it, he had other things on his mind at the moment. Like his own fiasco around chaotic nuptials.

"Don't mention it, Max," Alden answered. "You just needed a little nudge in the right direction."

"And you were there to give it to me. Like a true brother. Which is what you are, Alden. I mean that. You're just as much my family as my blood brothers."

The statement gave Alden pause. *Brother. Family.*

The realization hit him like a ton of bricks. All this time he'd been going about his days convinced he wasn't part of a family. When in fact he had been all along. Max was his family. All the Hartfords were. So was Mandy.

And so was Hannah.

He couldn't even recall when he'd lost sight of that truth. He'd convinced himself he wasn't cut out for such relationships. That he didn't want for any kind of family. Such a lie. When had he convinced himself of that fallacy? For the life of him, he didn't know. It was just as if gradually his fear had overcome his desire for connection the longer he was alone.

Except that he never really had been alone, after all.

He'd been such a fool. And he had to find Hannah to tell her just how foolish he'd been. Then beg her to love him anyway.

If someone had told him a month ago he'd be wandering the streets of Istanbul looking for his wife so he could return her wedding ring, Alden would have wondered which one of them might have lost their mind. But three hours after leaving Emir's office, Alden was doing exactly that.

With no luck.

He'd made his way to all the places they'd visited while in the city together. No sign of her. Now he was at the last place he could think of. Alden sat down on the bench next to the statue of Tumbuli and stared absentmindedly at the novelty shop across the street. The display window had an elaborate array of evil eye charms in varying sizes and colors. One was the size of a dinner plate surprisingly. Hannah might have gotten a kick out of seeing those.

She wasn't here either. Which left one very likely possibility—Hannah was currently already in flight. On her way back to the States. She'd left before he'd had a chance to even try and make amends.

He had no one but himself to blame. He wasn't sure how long he sat there when a small mewing sound reached his ears. Alden blinked and gave his head a brisk shake. Was that a meow he was hearing?

Okay. Clearly, he really had lost his mind because he was imagining a bronze cat statue was actually making cat noises.

Something soft and fluffy brushed against his ankle. He looked down to find a mound of fur moving over his foot. Leaning down, he picked it up. A small pink tongue darted out of the soft ball of cottony fluff. A set of emerald-green eyes blinked back at him.

A kitten.

She—or he—was barely more than the size of a baseball.

"Where'd you come from?"

He received another soft meow in response.

"How'd you do that?" The question came from a husky baritone voice across the way. The shopkeeper from the novelty store stood at the door, staring at Alden in disbelief.

"Do what?"

"My wife and I have been trying to catch that kitten for three days to make sure she's okay. She always gets away. But here you are, and she's practically crawling into your lap."

Huh. Alden shrugged. Darned if he knew why the little critter had chosen to grace him with its presence.

"I don't know. I guess she just likes me."

The man nodded and smiled. "And I would guess you just got yourself a kitten."

CHAPTER FIFTEEN

OLD HABITS WERE hard to break. Hannah had to fight the urge to tell Mama what she wanted to hear. But she was done being conciliatory. At least when it came to her professional life.

"This is a good decision for me, Mama. I need to see if I can make it work," Hannah said into the phone for what had to be the fourth time during their nightly call.

Her mother wasn't thrilled with Hannah's decision to work at a fashion boutique on Newbury Street instead of trying to get her old job back or searching for a comparable one. The boutique had given her a chance after she'd shown them some of her original designs. Eventually, she wanted to work up to displaying her very own creations on the exclusive racks. But the salary was nowhere near as good as what she'd been making as an accountant, a fact that seemed to be keeping her mother up at night.

And unlike before with her past career, now Hannah felt a spring in her step every time she went into work. She couldn't recall the last time that had ever happened. If ever. And she owed it all to Alden. Hannah would have never attempted to walk into a boutique with a portfolio of designs if it hadn't been for his encouragement and the inspiration that had struck in that fabric store back in

Istanbul. Still, it hurt just to think about him. Even with appreciation for the way he'd believed in her talent before she had done so herself.

"But what about all your expenses?" her mother argued, pulling her out of the melancholy thoughts.

"I have a roommate now. So my rent is half of what I used to pay. And I'm finding other ways to cut corners. But right now I have to go." Hannah hung up before her mother could come up with yet another argument.

Said roommate chose that moment to breeze through the door. Lexie gave her a finger wave from across the room. Mandy's sister happened to need a new place to stay because of her recent divorce. The unwelcome acknowledgment that she herself would soon be a divorcee too echoed through her head.

She pushed the thought aside before the ever-ready stinging behind her eyes could start. She'd done quite enough crying since boarding that plane by herself back in Istanbul.

"Get dressed, Hannah," Lexie said. "You are coming out with us and I'm not taking no for an answer this time."

Not this again.

"I'm really not in the mood. Maybe—"

Lexie held a hand up to stop her. "No arguments. You've done nothing but go to work, then come home and sulk this whole week. Don't make me sorry that I moved in here with you last week."

"I'm already in my pajamas."

Lexie tapped her foot impatiently. "So? You have a closet full of stylish new clothes that fancy boutique is letting you borrow. Go pick something and then make yourself presentable."

"Where are we going?" Hannah asked. Not that it mattered. She didn't want to leave the apartment to go and try to be social. And she certainly didn't want to take the risk that anyone would try and hit on her. She still felt too raw, too vulnerable. Thoughts of Alden kept invading her mind and she would no doubt compare anyone who approached her to her pretend husband. And anyone else was bound to fall woefully short.

"There's a new club over by Fenway. The food and cocktails are supposed to be out of this world. Now, go get dressed so we can see for ourselves."

Hannah made no motion to get up off the couch in the hopes that Lexie might give up on her quest if given enough time. No such luck.

"I'm waiting," Lexie declared, exaggerating the tapping of her foot until Hannah worried the tenants downstairs were going to come knocking on the door to complain.

Hannah sighed with resignation before uncurling her legs from underneath her and standing up. Lexie was clearly not going to let up. "Fine. Just give me a few minutes and I'll go get ready."

Lexie pulled out her phone. "I'll call for a ride share."

Twenty minutes later, they were in a late-model SUV heading toward the center of the city.

She could try to make the best of it. Maybe Lexie was right. Maybe it would do her good to get back out there. She certainly wasn't ready to date again anytime soon. But she could window shop.

The idea fled as soon as she'd thought it. Who was she kidding? Best-case scenario, this night was going to garner a nice meal and a tasty cocktail. Which she wasn't even going to be able to enjoy while she yearned to go back home and crawl into bed. Only to have the blasted dreams invade her sleep.

Dreams of Alden.

Try as she might, she hadn't been able to keep them at bay. They all ended the same way. With him walking away from her as she stood on the sandy beach of a remote island surrounded by turquoise blue water.

Enough.

The club was crowded and loud when they arrived. Hannah stifled a groan once they made it inside. When Lexie dragged her onto the dance floor, she went through the motions as best she could.

The last time she'd danced, she'd been doing her best to mimic the belly dancer as Alden watched her. A rush of heat flooded her cheeks recalling the heat that she'd seen in his eyes then.

Finally, after about ninety minutes, she couldn't fake it any longer.

She leaned into Lexie's ear, doing her best to raise her voice above the noise. "I think I've had my fill. I can make my own way back to the apartment."

"I'll come back with you," Lexie replied.

Great. Now she'd feel guilty for ruining her roommate's evening simply because she was a mopey mess. "It's okay. I'll be fine heading back on my own."

Lexie reached for her arm. "Hannah. I'm coming back with you. We can open up a pint of rocky road and do some girlie chatting."

Hannah couldn't help but feel touched at the other woman's consideration. See? She was going to be fine. She had a friend/roommate who was making sure to get her out of the apartment and then willing to hang with her afterward eating ice cream. She was finally taking a small step toward exploring a new career. Eventually, her broken heart would mend and she would move on even further with her life.

By the time they made it back to their apartment building, she'd almost convinced herself that moving on was possible.

Right up until all the positive thoughts came to a grinding halt. Lexie pointed out the car window as they came to a stop.

"Why is there a man sitting on our stoop?" she asked. "And what's in that big box he's got?"

The woman Hannah stepped out of the car with gave him the most intense glare as they approached. Alden wished he'd purchased a few of those "evil eye" charms to maybe ward off the clear dislike being thrown his way. He vaguely recognized her before placing her as Mandy's older sister.

But he couldn't spare Lexie much thought. His sole focus right now was Hannah. She was utterly, strikingly beautiful. And he'd missed her down to every cell within his body. He could only hope that she might have missed him too. If only a fraction as much.

"Alden? What are you doing here?" She glanced at her watch. "At this time of night, no less."

He'd never considered himself an impulsive man. But lately he hardly recognized himself. And now here he was, following the impulse to see Hannah.

"And what's in that box?" Lexie demanded to know.

He answered Hannah's questions to begin with. "I came to see you about something. And I guess I'm still stuck in that other time zone." He was also hung up back in the time they'd spent together overseas. He hadn't been able to get those moments out of his mind.

"Hello?" Lexie waved a hand at him. "The box?"

"Could we maybe go upstairs? Or even to a café?"

Lexie turned to Hannah, waiting for her to answer. "It's up to you, Hannah. Whatever you want to do."

As annoying as Alden found the other woman right now, he had to give credit where it was due. Lexie was obviously being protective of her friend. He couldn't begrudge her that.

Hannah hesitated for a split second before nodding her head. "Fine. But you have five minutes. That's it."

He would take it.

Of all the ways she'd imagined running into Alden again, finding him on her doorstep late one night hadn't been one of the possibilities that had come to mind. Now that he was here, she didn't know what she wanted to do more. Throttle him? Or throw herself into his arms and beg him to hold her for just a few moments before she let reality bring her back to her senses.

When they reached the apartment, Lexie used her key to let them all in while Hannah switched the lights on. Her hand shook, her core quivering with the jolt of seeing him again so unexpectedly.

"I'm going to give you both some privacy and go to bed," Lexie said. "Unless you'd like me to stay, Hannah."

As much as she appreciated the offer, she had to speak to Alden one-on-one. "I'll be fine. Have a good night, Lexie."

"Just promise me you'll tell me the contents of that box tomorrow."

Hannah made the universal motion of crossing her heart. "It's a promise."

She had a sinking feeling she might be able to guess

what Alden had brought with him. He apparently couldn't wait any longer to finalize their annulment. Or divorce or whatever it was. She couldn't even be sure at this point. Every time her phone rang since arriving back in Boston, she'd braced herself to speak to one of Alden's attorneys calling to tell her that she was once more officially a single woman.

"Was there no way to do this electronically?" she asked. And couldn't he have found a smaller box for the documents? "Most documents are signed that way these days."

"Signed?"

She pointed to the ground where he'd set the box down. "I'm guessing there are legal papers in there you need my signature on."

Before she got the last word out, she could have sworn she heard a soft mewing noise coming from the floor. And now that she was looking at it carefully, there appeared to be several small holes cut out of the cardboard. Hannah stepped closer to investigate, only to jump back in surprise when the damn thing moved.

"Alden?"

"Yes?"

"What's in there?"

"Where?"

Hannah slammed her hands on her hips. "What is going on, Alden?"

He actually had the nerve to chuckle! "Oh, I brought you something." Leaning down, he lifted the cover. Hannah felt her heart begin to melt when she peered inside. The smallest kitten she'd ever seen sat square in the center, licking its paws and mewing softly.

Without bothering to ask, she reached in and picked

it up, bringing the tiny whiskered face closer to hers. A tiny pink tongue darted out and licked her cheek. Hannah's heart was now officially complete mush.

"I don't understand," she began, not able to tear her eyes off the small wiggly bundle she held. "You brought your pet here?"

Alden chuckled. "She's yours. If you want her."

"You're giving her to me?"

He nodded. "Only, I was hoping you might agree to a package deal."

Hannah stood staring at him with her mouth agape for several beats. Alden felt a small pang of guilt for her reaction. Okay, maybe showing up with an adorable kitten was rather unfair. But in his defense, the little creature had approached him first. He'd just wanted to share his feline find with Hannah.

That and so much more. He wanted to share his life with her.

But first he had some groveling to do.

"What kind of package?" Hannah finally asked after a bit more staring.

He stepped closer to her, stroked a finger down her cheek. "One that includes me."

Hannah gasped, her jaw falling farther. She stepped away and gently placed the squirming animal back into the box. Alden pulled a small treat out of his pocket and tossed it in to keep her occupied.

He took both Hannah's hands in his as soon as she straightened. "I was a fool back on the island. There's no way I can make it up to you for how badly I reacted. But please know that I will spend the rest of our lives doing just that."

She blinked at him. "You will?"

He didn't hesitate to answer. "Yes. If you'll let me."

She clasped a hand to her mouth. "Then you're not here to finalize our divorce?"

He had to smile at her confusion. She still didn't seem to be grasping why he'd shown up at her door practically in the middle of the night. He obviously had to make it clearer.

"No, sweetheart. I told you, I'm here to give you the kitten I found in Istanbul. And ask you to take me on as well and, hopefully, any children we might have together. We can buy a family home here in Boston. Or anywhere you want to. As long as we're together. As a family."

"Oh, Alden." The way she said his name sent a wealth of emotion surging through his core. How in the world could he have even considered walking away from this woman?

"Hannah, I love you. I think I may have always loved you. During those high school dances, the homecoming games, and everything in between. And ever since."

Her eyes began to glisten with unshed tears. He could only hope they were happy ones. So he went on. "The smartest thing I ever did was marry you by mistake."

That earned him a small chuckle.

"The dumbest thing I ever did was to think about voiding said marriage," he added. "But luckily I came to my senses with some help from a couple of friends and a wiggly feline."

"How did the cat help?" she asked with an indulgent smile.

He shrugged. "As soon as she nestled up to me, I knew I had to bring her here and give her to you. She practically told me to."

Hannah laughed. "She did, huh?"

"That's right. She said it was kismet. She also told me to give you this." He reached into his breast pocket, pulled out the ring he'd slipped on her finger what seemed like a decade ago in Vegas.

Taking her hand, he slipped it back on her finger where it belonged. Where it would stay forever if he had anything to say about it.

"Alden, does this mean...?"

He kissed her before she could finish. "I think we should get married again. With a real ceremony this time. As good a job as Elvis did for us, I was thinking something a bit more formal."

"It would be nice if my mom could be there this time."

He stroked her cheek again. Now that she was here in front of him, he couldn't seem to keep his hands off her. He'd never get enough of touching her. Not in this lifetime.

"Your mother. Max and Mandy. Their brothers and sisters." He thrust his thumb in the direction of the bedrooms. "Even Lexie can come if you want her to."

Hannah's laugh sounded like angelic music to his ears. "Thank you. That's very generous."

"We'll have to figure out the best time and ways to get everyone there."

"Get them where? To Boston? That should be easy enough." Further confusion on her part. He was making such a mess of this, but all that mattered was that he was here now. With Hannah.

"Well, I was thinking someplace a bit more exotic. An island in the Mediterranean perhaps."

Her response was to wrap her arms around his neck and snuggle against his cheek.

A loud meowing sound coming from the floor echoed through the air.

"I think she might be getting hungry. Please tell me you have some tuna in the kitchen."

"She can have all the tuna she wants."

"I get the feeling we're going to have a very spoiled little tabby on our hands in a few short weeks."

"I have no doubt. What's her name?" Hannah asked between intermittent sniffles.

"Well, I've been calling her Chunk."

She giggled before answering. "After the cherished cat in Istanbul? Tumbuli."

"You remember, then?"

She nodded. "I remember every cherished moment we spent together, Alden."

Hearing those words shattered the last of his threadbare control. Alden couldn't hold himself back any longer. Pulling her tighter into his arms, he indulged in the feel of her, thanking his lucky stars that she was ready to give him another chance.

"We don't have to keep that name though," he whispered against her ear. "We can name her something else, if you'd like."

She shook her head, gifted him with a long lingering kiss that made him want to pull her onto the sofa behind them and keep kissing her until neither one of them could catch their breath.

"No," she answered after pulling her mouth off his much too soon. "We'll keep the name. It's perfect. Everything is perfect."

He couldn't agree more.

* * * * *

HOW TO TAME
A KING

JULIETTE HYLAND

MILLS & BOON

For Doreen.

Congrats on your retirement. Enjoy this next stage!

CHAPTER ONE

BREANNA GALANIS WAS glad she hadn't shared her doubts about her identical twin sister Anastasia's room design as she looked at the striped accent wall blurring into bright colors. It was striking. Not at all the gaudy image her mind had conjured when Annie had described it. Her sister's talent was wasted in the high walls of the Galanis family compound.

"This is gorgeous." Breanna clapped.

"I told you." Annie snapped a few pictures with her phone, then pulled the professional camera hanging around her neck to her eye. Her finger clicked over and over.

"You did." She wasn't sure their parents would approve, but then, she didn't know the last time they'd approved of anything the twins did. That didn't stop their mother from showing off the new designs to her friends.

They all assumed she'd found a hot new designer—and each had begged for their name. Her mother had refused to say it was Anastasia. Whether it was to make her friends jealous that she had access to something they craved or because she didn't want them to find out about Annie's gift, Breanna didn't know.

Probably both. Image mattered, after all. More than anything else in her parents' orbit.

Galanis women married well. They didn't have careers. Their job was to host parties, be armpieces and proof of the lavish wealth others coveted. In other words, showpieces in designer clothes, worn once and tossed away.

Aristocrats without titles—according to her father.

The view was outdated. After all, they were well into the twenty-first century. Breanna had wanted to run from their parents' control for years. She had her degree in early childhood education. She loved children, and would have been in the profession for years now if her parents hadn't intervened at every place she'd interviewed. She was also a skilled seamstress who thrifted and upcycled clothes, despite her parents' disgust of the "trade." She could sell clothes, teach classes, and Annie could open a design studio. Their life would be simple compared to the extravagant wealth they'd grown up with, but their lives would finally be theirs.

Anastasia wanted more of a plan. More concrete proof they'd be all right. She wanted a full portfolio of room decor designs before they left. So far, she'd remodeled ten rooms in the mansion, plus her and Breanna's bedrooms. This was the fourth "final" room.

"It's perfect." Breanna bit her lip, then forced her shoulders back. "And it's the last one, right?"

They could make a go of it. They just had to take the first step.

Annie's hands shook, and she lowered the camera. The happiness drained from her body as she looked at the colorful walls around her. Her gaze focused everywhere but on Breanna. "I was looking at my portfolio this morning. I don't have a kitchen yet."

"Annie…"

"I know. I know I said this was the last one. But we will have nothing. Mother and Father will cut us off completely. You tried to get a teaching position years ago. Father blocked it. He *will* do it again." Her voice caught, and she pinched her eyes closed. "People will balk at hiring me too, but design work… I can run my own business. Give us some income."

"I have my sewing. They can't take that. They can't control everything." Breanna said it with more certainty than she felt. What was the price of freedom?

"And we won't be alone. We'll have each other." Breanna was the younger sister by all of two minutes, but she'd always protected Anastasia. Annie was the one with the big dreams. The one who had plans...if she'd only start down the path.

Breanna was the extra. The interchangeable twin who asked too many questions but never pushed too far. Hell, she'd even accepted it when her parents gave large donations to the institutions she'd applied to not to hire her.

Breanna was determined that Annie got to have dreams outside the compound. She was too talented to stay. Too talented to only be someone's wife. Love, if it really existed, was wonderful—at least according to the storybooks.

Her parents treated their union like a chess game. A winner and loser, constantly making moves and trying to stay at least three steps ahead of each other. A winner and a loser and two daughters who looked identical for them to trade for the best offer.

Unless they left. "Annie—a kitchen?"

"Is a necessity in any portfolio. I have everything else. I should have seen it."

Breanna tilted her head and raised a brow. Annie had studied portfolios for months when coming up with the brilliant plan to ready her portfolio under her parents' careful watch.

Getting them to agree to redo their kitchen would be a lot of work. And a kitchen renovation...it would add months to the plan. Maybe even a year. They'd gotten lucky at Prince Alessio's Princess Lottery last year.

Prince Alessio had spent a year raising money for the arts by funding a princess lottery—with the prize to be his wife. Each week the price of the ticket had increased. The total cost for a year's entry was well over ten thousand pounds. Annie and Breanna were the only participants with a year's worth of entries. Statistically, one of their names should have popped out. Yet the universe had chosen another and given Prince Alessio and his new wife, Princess Brie, a happily-ever-after.

That kind of luck wouldn't last. Their parents would try again to find them a title. They needed to leave.

"Annie—we can—"

The door opened, and the twins snapped to attention as their father walked in. He was smiling. No. Their father routinely walked into rooms already halfway through an argument, but right now he was beaming. Glowing even. Whatever he was about to say would be bad news—for them.

It made her skin crawl. Lucas Galanis did not beam. His smiles were calculated to win a business deal. Whatever calculation he'd made, he planned to win today. Which meant she and Annie lost.

"Guess what, Anastasia?" The peppy words sounded congratulatory, but the authoritarian tone he used wasn't hidden. Her sister hated the use of her full name, but only Breanna ever called her Annie.

It wouldn't be hard for their parents to adopt the nickname, but in the Galanis family, everything was tinged with power. Annie preferred her nickname; therefore, the most powerful members of the family would refuse to use it.

Annie rocked a little and lowered her head. "What?"

"You're going to be the queen." His words were wrong. They had to be.

King Sebastian wasn't even looking for a bride. Though the press seemed to think every woman in his orbit was his future queen. One woman had even taken a job overseas just to stop the press from hounding her after an image of Sebastian smiling at her during a dinner function went viral.

The man was simply living his life. Except, *nothing to see here* did not sell ad space. Since Prince Alessio and Brie's happy union, the crown had been dull.

Sebastian had had a brief rebellious streak following his father's death. But most of those headlines were drowned out by Alessio's bride lottery. And the rebel Sebastian, whoever he'd been, had disappeared months ago. In his stead was the prince, turned king, she'd followed all her life.

The man was stoic. If the dictionary needed a picture of *duty* beside it, they could use King Sebastian. He never missed a meeting. Never stepped out of place at an event.

And never smiled.

"I can't be queen." Annie's words were barely a whisper, but their father heard them.

His smile slipped into the sneer Breanna knew so well. "King Sebastian chose you."

"He doesn't know her." Breanna's fingernails dug into her palms. There had to be a way out of this.

But if the king wanted one of them… The heat of the warm evening evaporated. Cold seeped through her body as she tried to piece together any plan. Breanna worked the system that was their family better than Annie. But in the chess game of her family, her father was the grand master.

Which was why all she had were *plans* to leave. Fancy ideas. A small bank account for a few months' rent. Thoughts. Discussion points. All of which were good. Until your bluff was called.

They needed to stand firm. The moment was here, and they had to rise to the occasion.

Now. Or never.

"He doesn't need to know her." What a sad, flippant statement. How could their father treat marriage, a lifelong commitment, supposedly, with so little concern? This was Annie's life.

But their parents didn't care about their daughters' lives. According to them, they'd been blessed with two identical beauties to give them access to a world that hadn't wanted them. Being rich beyond anyone's wildest dreams should have been enough. But Lucas and Matilda Galanis wanted titles. If they couldn't have them, then their daughters would.

Breanna looked to Annie, but her sister wouldn't meet her gaze. Her palm ached, but Breanna pressed on. She couldn't lose this round to her father. "He is marrying her. He needs to know her. To love…"

Red patches bloomed on her father's cheeks. She'd gone too far, but stopping wasn't an option. Not this time.

"Love is a childish game that gets you nowhere."

"Prince Alessio loves Princess Brie." Annie's head didn't lift as she pushed a tear away. At least she'd said something.

Their father's scoff carried in the beautiful room. "That isn't real. It's a media game. And even if it is real, what has he gotten from it? Outcast to a glass shop?"

Breanna personally thought Alessio and his "lotto bride," as everyone had initially called her, looked happier than ever. All the pictures were of them laughing or looking at each other like no one else's opinions mattered. Like the headlines that ran about them in the early days calling Brie all sorts of names were beneath their love.

Maybe that was staged, but it looked like Alessio had gotten freedom.

And it wasn't like they were thrown out of the royal family. Far from it, in fact. Alessio still regularly attended events. Brie was a constant presence on the tourism boards. He just had a life outside of the palace. A life of his own.

Something King Sebastian and his queen would never have.

Annie drew a deep breath, and Breanna knew what the resignation on her soft features meant. No. No. No.

The discussion of the room's design seemed so long ago now. In a place far away. The dream was floating away. It would be out of reach if Annie acquiesced.

"I'll do it." Breanna's voice was stronger than she expected. Stronger than she felt.

"Breanna."

She didn't look at Annie. If she did, she might let the tears pushing against her eyes fall. That could not happen. Breanna protected Annie. That was her role. She would not fail now that it truly mattered.

"If he doesn't need to know Anastasia, then he doesn't need to know me." Annie still had a chance for her dreams. She could make this happen, and if Breanna was queen, she could protect her twin.

As queen, she could ensure Annie's safety.

Their father tilted his head, weighing his options. A weird feeling as his daughter, but not the first time Breanna had stood under his hard gaze. "You are basically interchangeable."

She would not flinch. It was not the first time he'd looked at them as one person split into two bodies. Not the first time their parents boasted a "two for the price of one" statement.

"King Sebastian did not indicate he cared which of you met him at the altar. It's not like we can tell you apart anyways."

Really selling this, Father.

"Breanna. No."

"I had picked out a different spouse for you, Breanna." Her father's gaze shifted to Annie. "A lesser title, but…" Lucas considered his daughters his possessions, objects to be bartered for his own goals.

A future marriage partner had never been discussed. No consultations with the potential bride. Not in this family. She was only still under this roof because Annie was terrified of what leaving meant.

"But that union is not available until his divorce is finalized next year. So…"

So Annie has a year. A year to get out.

She could help in the lead-up to the royal wedding…and figure out how to get herself out of this predicament, too. She had at least a year, right? It wasn't like royal weddings happened fast.

Her father shrugged; one daughter for another hardly mattered. The outcome was the same. "Ready for me to meet the king?"

Breanna needed to move. Needed to get the next part over with before she lost the burst of courage. She walked over to Annie, pulling her close.

"I love you. This has to be the last room."

Her sister squeezed her tighter than ever. "I love you."

Her arms were lead as she dropped them and pulled away. "Time to meet a king."

King Sebastian wasn't surprised to see the guard hovering by the door. The security on the Galanis estate rivaled the palace's. At least his guards were better at remaining unobtrusive.

This level of security felt more like they were keeping him in, rather than guarding. He had no intention of running. After all, he was here for a bride.

One that wanted to be a queen.

And this house held two such women. The Galanis family had not been quiet regarding the twins' plans to marry into a title. It was rumored no one was even considered a viable match unless they were at least a viscount.

Anastasia and Breanna Galanis were the only two who'd had a year's worth of entries in his brother's princess lottery. More than twenty-six thousand pounds had been spent between them for a chance at the title.

They'd walked away unhappy that day, but today Anastasia would become a queen.

Anastasia…the name he'd drawn out of a hat this morning.

It seemed somehow poetic that Sebastian had given his brother, Prince Alessio, so much grief for his bridal lottery. In fact, on the day he'd pulled Brie's name from the lottery, Sebastian had urged him to cancel the charade.

That charade had turned tourism around, reinvigorated the local economy, and most importantly, resulted in true love for Alessio and Brie. Sebastian was under no illusion that today's twist of fate would grant him happiness.

He thought he'd found love once. Samantha, a woman chosen for him by his father. Beautiful, educated, the perfect queen. His father had planned to make the announcement of their union. Then a stroke had rendered him unconscious for weeks, before finally claiming his life.

He and Samantha had bonded during that stressful time. Hiding their growing affection away from the prying lights of the media. He'd selfishly let his brother and his lotto bride take all the heat to protect the woman he loved.

And then the illusion shattered. Sam refused to understand why the crown was so heavy. She'd wanted it…desperately. Not him.

The same was true for his new bride-to-be, but at least he was under no illusions this time. With no expectations of happily-ever-after for Sebastian.

He was the king. King—the only thing anyone saw. Hell, the moment his father died, the staff at his bedside had called the time of death. Then turned and bowed to him.

Only in death was the power of the title vanquished. The title his father had served with every waking breath—just passed to another. A fate he'd had no part in choosing and no way to break.

Celiana's throne held little more than ceremonial power, but every poll in the last decade showed that the vast majority of the population wanted to maintain their monarchy. His people wanted a king. A head of state that didn't rotate out like the politicians. A constant in a world of chaos.

And the poll was worthless anyway. There was nothing in the country's constitution or laws that allowed for abolishment of the crown. He'd spent a year looking, devastation seeping in when the truth hit him. If Sebastian stepped aside, Alessio would be crowned.

And with Alessio happily married, the pressure for marriage had been focused on him. Journalists, bloggers and random strangers hoped every woman he waved to or said hello to was his secret intended. One woman had fled the island after a photographer captured an innocent smile at a dinner outing. A simple interaction he couldn't recall the next day but that had altered her life forever.

Then a few weeks ago, he'd gone out for a stroll very early one morning, his guards at a close but not too close distance. A female jogger had raised her hand to him.

Someone had caught the interaction and uploaded it with sensational commentary that didn't match the moment. Social media had swiftly identified the single mother. It was like hounds descending on a target with no clue. It was cruel and unwarranted, and nothing he said seemed to make anyone listen.

At least after today those rumors would disappear.

He'd been raised to serve. This was what was expected of him. His and Anastasia's children would be next in line. But they'd know what was coming. Hopefully, he could find a way to prepare them better.

With time, he and Anastasia would become friends. That relationship had worked for his parents. Maybe not a great love, but peace in giving the kingdom the stability its residents craved was its own reward.

Wasn't it?

The door opened, and a striking young woman walked in.

Brown curls falling to her shoulders. A blue dress custom-fit to her hips. Soft caramel eyes that looked him over with more than a hint of hesitation.

"Anastasia." He bowed. This wasn't the way one planned to meet a forever partner. Except it was in many aristocratic circles. Luckily, the Galanis twins had been trained since birth to expect this.

"I'm Breanna." She let out a soft sigh, then curtseyed. "Your Highness."

"Breanna?" He cleared his throat. "I—I…" There was no diplomatic way to ask why she was here instead of Anastasia.

"I am to be your bride." She didn't lift her head, and she didn't elaborate.

There was no script for this. "I asked for Anastasia."

"Why?" Breanna lifted her head, the caramel eyes catching his gaze. A few freckles dotted her nose.

She was gorgeous. Fierce. Challenging a king within moments of agreeing she was to meet him at the altar.

"Why?"

"That is what I asked. Why Annie?"

Sebastian shrugged. "You both had a full year's worth of entries in the bridal lottery."

"For Prince Alessio." Breanna clenched her fists, and her stance wavered for just a moment, but she didn't break eye contact.

Not for you.

The words were unstated, but they echoed in the room. The pinch of pain that brought was not to be acknowledged. Alessio was the fun one. The one who got to have a life…and love. The one who broke the rules. The one allowed to break the rules.

Most of his childhood he'd spent annoyed that Alessio refused to follow the rules. That he questioned the life they'd been brought up in. Part of him was probably jealous that his brother had choices—not many—but more than Sebastian.

Then Alessio had stepped in for him when he'd fallen apart after the crown landed on his head. The bond they should have had as brothers growing up finally solidified. Better late than never. He would not subject Alessio to the crown, or any woman who didn't want it.

Anastasia and Breanna had wanted it a year ago. And she wanted it enough now to switch places with the woman he'd asked for.

"I promise a queen's crown is far prettier." He leaned a little closer, hoping his smile looked convincing. The press was waiting. This was the only plan he had.

The deep brown eyes ignored the comment on the crown, and she crossed her arms, then looked to the door and un-crossed them. "You still haven't told me why you chose Annie."

"I pulled her name out of a hat."

Silence hung in the room for a moment before Breanna hugged her stomach and let out a chuckle that soon turned into a belly laugh. "A hat. A hat. Our lives decided by what you plucked from a hat. What if you'd pulled a rabbit out, Your Highness? Would a bunny have met you at the altar?"

She wiped a tear from her cheek, but the laughs continued.

He couldn't help it. His own chuckle combined with hers. "If I'd pulled out a rabbit, I would have been honor-bound to at least offer it the crown. Luckily for Anastasia, or I guess you, I didn't pull a rabbit."

Breanna's laughs died abruptly. "Right. Lucky for me."

The tilt of her lips was perfect. Just enough teeth showing for a believable smile, but there was something about it that sent a knife through his heart. "If Anastasia would rather…"

"I won the crown, Your Highness. Fair and square."

Won. The air in the room shifted on those three little let-ters. Won. He was a prize. Nothing more. The Galanis twins wanted titles; everyone knew that. And she was getting the top one.

As she straightened her shoulders, the brief flash of pity, the question that maybe this was a misstep, disappeared. If Breanna wanted the crown more than Anastasia, then that was fine with him. Hopefully she wouldn't resent its weight too much after a few years.

"Your father was kind enough to let me use his office for a press conference. There are selected media there, and we will also broadcast the announcement of the engagement live."

"Now?" Breanna clutched her neck, a hint of pink creeping along it. "Press conference, now?"

"Yes. No time like the present. This is a marriage of convenience, after all. You get a crown. The country gets a queen. Everyone walks away happy."

Except me.

"And you get?" Breanna raised her brow, the challenge clear in her eyes.

If he believed in soulmates, he might get excited that it felt like she'd read his mind. Someone to share more than just the duty of it all. But wishing for love wouldn't make it appear. He was the king of Celiana. Nothing more.

"A partner to help me run Celiana." That was the truth. Most of it. He also got the press off his back and peace from constant rumors.

"Alessio and Brie love each other." Breanna swallowed, but she didn't break her gaze.

Another thing this union brought him. A way to crush the tiniest bit of hope that maybe he too could find love. That lightning could strike twice for the royal family of Celiana. But lightning wouldn't strike twice. He was the king. And this was his duty.

"They do. Which is good. Celiana has its royal love story. It doesn't need another."

"And what we need doesn't matter?" Breanna turned her head, her eyes widening as her father stepped into the room.

Lucas Galanis looked at his daughter, and his expression made Sebastian instinctively step closer to Breanna. He didn't touch her, but the urge to wrap an arm around her waist pulled at him. She was looking at her past, and he was her future. But he would not take an unwilling partner to the altar.

"If you do not want this—"

"Then Anastasia will be happy to meet King Sebastian at the altar." Her father didn't look at him. Some silent communication was seeping through the room.

This time he didn't hesitate. He wrapped an around her waist, surprised and pleased when she leaned into him.

"No. I am the choice. Not Annie." Breanna stepped out of his arms but pulled his hand into hers.

It was warm. Soft. A connection he wanted to lean into. Foolish dream, but at least they looked like a united front for the press. "Ready, Breanna?"

She didn't answer, but Lucas opened the door, and nodded to Sebastian—a far from friendly smile on his face. "After the royal couple." He bowed low, but somehow it felt almost mocking.

They started down the hall, her father a few steps in front of them. What was he supposed to say? What was the small talk etiquette of walking with your future bride less than ten minutes after you met her to announce a wedding? He'd had a lifetime of protocol training, and no one had covered this.

The buzz in the room was evident fifteen steps before they hit the door. The room was ready for whatever announcement was to come. Whether he and Breanna were was an irrelevant question.

He squeezed her hand as her father opened the door. Flashes of light hit them followed by a cacophony of questions. He'd promised them a statement, and the palace had said he would be taking no questions, but that didn't stop the determined lot from flinging them at the couple as he and Breanna stepped onto the podium.

"Good afternoon. I appreciate your patience as you waited for my bride and me." His fate… Breanna's fate…sealed in a single sentence.

The crowd seemed to lurch forward, and a wall of questions flooded them.

Sebastian raised a hand, the room quieting nearly instantly. "On Saturday, I will marry Breanna Galanis at the county offices at ten a.m. This will be a small affair, like many of the weddings our people have. We will hold a reception after at the palace for close family and friends. As I know many of our citizens are currently struggling with inflation and the cost of living, the amount that would have been spent on the royal wedding will be divided evenly between Celiana's food banks, and local shelters that help the unhoused find affordable housing."

He took a deep breath. "Breanna and I look forward to many years together in service to Celiana. Thank you."

Sebastian raised his free hand, very aware that he was fast losing feeling in the hand Breanna had a death grip on. He walked them both through the door they'd entered and back to the room where they'd met.

"Saturday. We are getting married on Saturday? How?"

"You already have a dress, the one you wore at the lottery result. You will move into the palace with me tonight. We will do the minimal planning we need to. Start the process of getting to know each other, and then we will marry on Saturday."

"Oh, just like that. Right. Of course." The laughter escaping her throat was nearly manic.

"If you're having second thoughts…" He wasn't sure where he was going with that statement. After all, the announcement was made. They were marrying.

"No. I just wasn't planning to pack tonight." She balled

her hands into fists and rocked on her heels. "So many things to put away."

That was an easy fix. Her father had ordered Anastasia's room packed up as soon as King Sebastian had arrived. The Galanis servants and the royal staff who'd traveled with him had certainly shifted the moment he'd learned it was Breanna who would be wearing the crown.

Given the efficiency of the team he'd brought, it was likely nearly done.

"My team started packing as soon as I arrived. I suspect most of the boxes are already loaded into the van. They are very good at their job."

"I'm sure they are." Breanna looked around the room, then nodded. "So, we get married."

Sebastian nodded, too. "We get married."

In three days.

CHAPTER TWO

THE ALARM'S INSULTING tone rocked the quiet room. Breanna reached for her phone, the shrill noise mocking the idea that she'd somehow found any rest after Sebastian showed her to her suite.

Between the exhaustion and brain fog following the announcement of their wedding, Breanna wasn't even sure of the path she'd taken to get here. She vaguely recalled something about him "fetching" her this morning. He'd probably even given her a time, but her brain hadn't absorbed the information.

Nope. All it knew was she was in the palace and marrying the king.

This weekend! How was this her life?

Her phone buzzed, the image of her sister popping up on the screen.

"Annie." Breanna sat up in bed, pushing her curls back. "Are you okay?"

That was one good thing. At least it was her in the palace. Not Annie. Their father hadn't won that round.

So why does it still feel like checkmate?

"I'm the one that should be asking that." Annie let out a soft cry. "Are you okay, Breanna?"

There was no good answer. She was dealing. That was probably the best she could manage. Particularly considering she didn't have a year to get out of this. Less than seventy-two hours stood between her and the throne.

"I'm handling it." Breanna sucked in a deep breath. "Now you."

"Not as well." She could picture Annie biting her lip on the other end of the phone, her eyes watering as she tried to sound brave for her twin. "Did they pack my portfolio in your boxes?"

Her portfolio.

My team started packing as soon as I arrived.

Sebastian had chosen Annie's name. They'd started packing up her sister's rooms. The portfolio she'd created. Their pathway out. Annie's pathway out.

It wasn't in Breanna's boxes. Because there were no boxes. Her room had been set up during her and Sebastian's dinner.

Breanna didn't remember any of the conversation. Maybe there hadn't been any. But when he deposited her at the door, she'd opened it to find the room exactly like hers at home, minus the cozy green walls Annie had chosen for her.

The laid-back beach house theme Annie selected was out of place against the royal ruby-red wall, but her bamboo chair was hanging from the ceiling. The houseplants she kept over her window were on the wire hanger she'd hung them from at home. The staff must have pulled it from the walls.

Even her sewing machine with the piece she'd been working on was set up in the corner of the room. The stitches not out of place at all. It was like her life had been picked up and moved across town.

Nothing to see here, just a complete change…and a wedding. Her chest tightened, but panicking was not going to do her any good.

The portfolio wasn't here. She was certain.

"Was your room tossed and messy?" She rubbed her free hand on her arm, trying to find some way to drive away the chill running through her. If the portfolio wasn't in Annie's room…if it was gone…

"No." Annie let out a sob. "I know they started packing, but they immediately stopped when you took my place. Everything is where it should be but the portfolio. I had it under my bed. The box it was in is there and empty."

Mother.

The woman was calculating. And she'd been conspicuously absent from the rest of the debacle with her daughters. A fact that was just now registering in Breanna's brain.

While their father was overseeing the announcement, she'd probably handled the packing. Going through their things. Recognizing that the hidden portfolio could only mean one thing.

"You need to leave, Annie." Her voice was strong. This had to happen now. Annie didn't have a year. Not if her parents considered her a flight risk. They had one soon-to-be-titled daughter, but two was better—at least to them.

"I can't. We will have less than nothing now. Without a portfolio, no one will employ me. And you as the former fiancée of…" Her sister's words died away, but Breanna could piece them together.

As the former fiancée of the king, no one would employ her either. They'd start from nothing. Less than nothing. Breanna might be willing to give it a go, but Annie wouldn't.

Her sister was the obedient first child. The one who never created waves. The one who bent and followed, even when it broke her spirit. Annie rarely said more than yes to her parents, hazarding a no only when she was sure that there'd be limited consequences.

To save her sister, there was only one choice.

Breanna looked around the room. Her room. Her forever. "And I am to be queen. So, you don't need our parents. You can redecorate the palace. Starting with my suite." She wasn't sure how to make that happen, but as queen, there had to be some perks, right?

"Breanna—"

"Leave, Annie. They can't come after the queen."

The queen. A marriage of convenience. There were worse situations. She'd never worry that her husband only wanted her because she was a Galanis.

She'd know forever that Sebastian hadn't plucked her name from a hat. She'd demanded the crown—and he'd decided she was good enough.

Story of her life. The second-born twin. The extra. The interchangeable bonus her parents got to use to their advantage.

The good news was it had trained to her to make the most of every bad situation. This was no different, and there were far worse situations to find yourself in.

Annie would get her dream. The one thing Breanna had always wanted was her sister's happiness. Annie's safety. And this was the best way to guarantee it.

She could be happy here. Or happy enough. It was all just a matter of mindset.

"Breanna."

"That's Queen Breanna to you." She giggled. It wasn't really funny. Or maybe it was. This was the universe's version of a joke. A pathetic one. But she'd make the most of it.

"Breanna…"

"I have a savings account. I started it years ago. There is more than enough in it for a few months' rental on a small apartment and some furniture. Pack, Annie. Promise me. I will send you the money as soon as you tell me you're gone."

"It's starting from nothing." Annie took a deep breath. "Nothing."

"Not nothing. Those are Father's words. Words designed to scare us. You are the sister of the queen."

A pause hung over the line. She wanted to pull the words out of her sister. But this had to be Annie's choice. Her decision. *Please.*

"You're right. Whatever is next has to be better than whatever this is. It has to be." Her sister said the final words more to herself than to Breanna.

Breanna looked at the ruby walls, so at odds with her tastes. Annie was leaving. It wasn't the way they'd planned, and they weren't together, but Annie would be safe. And in a few years, she'd be the country's top interior designer. Of that Breanna had no doubt.

"I'll send you a text."

"Great." Breanna's breaths were coming fast and hard, but hopefully her twin wouldn't hear the panic pushing all around her. "And as soon as you are a little settled, I need my room repainted. It's red. Ruby. Very royal."

"And very too much." Annie giggled. "Laughter, is that a good sign or a bad one? This is too much, Breanna."

It was. But they were on this path now. For better or worse. "Everything will be okay." Breanna said the words she always uttered when her sister was focused on the world falling apart.

"Or it won't." Annie let out her part of the phrase. "Those are the only two options."

"I choose." This was her choice. She was choosing Annie. "I am hanging up now. Pack and send me a text." Breanna swallowed the tears threatening. "I love you."

"Love you, too."

Then her sister was gone.

If she stood still, she'd give in to the wallow. The tears would flow, and she wouldn't be able to hold them back.

Walking into the suite next to her room, she looked at the overstuffed chairs and couch. Who would she host in here? No one.

"This is going to be my sewing room." Breanna put her hands on her hips, pretending this was a project that she wanted, rather than one forced upon her. Her twin was safe. Annie got her dreams. That was all that mattered.

* * *

The noises coming from the future queen's suite could be heard down the hallway. "What on earth is she doing?"

Away from the Galanis estate, Breanna had shut down. Whatever show she'd put on for the cameras had evaporated in private. He wasn't sure she even remembered the words he'd said on the ride to the palace. She'd sat through dinner, picking at the food, giving one-or two-word answers to everything.

The strong woman he'd met at the estate had wanted to be queen. The one across from him at dinner… He was less sure what this Breanna wanted.

She needed rest, and a good night's sleep. Sebastian had taken her to a suite not far from his. Technically the queen's quarters were connected to his, but his mother had never stayed in them.

His parents' relationship was one of cordial friendship, bound by respect. They'd done their duty with an heir and a spare. Put on a lovely show for the kingdom that made it appear they were ever so in love. In the palace, though, they'd lived separate lives.

Putting his soon-to-be wife in the queen's quarters felt like a step too far. And he'd already taken so many.

Standing at her door last night, he'd promised her that he'd pick her up today at nine, and they'd talk about next steps. If she was still in shock… Sebastian knew he'd offer her a way out. He wanted a willing queen. If she was having second thoughts, well, he'd cross that bridge when he had to.

He knocked, then opened the door to her suite. Sebastian stopped, his hand on the door handle as his mouth fell open.

Most of the furniture was gone. There was still a small couch and an overstuffed chair that he didn't recognize. The rest of the suite now looked like a fabric store.

"What…?"

"Good morning, Your Highness." Breanna turned, her

smile brighter than anything he'd seen yesterday. She looked happy. Ecstatic.

The perfect picture of a woman delighted to be in the palace. Good.

Her soft gaze held his. She was wearing what looking like old blue jeans and a flannel shirt, and her hair was pinned up in a polka-dot headscarf. Breanna was relaxed and busy.

And she was gorgeous.

"Good morning." He needed to say something else, but his mind seemed incapable of forming words.

Breanna tilted her head, then shrugged. "I hope you'd don't mind. But I figured I'd make this my sewing room. Give my bedroom a little more space."

"It's your suite." Sebastian cleared his throat. "I am glad the staff was directed to your sewing room." He'd given directions to make sure her room was packed and immediately unpacked. As little interruption to her life as possible.

There was already going to be so much change.

"I've never had a sewing room." Breanna crossed her arms, her eyes sparkling as they looked from the sewing machine in the corner to the cutting table in the center of the room.

Sebastian laughed. "Did you have a whole floor sewing suite? The palace is smaller than your estate, but there is plenty of room." If sewing made her happy, they'd clear all the space she wanted. Wearing the crown had some perks, after all.

Though he doubted she'd have a ton of free time for her hobby. A royal life was duty, meetings, events and then more duty.

"No, Your Highness."

"Sebastian. We are going to wed, after all." It was weird that moments ago he'd considered finding a way to grant her her freedom. But she'd been here less than twenty-four hours and was already redecorating. If she was happy to be queen, then he was content. Last night was simply overwhelming.

Understandable.

"Sebastian." Breanna hesitated for a moment. "Feels weird calling you Sebastian. Maybe after we've been married for a while."

"So, you didn't have a whole sewing floor? Was it more?" The Galanis compound could certainly hold more.

A small chuckle fell from her pink lips. "No, Sebastian." She tilted her head, like she was trying out his name for a second time. "I did not have a sewing room or a sewing floor or anything else. I had my room, which was large, but this—" she gestured to the craft table "—took up most of my free space."

There was more to that story. So much more. The way she parsed her words, weighing them. It was a strategy he recognized. One he'd used.

"I always assumed the Galanis twins would have their own palatial floors. To do with as they pleased. Any toy or hobby. Anything you chose."

Even a crown.

A curl slipped from her headscarf as she turned her attention to a yard of fabric. "You are the king, and before that you were the heir to the throne. Do you have a wing to do whatever you want with?"

There was something in her tone. A feeling of shared experience. A kindred spirit.

The Galanis twins were given the best of everything. Their parents' wealth granted access to places that were unimpressed by crowns. They were able to do anything they wanted.

And yet, neither had branched out from the family compound. Chosen their own path. They'd waited.

It had worked. She was to be a queen.

The thought cut him. She was getting a crown. That was worth holding out for...at least to some.

She placed a yard of fabric on a frame of some type. "Did you have a wing for your favorite activity?"

"Kings don't have times for hobbies." It was a line his father had stated more than once when journalists asked what he liked to do when he wasn't performing a royal duty. It wasn't a lie either. King Cedric had never had a hobby.

He'd given everything to crown and country. That didn't leave much for anyone else.

"That is not true, Your—Sebastian." Breanna put her hands on her hips. The action was protective, and her pink lips were set in such a way it seemed she wanted to battle.

For me.

"You are allowed a hobby, Sebastian." She reached for his hand, squeezing it.

Her skin was fire, and he craved the heat. When she dropped his hand a moment later, ice flooded his system.

Control.

No one did battle for Sebastian. He had a role. A duty. And he played the cards he was dealt.

Played them well. His body went through the motions even during the year his heart had rebelled. But Breanna smelled so sweet. Like cinnamon, apples, and allspice. And the way she looked at him made him want to believe in fairy tales.

Mentally he pulled that intrusive thought from his brain. It was just the hectic last couple of days. His heart refusing to fully accept what his mind already knew. This was a marriage of convenience between strangers.

She got a crown. He got a queen. Nothing more.

"I thought we should talk about our marriage. The union. The contract you signed for the princess lottery was a marriage contract. I had the lawyers look through it." They needed to discuss things other than hobbies. Or rather his lack of them. He woke early, worked until late, then repeated the process. That was all. Wishing for something different wouldn't bring changes. He knew his role.

"Lawyers. Right. I assume that means I've agreed to two

children and my full participation in the royal family until I die. After all, there is no divorce in the Celiana royal family. Some ancient law no one wants to overturn." Breanna walked back to her sewing table and started laying pattern pieces over the garment.

"I remember the words I signed. My degree may be in early childhood education, but one does not grow up a Galanis without knowing some legalese." She repositioned the pattern pieces.

He wasn't sure she was really seeing the pieces, or maybe this was all part of the process.

"That is the general agreement. Yes."

"So, you are here to talk about the heir part or the dutiful queen part?" She didn't stumble over the words. Said like they were nothing.

"The producing of an heir is part of the duty of a king and queen. An heir and a spare."

"No." Her curls bounced as she shot up. "No child of mine will be called a spare. Period. They are individuals. So, strike that word from your vocabulary, Your Highness."

Fire blazed in her dark eyes, and he nearly fell to his feet. He'd never been called a spare, but he knew the word had haunted his brother. The fact that Breanna was protective of their hypothetical children was the best sign he could think of.

"Consider it struck."

Her shoulders fell, and she bent over her table. He stepped beside her, rubbing her back. "Did you expect me to fight this?"

"Yes." Breanna stood, her body so close to his.

Emotions he hadn't let himself feel since his breakdown flooded his system. He wanted to laugh, to reach for her and bring out the chuckles he'd heard yesterday. Make her smile.

"I want my children to experience more than Alessio and I did. They deserve more."

"You do, too." Her hand brushed against his cheek.

The urge to lean into her, to say how much he hated the crown, was nearly overwhelming. But it wouldn't solve anything.

"We can conceive via IVF. The contract is for the marriage union, but you do not need to worry about sharing my bed." There were at least a dozen better ways to word that.

Breanna lowered her eyes and her hand dropped. "I see. Good to know."

"Breanna…"

A knock came, and his assistant stepped in before he could say anything else. A blessing since he had no idea what to say, and a curse given the tightening of her fists. At least one of the future queen's emotional tells was easy.

"Your Highness, Miss Galanis…" Raul bowed and then handed Sebastian a tablet. The bright words *Queen Bree!* radiated from the screen.

The headline was designed to draw attention to the similarities between Princess Briella and his Breanna. Briella and Alessio had an epic love story. The stuff of fairy tales.

And the exact opposite of this.

"Do you like the name Bree?"

"No." She stuck her tongue out, her nose scrunching as she shook her head.

So that was a definite no. They'd need to shut the press's nicknames down quickly. Once something stuck, it rarely unstuck.

"The press is likening you to Briella and the princess lottery."

"Princess Brie." Breanna cleared her throat. "I guess our names and situations being similar makes this a natural association. I mean, they don't know you pulled my sister's name out of a hat rather than the glass bowl your brother used for his wife. However, I do not like the nickname. I have always been Breanna."

"This isn't the same. Alessio and Brie love each other." They cared for each other. To each other they were everything. The whole world. If Alessio lost his title tomorrow, Brie would still love him.

Sam had confirmed what his father always said. Sebastian, without the crown, was nothing. Without the title, he had no place in this world. Everything about him revolved around a position he'd done nothing to earn.

"They didn't when he pulled her name from the glass bowl." Breanna tapped on the screen, making the text easier to read. "Looks like people enjoy your small wedding idea."

Shifting the topic was good. What was there to say? Neither expected the same to happen for them. "It makes a good statement. Makes us seem more regular when others have lost much in the last few years." The words felt off.

He wanted to acknowledge that many in the island nation were still suffering from the economic downturn. But the idea of having a giant celebration for such a union was unsavory. This was duty. Partnership. To spend Celiana's funds on such a thing would be unfair to the citizens.

"Royals caring. Always a good public relations call." Breanna stuck her hands in her pockets and rocked backwards. "So, umm… I don't think you just wanted to show us this." She paused. "Sorry, I don't think we've been introduced."

"Raul, my lady. The king's personal assistant." Raul bowed his head and held out his hand for the tablet. Once he had it, he tapped out several commands. "I wanted to go over a few things for the wedding. We got a list of your likes from your parents, but just checking. You want a bouquet of daisies and sunflowers?"

Breanna started to roll her eyes, then seemed to catch herself. "Only if you want me to sniff all the way down the aisle. Is there an aisle at the magistrate's? Or is it just a hallway?"

She shook her head. "Not the point. Focus, Breanna."

"Nice to know I am not the only one who talks to myself." Sebastian winked, wanting to overcome the negative feelings his early comments must have caused.

"A hard habit to break." Some of the tension leaked from her shoulders as she looked at him. "I am allergic to those. My parents tend to forget that Annie and I aren't exactly interchangeable. I am allergic to flowers; she can't get stung by bees. Anyways, I tolerate hydrangeas."

Interchangeable? They were identical in looks but still two different people. He couldn't focus on that now, though.

"Tolerate?" Sebastian shook his head. "No." She was marrying a stranger. The least he could do was give her flowers that didn't make her nose itch. "What flower can you be around easily?"

"Define *easily*." She looked at her feet, a hint of pink tracing her chin. "I can do ferns and pothos. I keep those in my room, but they aren't exactly royal wedding bouquet material."

Ferns and pothos. He knew the first. The second…surely a florist could figure something out?

"It's fine. It's not like I have to carry the bouquet for long. I can make do."

Make do. Words he was so familiar with. His whole life was concessions. Hers was now, too. Flowers for her bouquet were a choice that could be all hers.

"What about succulents?" Sebastian remembered seeing a beautiful design when Brie and Alessio were planning their union. Brie went with bright flowers for her bouquet, but the succulent option was stunning.

"Succulents? I mean, sure. I can also do cacti…they each have about the same amount of pollen. As close to zero as possible."

"Succulent bouquets are a thing. So, let's do that. Cacti would be a unique choice, but a little too prickly." Sebastian pointed to the tablet, happy when Raul picked up his cue to search for bouquet images. "Imagine the headlines if you carried cacti."

"Prickly queen! Touchy!" Her giggle was good, but those were just a few of the things the press might say.

He took the tablet and moved closer to her. She stepped closer, too. Not touching, but close. If this were a real relationship, he could put an arm around her. Instead, he swiped, showing off the different online options, watching her closely to see if any sparked her interest.

Breanna grabbed his hand as a small bouquet caught her eye. Her finger wrapped around his for an instant before she pulled back and cleared her throat. "These are pretty; let's do that."

Had she meant to touch him? Had she wanted more? Questions there was no easy way to ask a stranger, particularly in company.

"Anything else we should know?" Raul was poised, ready to take down any details.

Breanna seemed to purposefully step away from him. "I don't eat meat, and am not a huge fan of chocolate. Other than that, I am pretty easygoing. Promise."

"So, the steak and chocolate cake need to be canceled, too." Raul looked to Sebastian, the condemnation of her parents clear in his face.

Sebastian felt the same. This was not a traditional union, but Breanna deserved to make her own choices. "How about we go over everything and choose for ourselves?"

Breanna's shoulders relaxed, and she started to lean towards him before catching herself. "Thank you."

CHAPTER THREE

"You can still end this. You do not have to do this."

"I seem to remember saying something along the same lines, brother. You still pulled Brie's name out of the crystal bowl you made. It worked out." Sebastian didn't expect love for himself and Breanna. But they got along well enough, and she wanted the crown. This would be fine.

He straightened his tie for the hundredth time. "Why won't this damn tie stay where I put it?"

"Because you keep pulling at it." Alessio crossed his arms and looked towards the door, probably hoping that his wife, Brie, would make an appearance.

"Brie is with Breanna. She isn't going to come in here. It's royal custom for the princess to attend to the queen-to-be." Sebastian said the words with more conviction than he felt. He wasn't at all certain that Princess Brie would adhere to custom.

And it wouldn't be the worst thing if his sister-in-law arrived. Alessio could use the princess's calming effect. Though knowing Brie, she would have far more to say about today than his brother.

Alessio stalked to the mirror, pushing Sebastian's hands away from his tie. "Nothing about this is custom." His brother straightened the tie, then grabbed Sebastian's hands and pushed them into his pockets.

"Don't touch it!"

Sebastian wanted to pull his hands from his pockets on principle, but the tie was finally straight. "I think most of this actually is custom. I am just being honest about it. The fairy-tale stuff? The romance of royal unions—well, with present company excluded—we both know what it's really like."

"You can have more." Alessio threw his hands up, reaching for his own tie. "You deserve more. Just because you are the king. Sebastian—"

"Careful not to mess your tie." It was a pathetic joke, but what else was he supposed to say? Alessio got lucky.

Jealousy was pointless. He was genuinely happy for his brother. Brie was his match. But wanting it for himself wouldn't make it happen.

He was the king. That was all he was to almost everyone. Sure, his brother saw a different version, but the kingdom... even his own mother...saw only the crown.

The year he'd rebelled, he'd caused so much grief for Alessio. The fact that his brother had handled it perfectly didn't matter. Alessio had saved the kingdom. His and Brie's lottery had turned everything around. They deserved the happily-ever-after.

But Alessio should never have been put in that position. Sebastian had been raised for this role; he should have accepted it right away.

The frustration on his brother's face made it clear that Alessio had far more to add to this conversation. "Sebast—"

A knock echoed through the room, interrupting Alessio's next attempt. "Saved by the bell...or knock." He winked at his brother before walking over to the door. Sebastian pulled it open with flair, then stood there, not sure what to say.

Breanna was dressed in a floor-length white gown. The mermaid cut hugged her in all the right places. The scalloped top accentuated the swell of her breasts. Her dark hair was loose, curls wrapping her beautiful features, and her makeup looked natural. It was like she'd stepped from the pages of a bridal magazine.

In a few hours, she'd be his queen.

"Breanna."

"Well, hell." She crossed her arms, then looked around him and waved at Alessio. "Your wife was right, he's not in a tux."

"Umm…" Sebastian looked at his suit and waited for his brain to find any kind of statement. It was an afternoon wedding. At the magistrate's. A tux seemed out of place, but if she wanted him dressed in one, he had multiple.

Breanna hitched up her train and nodded to the interior. "Can I come in?"

"Isn't there a superstition about the groom seeing the bride in her dress before the wedding?" Sebastian wanted to reel the words back in as Breanna's face fell.

The hurt vanished in a flash. She shrugged and moved past him. "I think that curse only applies to those who aren't marrying out of duty."

Alessio made a noise and then started for the door. "I'll give you two a minute."

"No." Breanna held up a hand. "Brie said you should stay for this part."

This part?

His brother halted by the door. If Brie told him to stay, even through an intermediary, he'd do it. Until whatever *this part* was concluded.

"You are in a day suit. A lovely one. You're very attractive." A delicate rose coated her cheeks.

"I mean, you look nice. The suit. The suit looks nice." Breanna cleared her throat. "Wow. There really is no playbook for confronting the stranger you are marrying."

"Maybe we can write one." Sebastian playfully stroked his chin, trying to make his bride smile. *"No Big Life Decisions: Marrying a King in Three Days or Less."*

She tilted her head, "We need to workshop the title."

"Sure." Sebastian stuffed his hands in his pockets. "While we think of better titles, what is the problem with my suit?"

"I am in *this*." She frowned as she looked down at the exquisite gown, her fingers rustling over the beaded top.

"You look lovely." Such an understatement. Breanna sparkled as the light hit the jewels hand-sewn over the intricate gown.

"That is one of Ophelia's gowns, is it not? An original?" Sebastian knew most of the women from the princess lottery had rented their dresses. But the Galanis twins' gowns were specially made. With a year's worth of entries, the identical twins stood front and center as the odds of Alessio pulling out their names was high.

The twins were the focus of most of the early images on the day of the lottery, their bright, fancy dresses plastered everywhere. Commentators had discussed how their dresses even matched each other as Alessio drew the name, but he couldn't remember anyone saying if they looked upset not to hear their names.

"Yes. My and Annie's dresses were the most expensive gowns Ophelia has ever made."

"The price hardly matters." He doubted the price tag, even for two wedding dresses, had made a dent in the Galanis fortune.

"Except it does. People will talk." Breanna shook her head. "It is too fancy for this. Particularly with you dressed that way. The Galanis family upstaging the king."

The headline practically wrote itself.

"You want me to change?" He pointed to his closet. "My wardrobe is yours. Whatever you choose, I will put on. I have several tuxes." They weren't his first choice, but if that was what she chose, he'd put it on with a smile. "We can toss this offending day suit back in the depths where it belongs."

Breanna took a deep breath, her face softening. "You're very handsome, and the suit is lovely—as I said."

As compliments went, it was a tiny one. But coming from Breanna's sweet lips, it felt like he'd won a prize. "Handsome." He struck a pose, enjoying the giggle she let slip out.

She snapped her fingers. "Focus. This isn't the first time you've been told you're handsome."

"My future wife saying it feels different." He meant it. He didn't know why it made his insides gooey, but it did.

Breanna raised an eyebrow but didn't add anything else to that conversation. Instead, she pointed to her gown again.

"I can't wear this dress." Breanna took a deep breath. "We are having a small wedding. One similar to regular people, right?"

"Yes." Sebastian looked to Alessio, who'd remained painfully quiet during this exchange. But if his brother understood the issue, he wasn't giving anything away. Instead, he was looking at Breanna, a smile pulling at the corner of his lips. "I thought, given the cost of living crisis, smaller is better."

"Right. And this dress cost more than fifteen thousand pounds." Breanna sighed. "That is not a good look for that message, Your Highness."

He didn't like how the exasperated "Your Highness" fell from her lips.

"Breanna…"

She looked at the crystals lining the bodice. "I know you picked my name, or rather Annie's, because we had a dress, but this won't work."

What was the answer? They were heading to the magistrate's office in less than two hours. But she was right. If the cost leaked, and it would, the public relations team would be dealing with a nightmare.

"Do you have a plan to solve the issue?" Alessio had asked the right question. The one that should have popped from his mouth minutes ago.

Sebastian looked to Breanna, and nodded, hoping she had an idea.

"I have a dress. It's white—mostly. I made it from a dress I found at a thrift store a few years ago. It's simple, and I think it is the better choice. But if *you* want this…"

She had a simple gown. One she'd made. It wasn't exactly what people thought of when they imagined a royal wedding.

Though what about this was?

Breanna waited, then turned to Alessio. "Do you think I'm wrong?"

"No. And let me guess, Brie agrees with you." Alessio looked at his watch. "Brie's pretty good at estimating the press's response."

His fiancée's smile wasn't forced when Alessio mentioned his wife. Breanna sparkled, and it had nothing to do with the fancy dress. "She does. The princess is very kind."

"She is." Alessio nodded. "Do you need anything else from me?"

"No." Breanna shook her head, "You're free to go."

"Dismissed by the queen." Alessio bowed to the queen. This his gaze focused on Sebastian. "I like her." Then he was gone.

Sebastian had said the same thing about Brie to Alessio.

"Nothing about this is standard, but I figured you chose a couture gown for the lottery, and you won't get to wear it again." There was a law in place that kept the king and queen from divorcing. An ancient crusty script from a bygone era that parliament had never overruled.

The lyrical notes of her chuckle made him smile.

"I hate this dress. I didn't choose it. Mother did." She reached for his hands, then pulled back.

Mother did.

The words stuck in his head. That wasn't right. Breanna and Anastasia wanted titles. Everyone knew that. The press had followed their journeys for the princess lottery nearly as closely as they'd followed Alessio. A look inside the day of royal hopefuls.

Only after Briella's name bounced out did the Galanis twins' names fade from the press.

She wanted this. *But what if...*

"There was something else I wanted..." She looked at her feet, then straightened. "Kiss me." Breanna let out a nervous sound. "Wow, I probably could have stated that differently. Or maybe not at all, but too late now, so, yeah. We'll go with that. I want you to kiss me."

Her dark eyes flitted to the door, and color crept along her neck. "Breanna?" Kissing her wouldn't be hard. The woman was the definition of beauty. But her nervousness gave him pause.

"Have you ever kissed anyone?" The twins were waiting for a title, but surely she'd dated. She must have had suitors lined up around the family compound.

"Nope." Breanna bit her lip and let out a ragged breath. "I—I—I need to say something other than *I*, but my brain is overloaded."

Sebastian took her hand; the connection was firm but loose enough that if she wanted to pull back, it would take no effort. He was thrilled when she didn't. "Do you trust me?"

"I should say no. That is what makes sense."

Once more his soon-to-be bride was right. They were practically strangers, but he felt an odd sense of calm right now. Nerves should be popping; he should be fidgeting, but the only thing weighing on him was how to make this moment special for her.

"I trust you." She bit her lip, again. "Today is a lot, but I trust you. I do. Guess I am practicing for the vows." Her soft smile warmed his heart. "I do."

The phrase seemed to unlock part of his soul. The words

were sustenance on this day where everything felt more than a little surreal.

Using his free hand, he stroked her lip, pulling it from her teeth. "You are safe here." *With me.*

Yes, they were marrying. But he was not going to force anything on Breanna. They'd get to know each other. Learn to coexist and care for each other. It would take time, but she was safe. Always.

"Close your eyes." The words were barely above a whisper, but she did as he said.

A person only got one first kiss. Usually, it was fumbling and more than a little off as teens in the heady days of hormones figured out what the racing feelings meant. That was not the experience Breanna was going to get. But he could still make it memorable.

He squeezed her hand, trying to push as much reassurance through the touch as possible. "Breathe, honey." Sebastian let his free hand stroke her cheek.

Fire danced on the tips of his fingers. This was about Breanna. Giving her a memory. Still, his breath was picking up, and desire seemed to pulse on each breath.

Breanna.

So much of his life was out of his control. Even the woman before him wasn't his choice. But in this moment, it felt like the universe was granting something just for him.

"Sebastian."

His name. Just his name. Not his title, nothing else, fell from her sweet lips.

Finally, he pressed his lips to hers. He'd envisioned a short, nearly chaste kiss. A memory given to her, enjoyed by him.

Instead, the universe exploded. Breanna leaned into him, and his arms went around her waist without another thought, her hands wrapping around his neck.

Apples, lemons, sweetness divine filled his nostrils as his

soon-to-be wife's body fit against his. Time, space and everything in between vanished as he drank her in.

Then her mouth opened, and the taste of her nearly brought him to his knees. If the afterlife contained a paradise, the feeling of Breanna in his arms, lips pressed to his, would be the ultimate achievement possible.

"You cannot possibly wear that." Breanna's mother never raised her voice, but her tone right now was as close to hysterical as she could remember. "Your little hobby is cute when it is contained at home. But this is your wedding day. To the king."

"As though you wouldn't know what today is or who you are marrying." Princess Brie laughed and held up the champagne goblet. Her bright blue eyes sparkled as she met Breanna's gaze. "You are gorgeous."

Brie was saying all the things Breanna wanted to say to her parents but without a hint of bile or anger. Yet the daggers found purchase each time. The princess had skillfully put her mother in her place over and over again without ever raising her voice or getting testy. She was poised, confident and so sure that what she said would have the exact response she intended.

This was why Brie had broken from her powerful family. Started her own business. Created a name for herself. Even after marrying a prince, the patriarch and matriarch of the Alessio clan still didn't acknowledge the daughter, who outshone them all.

It was that willingness to take a leap that led Brie to carving her own path, while Breanna had made plans. But never followed through. Sure, she'd protected Annie, but she was still marrying a king she didn't know in less than an hour.

Sebastian. His name cascaded through her mind. Her hand reflexively found her lips where the ghost of the kiss remained.

Maybe first kisses were always like that. Maybe your body

felt like singing each time. It wasn't like she'd had any experience with it.

The boy she'd fancied at uni had stood her up for their first date. Later, she'd heard through the rumor mill that her father had paid the man quite handsomely to forget she existed. Whether it was true or not, and she suspected it was, all the men who'd asked her out afterwards seemed to be hoping they might also get the same fat check.

Life as a Galanis was privileged in many ways...but it did not come with freedom.

She hadn't expected his lips to feel so soft, so sweet, so refreshing. Kissing Sebastian felt like taking a sip from a fresh stream. Her body had nearly collapsed with want and need.

She'd pressed herself against him, lengthening the exchange. Desperate for another.

Focus!

Annie's hand pressed into hers, grounding her.

"I think she looks beautiful." Her sister cleared her throat, then continued, "That dress is gorgeous and looks nothing like the original dress you bought."

Her sister made a face. "It was hideous. I thought there was no way you could make it anything."

"I've thought that about your room ideas, too." Breanna pulled her sister close.

"You both have far too much faith in your abilities."

Annie straightened her shoulders, then looked at her mother. A week ago, those sharpened words would have bowed her spirit. Instead, she shrugged and twirled a finger through the curl by her cheek.

It was the only thing Matilda Galanis had said to Annie, and it was clear she wanted Annie to respond. Good for Annie that she was rewarding her mother with the same indifference she'd shown her.

The Galanis Trust had made it known that Annie was not

under their protection, and she'd been cut off. Which meant renting an apartment had been nearly impossible.

The only one they'd found was in a neighborhood people did their best to avoid. But the price was right, and the landlord had been willing to rent it on a month-by-month basis.

Breanna could have asked Sebastian for aid. But Annie had begged her not to. She claimed she'd needed to do as much of this on her own as possible. Breanna hadn't wanted to steal away any of her newfound confidence.

Breanna squeezed Annie's hand, then examined herself in the floor-length mirror. The dress was a vintage wedding gown she'd found at a local thrift store. The bottom had been stained, so Breanna cut it off, making this a tea-length gown. She'd added a crochet-like overlay, giving it a semiformal look. It was pretty, and handmade. It hung on her perfectly.

If she'd had a choice in the dresses she was allowed to pick for the princess lottery, she'd have chosen something like this. Light. Airy.

It didn't scream queen attire. Her mother was right about that. But it was perfect for her.

The sounds of the square's bell ringing echoed in the room. Time to go. Annie stepped to her side and kissed her cheek.

"You don't have to do this." Her sister's words were nearly silent, but the plea under them echoed into the universe.

Breanna put her hand on her sister's cheek. If she didn't there'd be no way for them to get Annie back up on her feet. Not for years…if ever. Her sister had goals and a plan, and the soon-to-be queen could protect her better than she'd ever hoped for. "I know."

Then she looked at her mother and Princess Briella. "I think that ringing is the sign that we are supposed to head to the magistrate's office." She'd not fumbled a single word. Pride and worry raced for first place in her mind.

Now, if I can manage not to stumble over my vows.

* * *

"You all right?" Sebastian's hand slid around her waist as she stood at the corner of the reception area. It was a light afternoon affair. Finger sandwiches, fruit, and for dessert, her favorite, lemon cake. It might be a normal reception. Except they were in the palace.

And a small gold crown was pinned to the top of her hair.

What a day. She started to lean into him, then pulled herself upright. He was her husband, checking on her. But they were still virtually strangers.

"Fine." The lie was easier than the truth. And it had nothing to do with the small crown Sebastian had placed on her head after she'd said *I do*.

No. Once more in her life, the upset was caused by the people who'd raised her. Or at least paid for the host of rotating nannies she and Annie loved and lost in their childhood.

Nothing about the day was right for them. The dress. The location. And now the reception.

They'd expected a huge party. Despite the press conference clearly outlining the fact that they were having a simple reception for close friends and family, they'd expected palace glamour. They'd wanted a queen for a daughter...but only if they could flash it to the world.

"This might as well be a pauper's reception. Where is the steak?" Her father's complaint carried across the room, and most of the heads turned in his direction.

Breanna started towards him, grateful that Sebastian moved with her.

"It's an afternoon reception, father." Breanna kept her voice low, hoping he might do the same.

Lucas Galanis got what he wanted. On the few occasions he didn't, hell tended to spill from its gates.

"Cucumber sandwiches, carrot and raisin sandwiches?

It's positively ghastly." Her mother huffed as she looked at the fare on her plate.

"There is smoked salmon, too." Breanna was a vegetarian. It was something she'd adopted after watching an online video when she was a teenager. Her father had called it a phase. A decade later, "the phase" was still intact. It infuriated him.

"And lemon cake," Sebastian offered, squeezing her side.

She'd never had anyone stand next to her while she tried to calm her parents. Annie had always avoided conflict.

Then she looked at her husband and felt her head snap back a bit. His eyes were boring into her father's. Fury matching her father's radiated in her husband's gaze.

Over what?

"Lemon cake." Her mother sniffed.

Sebastian's hand tightened on her waist.

Without thinking, she put her hand around his waist. They were a united front.

"Yes. Lemon cake." Sebastian's words were ice spikes, but neither of her parents appeared to pick up on the cool tones. "*Breanna's* favorite." The world seemed to shift, and the pressure on her chest evaporated. He was here. Choosing her side. Choosing Breanna. No one ever chose her.

Her mother let out a soft chuckle. "Chocolate is what *we* ordered."

Ordered. Like today was theirs. Their accomplishment. Their achievement. Not an irreversible life-changing moment for their daughter.

Before she could say anything, Sebastian offered, "It's *her* wedding day."

Her day. Hers. Such a simple statement that rocked her world. She leaned her head against his shoulder, enjoying having a partner for this exchange.

His lips brushed the top of her head, and she saw her mother's eyes narrow. They really didn't care if their daughter was happy. Maybe they didn't want that.

"Yes. But *we* are the ones that wanted to be here. Breanna didn't want the crown—" Her father looked at Sebastian, keeping his head tilted just enough for the king.

"Father—"

"He needs us, Breanna." He cut her off. "The country is a constitutional monarchy. They have no real power. He showed up on our doorstep for a bride, and we provided one."

And yet you wanted a daughter to wear the crown.

"Breanna, do you want your parents here?"

The soft question nearly made her laugh. Want her parents here? Of course not. She never wanted her parents around, but they were her parents.

Sending them away wasn't an option. Or it hadn't been before Sebastian put a crown on her head. "No?"

She hadn't really meant to say it as a question. It felt rebellious. Far more rebellious than anything else she'd ever done.

And liberating.

"Lovely. My wife, *your queen*, and I bid you farewell." Sebastian nodded towards the door. "Don't make me call the guard. In this palace, my word is final."

"Breanna, you don't mean to let him send us away." Her mother stepped towards her, but Breanna stepped back. Sebastian moved with her in unison.

"Where is Annie's portfolio?" It wasn't the answer to her mother's question, but Matilda Galanis was a smart woman. She knew the underlying question.

Her mother's eyes flitted to Annie, currently laughing with Prince Alessio and Princess Briella. She looked to her husband, then shrugged. "What portfolio?"

The lie was too much. Her mother knew what she meant. If the portfolio hadn't been burned, then it had been locked away. It didn't matter. The result was the same.

"Have a nice day." Breanna nodded to her parents, then turned attention to Sebastian. "Shall we dance?" A DJ had been quietly playing tunes, but no one had ventured onto the dance floor.

"Is that what you want?" Sebastian's gaze followed her parents' exit, then refocused on her.

No one, other than Annie, had ever asked her what she wanted. She was light. Happy. And she wanted to enjoy the moment.

"Yes. Let's dance!" She grabbed her husband's hand, trying to pretend that the king hadn't just kicked her parents out of their wedding reception. That this was just a fun afternoon get-together. The illusion would clear when Annie, Alessio and Brie all left. But until she was left alone with Sebastian—in the palace—Breanna could try to forget that she'd said *I do* to a king today.

A king. And a stranger.

Breanna hit her hip against his as the music bounced around them. His bride had kicked her shoes off five songs ago. Brie and Annie had followed suit. Only his mother still had her shoes on.

The dowager queen would leave her shoes on even if her toes were bleeding. But at least his mother was smiling. She'd even discreetly given him a thumbs-up when he'd told Breanna's parents to leave.

The fast song shifted to a slow tune. Briella and Alessio immediately went into each other's arms. A few other couples did the same while some of the singles exited the dance floor.

His wife stood still; her jeweled gaze watched him closely. Should he reach for her? They were married, but the fast dances let them be close without holding each other.

Did she want to dance in his arms? She'd put her arm around his when he was kicking her parents out. He'd kissed the top of her head, unable to resist. Breanna has pulled him onto the dance floor, but she hadn't touched him other than hip bumps and the occasional high-five since. And much of the dancing was in groups.

He was never more than a few inches from her. If she moved, he moved with her. And she'd done the same. He wanted to pull her close, hold her, but the day was already so much. They were husband and wife, but in title only.

The chords twanged on, and Breanna cleared her throat. "I am going to get a drink." She dipped her head to him, her eyes shielded.

Make a decision, Sebastian!

"I'll come with you."

Breanna nodded as she moved off the dance floor. There was nothing different in her posture, but he knew he'd hurt her feelings. It wasn't his intent, but the outcome was the same.

"Breanna." He said her name without knowing where he was going next. "Did you want to dance?"

"We've been dancing." His wife touched the crown he'd placed on her head after they'd said *I do.* "Your mother pinned this in perfectly. It hasn't moved with all the motion. She'll have to teach me how to do that."

"I am sure she'd be happy to." Sebastian grabbed two lemon drop mocktails, handed one to his wife and sipped his. The sugar on the rim blended with the tartness, but it didn't cut any of the awkwardness hovering between them now as they stood silently drinking the festive beverage.

The ease they'd had bouncing to the rhythms on the floor had evaporated. He wanted it back.

The slow song stopped, but the couples on the dance floor clung to each other for several moments after the final chords echoed. At most weddings, the bride and groom were center-stage.

But this wasn't a traditional reception in any sense of the

word, and the couples staring at each other with love were not the bride and groom.

His eyes again went to Alessio and Brie. They were whispering to each other as they moved to a beat no one else heard. No doubt saying the sweet nothings those in love spoke so easily. He looked to Breanna and barely caught the sigh in his throat.

A fast song kicked in. Good. They could get back on the dance floor.

"Breanna!" Brie bounced towards her sister-in-law. "This one is just for the girls." The princess stole the queen into the center of the floor with a host of giggles.

"Why did you stand there when your bride was looking at you, waiting for you to ask her to dance?" His mother's voice was quiet, but it carried an authority that made his back a little straighter.

The dowager queen looked at the dance floor. Her eyes rested on the queen and princess. "She wanted to dance with you. She is your wife."

"I froze." Sebastian finished the last of his drink. There was no use calling it anything else. The day was one for the record books. He was married to a woman whose parents insinuated she hadn't wanted the crown he'd thought she craved. It was enough to throw anyone off their game.

"Breanna wants you to show her how you pinned the crown so well. It hasn't moved." It was a bad segue but easier than anything else.

His mother sniffed but didn't offer anything else on that topic. "You will dance with her the next time a slow song comes on. Brie bought you a few minutes."

"Wha…?" He turned to see and caught Alessio's eyes as he waved to him from where he stood next to the DJ stand.

"He's helping you." His mother patted his arm. "He wants you and your queen to be happy."

"Do you think we can be?" He regretted the words as soon as they were out.

His mother looked to the dance floor again. "Happiness is much to ask for in a royal marriage. Contentedness. Maybe that will be in your reach."

Contentedness.

Was that what she and his father had had? Contentedness. Was that enough?

It would have to be.

The slow song began, and Alessio collected his wife. Sebastian started for the dance floor and met Breanna at the edge of it.

"May I have this dance?"

She looked over her shoulder, her eye following Alessio and Brie's rotations on the floor. Then she reached for his hand and squeezed it. "Only if you actually want it."

Of course his bride knew this wasn't by chance.

Not dropping her hand, he pulled her onto the dance floor and into his arms. "I very much do."

She slid her arms around his waist, gently swaying with him on the floor. After a moment she laid her head against his shoulder.

He breathed her in, holding her tight. Enjoying the moment a little too much.

"It's been a day." The whispered words were so soft he wasn't sure she'd meant to say them out loud.

His fingers stroked her back, and she melted against him a little more. They weren't so much dancing as holding on to each other as the storm of the day finally broke.

It didn't matter. They were together. Day one of a lifetime.

"We made it through the reception." She chuckled, "And our first family drama."

They had.

"What's next, Sebastian?"

"Next?" He looked over his shoulder at his mother, holding mini court with a few friends. She missed his father, but if he were still here, they would have stood near each other but never danced together. Two people who cared for each other but did not have a deep passion.

Two strangers who'd married.

Then his gaze fell on Brie and Alessio. They were holding each other, talking quietly, and laughing at a private joke. Two strangers who'd fallen desperately in love. A lightning strike.

Looking away brought more peace than it should. His brother and sister-in-law were happy. "We get to know each other." He smiled at his bride, seeing the uncertainty in her gaze. He and Breanna would be content. It would be enough.

It had to be.

CHAPTER FOUR

SEBASTIAN DOWNED THE cup of coffee, then poured himself another. He and Breanna had danced for hours last night. His legs burned with the memory of the exercise. But it was his heart that had kept him awake all night.

She'd held him tight through their final slow dance. Knowing the reception was nearly over. Today began the real story. Their life as king and queen.

But we are the ones who wanted to be here.

Her parents' words kept replaying in his mind. That couldn't be right. Breanna had won the crown from her sister. She'd wanted it more.

I think that curse only applies to those who aren't marrying out of duty.

So many phrases were burned into his brain from yesterday. As was the feel of her body against his. The soft scent of cinnamon apples in her hair seemed attached to his nose. Her downcast eyes as she'd quietly said I do in the magistrate's office.

The brush of her lips on his.

So many emotions to work through before the day had really even begun.

"I do hope you haven't drunk all the coffee." Breanna's voice was bright. No dark circles shadowed her eyes. She looked well-rested.

His mind couldn't seem to align the words her parents had

thrown at him yesterday and the bubbly woman pouring her own cup of coffee beside him.

"Not to complain, but is there any coffee syrup hiding anywhere?" Breanna looked to the cabinets like she was considering opening them but holding back.

"Not in this kitchen." Sebastian pulled up his phone, ready to text her order to the staff. The fact that she hadn't asked for syrup when she first arrived was frustrating. But she was asking now. "What do you want?"

"This kitchen? So how many kitchens are there?" Breanna went to the fridge, found some milk, poured it in, and then added more sugar than he'd ever seen someone put in such a small cup.

"Several." Take Breanna on a tour of the palace…today's task. "This is my, *our*, private kitchen. There isn't staff for this one, but it's always stocked with what I—we—want. I just need to know what that is."

"Do you cook?" Breanna slid onto one of the high stools.

"Yes, when I have time." Sebastian took a deep breath because part of him wanted to shake the phone in her face and demand the answer to the question he'd asked and she'd now dodged several times.

"What syrups do you like, Breanna?"

"It's no big deal." Breanna put her elbows on the counter, then rested her chin in her hands. It was adorable and infuriating at the same time. "So, what do you like to cook? Eggs? I swear that is what the movies always show. The man makes the girl scrambled eggs in the morning and everyone swoons—he can cook."

"I will answer that question when you tell me what syrups you want stocked in here. If you don't tell me, then I will have the staff order one of everything."

She laughed and gestured to the kitchen. "This kitchen is huge, and I still don't think you could fit one of everything."

"I guess we get to see then." Sebastian started typing.

Her hands were warm as they wrapped around his wrist. "It's not a big deal, Sebastian. And its early. Don't disturb the staff on my behalf, please."

Tears hovered in her eyes. "Please."

He set the phone down and walked to her without thinking of the next steps. Sebastian pulled her into his arms. She was still sitting on the stool, and her head barely came to his shoulder. "It's coffee syrup, Breanna. It's not earth-shattering, but it's something you want, so I will put in the order this afternoon. You will have it tomorrow."

She nodded against him and sniffed. "This is silly. I don't know why syrup is sending so many emotions through me."

It wasn't syrup. It was everything else coming through something that didn't matter in the universe's grand scheme. He'd had similar breakdowns when the crown got too heavy. Worrying over something minor was easier than addressing the elephant in the room.

"A lot has happened in four days." That was an understatement. He stroked her back, then leaned his head against hers.

No words. Just two people who fate had tossed together. He kissed the top of her head and took a breath. If the wedding orders her parents put in were any indications, the Galanis twins weren't allowed their own choices. But she could have them now. "What kinds of syrups, Breanna?"

"Your comment on filling the room isn't that far off. I love syrups, vanilla, mocha, chai, white chocolate, brown sugar cinnamon, seasonal favorites like pumpkin, peppermint, lavender."

"I know pumpkin and peppermint, but lavender?"

"More an add-in for tea. It's easiest to find in spring." She pulled back.

His arms ached to reach for her. To hold her again. To wipe away the hurt she hid too quickly in her eyes.

"Brown sugar cinnamon and chai are my favorites."

Then those would be here tomorrow. And a few others. He'd let the staff know to add a different new one each time a bottle was empty. That way she'd eventually have a nice stock without feeling like everything appeared all at once.

"All right. Was that so hard?"

"No." Breanna reached for the coffee mug.

"I have something for you." Sebastian had meant to wrap it, but the little box sitting on the cabinet would drive most of her days.

Breanna grinned. "A present?"

Yes. And no. "I thought this might come in handy." He pushed the box towards her.

"Handy. Interesting wording from a king." Breanna opened the box and nodded at the silver watch. It was delicate and well-made. But as her gaze roamed over it, he wished there'd been anything else in the box. A necklace or ring or...something.

Something that didn't scream *Sorry, but from now on the clock will rule your life. Time will be your enemy because there is never enough of it. Minutes will fly and hours evaporate.*

"Sebastian?" Breanna's hand was on his cheek. "It's a nice gift. I suspect I will need a good timepiece to make sure I am where I need to be."

Sebastian nodded, then looked at it. "Yes." What else was there to say?

"Thank you." Breanna brushed her lips against his cheek, then put the watch on her wrist.

"So." She held up her arms as she spun in their kitchen. "What do you cook?"

There was no quick answer to that. He cooked a little of everything. Sebastian loved trying new recipes, creating his own. He was skilled enough now that most of the creations tasted good. That had not always been the case.

"Anything. I can make a mean scrambled egg." Sebastian winked. "Since traveling to Japan last year, I've started some days with *gohan* and an egg."

"So cooking is your hobby?"

"No. Cooking is just cooking." Sebastian headed to the fridge. "Do you eat eggs? These were never fertilized." One of his university professors had gotten very upset during a lecture about the different kinds of vegetarians. He didn't remember what started the man's forty-minute off-topic discussion, but he remembered the type the professor outlined.

He looked over his shoulder, and she was smiling. "If they were never fertilized, yes. No one has ever asked."

Another punch in the gut. No one had asked his wife a basic question about her choices. He was used to that. As King, everyone assumed you got what you wanted. The reality was you got what others wanted for you.

Breanna hadn't worn a crown until yesterday. There was no reason for her not to be asked. Except for the Galanis family not caring what their daughters wanted.

"All right, well, I have rice in the steamer, and we can add the egg for protein. Then, time to get to know each other."

"Wonderful words to hear from your husband." She raised her coffee mug in a mock toast.

"So, you want to play twenty questions?" Breanna took a bite of the rice dish. It was savory and filling, but her stomach had no intention of settling. Get-to-know-you time was meant for dating. Meant for figuring out if you matched.

There was already a simple gold band on the ring finger of her left hand.

Sebastian's gaze was intense. The man's blue eyes seemed to say things that she suspected he had no intention of sharing.

"Let's think of it as more of a coffee date." Sebastian went to the machine and topped her mug off. Then he opened the sugar jar. "You tell me when."

He put one heaping spoon in. It looked just like what she'd done. He'd paid attention. Why did that make her want to cry?

"That's good." Breanna's voice, broke but Sebastian didn't acknowledge it.

Her husband was kind. That was a good thing. A brilliant silver lining.

"Did you want to be queen?" Sebastian passed her the mug.

It nearly slipped through her fingers. There was a simple answer. Two little letters that changed nothing. What was the point of answering it now?

"That is not a coffee date question, Your Highness." She took a sip of her coffee, set it aside, then leaned her hands on the table. "Though to be honest, I've never been on a coffee date."

Or any date.

"Still, I think it's supposed to start with hobbies or favorite colors or what you were like growing up." Breanna playfully wagged a finger at him. "You like cooking. Do you enjoy baking too?"

Sebastian made a face.

"Was that grimace about me shifting the topic or about baking?" She leaned forward, enjoying the grin that appeared anytime she got close. Did he know he was doing that?

The king reached out and took her free hand, loosely playing with her fingers. A simple motion that shouldn't send heat racing through her.

"Maybe both."

"I had a roommate in college who loved to bake. She made cookies, cakes, the most beautiful pastries. Ask her to cook pasta and she'd throw up her hands. No interest. You'd think we were torturing her with such a suggestion!" She wrapped her ring finger around his, their matching gold bands glinting.

Small lines appeared around his eyes as he laughed, again. It filled the kitchen, and her stomach let go of some of the tension that seemed to be her constant companion.

"I feel that way about baking. It really is more science than anything else. No thank you."

"So, you didn't make the lemon cake for our wedding reception?" Breanna laid a hand over her chest, mock surprise making him laugh harder. It was a nice sight. The king in public was so controlled. So dutiful.

In his own kitchen though, he could laugh. When they were alone, she wanted this man.

"If I made it, it would have looked more like a lemon mush than cake."

"Lemon mush… I bet it still would have tasted lovely." Brenna didn't care so much about what the cake looked like. Until he'd kicked her parents out, their reception was a horror show. After?

Well, after they'd danced and danced. It was fun. Then the slow songs had started. She'd waited for him to take her hand for the first one, then made a quick escape when it seemed he didn't want to.

The second song, and the third and fourth, she'd spent in his arms, a feeling of safety seeping through her. Clearly the long day had scrambled some of her senses.

"Your Highness?" Raul walked into the kitchen and stopped. "Sorry, Your Highnesses." He nodded to Breanna. *Your Highness.* She doubted she'd ever get used to that.

"It's early for the look of concern, Raul." Breanna held up her coffee mug. "Want a cup of coffee before you spill whatever difficult thing is on the tip of your tongue?"

Raul and her husband both stared at her with open mouths. "Do you not normally get asked to join the king and queen for coffee, or are those looks for something else?"

"I know the schedule says get to know the queen. But we have a situation." Raul looked at King Sebastian.

The queen. Not Breanna. The queen. Anyone could have fit that description provided they had a dress and willingly signed a contract. She was just the one he'd picked—or the one he'd been forced to pick when she'd exchanged places with Annie.

Breanna blew out a breath, trying to focus on the comment from Raul.

"An emergency?" It wasn't. At least, not a real one. Raul was stressed but not bent in trauma. Sebastian, and now she, had duties as royals, but they also needed a life.

"Uh—"

"If you have to think on it, then it's not." It was day one of being queen. Maybe she shouldn't assert herself now, but if she didn't start right away, she might lose the gumption. Her husband needed a hobby and time to be Sebastian, not just the king.

And she refused to wear her crown, metaphorically or otherwise, before nine, unless it was absolutely necessary.

"So, coffee time. The king and I are not responding to business before nine a.m. or after eight p.m." She wasn't sure the times would stick, but whether they fluctuated or not, the idea was what mattered.

"Breanna," Sebastian's voice was soft, not quite a rebuke, but close enough.

Ignoring the twinge in her stomach, she went to the small mug stand and grabbed one for Raul. "We don't have syrups." She made a playful face at Sebastian, but he didn't react.

The king stood before her now. The duty-bound man who gave her a wristwatch the day after marrying her.

"So, cream and sugar or black?" Her voice wobbled, but she kept the smile on her face.

Raul looked to Sebastian, but the king didn't say anything. "Um…black, Your Highness."

"Breanna. Call me Breanna." She passed him the cup.

"We have a duty, Breanna." Sebastian was ramrod straight. The man who'd played with her fingers and kissed her head when she was panicking this morning was lost. But he was there, she'd seen him. He just had let go a little.

"We also have lives." She held up her hand before Sebastian could say anything else. Maybe she hadn't wanted this life. But she was making the best of it. Period.

"Raul, tell me about yourself." Color drained from the man's face, and she sighed. "All right, take a deep breath. We will start the actual work in an hour. Until then, we were talking hobbies. Sebastian claims he doesn't have any, but we both know it's cooking, right?"

This time Raul didn't look to the king. Instead, he laughed, and she saw Sebastian take a deep breath. Her husband was not used to putting off work.

Even the day after their wedding. She tried not to let that sting. This was a marriage of convenience. In the twenty-first century, it looked a little different, but that didn't change the truth. Her husband didn't want her.

He'd wanted a bride, and a queen. The person standing there didn't really matter. As exchangeable as pieces of paper placed in a hat.

But she needed to have some boundaries. Something to ground her.

"Yes. And I assume based on the sewing equipment the team brought to your room, you like creating new things."

It was more than that. She liked finding and repurposing old things. Rehabbing clothes that others thought were too outdated or damaged. Almost one hundred billion garments were made a year, and nearly ninety percent of materials ended up in landfills. Less than one percent was rehabbed or recycled, but she was trying to do her part.

It was a stance her parents refused to understand. Yes, her

closet could contain a new outfit every day. A couture item designed just for her never to be worn again. Her family's budget wouldn't even notice a dent.

But what was the purpose of that?

"Breanna, we really need to discuss the situation." Sebastian motioned for Raul to continue.

This time Raul didn't look to her for confirmation. Instead, he reached for the tablet next to him and started reciting off the "issues."

None of which sounded like they were more than the average headache. A frustration, but hardly something that had to be started right away.

In the passing moments, it had become clear that she wasn't needed. She looked at her new watch, then slid off the stool. She waited to see if her husband would say anything, then hoped to hear his voice as she walked to the door.

He never raised his head from the tablet.

A day after her wedding and already an afterthought...

CHAPTER FIVE

"WHAT DO YOU THINK, Breanna?" Sebastian lifted his head from the tablet and was shocked to find her gone. "Breanna?"

Color crept up Raul's neck. "She left."

"Left?" Sebastian shook his head and tried to remember if she'd said goodbye.

"About twenty minutes ago, Your Highness."

Twenty minutes.

He pushed his hands through his hair and looked at her coffee mug sitting in front of the stool where she'd sat joking with him about hobbies and setting a schedule. How could he have missed that?

Except he knew how. When he focused on duty, he drowned everything else out. It was a trick he'd learned as a child, that way his focus never drifted to things he'd rather do. Instead, his mind stayed in the present. Laser-focused on the responsibilities given him though a roll of the universal dice of fate.

It worked well when he was a child. Even as an adult—but as a husband it left more than a little to be desired.

"I think we are done for now. Reach out to Alessio. The art nonprofits usually like having him at their events. I agree that more notice would have been nice, but everyone gets busy, and things fall through the cracks. I am not surprised the requests for royal attendance came late."

Raul made a few notes. "If Prince Alessio and Princess Brie are unable to attend?"

"Then I will figure out how to be in three places at once." He and Breanna were already scheduled to make appearances at two other locations that day. A ribbon cutting and a speech given by a local celebrity on a topic he couldn't quite remember.

Breanna liked fiber arts. That was something she could highlight as the queen. Show off her pieces and work. Encourage others. Between her and Alessio, the royal family was quite artistic.

Sebastian pushed himself away from the counter. He needed to find Breanna. This was supposed to be their day together. Time to get to know each other.

And he'd let duty get in the way. It was necessary, but he could have explained better.

He quickly rinsed the mug, hung it back in its place, then went to find his bride. She'd be in her rooms. Mostly because he hadn't taken her on a tour of the palace yet.

There were many excuses he could give for that, but none of them mattered.

He raised his hand, knocked on her suite door. Her voice gave him entry, and he opened the door.

Breanna was bent over her large workbench. The ugliest dress he'd ever seen lay on top of it. He stood there waiting for her angry snap. He'd earned this one. Whatever she wanted to let out, he'd take it.

But the silence carried on, and his wife's eyes never left her project.

Finally, she grabbed some tool, and then started doing something to the garment on her bench. The sleeves fell away, but it didn't improve the garment's look all that much. "Did you need something, Sebastian?"

"It's all right if you want to yell at me." Maybe she wanted permission? His father often gave it to his mother when they had a spat. Sebastian didn't remember her ever raising her voice, but the option was there.

An option Samantha had never needed. When she'd felt like lashing out, she had not held back. She'd told him all the things she'd change when she was queen. How he'd not recognized that was all she wanted was beyond him now. *Love blinded you.*

The tool clattered to the table. "Why would I yell at you?" Breanna's dark eyes looked genuinely shocked.

"I ignored you." Heat stole along his collar. Married less than a day and he'd ignored the woman in front of him when they were supposed to be getting to know each other. Duty came first, but he should have noticed her leaving.

"An apology would be nice. But why yell? I know what this marriage is. What I am." There was no malice in the words. No emotion at all.

Just an acceptance that nearly sent him to his knees. Funny, he'd always thought anger was the worst emotion. But her quiet statement hurt more than any angry words Samantha had thrown at him.

"Breanna, I am so sorry. I got caught up in the emergency."

"No." She leaned against the table and crossed her arms. "I appreciate the apology, but that was not an emergency."

He didn't want to squabble, but he needed her to understand their roles.

"What might not look like an emergency to those not wearing crowns has to be treated as an emergency by those who are."

One of his father's favorite refrains.

"I know a gala event might not seem like an emergency."

"No." Breanna shook her head. "A gala event is *not* an emergency."

He smiled, but he knew the motion was tight. "It is to the nonprofit."

"No." Breanna laughed. "It is not."

"Everyone is struggling."

"No, they *are not*." Breanna pushed away from the table. "Princess Brie's tourism board has brought back all the tourists we lost during the recession, plus others who've never visited. Yes, there are those still struggling, but it is not the same situation the country was in a year ago. And *no one* throwing a gala is in danger."

"The nonprofit—"

Her hand pressed against his chest. "Would not be spending hard-earned coin on an expensive gala when they are in danger. That is something you do when you have money to spare and are looking for bigger donors. It is a *good* sign."

Her words struck him. He knew what was required of him as a prince, and a king, but Sebastian's life was as far from normal as possible. Attendance at events. Hosting diplomats. Staying politically neutral. It was a delicate balancing act.

But his day-to-day looked nothing like that of the people of Celiana.

"The last few years—"

"Were rough." Breanna ran her finger along his chin. "But that changed when your brother married Brie. The choice to have a small wedding for us was a good one." She swallowed, looking away for a moment.

He couldn't blame her. Brie and Alessio's wedding had been a giant party. Even though they'd made sure the cost was far from the weddings most expected of the crown. It could have been had in the smallest room on the island, with no music, and the happiness from his brother and sister-in-law would have carried the event.

The same couldn't be said for the affair they had. Even though he'd enjoyed dancing with Breanna most of the evening. There was no love in the air. No music created by two souls who never wished to be parted.

"People are still focused on replenishing savings, but they are not struggling like they were. So, it was a good idea." Whether his wife was trying to convince herself by repeating the idea or convince him didn't really matter.

Rationally, he knew that made sense. And he'd seen the metrics from the tourism industry, and others. It was good. But it wasn't the full story of the crown.

A life of service. Always. That was what the king and queen of Celiana owed the country.

"That doesn't change the fact that we need to be at events." It was their role. Draw attention to projects needing it—the power of influence.

"Which events do we pass along our regrets to?" Breanna raised her chin, her eyes brimming with challenge as she crossed her arms. He wanted her to touch him again, to comfort him.

"We don't." He hated the stress he saw fly through her eyes. But influence was a fickle beast. A cup overflowing could dry up with the wrong words or missed opportunity. He wore the crown, but the influence his father had cultivated, the embers his brother had kept warm when he'd floundered…it could disappear.

Sebastian didn't care about the influence for himself, but the nonprofits, the tourists, the people gained something from it. He would not strip that from them for his own selfish desires.

Breanna laughed, though the bell-like sound held no humor. "Seriously, Sebastian, you do get to have time off. You are just a man, after all."

"The crown does not rest."

Dear God, it was like his father's soul had just overtaken him.

The man's presence even a few years after his passing was still felt everywhere.

"That is nonsense."

Breanna wasn't used to a life of duty. The Galanis family had more money than nearly everyone on the island. Her family did not care what their influence brought for others. He doubted Lucas Galanis was capable of thinking of anything besides his own bank account.

Breanna and her sister had wanted for nothing.

Except affection.

His life had been similarly privileged, similarly lacking in affection from his father and to some extent his mother. But it was duty, not coin, that drove his father's ambitions. The deep knowledge ingrained in each royal that they worked for the people of Celiana.

He'd had one vacation. A few days skiing before his tenth birthday. A last hurrah before the real work of his life started. Was that unfair? Sure. But fairness was not what this world was built on.

During the year where he'd rebelled, he'd still attended the events required of him. Alessio had had to pick up most of the day duties, and he'd figured out a way to get the country out of the economic depression with his bride lotto. However, he'd arrived when he'd absolutely had to. Even the night when he and Samantha had broken up, he'd gone to the state dinner. Broken. Bitter. And late. But still in attendance.

"It can be fun. As queen, you can focus on specific charitable events." He pointed to the dress. "There are many arts functions that would love to display any of the garment talents you have."

Breanna shook her head. "No. This—" she gestured to the dress "—is just for me. Mine. Something no one can take from me."

He wasn't trying to take it. Just expand it. Use her knowledge and expertise to help others. She was queen now. She'd met him at the altar. Chosen this path. "You're the queen now. Nothing is just for you, anymore."

"We shall see about that."

He didn't argue. She'd come to understand the truth soon enough. "Would you like a tour of the palace?"

She closed her eyes for a moment, then turned a brilliant smile to him. "I suppose it is a good idea to know my away around my home."

"Home." He chuckled. "I don't think I've ever referred to the palace as home. It's not really mine, after all."

Once more the truth slipped out. He was typically very good at keeping his personal truths locked away. Sometimes he pushed them far enough away he almost forgot they were there.

Almost.

Breanna didn't push back though. Instead, she put her tools away, then looked at him. "Ready when you are."

CHAPTER SIX

THE TINY CROWN on her head didn't weigh much. Rationally she knew that. But it still felt like it was digging into her scalp as she greeted yet another guest at the fundraising event that she was more certain than ever was not an emergency.

"You are doing well." Sebastian's words were soft as he leaned over and pushed a hair that had fallen from the elaborate updo from her face. His fingers brushed her cheek, lingering for just a moment before turning back to the guests.

Well. A word her father had used to make sure she and Annie knew they could do better. Four letters that fell far short of best. And if you weren't the best, why bother?

Sebastian meant it that way, too. Not in the cruel manner, but in the "helpful" you-will-get-there way. The supportive king instructing his brand-new queen. There was no anger. No upset.

Because he'd expected his pick to struggle with the adjustment at first. This wasn't an issue with Breanna. It was an issue with "the queen."

An interchangeable bride the crown would sculpt. Anyone could be standing here and Sebastian would support them.

"You look tired." The woman's kind words were sweet as she squeezed Breanna's hand.

"I'm fine. But thank you."

The woman moved to Sebastian. Her statement not one

of a real concern, but a passing phrase. But it meant others could see her forced smile.

But how could she offer more? Her toes ached and her head pounded. She'd been on her feet for almost fifteen hours straight. Exhaustion had stopped nipping at her heels hours ago.

Now it was the pure force of pride keeping her upright. She was not going to collapse in public. With any luck, their commitment was over as soon as the receiving line ended. After all, the event had ended almost an hour ago.

Raul came up and offered Sebastian, and then her, water. "The receiving line just closed at the other end. It should be done in about an hour."

Breanna couldn't stop the harsh laugh escaping her lips. An hour. *An hour.* Sebastian stepped closer and put an arm around her. She leaned into him. Needing to give her feet some relief from the torture devices on her toes.

"It will be all right." His words were kind, but they did little to help her in the moment.

How did he manage this? They'd been on the go every moment since their wedding. She was maintaining some boundaries. Refusing to start her day before a certain hour might not seem like much, but in the palace, it was rebellion.

She wasn't sure Sebastian had any boundaries at all. The man said yes to everything.

"Take a deep breath." He shook the next person's hand. His arm on her waist tugged just slightly. He was offering to pull her close. Giving her some of his strength. Not pressuring, but the unspoken offer was clear.

She took it. Desperate times called for desperate measures. And standing close to her husband, enjoying the scent of him, the comfort he offered, was as far from desperate as possible. "I need different shoes."

Sebastian looked at her feet, then motioned with his free hand back to Raul. "Find the queen some flats."

"Oh." Raul was off before Breanna managed any other words. She'd meant the statement as a reminder to herself to wear flats for the next event. Like she'd have a choice. Her toes might rebel if she tried to put them in heels tomorrow.

She'd watched her husband swallow a yawn as he reached for the next guest's hand. The man was skilled at hiding exhaustion, but if you looked for it, it wasn't hard to see. He gave the country everything—he needed something for himself.

"The queen is stepping into her role quite nicely." Sebastian nodded to the gentleman, then turned to greet the next guest.

The queen. Not Breanna. Here she was the title. Nothing more. Anyone with the crown and the title could be here, and the line would form.

When the end of the line came into view, Breanna bounced, then winced. Wherever Raul had gone for flats, it was a futile effort now.

She started to lean her head against Sebastian's shoulder, then snapped it back up. Getting support from him was nice. And she needed it. That did not mean she needed to rest her head on his shoulder.

"Almost done." He squeezed her as the final two people came into view. "We helped raise a lot of money tonight. You've done wonderfully."

They'd done well. But money would have come in without them. Maybe not quite as much. People had purchased tickets to the fundraiser long before the king and queen's attendance was announced. So, the nonprofit would have made a hefty profit.

Then Sebastian had offered a reception line as a fundraiser. Now the pot was overflowing. Literally. A nice perk for a group that wouldn't have to fundraise much for the next year but hardly an emergency. If everything was an emergency, then nothing was.

Her husband needed some boundaries. If only for her own sanity.

Sebastian gave their goodbyes to the organizers as she smiled. The neurons not focused on the pain radiating down her feet were an exhausted mush too far gone to say much more than have a nice night. They waved and started towards the car.

She took two steps, then let out a sigh. "Hold up." She put a hand on her husband's shoulder and slipped one heel, then the other, off her feet.

The cold tile was heaven. "Ooh." Her toes rejoiced as they were finally allowed a little more freedom. Her hose refused to give them a full range of motion, but she'd take what she could get.

Breanna resolved to donate these torture heels. Those monstrosities were never going back on her feet. Never!

"We aren't at the car yet." Sebastian looked at her bare feet, then into the distance she had no plans on crossing in the heels.

"I know." She patted his arm, then started towards the car. "But I refuse to hobble my way there. I can't stand the way those things—" she glared at the offending shoes "—find every possible way to make my feet scream!"

"You'll tear your hose."

"Congratulations, Your Highness." Breanna giggled, exhaustion making her a little punchy. "I think you found the argument least likely to move me."

If she had her way, the hose in her top drawer would vanish. Flimsy material that was confining was the work of black magic—you would not convince her otherwise. Yet the dowager queen never set foot outside the palace without nude hose covering her legs.

It was expected of queens. For reasons no one could explain to her because hose weren't even technically invented until 1959. A fact she had not known until she was adding it to her arsenal of reasons why she had no intention of keeping up that tradition.

"The car isn't far." Sebastian took a breath. "What if you hurt your feet?"

She looked at him, really looked at him for the first time this evening. The lines under his eyes were darker, and worry lines were etched along his lips. Without thinking, she raised her free hand and ran her thumb along his chin.

His sigh echoed in the empty room, and his head leaned against her hand, like she was pulling a little of the exhaustion from his tired frame.

She took a breath and softened her tone. "I appreciate the concern. I do. But these heels will hurt my feet more than the pristine floors. And sometimes it is fun to be spontaneous. Take your shoes off, Your Highness."

Sebastian chuckled but shook his head. "A king is supposed to keep his shoes on."

"Says who?" Breanna stuck her bare feet out from under the full-length gown she had on. "Your queen is almost barefoot."

"She is." He stepped towards her, and the air in the room vanished as he smiled at her. He was close. So close.

"My queen is very cute almost barefoot." Huskiness coated his tone as he closed the bit of distance between them.

Was he going to kiss her? There was a glint in his eyes. A mischievousness.

She wanted him to. "Come on, Your Highness?" Was she daring him to take off his shoes? Or kiss her.

"Breanna." Sebastian paused then scooped her up.

"Ooh!" She instantly wrapped her arms around his shoulders. The relief in her digits sent a groan through her as she flexed her feet. He hadn't kissed her. That was fine. Picking her up was sweet. It was.

The tiny burst of disappointment was just from exhaustion.

"See." His lips were so close to hers. "You needed—" he pulled back, a yawn escaping his mouth "—the relief."

"Yes." She kissed his cheek. For a moment she could pretend this was a date. Or a fun night out. That they were just two people having a good time. Caring for each other.

Not a husband and wife…a king and queen…who barely knew each other.

"But you are exhausted, too. Who takes care of you?"

"I am the king." Sebastian nodded to the man opening the door and waited a moment as the other doorman rushed to the waiting car to open that door.

He slid her into her seat, and the relief in her aching back nearly brought tears to her eyes.

Sebastian climbed in next to her and told the driver they were ready. It would be easy to close her eyes and drift into sleep until they were at the palace. But she had so little alone time with the man she called husband.

"Who takes care of you?" Breanna pushed again.

"I told you." Sebastian closed his eyes and leaned his head back. It was like the final charge of his internal battery was gone.

"No." Breanna shook her head. "I am king."

His eyes popped open and he chuckled, his hand reaching for hers. "That sounds nothing like me."

"The words are an exact replica." Breanna squeezed his hand. "Who takes care of you?"

Sebastian pulled her hand to his lips, quickly brushing them across her knuckles. Her breath caught.

"I am the king." He let out a sigh so heavy it sounded like

it carried the weight of the country. "No one needs to take care of me."

He closed his eyes again.

All her words were trapped in her throat. What was she supposed to say to such nonsense?

"Everyone needs care."

The only response she got was soft snores, but his hand still cradled hers.

CHAPTER SEVEN

BREANNA REACHED FOR her toes, groaning as the muscles in her lower back cried out. She was active. She'd biked nearly every day and lifted light weights. The only trouble she had was heavy menstrual cycles, which were now well-controlled with an IUD. She was at peak physical condition according to her doctor at the appointment she'd had a month before Sebastian arrived at her door.

And the crown had worn her into the ground in weeks. Her feet had more blisters than toes, and no matter the amount of stretches she did in the morning and before bed, her body ached when she woke. How did Sebastian maintain this life?

He doesn't.

The thought pierced her mind as she looked over the schedule her assistant always forwarded just after midnight. A full day—like every day.

And like most days, she wasn't seeing her husband until a dinner engagement they were attending with Prince Alessio and Princess Brie. The man was gone before she woke.

Off to some meeting. Attending some function. Working on a task that didn't really need doing. How many things could a king really be expected to do before eight? Apparently far too many.

"Breanna?" That was her husband's voice. But according to his schedule, he was supposed to be handling personal correspondences this morning. A mountain of letters arrived with each post. He'd respond to so many that tonight he'd stretch his fingers when he thought no one looking. Bending them, flexing and balling them into a fist. Hurting but saying nothing.

She turned to look at the door to her work room. "Yes?"

Her husband stepped into her room, and she smiled. He was here. To spend some time with her. Since the morning after their wedding, they'd really only seen each other at events. In the car and in a few passing moments in the hall.

He was kind, asking after her needs. He'd never gotten close enough to make her think he was going to kiss her though. That night at the fundraiser was a one-off moment. Maybe she'd been so tired, her memory was playing tricks on her.

Her husband checked in on her. Far more than her parents had ever managed.

Part of her almost wished he didn't bother. If King Sebastian refused to acknowledge her, if it was clear that she was just a thing he needed to support his throne, to stop the constant wave of people harassing women even loosely attached to him, then she could adjust. Accept the life she had to protect Annie.

After all…filling a role was something she'd always done. Quiet daughter. Respectful daughter. Exchangeable daughter. If only the location had shifted, from the compound to the palace, she'd adjust easily.

But he cared for her when she was tired. Kicked her parents out of their wedding reception when it was clear that they were cruel. Got her coffee syrups and made veggie dishes that were clearly marked in the fridge—when—she had no idea.

It was the grounds for so much more than they had.

He was overburdened. If she found a way to give him peace, found a way to have him accept the need for boundaries, they had a chance to not spend the rest of their lives as strangers.

To give themselves a chance at more. Surely that chance was something they should reach for.

"Sebastian. Are you here to join me for coffee? I got my cup from our kitchen a few minutes ago. I can ring—" The words died on her lip as a woman who couldn't have been more than five feet tall stepped from behind him. Around her neck hung a measuring tape, and she had a box filled with tools Breanna didn't recognize.

"Where can I set this, Your Highness? It's heavy." Her thick accent accentuated each word.

"Of course." Breanna moved quickly folding her project but careful to make sure the pins holding the material in place stayed where they were meant to be. "You should have asked the king to carry your things."

She winked at her husband and immediately hated the joke as his shoulders stiffened.

"I offered Olga more than one chance to let me handle the box. She's as stubborn as my wife."

"Then we shall get along fine." Breanna clapped her hands, hoping this jest would remove some of the tension in his body.

Olga hmphed as she set the box down and then looked at the queen. The woman's eyes were sharp, but the assessment held no malice. After the weeks she'd had in the palace, it was refreshing.

"You are tallish."

Ish? Breanna wasn't sure what to make of that. She was a little over five foot seven. Average height. Though to a woman who had to look up at the world, she supposed most people qualified as tallish.

"Good feet." She pointed, then started pulling things from her box.

"They don't feel so good." Breanna glared at the sores on her toes, then made a silly face at her husband.

"Because your shoes don't fit." Sebastian stepped beside her. Not quite touching but close enough that if she moved even a little, they'd brush sides.

Except he didn't get any closer. It was silly to be upset by that. But the flicker she'd felt at the fundraiser had been snuffed out.

If it was ever there to begin with.

"They fit before I stood in them for hours on hours on hours on hours."

Her husband held up his hands. "I get it. I should have put a cap on the receiving line."

That was more than she'd expected him to acknowledge. "Yes. You should have." She bumped his hip with hers. Why did she want to touch him?

Sebastian wrapped his arm around her waist, just like he'd done the night they'd met, and that night in the receiving line. But unlike those times, he pulled away quickly. Like she'd burned him. Or more likely, because he didn't want to touch her.

Her chest burned as she sucked in a breath. Trying to focus on the task at hand.

"So I am here to fit you for shoes. Perfect ones. Ones that will not do that." Olga tsked as she pointed to the sores on Breanna's feet.

"They wouldn't if I wasn't standing so long."

"But you are queen." Olga said the words, but it was Sebastian's nod that tore through her.

This was the expectation. This was what she was supposed to do. She was supposed to stand all the time. Supposed to put everyone's needs before her own.

She'd done that her whole life. Breanna was good at it. But there'd been downtime, too. Time for herself. Filled with thread and bobbles, and laughter and rest.

Celiana was important. The royal family was important, but they were more than their positions. Weren't they?

Sebastian was more than the title. More than the king. The crown didn't have to be the only thing people saw.

"So, I need shoes that will let me stand for hours every day." She pointed to Olga's box. "What magic is in there to allow such a thing?"

Olga pulled a few things out and started gesturing for her to sit. A woman of few words, but the demands were clear.

"I need to see to my correspondence."

"Oh. I thought you'd stay?" If only there were a way to bite back that request. She'd hoped he'd adjusted his schedule. More than just to drop a shoemaker at her door and wish her good morning.

"Behind schedule. I'm going to have to skip lunch to get it all written up." He lifted a hand and headed for the door.

"Sebas—" But her husband was already gone.

She followed Olga's demands while plotting out her next move. One thing was certain. Sebastian was not skipping lunch.

Sebastian shook his hand, then rolled his wrists, even though he knew it wouldn't stop the pins-and-needles feeling trickling from his elbow to the tips of his fingers.

His schedule was off today, but the trip to see Breanna was worth it. The image of his wife popped into his head. He'd wanted to kiss her the night of the fundraiser. Wanted to pull her close, hold her and never let go.

But he'd promised her separate lives. A king and queen in title. Lives of their own. He couldn't ask for a change when she was a newly minted queen. She was overwhelmed. Finding her place.

He would not take advantage of that.

Sebastian stifled a yawn. No one was here to see the exhaustion, but the habit was ingrained in him. Only Breanna had seen him yawn in years.

"Kings do not get tired. They are perfection for their people."

Words his father had said during their early-morning

walks, back when he'd still complained about the exhaustion that was his constant companion.

He read the letter over, for the third time. Nothing seemed to stick this morning.

The door to the office opened, but he didn't look up. If he allowed himself to get distracted now, then he'd never get through all of this. Sebastian's schedule was already pushed to the extremes today.

"Sebastian?"

"Hello, Breanna. Did Olga finish your shoes?" He tried to read the letter in front of him and figure out a quick way to sign a response.

If only the letters on the page stayed still.

"Sebastian, I can hear your stomach gurgling from here." She stepped to the desk and took the letter from his hands. She looked at it, then leaned over him, taking the pen from his other hand.

Breanna's scent infiltrated his nose. His body tightened, then softened, like a strong breeze that suddenly shifts. He took a deep breath, letting himself settle. She was here. His wife.

"Now sign your name." Breanna pushed the pen back in his hand.

He blinked, then looked at the short note she'd written on the paper the staff had left for this letter's response.

Happy birthday, Serena. Sixteen is a wonderful time. We hope that your days are blessed with adventure and growth. Enjoy!

A birthday letter. A note that should have been so easy to push out. Yet he'd read the words multiple times without his mind clicking. Shame there wasn't time for a nap.

He quickly signed his name above Breanna's.

"Serena won't know it, but this is the first letter signed by the queen."

"Uh-huh." Breanna grabbed the rest of the correspondence.

"Wait. What are…" Sebastian stood as she started towards the office door. There were at least a dozen left to go. Probably more.

Breanna opened the door. "Come on. He needs to eat." She sighed then looked over her shoulder. "Raul wants you to know that I am forcing this issue and that he had nothing to do with it." She looked back through the door. "Does that cover it?"

It must have, because Raul marched in with a tray of food, set it on the table by the unlit fireplace, and vanished.

"You need to eat." Breanna grabbed his hand and pulled him towards the table.

"I *need* to—"

Her finger lay over his lips. "You need to eat. So that is what we are going to do, Your Highness."

"Your Highness…? Guess you're cross with me." Sebastian sat at the table, happy when she sat on the other side.

Breanna lifted the lid of the plate. "Not cross. Worried."

He opened his mouth, and she held up the finger that had pressed against his lips moments ago. "If you are about to do anything other than eat the veggies, hummus and egg salad, you can do it after."

She dipped a veggie in hummus took a bite, then motioned for him to do the same.

Tightness hovered in his throat. He was the king. No one looked after him. No one.

"Thank you."

"You are welcome. Now, eat." She pointed to his dish. "You look like hell."

"Only Alessio ever tells me that."

"Well, I am your queen, so…" Breanna huffed as she drove her fork into the salad.

They ate in a comfortable silence as he wolfed down the lunch she'd had prepared and let out a soft sigh. He felt better. "Thank you."

"You are welcome." Breanna smiled, then pointed to the desk. "How about I sort while you sign."

"Teamwork?" Sebastian started to reach for her hand, but stopped himself. "Umm, I don't want to hold you up. You don't have to help."

"I am offering. There is a difference." She looked at his hand, the one that had not reached for hers, then stood and grabbed the pile, sifting through the letters quickly.

He followed, very aware of his bride's presence at his side as she handed him one letter at a time.

"Birthday."

"Anniversary."

"Graduating with a master's degree in biochemistry. Wow."

He signed each one with a quick note, and the pile was nearly gone before he realized it.

"Wow." Breanna read the last one.

"Another graduation?"

Sebastian started to reach for it, but she shook her head. A look he couldn't quite interpret coming over her eyes.

"No. Anniversary. Fifty years. Fifty years. Their daughter requested the note. She gushes over how her parents are soulmates. How lucky she is to watch their love." She let out a breath. "Must be something special."

Something we don't have.

She didn't say the words but passed him the note.

He wrote a quick congratulations, aware of the shift in the room.

"Do you believe in soulmates?" The question was out, and he wished there was a way to pop it back in. That was a question to ask on a date. Or with a friend. It was not a question to lay at his wife's feet.

A wife he'd known for weeks. A wife he'd married days after a public announcement. A wife he rarely saw.

"No." There was no hesitation. "I am glad that others believe, but no. I do not feel like there is one perfect person in the world for me. Relationships take work. Good ones involve friendship and respect."

There was no way to ignore the pinch in his stomach that she didn't mention love or caring in her thoughts on marriage. Why should she? It wasn't what their marriage was built on. No, they didn't even have friendship. Though the respect was there. At least on his side.

Breanna sat on the desk, now clear of the notes he'd thought would take twice as long. "You have thirty minutes until your next appointment." She grinned as she tapped the watch on her wrist. The gift he'd given her the day after their wedding.

It was a nice watch, but he couldn't help but wish that he'd given her something more Breanna. Something that said he knew her.

Except outside of liking to sew and wanting to sleep in until seven, he knew very little about his wife.

"So what shall we do with the extra thirty minutes?" Breanna raised her brow as though she was asking something truly scandalous. "We could think of it as playing hooky."

"We could." He leaned closer. "The king and his queen."

"Or Sebastian and Breanna. There is no one here right now. No crowns." She patted her head, then patted his. "Nope. No crown."

"Had to check?" He laughed and put his hands on her hips. Heat, need and things he shouldn't want raced through him.

"It does seem like one might live on your head all the time."

"Very funny, *Your Highness*." He laughed, pulling her into his lap. His touch was light. If she wanted to move, she could. This wasn't in the script of their separate lives' union. But then, neither was her showing up with lunch and making him eat.

What if they could have more?

Breanna poked his forehead. "You are lost in thought. Want me to move?"

"No." His arms wrapped around her.

Kiss her. Kiss her.

The mantra repeated in brain, screaming at him to take the next step.

Then phone on the desk buzzed, and he could tell by the instant fall of her face that she knew something else was popping in. He could ignore it. He could.

Except…this was the life of a king and queen. The call of duty for one who knew nothing else. If he failed in his duty, others got hurt.

This was his life. All he was.

Sebastian took a deep breath, pushed on the speaker, and heard Raul's out-of-breath sigh. "Any chance you can do a short video call with the director of Leaps for Launch?"

"Leaps for Launch?" Breanna asked as she slid off his lap. Whatever moment they'd been about to have was gone.

"A new nonprofit." Raul answered for him through the phone. "They are trying to set up micro loans for small businesses. A real leg up, but the idea is having some trouble gaining ground. Royal backing is good, but a businessperson would be better."

"Right now, all we have is royal backing." Sebastian reached for the pen he'd used to sign his name to dozens of letters. Now it was note-taking time.

"Not like royal backing is nothing." Breanna moved around the desk, resignation clear on her features.

"Raul." Sebastian looked at Breanna, smiled, then continued. "Give me five minutes to check in with my wife, then patch the call through."

He hung up the phone. "Thank you for your help with the letters and for lunch."

"Of course." Breanna crossed her arms, then uncrossed them, then crossed them again. The easiness they'd had before Raul's call vanished.

"If you need a businessperson, why not ask Brie to reach out to her brother? He's broken with their parents now. Beau might be willing to provide some backing."

"His break with the Ailiono is fairly recent. He and Brie haven't had much of a chance to get to know each other in their new relationship. He might not be up to it." But if he stepped in as a backer, it would send a powerful message to the island.

But would he?

Sebastian hadn't interacted with Beau Ailiono much. Beau was as much his father's protégé as Sebastian was his father's. Neither side was discussing the cause of the break, but given what Brie had experienced, he was inclined to side with Beau.

"The answer to every unasked question is no." Breanna shrugged. "What if I reach out to Brie and see what she thinks?"

A wave of appreciation washed through him. He didn't need to add anything to the mental list that seemed to run miles long through his soul. A to-do list that the king had no power to ever finish. All the checkmarks only vanished when another took his throne.

"That would be very helpful." Sebastian nodded. "Thank you." He looked at his watch. "We still have two minutes."

"Right." Breanna balled her fists and then looked over her shoulder at the door, "I will gift those to you, Your Highness. Spend them well."

The ache in his stomach now had nothing to do with hunger. He wanted to go after her. Ask her to stay with him for the day, chat, do fun things. Things that weren't on his schedule.

The phone rang, and reality slipped in. Duty called...literally.

CHAPTER EIGHT

"YOU LOOK LIKE HELL. I know no one else will say that. But it is still true." Alessio's muttered words were soft enough not to draw attention to them from other bystanders, but the bite was still strong.

"My wife said that exact thing this morning." Sebastian chuckled as his gaze found Breanna. She was dressed in a floor-length red beaded gown. One shoulder was bare while the other had a cap sleeve. It was elegant, queen-like. With a slit up the side that made his mouth water every time his eyes landed on her.

Alessio lifted his champagne flute in her general direction. "Then to our new queen."

Sebastian followed the motion. "To the new...queen." The word *queen* was heavy on his tongue. Breanna was more than that. So much more.

At least until he put the crown on her head.

"But you still look like hell." His brother blew out a breath. "You need to rest more."

"Said so simply." Sebastian tipped his head to one of the guests as they made eye contact. Tonight was more about the politicians and their goals for Celiana, but the royal family's attendance was still expected.

Expected. One of his father's favorites. Such a foul word. One that drove everything about his life. About Breanna's life.

He hated the word, but also knew that if he didn't play this role, then someone else would have to.

Someone else had.

The man beside him now. The man that it would fall to again if he failed.

"The crown—"

"Is heavy." Sebastian slapped his brother's shoulder as their wives walked up. He had no intention of continuing a conversation for which there was no resolution.

Brie slipped into Alessio's arms; he squeezed her tightly. While Breanna stepped close to him. A respectful distance between the two.

This afternoon she'd been on his lap. Laughing and joking. And looking oh, so kissable. For a moment it felt like the contract they had wasn't needed. Like maybe…

And he'd taken that phone call. Had to take a phone call.

He couldn't stop the sigh echoing from his lips. It would be so easy to want what Alessio and Brie had. To reach for Breanna and hope his queen wanted the same. But duty demanded he put the kingdom first. No one should settle for being second to that.

"Brie is going to reach out to Beau about Leaps for Launch." Breanna whispered as she waved to a guest who was walking their way.

"Do you know him?" Sebastian asked. The gentleman was a giant. A damn handsome giant. A well-known playboy strolling towards Breanna.

And his wife looked happier than he'd ever seen her.

"Yes. That is Hector Stevio. I thought everyone on the island knew Hector." She pushed on Sebastian's arm.

Knew of him was probably a better statement. And she was practically bouncing.

"Look at you!" Hector stepped up and bowed to the queen, then turned his attention to the other royals, bowing to them.

"I think you are supposed to bow to the king first." Breanna laughed and then offered her hand to Hector.

Sebastian took a deep breath as he watched his wife visibly relax. It was hard not to wish that she smiled at him like that.

"I guess you shall have to school me in royal protocol, Your Highness." Hector winked at the queen, then dipped his head to Sebastian. "Your Highness."

Sebastian nodded, his eyes glued to the playboy who'd dated most of the island's leading men and women. Hector was famous, or infamous, depending on the storyteller, for his parties, his businesses, his life. The man could turn a piece of straw into gold. Then the business got boring for him—at least that was the story—and he sold it.

Started the game over. Never satisfied.

And now he was looking at Breanna as though she was the top prize in the room. Which she was.

"The dance floor is empty, my queen. Can I have this dance?" Hector offered his hand to Breanna.

His wife placed her hand in the playboy's hand and walked with him to the dance floor. Hector pulled her close, and the air evaporated from the room. Breanna was glowing. She was happy. There was no hint of hesitation.

Something the weeks in the palace hadn't granted her. Something he didn't expect to ever be able to fully give her. She had a crown, a title and duty.

Just like him.

"Breathe, brother." Alessio passed the champagne flute to one of the waitstaff. Then took Sebastian's and passed it over too, waving away the offer of more for both of them.

"They are childhood friends." Brie leaned around her husband, her brow raising exactly as his wife's did. "She is trying to get his help with the Leaps for Launch, too. But given his reputation for spinning something up and then selling it, she thinks Beau might be a better spokesman."

"That's nice." Alessio's grin was clearly meant more for Brie than him. "Isn't it, brother?"

"Yes. Nice." Sebastian muttered, trying to ignore what could only be jealousy flowing through his veins as Hector pulled his wife closer, leaned forward and whispered something in her ear.

Breanna laughed.

She was enjoying the moment. He was jealous.

Jealous. Such a dumb emotion considering the union he'd offered her. It might make sense if he'd held her close instead of taking that phone call. But he'd done as he had to and put Celiana first.

Now, he couldn't stop the worm from slinking down his veins. Breathe. He needed to breathe. The dance would be over soon.

Soon.

A few more couples ambled onto the dance floor, and Alessio offered his hand to his princess. "May I have this dance?"

"I thought you'd never ask." Briella placed her hand in her husband's but stopped before Sebastian. "Rather than standing here grumpy, you could always cut in."

"I just might." Sebastian raised his chin, enjoying the challenge in his sister-in-law's features before turning his attention back to his wife.

Breanna was enjoying herself. He wouldn't steal that from her. But he would claim the next dance.

As soon as the song ended, he was by her side. "Do you mind?" He held out his hand, and his wife's fingers locked through his. His breath eased a little as she squeezed them.

"Your Majesty," Hector bent his head, then turned back to his queen. "I told you, Breanna. You owe me." He winked, then headed off the dance floor.

Sebastian tilted his head as his wife stepped into his arms. "Why do you owe him?"

"He bet me that you would interrupt either before the song finished or just after. I told him that was ridiculous, that you probably didn't even notice I was gone." She smiled, but her eyes didn't light up.

"Breanna." His fingers tightened on her back, pulling her a little closer. He bent his head, so his words were only for her. "I watched you the whole time. I knew exactly where you were. I wanted you for the next dance the moment you were on the floor."

And every dance after.

Breanna's smile was almost as bright as it had been for her friend. Almost. "I do hope you're happy. Hector wins a date night—"

"A date night?" The words came out harsher than he'd planned.

"Yes." She chuckled, though her features were not as free as they were with Hector. "Dinner, though, I think we are making dinner? Not sure on the exact idea yet. But it is for a few hours in a couple of weeks or so. Again, the details are still a bit up in the air. I shall have to clear the schedules."

She enunciated the word *schedules* and he tried to find some way to figure out what it meant that his queen was going on a date with one of Celiana's most notorious playboys. The man's dance card was full, but he'd never courted a married woman. At least not openly.

"That will certainly make the headlines."

"I think that is Hector's plan." Breanna sighed as he pulled her a little closer. "The king and queen at his date night extravaganza or whatever he plans to call it."

"The king *and* queen." Sebastian blinked, and his footsteps faltered.

"Careful, you might step on my feet, and the lovely shoes

Olga is crafting aren't here yet." This time her eyes lit up as she grinned at him.

The music slowed, and Sebastian closed the tiny amount of distance between them. "You knew what I was thinking, Your Highness." The sweet scent that was just Breanna infiltrated his nose.

"I did." She laid her head on his shoulder. They'd had one dance like this at their wedding, but his wife hadn't rested on him since. He hadn't known it was possible to miss something so much without realizing it.

The music lilted around them, and for a moment it was just the two of them in the world. His lips found her head. This wasn't what he'd promised her. But right now, he wanted so much more than a dutiful relationship.

"So, date night for some new venture for Hector. I think we can make that work." His lips brushed her hair again.

"I used to give Hector a hard time when we were in school together. Told him he couldn't settle on just one thing. He had to try everything. He skipped the traditional lemonade stand and started by selling a computer code that helped students do their math homework—according to Hector. Help the students cheat, was what our teachers said. That one nearly got him expelled. Then it was 3D printing and..." She shifted in his arms as the words failed to come to her.

He didn't loosen his grip, though if his wife stepped away, he wouldn't stop her.

Instead, she smiled at him. And his heart tripped in his chest.

"I can't remember. There have been so many. Hector has an idea. He chases it, and the rest of the world just seems to follow."

"We are alike in that way." Sebastian kissed the top of her head. He couldn't stop. He was drawn to this woman. A woman whose name he hadn't picked out of a hat. A woman he'd married just days after meeting her. A woman who should want more than him. Deserved more than him.

"No." Breanna pulled back as the music shifted. "Hector has ideas and he grows them into something. We have crowns that turn the eye."

There were no words to cut through that truth. Breanna didn't look sad or unhappy. It was acceptance on her features. Something he should be grateful for.

Instead, all he could think of was that the crown had stolen her ventures. Every single one of them.

The pop beat banged out, and Breanna laughed. Her hair bounced as lights hit her crown, her hips swaying to the beat. "Think you can keep up with these moves, Your Highness?"

"Of course." The heaviness around them parted. The worry retreating to the back of his mind. Pushed away, but never truly gone.

Breanna watched her husband's throat move and wanted to shake him. The man was exhausted. And yet, even here alone with his wife, he was swallowing his yawns. As if the image he presented could keep the exhaustion at bay.

"I might just fall into bed for the rest of the weekend." Breanna laughed as she stood in front of her door, hoping he might agree with her. Smile at her like he had in his office this afternoon or on the dance floor an hour ago.

"If you need a break, we can schedule one. Not several days, but a day here and there."

She didn't bother to try to stop the rolling of her eyes. "Ooh, a whole day to myself. Wow." She put her hand on her chest, mostly to keep from shoving it into his shoulder.

"Breanna—" A yawn interrupted whatever diatribe he wanted to give her on duty.

"You are exhausted. What time do you get up? It seems

to be a guarded secret." No matter who she asked, all she got was a shrug.

"Early." He leaned forward like he was going to drop a kiss on her lips.

Her breath caught. So many times over the last few days, she'd thought he wanted to kiss her. But he never followed through. And he didn't now.

Maybe she was the only one wanting kisses.

She crossed her arms, willing him to let her be a partner in more than just the public-facing activities of the court. Maybe they weren't like Briella and Alessio, but they could be more than strangers. Could be friends, at least. Even if her heart cried that it wanted more.

"I'm fine, Breanna."

"That wasn't the question I asked. And you aren't. You are exhausted. Let me help. It's why you wanted a queen. A partner. A person standing here." *Annie. Not me.* Though he hadn't wanted Annie either. Just a body. A person to stand there.

But she wasn't just going to stand there. "Sebastian…"

He let out a sigh, like he truly believed that this was his life and there was nothing more. "I'm fine." An edge hardened in his tone.

"I'm not sure you'd know if you weren't." Breanna raised her hand, cupping his cheek.

His face softened as he leaned into her. Rested himself on her palm. His breathing slowed, but he didn't let himself hold the position for long.

Far too soon, he raised himself, and the king stood fully before her. The mantle the only thing present now. "I would. I did. Last year. I broke. I lost myself. Alessio and then Briella took the hits. The press—" He cleared his throat, shaking his head and if he was trying to dash away the memories.

"The press was vile to Brie. But you are not responsible for that."

"I am. I was the one who was supposed to marry. It was my father's plan. A marriage, a union to make sure the Celiana royal love story he and my mother presented stayed true in the minds of the people. I refused. I wanted to take time to get to know the bride they'd selected. To try for a real union. Then Father passed, and Alessio stepped up with the princess lottery."

"They are fine now. They love each other." He was in a way responsible for that. If he hadn't refused…

"Just because lightning struck for them does not take away that it should never have happened. I understand now what it means when I break and who it might hurt. Alessio, Brie. You."

"Sebastian."

He ignored her, pressing on, "I promise. I am fine."

It was a lie. But she didn't think he was saying it intentionally. No, her husband believed that he needed to break fully to be less than fine.

"Good night, Breanna. Rest well." Then he bowed and left her at her door.

The handle was cool in her hand as she watched his retreating form.

The Sebastian escorting her to her room was the king. Not the man who'd danced with her on the floor tonight. The man who'd smiled and held her close. The man she'd ached to kiss.

That man deserved freedom from the shackles of the other.

Her own yawn interrupted her thoughts. That was a question for a brain more awake than hers. A question for tomorrow.

There was a solution. Breanna just had to find it.

CHAPTER NINE

Today's agenda is quite full, Your Highness.

LETICIA, HER NEWLY hired assistant, always sent her text to arrive at one minute past midnight. It was the first thing she saw upon awaking. The reminder, as though she needed it, that she was the queen of Celiana.

Sebastian's partner...but only when it was the schedule.

Start time five past nine.

At least she'd managed to keep her schedule start time to nine in the weeks she'd been here. A boundary she'd had no luck getting her husband to follow through on.

Husband.

She'd set her alarm fifteen minutes earlier every day for the week. But even arriving in the kitchen at four fifty yesterday, she'd found only the hints of his presence. A freshly rinsed coffee mug, a note from him about the breakfast fixings he'd left for her in the fridge.

Did the man sleep?

If so, she'd yet to see evidence of it. That wasn't happening today though. They were having breakfast, talking, relaxing, and he wasn't starting his day until nine.

She'd even worked that in with Raul. Probably. Sebastian's assistant had agreed he needed a break and was willing to help. But she'd seen the underlying worry in his face.

So, assuming Raul was willing to follow through on the

promise he'd made to the queen. Assuming she could figure out when he rose. Sebastian was resting today.

But that meant she had to catch him in the kitchen.

She looked at the watch he'd given her. Five past midnight. Blanket and pillow in hand, she was going to the kitchen.

One way or another, the king was going to spend a few hours with her today doing nothing.

"Breanna!"

The call was loud, but her brain was too mushy to truly capture the voice. She wrapped the blanket around her as cold seeped through her. Tired.

"Breanna!"

Kitchen, Sebastian, tired. All three words rattled in her mind before finally syncing. He was in the kitchen.

She popped up, looked at the clock through bleary eyes and groaned. "Three thirty. Three thirty in the morning. What the hell, Sebastian?"

"I don't know what you mean. Why are you on the floor? With a pillow and blanket? How long have you been here?"

"Oh, no," Breanna pushed up on her elbow, stood, then pinched the bridge of her nose. Exhaustion gripped her, but she was not losing her train of thought. "I started the question session, so I get the first answer."

"There is no answer to, *'What the hell, Sebastian?'*"

Not true. There were many answers he might be able to give, if he just thought about it. "I think you know very well what I mean, Your Highness."

"You only call me that when you are frustrated. Do you want a cup of coffee?"

"No. Because it is bedtime. We should be asleep." Coffee at three thirty? *No, thank you.* "*You* should be asleep."

Her husband looked to the coffeepot, his fingers moving like he needed caffeine or he might lie down on the floor with her. "I've started my day at three for as long as I can remember."

That was heartbreaking.

"My father started at the same time. He woke me and we had coffee, then got on with the day." Sebastian started towards the coffeepot, not managing to cover his yawn. The only thing keeping the man running was routine.

"At what age?" She grabbed his hand; he was not going to start the coffeepot. Not right now.

"Huh?" He looked at her hand around his wrist, then back at her. "It's fine, Breanna."

No, it very much was not!

"At what age?" She'd repeat the question as many times as necessary to get an answer.

He started to push a hand through his already done hair, but caught himself. Even at three thirty in the blasted morning, the man didn't want to ruffle the king's appearance. "I don't know. Sometime around ten or eleven, I guess. The crown——"

She tightened her grip on his wrist. "If you are about to say the crown does not rest, I swear…" Her parents were controlling. They believed their daughters belonged to them. It was horrifying. Sebastian's father had convinced him that he belonged to an entire country.

She pulled on his hand. "We are going back to bed."

The words were out, and she heard exactly how they sounded. "Not like that, though!"

"Breanna——" His voice was soft, low, and despite the exhaustion pulling through her, she wanted to lean into him. Kiss away his frowns and make him believe he was worth more than what his title gave him.

The man was her husband. He was also a workaholic and still a near-stranger. "Do not *Breanna* me. You need sleep. *I* need sleep."

"I don't." He used his free hand to cover his mouth as another yawn escaped.

If only there were a way to reach into the afterlife. Because Breanna very much wanted to have a discussion with King Cedric. At least his mother was still within her reach. Because this was ridiculous.

But getting angry right now was not going to solve anything.

"I'll make you a deal. You lie in my bed for fifteen minutes." She grabbed her phone, opened the clock app and put it on a fifteen-minute timer. "I will start this the second your head hits the pillow and you close your eyes. If you are still awake when the alarm goes off, I will not stop you from starting your day when others are stumbling home from the bar."

"You're tired." Sebastian lay his hand over hers on his wrist.

"I *am* exhausted. And I had to sleep on the kitchen floor to even find out what time *my husband* wakes. So yes. I am exhausted and a little furious."

"At me?" For a moment he looked so young. So lost. So much like the boy he must have been when King Cedric dragged him from bed, plied him with coffee and told him his soul belonged to a kingdom.

Breanna stepped close and shook her head. "No. I am furious at your father. But we can discuss that in a few hours. Right now, we are both running on fumes."

"I'm used to it." He grinned, and the twinkle in his eye would have been adorable if she didn't think it was wholly tiredness pulling at him.

"Then lying down for fifteen minutes will not cause a problem."

He looked at the coffeepot. "Let me set it up." He moved fast, his hands flying in an easy motion that he'd done thousands of times.

The drip started. She pulled on him. "Now."

He looked at her and then the coffeepot. "At least the coffee will be here when I get back." He dropped a quick kiss on her nose, surprise dotting his features as he pulled back. "Right. Fifteen minutes, Breanna."

"Fifteen minutes, Sebastian. From the time you close your eyes!"

Bending down, he collected her pillow and blanket and nodded towards the door. "After you, Your Highness." His gaze was bright.

Maybe she was wrong. Maybe he wasn't as exhausted as she thought. Well, then her alarm would go off and she'd find some other way to get the king to relax.

Opening the door to her suite, she took a deep breath as her bed came into view. This was mostly a spontaneous plan. She wanted him to take a break, but she'd not truly expected to find him up so early. And now they were in her bedroom.

Sebastian put the pillow on the bed and crawled in. "The timer starts the moment my head touches the pillow."

"When you close your eyes." She'd been a child who hated bedtime. She knew the tricks to staying awake. And she suspected Sebastian did, too. For very different reasons.

"You coming to bed, too? You're exhausted."

"If I lie down, I will fall asleep. And then the alarm will go off and wake us both."

"I will still be up in fifteen minutes." So sure of himself.

"Then me sitting in this chair doesn't cause a problem." Breanna raised her chin. The king was stubborn, but she could rise to the occasion, too.

"Fine." He lay down, let out a sigh, then closed his eyes.

Breanna started the timer. And shut it off at the four-minute mark when Sebastian's light snores echoed across her chamber.

The man needed rest. And if no one else was going to get it for him, then she would. She sent a quick note to Raul clearing his schedule for the morning. Then Breanna stepped beside the bed.

The lines around his eyes were gone. He looked peaceful. A stray piece of hair fell across his face, but she dared not touch him.

"Good night, Sebastian." Breanna's words were more in her head than spoken. She grabbed a blanket, curled up in the oversized chair, closing her eyes, and let sleep take her, too.

Sebastian knew as he rolled over that the fifteen minutes had passed long ago. He rubbed the back of his hand against his head, then looked at his wrist. His watch was gone.

No. He blinked. He put it on every morning, first thing. It was part of the routine his father had kept. And Sebastian kept. Bed at eleven, up at three. Clothes already set out. Watch on the dresser.

Sitting up, he looked to the window. But the heavy curtains were pulled, giving no indication of the time. How long had he been out? What meetings had he missed? How far behind schedule was he?

Rolling out of bed, Sebastian reached his hands up, stretching. He needed to get moving, but he couldn't argue that he didn't feel great. Apparently, his body craved the nap.

Walking into his wife's study, he wasn't surprised to see her standing next to her workbench. The woman seemed glued to that space when she wasn't on official business.

"Are you feeling rested?" Breanna set her tools down and smiled at him. A full smile. Like the one he'd seen her give Hector. But this was directed at him because she'd won the bet.

It was like winning the lottery. His whole body seemed to sing as her smile radiated over him.

"I am. Feel free to say told you so." Sebastian had earned the call-out. He must have been completely out for her to remove his watch without him noticing.

Her dark curls bounced as she tilted her head. "Why would I say told you so?"

He waited for the laughter, or some other trick. That had been Sam's go-to. A laugh to lighten the mood before a devastating comment. She'd excelled at weaponized words.

Something he'd only realized after their terrible breakup.

Breanna looked at him as he waited for the shoe to fall. Better to get it over with than for it to fall later when he wasn't expecting it. "It's okay. I earned it."

"Why did you earn it?" Such a simple question.

He'd failed today. For the first time in more than a year, he'd missed meetings and caused havoc. All because he couldn't operate as well exhausted.

"Because you were right." His father was always right. And his mother. Hell, even Alessio stepped in after his father's passing when Sebastian had fallen apart and made all the right choices.

King Cedric had made it look easy. His mother was excellent at navigating aristocratic politics, and Alessio had come home from abroad and stepped right into the hole Sebastian had vacated.

He'd been raised for this life. Trained—literally at dawn. Yet he was constantly feeling like he was failing. Living up to his father's legacy was draining.

"It's not about being right. It's about taking care of people."

Taking care of people. That sounded nice. But it was his job. He took care of Celiana. He didn't need anyone looking after him.

"Yes, you do."

Breanna words made his head pop back. "What?"

"You were thinking that you don't need anyone looking after you." She crossed her arms; her bright gaze bore into him. "I can see it written on your face."

"I am the king, and we…" He gestured to the space between them. "We are married, but…"

So many things hung on that *but*.

His wife's stance softened. "Even when the marriage is nothing more than a contract agreement."

She took a deep breath, closing her eyes. Did she want more? Was that even possible? Would hoping for it destroy him if he was wrong?

Yes.

"Breanna." He wasn't sure what to say. No words came to his well-rested mind.

"You slept for nearly twelve hours. Do you know how exhausted you have to be to do that?" She moved around the sewing table and stepped right in front of him.

"Twelve hours?" His brain was firing, but it couldn't seem to calculate everything that meant.

Breanna put her hand on his chest. The motion was soft, but he got the distinct feeling that she'd shove him if he fought her right now. "The entire weight of this country does not rest on you, Sebastian. And even *if* it did, you still deserve some rest."

His hand lay over hers and he leaned his head against hers. This was a lot to take in. There were meetings to reschedule, but right now all he could muster was, "Thank you."

"You're welcome. But, um…" Color traveled up her neck as she pulled back a little. "There is more. I…um…"

"You are saying 'um' a lot." Sebastian let out a chuckle.

"I cleared your schedule for the next two weeks." The words were said so fast he almost didn't catch them.

"That is a funny joke." He laughed, and then the chuckles just kept coming. Two weeks. Tears of mirth started down his cheeks. Two weeks off as the king. Sure.

She might as well as said that they were going to the moon tomorrow. It was as feasible.

"I did." Breanna stepped away, and he ached to pull her back.

"Breanna, two weeks? I'm the king. You are the queen."

"Thanks for the reminder. If we were a normal couple, a two-week honeymoon would be a luxury, but it would raise no eyebrows. This is the same."

"Honeymoon?" The word hit his heart and the simple meaning behind it. Honeymoon. Something nearly every couple took. Something he hadn't even thought of. "I didn't think—"

"Of a honeymoon for us. Yeah. I know." She focused on the fabric on the table, not quite covering her sigh.

Darn it.

He'd hurt her. Not intentionally, but that perception was what mattered, not intent. Rule one you learned in the palace.

"Did you want a honeymoon?" He'd assumed she wanted the crown. Assumed she'd beaten her sister for it. Assumed that he was just an accessory.

Assumed a lot, if he was honest with himself.

"What I want stopped mattering long ago. If it ever did." Breanna grabbed the shears and trimmed an edge.

If it ever did.

"You didn't really want to be queen, did you?" He'd suspected it after their wedding. Worried over it. But he wanted her to say it. Though he had no idea what he'd do with the information.

The scissors in her hand seemed to slip just a bit. "What are you going to do with two weeks off, Your Highness? I suspect it is your first vacation."

Deflecting the question. Breanna was nearly as skilled at shifting the topic as him. But right now, he didn't have time to force the issue.

"I don't know." Right now, he needed to talk to Raul about scheduling their honeymoon. If he had two weeks off, they were not hiding away in the palace. He could at least give his bride a vacation.

CHAPTER TEN

"WHERE ARE YOU going on your honeymoon?" Annie's peppy voice was a good sign. It was the first time she'd sounded like herself since she'd fled their parents' mansion.

"It's just a story for the press, Annie." One she'd cooked up as she'd watched her husband sleep soundly. It had taken her longer to convince Raul to leak the news to the press. The man was as on board with Sebastian taking a rest as her. Maybe more so, but he was also steeled in tradition and protocol.

Only her promise to post it on a piece of paper on the palace wall if that was the only way to accomplish it had caused him to bend. She'd approved the press release from the public relations office then waited…and waited…for Sebastian to wake.

And she'd not seen him since he'd left her room after she told him about the two-week vacation yesterday. Their first fight. Though it didn't have much bite behind it. For fights to matter, you had to matter.

She was a name not drawn out of a hat. A woman to wear the crown. One easily overtaken by a phone call.

Breanna blew out a breath. As much as she'd love to soak up the sun on a beach, read a fun novel and think of nothing, she had no illusion that they'd go anywhere. Though Breanna planned to get to know her husband during this forced isolation period.

If he didn't have work to focus on, then he could focus on her for at least a few minutes. Right? They could have a real conversation. Not one timed to fit into his always busy schedule. Not one easily interrupted by nonsense masquerading as emergency.

"A story, Breanna." The disappointment flowed through the phone connection.

Disappointing her parents was a common thing; disappointing Annie always cut. But letting her sister know how much she wished there was some truth to the story was not an option.

They weren't a real couple, but she wished he wanted to spend time with her. It shouldn't matter. Her family had never spent much time with Breanna. The bonus twin. The one who meant her parents got a two-for-one deal.

She'd survived by pretending, accepting, and finding the silver lining.

And it was going to be her life forever. That was the part that stung. The knowledge that she'd never have the fairy tale. Not that the fairy tale truly existed.

"Well, in your mind you can imagine me in a bikini on the beach, reading a sex-filled romance novel while the sun kisses my skin."

She heard a noise and turned to find her husband standing at her door. His head was bent over his phone. Had he heard her? Probably not. The man was focused on whatever was on the screen, not her.

"I need to go, Annie. I want to see pictures of the changes you made to the apartment when you get a chance." Her sister had cut a deal with the apartment manager. He'd pay for supplies, and she could upgrade her unit and the three empty ones. It would let him raise the price of rent and give her a start on replacing her portfolio. It was a brilliant idea.

And one Annie had come up with on her own. Her sister

was getting her freedom. That was worth everything. Even marriage to a king she still didn't really know after weeks of being his wife.

"Good afternoon, Sebastian." The small line that appeared on his cheek when he was trying to hide a frown stood out. "I suspect you are here about the honeymoon story."

"I admit that it surprised me to find my queen has already managed to get the staff on her side." The words were said with a little bite. Surely he knew the staff was looking out for him, too. They were all worried about him—if only he could see that they cared about him. Not the crown.

Breanna plastered on the smile she'd used at home far too often. "It was a good plan, though. Right?" She was actually pretty proud of the calculation.

"It was." He looked at his watch. "You have thirty minutes to pack."

"Pack?" Breanna laughed. Was he kicking her out? Just for making him take a vacation.

"Yes. Pack. For the beach. Make sure you put the bikini in."

"Bikini?" He had heard her. He wasn't focused elsewhere. Was this a joke? A way to poke fun at a queen who'd overstepped her place?

Sebastian tapped his wrist "Twenty-eight minutes, Breanna."

"Where are we going?" How was she supposed to pack if she didn't know what was expected?

"On a honeymoon." Sebastian winked, then headed for the door. "I need to change something in my bag." He hit his watch one more time. "Twenty-seven minutes," he chuckled as he closed the door.

Checkmate.

His wife had successfully found a way to make him take two weeks off. Releasing the honeymoon statement while he was still deep in the land of Nod was a stroke of genius. And a honeymoon was a good idea.

It wouldn't be traditional. No matter how many times his wife appeared in his dreams, how many times he replayed the kiss on their wedding day. The dances they shared. The laughter in those stolen minutes. The feel of her while she was pressed against him.

He'd sworn to have a marriage of convenience. To give her a life with no expectations of sharing a bed with man who'd chosen her sister's name from a hat.

But they were going on a honeymoon. A long-overdue extended get-to-know-you session. His plans to head to the mountains to ski had changed as soon as he'd heard her chattering with her sister.

"Imagine me in a bikini."

It was all too easy for him to piece together the image. His mouth had watered. Spending two weeks with Breanna on the sand wearing a hopefully skimpy bathing suit would be its own form of torture.

That would have been enough of a reason for him to text Raul to change the location for this trip, but the wistfulness in her voice had stolen away his breath. The hint of wanting something. He knew that sound, the plea only his heart recognized.

She'd said that to the one person she trusted. Her sister.

"What I want stopped mattering long ago—if it ever did."

He loved skiing. The few day trips he'd managed to make as a child and teen were heaven. During his year of rebellion, Sebastian had spent more time on the slopes than at the palace.

But if her first choice was the beach? Well, she was the one who'd plotted this honeymoon out. It should be her choice.

Breanna walked up the hallway with a backpack and a small carry-on rolling bag.

"Where is the rest of your luggage?" His mother went on an overnight with more luggage than Breanna had on her.

She looked at the roller, then back at him. "You said pack for the beach. Bathing suits and shorts don't take up that much room."

His mouth watered, and he had to take a breath before he could answer. Control. His wife was gorgeous, and the idea of spending two weeks with her barely clothed...

Focus.

They could always purchase items if she needed them. The benefits of royal life.

"I do need to stop by a bookstore." Breanna smiled. "I am all out of—"

The pause hung in the air. He'd heard her words to Annie. All of them.

"Sex-filled novels?" Sebastian winked. The idea of his wife reading such novels was its own turn-on.

"Yes." She didn't look away. No color crept up her cheeks. Good. This wasn't something that should embarrass her.

"Do you know what you want?" Sebastian pulled up his phone. They could order whatever she wanted and have it sent to the beach cottage. It would be there, wrapped in nice packaging before they arrived.

Her fingers wrapped around his wrist, and she pulled his phone from his hand. The touch was gone before his mind could fully register it, but the heat it left behind scorched his skin.

"I have my TBR on a website dedicated to books. But that isn't the same as a shop."

"TBR?" Sebastian read occasionally, but he wasn't aware of a specialized lingo in the reading community.

"To be read pile." Breanna shook her head with a vigor that screamed, *How can you not know that?* "Mine is infinitely long, but I will always add to it."

"So, pick a few things off of it." Sebastian started to reach for his phone again but stopped. There was wonder in her eye. A look that was purely Breanna.

Have I ever looked like that? Excited? Free? No thought of the place or the crown.

He knew the answer. And the fact that time would likely steal the excitement from the woman in front of him tore through him.

"The fun of book shopping is the store. Walking down the aisle, picking up something with a fun cover or great title. You don't know what you want until it calls to you from the shelf." Breanna was nearly bouncing. "I know we are royals and everything, but surely there is a way we can stop at a store?"

Now she was bouncing. "You might even find something to keep you busy this week. Something besides work correspondence!" Her face was bright and excited.

And he was about to crush it with reality.

"As you say, we are royals. You are the queen. Stepping into a shop isn't as simple as just stepping into a shop."

Her face shifted, "I understand, but I mean, I am also…" Her voice wobbled. Then she lifted her chin. "We have to have a process for doing so. When you go…"

He watched the wheels turn and the realization cross her face. "I don't go anywhere that isn't preplanned. Everything is controlled, and nothing is ever just for fun. It's to promote a shop or raise awareness of a cause."

"Duty thy name is Sebastian." Breanna pulled at her neck, then reached for her phone. "I guess the TBR list it is." The laugh that fell from her lips wasn't crisp. It wasn't fun or happy.

Resigned.

That was the word for Breanna in this moment. Resigned. No anger. No frustration

She pulled up an app, clearing her throat. "I guess the top five on here are a good start."

He took a screen shot of the top ten and sent it to Raul with instructions for them to be delivered to the beach house before them.

"Wonderful." He pointed to her bag. "Really sure you don't need to add anything else? We're going for two weeks."

"Really."

All right then. He held out a hand, his body relaxing as her hand fit into his. "Time for a honeymoon."

Whatever that means.

The blue bikini was skimpier than she remembered. All of the bathing suits Breanna had brought were skimpier than she remembered. Annie used to joke that Breanna bought as little material as possible as though that would let her soak up more sun.

Which was technically true. And if this was a traditional honeymoon, the bright blue string bikini—well, this would make most people's mouth water.

He'd told her that he'd watched her with Hector. Hector swore Sebastian was jealous. But how could he be?

Breanna was hoping for kisses. Sitting in his lap like a fool, only to have the phone give her husband a reason to be free of her. Oh, he'd offered five minutes, but she hadn't wanted that. No matter how many times she thought he was about to drop his lips to hers, the most he ever did was lightly kiss her head. A sweet motion for those watching, probably.

And on their "honeymoon," they had separate rooms.

"Technically, I don't have anything with more coverage." She looked at her bed and sighed. There was no way she was spending this vacation inside.

In my own room.

She opened the door to her private beach entrance, pushing back the tears that were pulling at her. A private room. A private entrance. All to herself…on a honeymoon.

If she gave herself time to think on that, her heart might break. Silver lining, Breanna. She was on the beach. She was away from the palace. Away from the schedule.

The sun hit her face, and Breanna's heart lifted a little. The beach called to her. She had a book—freshly delivered—and a lounge chair calling her name.

Strolling up to the chairs, she was shocked to find Sebastian already in his. Washboard abs ordinarily hidden by suits and tailored shirts were on full display. He looked like a man who had stepped from the pages of one of her books.

Maybe being around her hot, mostly unclothed husband for two weeks wasn't the best plan.

"It's nice out, but the sun is bright. If you want me to get the umbrella—" Sebastian turned his head, his words stopping as he stared at her.

Guess the bikini was as head-turning as she thought.

"I like the sun. Annie says I crave it." It was one way they were different. Annie liked cloudy, rainy days.

"My parents could always tell us apart in the summer because I had a tan." It was the only time in the year the girls weren't interchangeable.

"Only in the summer?"

Her husband's tone was sharp, but she just shrugged. Mistaking their daughters' names never bothered their parents—if it bothered the girls, then that was their problem.

"Identical twins. Interchangeable and all."

His hand was on hers in an instant. "You are not interchangeable."

"Sure I am. Even on the day you came looking for Annie I was. It's okay." Mostly it was. It was her life.

Sebastian's thumb ran along her wrist, the movement sending little spikes of energy up her arms. "I am glad you were the one who came into that room, Breanna."

Her name rumbled from his lips. Her name. Not her title. His muscles were relaxed, but her eyes couldn't seem to stop from staring. What would it feel like to run her hands down them? Drag her lips across them?

Not like she'd find out in the private room she occupied. He was glad it was her. He was holding her hand, but not pulling her any closer.

Get it together.

Breanna slid onto the chair next to his and pushed her sunglasses back on her head. Time for some sun, and she didn't want to risk tan lines around her eyes with the glasses. That and forcing her eyes closed would make sure she couldn't drool over the physical attributes of her husband.

"Annie is the one who stands out—even looking just like me."

"What is that supposed to mean?" Sebastian shifted beside her. Maybe pushing up on his elbow? If she was sitting on the other side, she could get a great view of his butt. Of course, if her chair was on that side, he would have turned to look at her that way. So, the hypothetical situation where she drooled over his backside was flawed from inception.

She heard him twist again but didn't open her eyes. "It means what it sounds like it means." Breanna wasn't sure what the question was about. And her mind had very little available space for anything more than picturing her hot husband who she'd barely touched during their month together.

Seriously, fantasizing about how to get a glimpse of the Adonis's butt. Yep. There was no way she was daring to open her eyes. At least with the sun's rays dancing on her skin, she could pretend the heat wasn't embarrassment crawling up her body.

Sebastian's hand stroked her arm, and she nearly shot up. Only a lifetime of ignoring her wants kept her in place.

"Breanna." Her name was soft as he rubbed a thumb across her arm.

Goose bumps appeared despite the heat.

"Breanna."

"Yes, Sebastian?"

He waited for a moment. Probably seeing if she'd open her eyes. Nope, not happening.

"Why does Annie stand out?" The words were barely above a whisper.

Why was this the first conversation they were having? It was sunny. They could talk of books. Of places they'd visited. Him for official business. Her for family business trips. They could talk about anything. But no, he wanted to know this.

If she didn't answer, he'd press. She knew that. But right now, it was a soft question. A plea. "Annie was the daughter to secure a good marriage. I was the extra. A two-for-one deal, they liked to say. And she is so talented. She is going to make a name for herself. All for herself."

Sebastian didn't say anything, but the pressure on her hand increased.

She hadn't meant to say anything else, but now that the first words were out, her mouth seemed incapable of controlling itself. She'd never told anyone how it felt to be the extra. How much she wanted a different life.

She'd wanted to teach. To disappear into a classroom. Educate the next generation. Something so small. Meaningless to her parents. So meaningless they'd stymied every attempt she'd made to get into the classroom.

"And you?"

If she opened her eyes, the words would likely stop. She'd lose the ability to form them. But she'd also have to see the pity in Sebastian's eyes.

"My dreams were smaller. A classroom decorated with bright colors and little students who wanted to be in circle time. Or didn't. At that age, sitting still is not a skill most little ones have. My student teaching days were my happiest. But teaching is not a profession for Galanis women. Not when we can marry well, according to my parents."

She laughed, but the lack of humor wasn't lost on her. "Anyways, Annie is brilliant with colors. She has dreams. She's an interior designer. One day everyone on this island will know exactly who she is—for her work—not her name."

"So when I pulled her name from the hat…" Sebastian's whispers chilled her skin.

"She was going to marry you. I saw it. All the work she'd done to get her portfolio ready. Our escape hatch." She cleared her throat. "Anyways, I pointed out that you didn't know her so you couldn't mind if we switched the script. We look the same, after all. And you didn't know us. Which was true."

"Breanna." Her name. The twin he hadn't meant to meet at the altar. Why was this bothering her now? They'd been married a month. A month as his queen. A month of accepting that this was her life.

And she was doing a good job. Or she had been. Until she'd stepped onto this beach.

"I don't say that to make you feel bad. I say it as the truth. Annie has a dream." Breanna sighed as she remembered the first room Annie had ever redecorated. A spare room her mother had no use for. A room designed for failure.

Her parents had only let Annie try because Breanna would not stop pestering. And then the finished product was gorgeous. It was still the room her mother had all the guests sleep in. Not that they'd ever praised Annie.

But others would.

"And your dream was a classroom?"

Rolling over, she opened her eyes, letting the grin swimming in her soul appear freely. "No. My dream was for Annie to get her dream. And she is going to. She has an apartment now. She is decorating it, and the empty units, with her landlord's approval. Maybe it isn't the fancy portfolio our parents stole, but it's something that can't be taken from her."

"But what was *your* dream?" Sebastian's hand gripped hers. Heat bloomed beneath it.

She lifted it, placed a soft kiss on it, then rolled onto her back. "That was my dream. Now my dream is to get some sun." There was no point discussing this. She'd made her choice.

This was her life now. She was a queen. Annie was free.

Maybe this wasn't the life she'd envisioned. She'd never step into the classroom as a teacher. Never see little eyes light up as they learned their letters and numbers. But she'd make the same choice again without question.

CHAPTER ELEVEN

"WANT TO ORDER some lunch?" Breanna stretched on the lounge chair next to him. She'd occupied it nearly every moment since they'd arrived yesterday. Flipping when the timer on her phone went off. Or running into the sea for a quick dip. "Or would you rather cook?"

The sun kissed her skin in ways he could only dream of.

"What would you prefer?" He had a fully stocked kitchen here. Outside of sushi, he could fix up just about anything she requested.

His wife sat up. The pink polka-dot string bikini left so little to the imagination, if he was standing, he might drop to his knees in worship of the beauty beside him. She was delectable.

The blue bikini from yesterday had played the main role in his dreams last night. Today, his fingers ached to travel down her stomach. Circle her belly button, see what sounds she might make if his lips followed the same path.

None of which was going to happen.

"I do not enjoy cooking, so fixing my own food on vacation is not high on my priorities." Breanna moved her hand like she was going to push his shoulder, but he caught it and held it.

Her eyes flicked to their combined fingers, but she didn't pull back. "However, you do enjoy it. And this is your vacation. Do you want to cook?"

She'd put his needs first. Again. It was a pattern that he should have seen faster. One he might have seen if he'd spent more time with his queen. The woman put others first. It was an admirable quality.

But it didn't mean you had to give up everything you wanted. Outside of sewing, did his wife even know what her preferences were? Had she ever had dreams that revolved just around her?

Just because she was an identical twin didn't mean she didn't get to be an individual.

"What is your favorite food? The day after our wedding, you asked about me, but I learned little other than you like a little coffee with your syrup in the morning." Her laughter filled his heart as she swung their combined hands.

"My coffee is not that full of syrup." She stuck her tongue out, then laughed.

His statement wasn't that far from the truth. His wife put at least four squirts of coffee syrup in each mug. He watched her create combinations that he'd never consider. Sometimes it was clear she had a drink she was recreating. Other times it seemed she was just flying by the seat of her sweet tooth.

"What is your favorite food, Breanna? I know you like lemon cake, and I will make that if you like, but one cannot live on dessert alone."

"Not sure that is true." Breanna pulled her hand back, and even though he wanted to reach for it again, Sebastian let it be.

"I can't make it if I don't know it." This was such a simple question. One most people could spout off with no thought.

"I like vegetable lasagna. Our cook used to make it once a week so I had something besides salads for dinner." She rolled her head, shifting in the chair. Discomfort was clear on her features.

This was about food; it wasn't hard. Or it shouldn't be. And the statement's meaning struck him. "Did you not have veg-

etarian options at dinner?" The Galanis estate was famous
for the luxury dinners they served investors. Sebastian had
attended more than one event at the estate with his father.

He racked his memory for anything about those events,
but they were a blur in a lifetime of service. He wasn't even
sure he'd seen Breanna and Annie there. Though they were
probably in the sea of people.

"My parents did not support my choice." She stood and
walked towards the sea.

He followed.

"That can't be surprising, Sebastian. Unless you and Raul
had intervened, I would have eaten very little at my own wedding reception." She strolled into the waves, then turned and
splashed him.

Water dripped down his face as she squealed and sent another small wave towards him. He cupped some water and
tossed it her way. Her laughter increased.

The moment was fun, and happy. A honeymoon moment—
and once more she'd redirected the conversation away from
her. He splashed some more water her way, then reached for
her waist and pulled her towards him. "What is your favorite food, Breanna? I am not letting you go until you tell me."
Sebastian dipped his head and kissed her forehead.

He'd done that many times. It was never thought out, and
not what he truly wanted, but he didn't want to push her for
more than she'd signed on for. Even if he craved more.

Water slipped off his wife's face, and she didn't pull away
from him. Instead, her hips pressed against him as the waves
broke around them.

"You plan to hold me until I tell you my favorite food, Sebastian?" His wife moved her head, her lips so close to his.
"Not sure that is much of a threat."

The sun's heat had nothing on the flames pouring through
him. Steam should have risen from the ocean water as his

mind replayed Breanna's comments back to him. "Breanna." His brain seemed incapable of forming any other thought besides his wife's name.

"Sebastian." Her arms wrapped around his neck. "How long do you think we'll just stand here? High tide comes in shortly. Then what?"

"What if I cut you a deal?" He stroked her back, enjoying the feel of her in his arms.

"A deal?" Her arms tightened just a little, and her hips brushed his again. The sun glinted off her dark hair. It was like he was standing with a fairy-tale creature. One he desperately wanted answers from. Though the question was far too simple for a fairy tale.

"Sebastian." Her purr echoed with the waves.

Maintaining his focus was a never-ending battle. "A deal." He cleared his throat, the action doing nothing to clear the thoughts of trailing his lips down her throat. "You tell me your favorite dish; I fix it. Then we spend the night cuddled on the couch. You pick the movie."

"I told you." She pressed her lips to his. The connection lasted barely a second. "Veggie lasagna."

"No. You said the cook made that once a week so you didn't have to eat salads. Not the same thing. And if you shrug that off—"

"You'll what? Kiss me into submission?"

Tempting. Oh, so very tempting. And if he didn't think she was using this to make him try to forget about herself, then he might just offer that. But this was important.

Even if she didn't think so.

"I won't cuddle on the couch." He wasn't sure how they'd slipped from serious conversations to playfulness, but he was embracing it. There was more than one way to get an answer. And sometimes humor worked best of all.

The Sebastian he'd been a year ago bolted from the cage

he'd locked him away in. "Or maybe I will spend the whole movie talking. Just interrupting and asking questions."

"You wouldn't." She threw one hand over her heart in playful surrender, but the other stayed wrapped around his neck.

"I guess I don't know. I ate a lot of salads, so definitely not that. At home it was lasagna though...my college roommate, Binna, used to make this potato dish. It..." She closed her eyes.

This was a moment he recognized. A dish that touched you. That made you feel something. It was something chefs worked for years to achieve. He'd once made a lamb stew that had brought tears to his eyes as the flavors mixed together.

Food had power. It held memories...good and bad.

"Describe it to me." He whispered the words against her ear as the water rose around them, binding them together. His fingers stroked her back. Staying a respectful distance from the top of her bikini bottom.

She brushed her lips against his, again. It was like they were going with the motions. This place was out of time and space. Just for them.

"Breanna." Her name was power. He ached for her to deepen the kiss, but he wasn't going to push this.

"Sebastian." Her lips passed his again. Then she seemed to remember they'd been talking about food.

"Binna used a giant pot with a lid. Not a sauce pot but something she'd brought over from Korea. But you could find it anywhere. She joked with me once that I knew so little about cooking, I thought the pot was something special. She had a name for it, but one of the other roommates called it an oven of some kind."

"A Dutch oven." It wasn't an uncommon method for making a stew. In fact, he'd crafted several in the one he stored in his kitchen.

"Yep. That's it. Binna's dish was called gochujang potato stew. I have no idea what the recipe was, and I wish I'd asked. Unfortunately, we lost touch after graduation. I heard she works at some big pharmaceutical firm in Germany now. The spices were strong, and I remember she was worried the scent would upset people."

"Did it?" Food was home. It was also something people judged. At uni, a young man had talked about how the kids at his school bullied him for the ethnic food his mother packed each day. A reminder of home for her. Something that made him different during a period everyone wanted to fit in.

Now he owned one the most successful restaurants on the island, and people paid a good bit for the Vietnamese cuisine others had judged.

Breanna shook her head. "It drove them to our door, but in a good way. It was so aromatic and yummy. Whenever people smelled it, we'd have them begging for a taste. I think Binna could have funded university by selling the stew."

"Well, I know how to make a gochujang stew, so I just need to see if there is gochujang in the spice cabinet here. I keep it in my kitchen at the palace. I'm not sure I have the exact potatoes Binna used, but it is a fairly standard dish, so we can play around and see if we can recreate it."

"Seriously?" Breanna planted a solid kiss on his lips before pulling back. "Oh."

It looked like all the blood in her body might be running to her face. "You're turning red." Sebastian dropped a playful kiss on her nose. "Don't want my bride getting sunburned."

"It has nothing to do with the sun, Your Highness." Breanna kissed his nose, recreating the movement he'd used.

He held his breath, and when her lips met his this time, there was no hesitation. A strong wave pushed against them, and rather than pull back, she wrapped her legs around his waist.

She opened her mouth, her tongue sweeping his, and the

world melted away. She tasted of the ocean, sun and future. Breanna. His wife. His queen.

The kiss was over far too soon. She dipped her head, then grabbed his hand and pulled him towards the beach. "Let's see if you have the spice."

If perfection ever needed a new descriptor, it could use this moment to build it. He wanted to stop time. Be just Sebastian and Breanna forever.

Spices and ocean air might be her new favorite scent. She had no idea how she'd recreate it, but the spice smell meant she wasn't surprised to find Sebastian standing in the kitchen tossing a few things into the Dutch oven he'd found in the back of a cabinet yesterday.

"I figured we'd eat leftovers today." They had at least enough stew for a second serving. His gochujang potato stew wasn't the same as Binna's, but it was good. And the fact that he'd made something for her, something she wanted…it was a feeling she couldn't describe.

Which was why she'd jumped into his arms yesterday. And kissed him. It was spontaneous. But it felt right. Like she'd been waiting her whole life for a switch that was finally on. He'd kissed her back. Really kissed her.

Maybe he'd finally initiate a kiss. A real one instead of brushes against her forehead and nose. Their relationship was finally shifting.

Relationship. She wanted to laugh at the word. They'd gone from married strangers to people who'd shared a confidence beside the sea. It should feel awkward.

Should feel weird. They were married. Staying in separate rooms. But kissing and touching and…and figuring out what they were. It was certainly a unique way for spouses to play get-to-know-you.

Still, it felt right.

"We can have the stew for lunch. But I'm making some lentil curry for dinner. It will be perfect after cooking all day." Sebastian tilted his head towards the coffee. "I just made a fresh pot."

Just made.

"How long have you been up?" These two weeks were supposed to be about him resting. He couldn't do that if he was rising at three.

Sebastian bent his head.

The sudden focus on a dish she guessed he'd made dozens of times and the rapid spin of the spoon broke her heart. "Sebastian." He'd spent his entire life in service. Even on vacation, he was still serving. Except instead of a country, it was a focus of one. But what about what he wanted? What he needed?

She walked up behind him, wrapping her arms around his waist. She laid her head against shoulder. "What time, honey?"

The endearment slipped out, but she wasn't going to focus on that now. They were helping each other. Giving each other rest. A place away from the lives they'd grown up in. A fresh start, hopefully.

"I managed to stay in bed until five."

Managed...

"Okay. But what time did you wake up?" She was a master of wording, too. One did not grow up in the Galanis household without learning more than a few phrasing tricks.

He chuckled, but there was no humor in the sound. "My wife is keen to my tricks already. I thought that was something that took time to develop in a marriage."

She squeezed him tighter. There was no judgment here. Just concern. "Sebastian."

"Three forty-five." He uttered the time and shrugged against her. "It's like my body needs to be up and going."

His voice was coated in exhaustion and frustration. "Sorry."

"You don't have to be sorry." His body was following the only routine it had ever known. The routine that had been forced onto him as a child. She couldn't get mad at that. At least not at him.

He stirred the dish, but she didn't let go. She was here for him. "During my rebellious year, I used to slip my security early in the morning. It drove Alessio mad. He accused me of trying to get hurt. Brie gave me an exceptionally strong talking-to one day. Told me I was hurting him."

And that would have nearly killed him. Sebastian cared for everyone. Full stop.

"Anyways, even when I was pushing back on the duty I was born for, I couldn't manage to keep myself in bed. What kind of rebellion involves being up before the dawn?"

"Not a very good one." She kissed his shoulder. "Somehow, I can't imagine you as rebellious. I mean, I remember that year. I know you call it failure and other ridiculous things, but please!"

Sebastian turned in her arms, wrapping his arms around her waist. They stood there, in the kitchen. His lips pressed to her head. "And what would you know about rebellion, Breanna?"

"Oh." She pulled back, then kissed his cheek. "I have rebelled a time or two." She laughed and kissed his shoulder again.

"I doubt that, very seriously, *Your Highness.*" This time his chuckle had a true lilt of humor.

She pushed on his shoulder, breaking the connection and offering a very fake pout. "How dare you say that." She grabbed a mug of coffee, dropped four pumps of brown sugar cinnamon syrup in it, then hopped on the counter.

Sebastian nodded his head the way she'd watched one of

her uni professors do when about to press an important point. Her husband was getting ready to ask a very deep question. "Tell me one truly rebellious thing you ever did?"

"Hmm." She put her finger on her chin, playfully looking at him. "I need to think about what secrets to give away. Tell me what you did, *Your Highness*."

Sebastian went to the fridge and pulled out two jars. "Overnight oats made with almond milk and dried fruit."

"Ooh." She grabbed a spoon from the freshly washed rack and opened her container. "So good."

Sebastian took a bite of his, then pointed a spoon at her. "I broke off the relationship with the woman my father wanted me to marry. A year-long affair just…" He snapped his fingers, and a look she worried was wistfulness floated on his features.

A girlfriend. Whoever she was, there'd never been any hint of her in the press.

There was no sign of animosity in his voice. No dismissive tone for a relationship that hadn't worked out. Did he miss her? Was she who he'd really wanted to wear the crown and the reason he'd settled for Breanna?

Words escaped her.

"The night of my first state dinner, I told Samantha that I hated the crown. Hated the responsibility and wished I'd never been born heir to the throne."

He took a deep breath. "And she said she didn't understand that because without it I was a nobody. The crown was the only thing that made me special. Pretty sure it just popped out and she tried to walk it back, but… I could see it was the truth."

That was horrible. "Sebastian." She wasn't sure what else to say. "You—"

"I don't want to talk about Sam. She's gone, and luckily

the nondisclosure agreement my father worked out was iron clad. The man had some good ideas."

His voice was set. But the look on his face broke her heart. His title was such a small part of him. But they'd discuss that another time. "Well, that doesn't count."

"Excuse me." Sebastian stepped between her legs, and she dropped a kiss on his lips, happy that he was grinning.

"You broke off a relationship that didn't work. Sorry, Your Highness, but there is nothing rebellious about that. Very standard stuff, actually."

Her husband's eyes rolled to the ceiling. "Fine. I arrived almost three hours late to my first state dinner. It made Briella the villain in a media narrative that still floats to the surface now and then."

Not anymore.

Breanna knew the articles printed about them were less than congratulatory. More than one op-ed had run about the king so openly agreeing to a marriage of convenience. As though he'd been forced into it, rather than marching into her home after choosing Annie's name from a hat.

Alessio had a lotto bride. King Sebastian had the leftovers. The headlines practically wrote themselves.

"Enough about me. What mischief have you ever gotten up to?"

"I orchestrated my sister's escape."

"Doesn't count." He mimicked her voice, and she couldn't stop the giggle. "I already know that." Sebastian turned the stovetop to Warm, then reached for her hand. "Come one. We can finish breakfast on the patio."

"I told you I changed places with her." Breanna said as she followed him outside. "I didn't tell you that I used a secret fund of money to get her an apartment. That I helped make sure she never has to contact our parents again. Their two-for-one deal is forever outside their reach."

Breanna laughed. "They hadn't fully realized it by the wedding. They refused to talk to her, thinking that would bring her back. Nope. She's gone. Then my husband—the king—ordered them out." She put her hand to her lips and blew a kiss.

No words fell across the small table for what felt like forever. "I think that counts." She scooped the last bits of oats into her mouth and held up the spoon.

"That isn't rebellion, Breanna." Sebastian's words were soft. "It's survival."

Survival. Three syllables; three tiny daggers she didn't want to acknowledge.

"Want to go into town today?" Breanna pointed to the beach. "It's a beautiful day. Though I suspect every day is beautiful here."

"Breanna—"

"Shopping sounds fun." That wasn't really true. She'd never been a fan of shopping. Except for books and in thrift stores. Those places she could spend hours in.

"We can go shopping later in the week. I have to get security set." Sebastian's brow burrowed as he reached his hand across the table, wrapping it through hers. "But I have an idea."

"More talking…" Breanna had wanted to get to know her husband. Wanted to care for him—it was what she did. But him seeing through her own armor…it was exhausting.

"Yes. But about food." Sebastian put his free hand over his heart. "I am making the curry for dinner, but do you want to make bread?"

"Isn't that baking?" She made a playful face. "I was under the impression my husband did not like baking."

He stuck his tongue out. "I like making bread. But yes, I guess, technically, it's baking. But it's a process. A long one. We can make the dough. Knead it, then sit in the sun or play in the sea while it rises. If you think about it, it's the perfect vacation bake."

"I've never made bread." Breanna ran her thumb along his hand, enjoying the connection but wanting to be away from the chairs, where she seemed intent on spilling secrets she didn't even share with herself.

"But sure."

Breanna beat the dough. Her dough had passed the right stage for rising minutes ago. The bread was going to be hard. But this exercise wasn't about perfect bread. Even hard, it would still be good for croutons and dipping in sauces.

She needed to work out her anger towards her parents. Anger she'd not even allowed herself to acknowledge.

He did, too, but his wasn't decades long. Though if Lucas and Matilda Galanis thought they could profit from having a daughter with a crown, they were sorely mistaken. Money bought lots of things. Power, security, influence.

Things a king had, too. And while he couldn't strip the Galanises of power and security, he could limit their influence significantly. At least in the aristocratic circles they craved. His wife was not part of a "two-for-one deal." She was not interchangeable.

She was amazing, and he was lucky she'd switched places with her sister. His wife sacrificed herself for everyone else. Even a husband she barely knew. From this point forward she needed to be herself. Whoever that was.

"How long am I supposed to beat this?"

"The baking term is to knead." Sebastian chuckled. "Though I think what you have done to that bread counts more as beating than kneading."

Breanna looked up, her mouth falling open. "Wait. Did I do this wrong?"

"Not at all." Sebastian grabbed the oiled bowl he'd prepped for the bread to rise in. "Just put it in here."

Breanna gave him a look he couldn't decipher as she dropped the dough in the bowl. "I feel better." She looked at the dough she'd pummeled, then at him. "Thank you."

"I may not like baking, but making bread is a healing process. Not sure why, but it is true." Sebastian shrugged. He'd created many hard loafs in the last few years.

"You know what else is healing?" Breanna tilted her head, and her fun smile reappeared.

"Should I be worried?" Sebastian saw her hand move to pile of flour she'd used for the bread the instant before it landed on his chest.

"Flour fight!" Breanna giggled as another pile hit his pants.

Flour dust filled the air as he reached for a handful. His toss landed on her shoulder, the dusting cloud dropping specks across her nose and cheeks. She squealed, and happiness burst through his body.

When Breanna grabbed the last handful from the counter, he raised his hands, providing her with a full target. "Give it your best shot, wife."

Wife.

A flash passed over her eyes, but she didn't launch the flour. Instead, she sauntered towards him, the flour tight in her hand. "Husband." She wrapped her arms behind his neck and raised her brows. "There are two options as I see it."

Her husky tone triggered goose pimples on his arms. "And those are?"

"I can drop this flour in your hair. See what you will look like when we have been married for decades and you have passed gray and gone on to white hair."

"That would make quite a mess." Sebastian squeezed her waist. He thought he knew what option two was. And he'd choose it over anything else. But if he was wrong, or she chose to dust his hair with flour, that was fine, too.

"You could kiss me." Pink rushed to her cheeks, but Breanna didn't break her gaze. "Really kiss me."

Sebastian pulled her as close to him as possible. "If I get to choose—" he ran his hand up her back, leaning as close to her as possible "—it is the easiest choice of all." He dipped his head, dropping his lips along her jaw. They were coated in flour, but he didn't want to miss this opportunity.

He took a deep breath, then pressed his lips to hers. This wasn't the hesitant kiss they'd shared right before their wedding. It wasn't the passing glance they'd shared over the altar. Or even the flirty fun they'd had in the sea.

This was the future. It was sweet, passionate, and timeless. Everything he'd dreamed of. Sebastian ran his hand across her skin as his tongue danced with hers as though they'd done this hundreds of times.

She pressed her hands to his back. The handful of flour dropping to the floor behind him…and probably splashing across her skin, too. Another thing that didn't matter.

"Sebastian."

His name on her lips, breathless. Desire exploded through him. He wanted to kiss her, everywhere. Spend the rest of his day worshipping her lips, her body, everything.

She slipped a hand under his shirt. The light touch of her fingers set his skin ablaze. He followed her motion, slipped his hand under her shirt, mimicking each of her strokes.

"We are getting flour all over." Breanna's silky voice matched this moment even though her words were the stuff of comedy.

"We are." Sebastian ached to scoop her up. One word from her and he'd take her to bed and spend the next several days learning every inch of her. Memorizing what made her sigh with satisfaction and pant with need.

"We could rinse off in the sea." Her lips slipped along his neck.

He'd never had trouble finding words, but when his wife flirted with him, the synapses refused to fire.

"First one to the water wins." Breanna kissed him, then took off running. She was out the door and onto their private beach before he turned.

There was no way he was winning this race, but each of her giggles felt like a trophy.

CHAPTER TWELVE

SEBASTIAN WASN'T BEHIND HER. At least not yet. That final kiss had thrown him, but her husband would follow soon. Still, the delay was the only reason she had the courage to take on the truly rebellious act of dropping her shorts, T-shirt, and bathing suit before racing into the surf.

He'd said she wasn't rebellious. But she could be. She'd show him.

She planned to carve her own path as queen. And she doubted queens took naked dips in the sea after food fights with their husbands.

Turning to the beach, she saw the moment her husband discovered her pile of clothes by the chair she'd occupied most of this vacation. All the momentum he'd had from running evaporated as he looked from the water to her clothes, then back at Breanna. If he'd been a cartoon character, his eyes would have popped out as the sand flew up around him.

She splashed a little but did not rise far enough up for her breasts to exit the water. The bloom of heat she feared was embarrassment was pushing at her mind. Breanna was not going to give in to it. She'd started this. And she was finishing it.

Maybe a rebellious queen was the exactly what King Sebastian needed.

"Come in, the water is very nice. You can keep your clothes on, if you like." He could, but she wanted him to strip. Wanted to run her hands over all of him. Give in to the emotions she felt every time she was near him. Tame the heat that refused to cool whenever his hands were on hers.

The king looked at the pile again, then pulled his shirt off. His abs gleamed in the sun, and Breanna licked her lips.

No one was ever going to say that King Sebastian of Celiana wasn't the most handsome king to sit on the island's ancient throne. His hands went to his shorts. Then he paused and looked at her.

"You will have me at a disadvantage if you leave your shorts on, but I will understand."

I might die of embarrassment, but I'll understand.

Sebastian smiled, then walked into the water. His bathing shorts still firmly on.

Hell.

As he stepped next to her, she fought back the urge to cover herself with her hands. Rebellion wasn't all that good if you didn't commit.

"How is that for rebellion?" She winked, then slid under the water, running her hands through her hair.

When she surfaced, she raised her hands, patting her soaking hair. "Did I get all the flour out?" Her nipples were just below the surface, but easy to see in the crystal-clear water. And the primary focus of her husband.

He blew out a breath. "Breanna—"

Her name. Only her name left his lips. It was like a meditation as he stared at her.

"Sebastian." She swam a little closer. "You didn't answer my question."

"Question?" He titled his head.

She couldn't stop the giggle. "I *asked* if I got all the flour out of my hair. Aren't you paying attention?"

"I think my wife knows very well exactly what attention she is drawing out of me." The huskiness of his tone sent little waves of desire through her body. She'd never had someone so in thrall to her.

He lifted his head, purposefully looking at her hair. "I don't see any more flour."

"Anywhere?" She twirled, breathing deeply, fearful that her nerve might evaporate any moment.

Sebastian's gargled sound as she spun slowly in the water made her giggle. Power. Excitement. Happiness. In this moment she was simply Breanna. Not one of a pair.

All the emotions swirled in her body as she waited for his answer and met his gaze. "Well?"

His Adam's apple bobbed as he swallowed, then cleared his throat. "No more flour."

She swam close enough that her breasts were nearly touching his chest. "You have a little on your cheek." She dipped her hand in the water, even though it was already wet, then ran her fingers along the streak, wiping it away.

She didn't lower her hand. Instead, she traced her finger along his chin, enjoying the hint of stubble there. "You don't shave as close when you aren't at the palace. I like it."

"Breanna."

There was her name again, followed by nothing else.

"Sebastian." She mimicked his tone. "I like when you kiss me."

His hand was around her waist in an instant. He pulled her close, her body, her naked body, pressed against him. "Your wish, my lady."

She might not have a lot of experience with men—or any—but she understood how the human body worked. Breanna knew how to give herself an orgasm and knew that the bulge on her hip meant her husband was incredibly turned on.

"I think I am going to enjoy having a wife that runs naked into the water. We certainly couldn't do this on a ski slope." Sebastian dipped his head to hers and placed both hands on her butt, lifting her out of the water as his tongue danced with hers.

She wrapped her legs around him. Her body knew what she wanted; her mind would just get in the way.

Waves cradled them as they clung together. Here and now, it was only Breanna and Sebastian. The past, present and future didn't matter.

Nothing mattered except the feel of his lips on hers, the dance of his fingers on her skin.

"Breanna."

Her name sounded different this time. A force rather than a meditation. A breaking. Reality seeping back into their lives.

She pulled back but let her fingers run through his hair. Touching him was a necessity she couldn't understand even as she knew he was about to end whatever was happening here.

"We need to go back inside the cottage." His voice was tight as he pulled back. The moment over.

"Right." She nodded. "The bread is probably ready for the oven."

"I very much doubt the bread is ready for the oven." His lips were so close but not on hers. Not where she wanted them.

Before her brain could muddle through any words, Sebastian continued, "I want you, Breanna. My desire burns. Come to bed with me?"

"Breanna." Sebastian breathed her name against her ear as she clung to him through the waves. For the rest of time, he'd remember the moment he'd stepped into the sea with his naked bride.

The only reason he hadn't fully stripped was that he'd needed some kind of barrier between him and the stunning sea creature waiting for him in the surf.

"I like how you say my name." Breanna ran her fingers along his chin.

She liked the stubble there, too. His father had instructed him to shave multiple times a day. A prince and king must always be presentable. And stubble or a beard…apparently those didn't fit a royal image.

The first morning, he'd held the razor, then put it away. He was on vacation, after all. In the realm of rebellion, it wasn't anywhere near dancing naked into the sea. But it felt nice.

"Breanna." He let the syllables drip off his tongue before he pressed his lips to the top of her ear. Salt, waves and the scent that was simply his wife invaded his senses. His bedroom seemed so far away, but she deserved her first time to be slow. Sensual. Memorable.

Not a romp on the beach.

"Just like that." Her hands dipped to the waistband of his shorts, her thumb running along the top.

"Again, you have me at a disadvantage. You *are* clothed."

"No." He nipped her ear. "It is *you* who has me at a disadvantage, Breanna." She was the only thing he could think of. Her slick body set his ablaze.

He stepped up to the cottage, and Breanna reached over and turned the door handle.

"Teamwork," she whispered as her fingers ran through his hair.

Teamwork.

He liked that.

Moving through the cottage as quickly as his legs would carry them, Sebastian let her open his bedroom door, and he kicked it closed behind him. Capturing her lips, he gently laid her on his bed.

Stunning didn't begin to describe the siren on his bed. Her wet, dark hair splayed across his pillow; her pink lips were swollen from kisses. Her nipples tightened as he twirled a thumb around each.

"Sebastian."

His name. The power behind the sound of it on Breanna's sweet lips nearly sent him to his knees. Letting his fingers dance across her glorious curves, he listened to each hitch of her breath. Studied each movement that made her arch against him.

Greed was the best description for the urge within him. But it wasn't his own release he needed. Sebastian craved the knowledge of Breanna's needs. Her wants. The touches that would make her say his name with such perfection.

Dipping his head, he trailed his lips along the same path his fingers had traveled just moments before. Breanna's hips arched, and he took the offering.

His mouth found the right spot, his fingers trailing along the insides of her thighs.

"Sebastian." The pant was perfection as she crested to completion. "Sebastian. I...want...you."

Every bit of control fled his body.

He stood, stripped, and moved on top of his wife. She wrapped her legs around his waist, and it was only as he was pressing against her that the rational thought of contraception broke through passion's fog.

"I don't have a condom." He kissed her neck. This was supposed to be a honeymoon in name only. Only in his dreams had he allowed himself to contemplate this moment.

Breanna let out a breath. "We *are* married, and I have an IUD." She kissed his lips, then pulled back. "But if you want to wait..."

He did not. "Breanna." Sebastian kissed her, joining them and losing himself in the blissfulness that was his wife.

CHAPTER THIRTEEN

BREANNA STRETCHED IN the kitchen. She'd fallen asleep in Sebastian's arms and stayed there until just after six this morning. Her husband was still snoozing. It was the biggest win.

Maybe having company in his bed was what he needed to stay put. If that was a sacrifice she needed to make, it was the best one the universe had ever asked of her.

She smiled as she fixed a cup of coffee for herself and then another for Sebastian. She'd love to let him sleep, but he'd promised her a trip into town. Breanna grabbed a muffin. The top was a little hard. It was still good, but not as fresh as when it had been delivered a few days ago. But neither she nor Sebastian wanted to bake muffins.

It would work for today, and while they were in town, they could make sure they stopped at a local bakery. She'd enjoyed the last several days alone with him. But she was also looking forward to checking out the local bookstore.

Breanna needed to get moving, or rather get her husband moving. So, she tossed the muffin on a platter she'd found, then headed for the dark room.

"I smell coffee." His words were slow, and his eyes weren't open. The sheet was loosely covering his bottom half.

Her body heated, and the urge to spend the rest of the day right here was nearly overwhelming. But they'd asked security to take them. And a few of the stores in town were planning on their arrival. Inconveniencing others wasn't a good look, especially for royals.

Particularly for such a reason. *Sorry. Can't come, the queen and king are too busy getting busy* wasn't really a statement she wanted anyone to type up.

Sebastian sat up and grabbed the coffee.

He took a deep sip and met her gaze. "I slept in."

"You did." Breanna laughed as he grinned over the mug. "I think we may have found a way to keep your butt in bed."

His eyes sparkled as he looked to her. "I like having your butt in bed." He reached for her, but she pulled back.

"I let you sleep as long as possible, Your Highness!" She tapped the watch he'd given her. "But if I let you touch me..."

She swallowed as he sat up a little straighter. The sheet slipped even further. Her husband, ruffled from a night of good sleep, was sexy as hell.

"If you let me touch you?" His gaze dipped to her breasts.

Her nipples tightened as the memory of him stroking her filled her. "If I let you touch me, you know exactly what will happen."

Sebastian playfully raised his eyebrows twice, then took another sip of his coffee. He was a dream.

"I also brought you a muffin, though it's not super fresh." She held up the platter and tried to remind herself that they had security arriving in less than an hour. That was not enough time to spend in his arms. Though a Sebastian unconcerned about his daily schedule was also hot as hell.

Sebastian leaned forward. His lips met hers, and she melted. Luckily, he pulled back.

"I could get used to my wife bringing me breakfast in bed. Give me one sec." He winked, then slid from the bed, walking to the bathroom.

She didn't look away from his retreating naked form. He was delicious.

Sebastian returned quickly, now wearing a pair of loose slacks, his hair combed but still shirtless. He leaned against the doorframe and looked at the muffin. "I think I'll pass on the three-day-old muffin. We can pick something up in town."

She put the platter on the dresser and wandered to where he was. "Sounds like a plan."

His arms wrapped around her waist, and his mouth found the spot just below her ear that made her knees go weak. "Sebastian."

"I do enjoy when you say my name." His tongue licked the spot, and then he pulled back. "You're right. We can't start this when today's adventures await us. One of them might even include a bookstore."

"Sebastian." She grabbed his hand, pulling him to the front of the room. A bookstore. Something for her.

"Security is here." Sebastian pointed to his watch. Then the door and the knock followed less than a second later.

"Impressive." Breanna smiled at the security guards as they stepped through the door. It was also sad. Sad that he had his life timed down to the minute.

"Nice to see you." Sebastian nodded to the group as they bowed to him. "My wife wants to spend as much time in the bookstore as possible, and we need to get some goodies from the bakery. But what else is on the agenda?"

Breanna saw the subtle tilt of the security staff's heads. Their dark glasses hid the movement of their eyes, but she wondered if several had raised brows. Sebastian was relaxed. Yes, he was talking about agendas, but not with the stiff air he'd had at the palace.

The head of security nodded to them. "Your honeymoon seems to be going well."

Her cheeks were fire as Sebastian slid his arm around her waist. "My wife has proven to me that vacations are a good idea. We'll have to pencil them in each year." He kissed her forehead.

She knew the head of security was outlining the day. Knew he was explaining the adventures and schedules they needed to keep to. But her brain refused to focus on anything other than Sebastian saying they'd have to pencil in vacations.

He was willing to schedule the vacations. Willing to take time off. Yesterday was fantastic, but today felt like she'd truly won a lottery.

"Ooh." Breanna patted his hand as they walked towards the bookstore. Cameras clicked around them, but his wife's eyes did not leave the blue door of the not-so-tiny bookstore. "This is going to be so fun."

"It is." Sebastian leaned over, kissing the top of her head. Touching her was intoxicating, but watching her get excited for herself brought forth an emotion that there was not a descriptor for.

Stepping through the front door, they left the crowds outside.

"Your Highnesses." The owner of the store and her two employees stepped forward. "We are so glad you came in. I am Lila Patri. Welcome to my store."

Breanna reached for Lila's hands, then the workers standing on each side of her, giving each individual attention as she shook their hands. She was so good at this. Like she was built to be a queen.

"You get to work in one of the best places ever!"

The sincerity of her tone seemed to bring tears to Lila's eyes. "This was my dream as a girl. Owning my own shop full of books from wall to wall. It took until I was fifty to see it to fruition. Spent most of my working life as a public relations manager. Now, though…" The woman gestured to the walls of books; her was happiness clear even if she couldn't put everything into words.

"Dreams are important." Breanna nodded to the owner. "What is your favorite thing about owning the shop?"

Lila looked to him, but he just nodded for her to show his wife around. "I am not sure I can pick just one, Your Highness."

"Breanna. Please, call me Breanna."

He stared at his wife and Lila as they wandered around her store. The king he'd been before they'd gone on this honeymoon would have known down to the minute how long they had to be here. After all, there was a plan for this shopping trip. One he'd asked Raul to work out before their arrival. But Breanna was interested, the owner clearly wanted to show off her store, and he needed a minute to process Breanna's words.

Dreams are important.

Such a simple phrase. One he'd murmured hundreds of times at events for students, workers, the general public. It was true.

And his wife had never had a dream for herself. Her dreams were all for others.

"Are we ready, Your Highness?" Lila was standing next to Breanna, holding a pad.

"Ready?" His wife looked at him, and the door. "I thought we were browsing for a while."

"You are." Sebastian swallowed the emotions boiling in his throat. Before she could worry there was something jam-packed into their schedule, he grinned. "This bookstore has a fun activity. When I heard about it, I knew you had to try."

Breanna raised a brow. "Activity?"

"Yes." Lila looked like she might bounce away with joy. "This. This is the favorite thing."

"Today." One of her assistants laughed as she gave her boss a big grin. "She says that about all sorts of things."

"Why don't you explain?" Sebastian nodded. She clearly wanted to, and it was her store and activity. No need for him to step in. Though he had a role to play.

"Oh." Lila clapped. "Thank you. I saw a television show once where everyone ran around with a shopping cart. As a kid, I wanted to do it so bad, but in a bookstore."

"You have shopping carts?" Breanna looked at the aisles. They were tiny and stuffed with books.

"No." She bit her lip and leaned in conspiratorially. "I wanted to do it that way, but there isn't room. It was either less aisles or more books."

"Oh, easy choice! Always more books." His wife chuckled, and he thought Breanna and Lila might have been fast friends if she wasn't queen. In this role, there was always a power imbalance that made true friendship nearly impossible.

"Exactly." She motioned to Sebastian. "So, the king is your cart."

He made a show of pumping his muscles, and everyone laughed. "Not sure that is what I was going for." Sebastian made a playful pouty face as Breanna leaned into him.

"You are fine." She kissed him, lingering for just a second. How a few days alone could change so many things.

"You get to walk around for fifteen minutes. Take stock of what you want then. At the end of the fifteen minutes, you get five minutes to pick out as many as you can. The only catch is that Sebastian must be able to carry them all to the checkout without dropping them. Anything in his stack will be twenty percent off."

"Ready?" Sebastian held up his wrist, tapping on the watch. This would be the best use of it he'd ever had. "Set."

Breanna's eyes roamed the store. She was already breathing fast.

"Go!"

She took off. Not running but moving very quick. She

slowed as she reached the romance section and started to pull a few books forward.

"That might be cheating." He laughed as she stuck out her tongue.

"I listened to the rules of this game. No one said anything about not being able to touch the books while I looked around." She raced down the aisle to the general fiction area.

"True." He chuckled as he kept up with her. "Not sure my muscles are going to be able to handle this."

"Better start stretching!" Breanna giggled as she rushed for the hobby section and pulled a few books on sewing and one on crocheting animals. Then it was on to the education section.

There she pulled a few books on early education and lesson planning.

He stopped to look at those titles.

Build Your Classroom for Student Success
Burned Out and Busted: The Road Back for the Exhausted Educator
Everything You Need to Know About Lesson Planning in the Digital World

The titles made zero sense for a queen. She had a degree in education—one she'd never use.

He looked at the three books she'd pulled. Did she want those? She'd wanted to teach. But that was out of her reach now. The queen couldn't walk into an elementary classroom as a regular instructor. It would cause havoc.

Still, there had to be a way to give her something of her own.

"How much time do I have left on my expedition phase?" Breanna was across the store.

He looked at his watch, but before he could answer, Lila called out. "Two minutes twenty seconds, Your Highness."

"Lovely!" She bounced back over to fiction and grabbed a few more titles there. Then raced to the starting line. "Let's go, Sebastian."

"I think you still have a minute or so left?" He looked at his watch as he walked back towards her.

"I know." She pulled one leg up to her back. Then the other. Stretching. "You ready?"

"Honestly?" He shook his head as his wife readied herself. "I'm a little terrified of you right now. Swear you won't hold it against me if I can't carry everything."

Breanna looked him up and down, and playfully held her hands out, measuring his torso. "I think you will do just fine, Sebastian."

"Promise me." This was the first time he'd seen her do something that was just for her. Something she wanted. And if he couldn't carry the whole load. He didn't want to fail at this. Fail her.

She stepped into his arms and kissed him. Lila and the assistants let out a sigh behind them.

"You are going to do fine." She tapped his nose and looked at Lila. "Let's do this!"

Lila could not have asked for a more excited customer. "All right." She nodded to the queen and held up a stopwatch. "You have five minutes, and the king must be able to carry the books."

"Oh, he will carry the books." Breanna laughed and then ran as Lila shouted *Go*.

Books piled into his arms. It was a flash, and he was staggering behind her, letting her shift the books as she added more. Her ability to stack and add was truly impressive even though his arms were burning when Lila called time.

"I can barely see over the top." Sebastian didn't dare laugh or do anything that might jostle the mountain of books in his arms. His muscles were shaking, and he could barely make out the path to the checkout desk, but he was not going disappoint his wife by dropping her precious cargo.

"You just have to set them on the counter." Lila's voice guided his way, but he could hear the surprise in her tone. She was expecting a catastrophe, too.

Breathe. Step. Breathe. Step.

"Almost there." Breanna stood beside him. Calculating the distance or the likelihood of a topple, he didn't know. And there was no way he was turning his head in any way to upset the delicate balance.

Breathe. Step. Breathe. Step.

"Made it." Breanna clapped as he set the pile on the counter. "Nice job." She squeezed him tight, then moved to the other side of her bounty. "Ready for the picture."

"Oh." Lila made another noncommittal noise. "I was under the impression that you didn't want a picture." The proprietor's eyes cut to Sebastian before landing on Breanna.

Breanna pointed to the wall behind the counter. It was covered in pictures of women, men and children posing next to their bounty. None of it quite as hefty as the queen's, but the smiles all brilliant. "It's part of the process, right? I mean…" His wife's gaze cut to him.

"I think Raul thought you might like privacy on your picks." Sebastian shrugged. "You're the queen, after all."

"I want the books shared. I picked local authors, books I have loved, books I look forward to loving, and nonfiction topics that are important to me. These will sell out if people know the queen bought them. Both in Lila's store and online. The authors will reap so much from the free publicity."

"Were any of them your choices?" His tone was rougher than he meant, and he saw Lila step behind the counter, giving them a little distance. This was a gift for Breanna.

For her. Just her.

"Of course." Breanna pointed to the top book. "This one

is a local author that sells at the booths in our market, next to a stall that sells the cutest purses. I think Brie actually has one of the purses. And this topic—" she pointed to the burn-out book "—is vital for educators."

She pointed lower. "Did you know there are studies that show most teachers leave the field in the first three years?"

But what about books for her?

"Oh." She grabbed a bright blue one with a winged crea-ture on the front cradling what looked like a human woman. "This one is simply a pure delight of gooey sex that every-one should read. It should be a bestseller in its genre but…" Breanna shrugged.

"So yes, I did pick these for me, but there were other thoughts, too. I am the queen. We have a duty. Something you are so fond of repeating. You chose a queen that wanted the title and the duty that came with it." She huffed and looked around him.

She was right. When he'd walked into her parents' man-sion weeks ago, he'd wanted someone who wanted the title. Someone who would let her life belong to the country so she could be called queen. Someone who was doing exactly what Breanna was.

"Sorry, Lila. We don't normally argue in front of people." Breanna bit her lip as color traveled up her neck.

"We don't normally argue." Sebastian added.

"Not sure that is true."

His mouth opened, but he didn't know what to say. Luck-ily his wife was rushing past it, too.

Breanna pointed to the books. "This was a lovely treat. I got to run around a bookstore picking things out. I got to watch you carry them without tripping, and now, I want to finish this. And yes, it will help others, but these are also my choice."

"But you've already read at least that one." He pointed to the book with the winged creature.

"Yes, but it was downstairs when your people gathered my things. So, I need a new copy. I've reread it at least a dozen times. It's like an old friend. You get it, right, Lila?"

"I do." Lila's answer was quick, and he suspected the shop owner would normally chatter on about all the books she also considered old friends. Dissect what made the characters or plot memorable. Make recommendations for future friends.

None of which she did now. The assistants had disappeared to the stock room. Likely sent there by Lila when this disagreement started. He saw the shop owner look in the back and suspected she was considering if she needed to do the same.

He'd instructed the staff to pick up her room and put her belongings in the suites she occupied in the castle. Told them it needed to be exactly as it had been. A ludicrous order.

And she'd never mentioned that they didn't have all of her things. In fact, the only complaints his wife had issued regarding herself were that her feet hurt. And only after she could no longer stand in her shoes.

Duty was his life, and he'd picked the perfect partner for it. Except he could see the life she'd live. The duty that she wouldn't let overwhelm her like it did him. But that would claw at every part of her life.

Because of him. Because of his title and hers.

"Smile and take the picture, please." Breanna's dark gaze was holding back tears. She'd thought of something lovely. Something helpful. Something that would make a difference in many creatives' lives. And he was trampling on it.

"Of course. I am sorry, Breanna." He stepped next to the books and she stood on the other side.

"Smile." Lila stood in front of them, holding her phone up. "I will post it to social media and then print it for the wall."

She looked at the image, swallowed and then pointed to the stack. "Umm…the light isn't quite right. Queen Breanna can you move your head just a little that way?" She gestured for her to turn her face more towards the books.

It was a trick his father had used frequently. One a public relations manager turned bookshop owner would certainly know. A smile that wasn't as bright could be hidden with the right tilt of the head. The right focus.

He'd stolen his wife's smile with his worries over her books. There was no way for him to kick himself, but he'd find a way to make this up to her. Some way.

CHAPTER FOURTEEN

ROLLING OVER IN her bed, she reached for her husband but knew he was already up. They'd returned to the palace three days ago. And he'd risen well before six each day.

At least he wasn't putting anything on his schedule until eight. It was a small win and one she hoped would stick.

"You're awake." Sebastian swooped in with a breakfast tray and a big smile. At least he still looked rested.

"Yup." She looked at the clock then at him. She wasn't going to ask it directly, but if he volunteered the wake-up time…

"Earlier than yesterday but after five." He shrugged, then set the tray in front of her. "The good thing about me waking early is that I can make you breakfast in bed."

He leaned over, brushing his lips against hers. The quick nature of the kiss left her wanting for more. And as happy as she was to have breakfast in bed…again…she'd prefer to wake next to the man she'd married.

"Today's delight is breakfast tacos. Made with flour tortillas, avocado, seasoned tofu and some cheese." He bowed, so pleased with himself. He was cooking. For her. It was nice.

Sweet.

Before their honeymoon, she'd have given anything to have such attention. Now though. It felt off. Like he was worried she might float away.

She wanted him, but the authentic man.

"Thank you." Breanna looked at the tray. "No plate for you?" There hadn't been one for him yesterday either.

"This is just for you." Sebastian smiled as he moved to open the curtains. Bright rays fell across his face. Light bounced off the hints of blond in his dark hair. Mentally she snapped a picture, wishing her creative side leaned towards painting.

"If you wake at five, wake me. I'll come to the kitchen with you. We can cook together." Breanna took a bite of the taco. It was delicious. Like everything else he made in his personal kitchen.

Sebastian nodded as he looked out the window, but she knew that he wouldn't. He'd sneak out, letting her sleep. Then bring her something sweet or savory.

She finished the taco, grabbed the platter, got out of bed, and set it on the dressing table. Then she went to where her husband still stood.

"What are you thinking?" She wrapped her hands around his waist, grateful when his fingers locked with hers.

Sebastian took a deep breath. "Honestly?"

"Of course." She wanted the truth, but the breakfast tacos in her belly seemed to flip. "Tell me." She pressed her head to his shoulder, glad that he was turned away from her so he couldn't see the worry she knew was etched on her face.

"I was wondering what you might have done if you'd gotten to teach." He turned in her arms, pulling her close. "If you'd have used your sewing skills to wear fun outfits to go with the lecture."

"Lecture." She laughed. "I was an early education major. I would never have given lectures." She kissed his nose. "Most days I probably would have come home sticky."

He pulled her closer, like he didn't want any distance between them. "I'm serious, Breanna. You would be getting ready right now. Packing a lunch and probably thinking over how to make sure each student excelled for the day. I bet your classroom would have been bright and colorful."

"Annie would have ensured that color was everywhere." Breanna lifted her head, hoping he'd kiss her. Focus on today, on where they were now. Together.

The life he'd described was never going to be hers. Yes, she'd trained for it. Yes, it was something she'd have enjoyed. Probably excelled at. Yes, her upcycled outfits would have played a role.

In another timeline, in a different place, that Breanna would have been happy.

But this Breanna, the woman she was now in this place, was happy, too.

"I think I'd have enjoyed the classroom. My favorite age was third grade. They are learning to read small chapter books. Still excited to be in school. We'd have painted and sung math songs."

His shoulders slumped.

"But—" she held him tightly "—I am happy here, too." It wasn't hard to say. This wasn't the path she'd have chosen for her life. Maybe that was good.

Life was made from the unexpected. The gifts you didn't know you needed. The people you never expected to fall into your life. To love.

Love.

The word hit her mind, hammering its truth through her. She loved Sebastian. She didn't know how it had happened. How she was so certain that her heart belonged to him.

This wasn't the life she'd asked for. It was better.

"Sebastian." She stepped back and waited for him to turn. "Sebastian."

Finally, he turned, but it was the king standing here now. The shift was subtle. Less movement in the jaw. Eyes hiding emotions.

"I am happy here. Playing a what-if game can be fun." In the right circumstances, she mentally added. "But it gets us nowhere. After all, what if you weren't the king? Would you be a chef? You'd handle the hours well."

Breanna smiled, but the king didn't show any signs of finding fun in the words.

Instead, he adjusted, like the mantle he'd worn since birth was sliding fully into place. "I never had any choices."

"Neither did I." Breanna lifted her hand, running it along his chin. "But we have choices now."

"Do we?"

"Yes." She didn't stamp her foot, though she desperately ached to add emphasis to the moment. "We are the king and queen."

"I know."

"Do you?" She stroked his chin. The five o'clock shadow he'd worn at the beach house had disappeared the morning they'd packed up to return to the palace. "Do you know that you can choose?"

"Breanna."

She laid a finger over his lips, stopping the argument she saw brewing in his eyes. "You can choose if you wear the title of king. Or if it wears you.

"Here and now, with me, we are just Sebastian and Breanna. In these rooms, with no one watching. There is no crown. Okay?"

He nodded, and she let out a sigh of relief before removing her finger from his lips.

She replaced it with her lips. He stood still for a minute, then wrapped his arms around her waist.

Breanna drank him in. These moments were the best moments with Sebastian. Her husband. The man she loved. The man she wanted to be happy. They'd wear crowns the rest of their lives. But in this room, with each other, they'd just be Sebastian and Breanna.

"Starting the day with kisses from my wife is certainly my favorite way to begin the day." His fingers caressed her cheek.

He'd started his day alone in the kitchen, but she had no desire to point that out right now. "It's my favorite way to start the day, too."

"Any idea what we are doing for this date night?" Alessio slapped Sebastian on the shoulder as he stepped up to the table Hector had put Sebastian and Breanna's name plate on.

"Nope." Sebastian looked at the tables, each with the name of a couple. Just their name. No titles. "Breanna agreed to this when they were dancing several weeks ago. I guess he bet her that I'd be jealous."

"Were you?" Alessio's gaze went to his wife, who was laughing with Breanna and Hector over something.

"Yes." There was no need to lie, particularly to Alessio. "I didn't have any reason to be. Not just because there is nothing between Breanna and her friend, but because I didn't really know my wife at the time."

"And now that you know her?" Alessio grinned, his eyes saying there was no need for Sebastian to confirm the feelings.

He looked over to his wife. Annie had joined Hector, Brie and Breanna. The four were in a world all to themselves.

"Quite the group." Beau, Brie's brother, stepped up.

A queen, a princess, the sister of a queen and a party planning entrepreneur. A group bound together by friendship and family. Not titles and rank. Something his wife might have easily had with so many others, if he hadn't marched into her home demanding a bride.

"Any idea what we are doing tonight?" He needed to change the subject. Needed to focus on something, anything other than the feeling that he'd stolen something from Breanna he could never replace.

"Nope." Beau shrugged. "Briella told me to be here. That I was on a 'date' with Breanna's sister, Annie. Whatever Hector has planned is a couple's event, and they needed to round out the numbers. So here I am."

"Brie." Alessio crossed his arms. The nickname was the princess's preferred name and the only one anyone besides her family called her.

Color traveled up Beau's neck as he nodded. "Brie. I know that, and I will get better at it."

Alessio nodded, a man in love with a woman who wanted nothing more than to protect her.

Once more Sebastian's eyes found his bride. She looked over at him, smiled, then waved. The world narrowed to her dark curls, the curve of her lips, the light he knew was dancing in her eyes. All he wanted to do was make sure she had everything.

Was this what Alessio felt when he looked at Brie?

The all-encompassing urge to give her whatever she needed. The desire to make her happy and never let her down.

Love.

He was in love with his wife. With the woman he'd trapped into becoming his queen. A role from which there was no exit.

"You are thinking very deeply." Breanna was beside him, her lips brushing his. "He gets this far-off look when he is worried." She winked at Alessio. "But there are no worries here tonight."

She kissed his cheek and pointed to their table. "Showtime." Her fingers wrapped through his as she pulled him to their table. "This is kind of our first date."

Not kind of. It was their first date. And even in this, she was helping out a friend.

"What are we doing?"

Breanna's face lit up as a group of people, each carrying a box, walked out, depositing the closed boxes on the tables.

"Do not open the boxes until I give the instructions." Hector was standing in the center of the four tables, the ringleader of whatever circus he'd designed.

"You are going to love this." Breanna clapped as Hector gestured to the boxes.

"So, you are in on the activity?" Sebastian put his hand around her waist, enjoying the feel of her laying her head against his shoulder.

"Of course. This is based off some game show he saw a while back. When he told me the plan on the dance floor, I knew we had to be the first to give it a go. There are all sorts of activities, or at least that is his plan, but when he told me about this one—I knew you had to try it." Breanna bumped her hip against his hip. "Now, pay attention."

Hector turned to the table behind him. "Tonight, we cook." He gestured to the three flags on the table. "Sweet. Savory. Spicy. When I say go, one member of your team will run up here and grab a flag. You then have one hour using the items in the box to make a dinner item that is what your flag suggests. Ovens are behind you, and there is a hot plate in the bottom of your box. At the end of the hour, we will judge the dishes, and the winner gets a prize."

Breanna clapped. "This is going to be so much fun. Can I please run?"

"Of course." Sebastian squeezed her tightly. "Try to get anything besides sweet."

"Annie, you and Beau need to get something besides sweet. Otherwise Sebastian will win," Alessio called out. "Unless anyone besides the king is hiding a secret talent for cooking. But the man hates making sweet things."

"Not true." Sebastian stuck his tongue out. "I just don't *like* to make sweet things."

"Not sweet." Breanna stepped beside the table, her knees bent, ready to dash into the fray for him. "Don't worry. I got this."

"Go!"

His wife took off, reaching the table a full second before anyone else. She grabbed the third flag, the savory one, and bounced in front of Alessio, smiling as she headed back to their table.

"May as well pass the trophy to the king and queen now." His brother playfully rolled his eyes as Brie came back holding up the sweet flag with a huge smile for her husband.

Annie had spicy, and she and Beau both looked a little lost as they gazed at the flag and their box.

"Let's do this." Breanna planted the flag and then started pulling things out of the box. "I have no idea what these spices are, but my husband does." She grabbed the chef's hat in the box and placed it on his head. "Tonight, I am your lovely assistant."

His throat closed as the words left her mouth. That was the plan. For her to be his lovely assistant. A queen to get the press off his back. A role anyone could play if they followed the right script. An interchangeable person to give the people of Celiana what they wanted. A lovely assistant.

But she was so much more. So very much more.

"What if you cook tonight?" The words left his mouth before he even knew what he was saying. Lifting the chef's hat, he held it out to her. "You cook, and I will be the lovely assistant."

She looked at the hat, then at him. "You are very handsome, but don't you want to show off your skills?"

"I am here to have a fun date night with my wife. That is all I care about." He kissed her cheek, then set the hat on her head. "That looks good on you. Though everything looks good on you."

She lifted on her toes, pressing a kiss to his ear before whispering, "I think you like it best when I wear nothing at all."

"So true." He leaned toward her, straightening the cap. "Tonight isn't about winning. It's a date night. Just for the two of us."

"I have no idea what I am doing, Sebastian." Breanna held up the rosemary and peppermint. "I mean, I know these are herbs, and this one—" she sniffed the peppermint "—is mint."

"I got you, and you got this." He stepped beside her and looked at the ingredients. "How about a veggie pot pie?"

Breanna looked at the ingredients, too, and then laughed. "I am looking at these like I have any other idea." She gave him a little salute as she giggled. "All right. I'm the cook."

"It almost feels like cheating." Breanna sighed as she sat beside Sebastian on the little couch.

Their pot pie had gone into the oven ten minutes ago. It needed another ten, and then they'd just leave it on warm.

Brie and Alessio were whipping up what looked to be brownie batter with a fancy icing. Annie and Beau hadn't even started whatever they planned to make. Probably not the best sign, but her sister didn't seem overly distressed by whatever was causing their delay.

One of the great things about pot pies was that they only took a few minutes to whip up. Particularly when the host provided a premade pie crust.

"It's hardly cheating." He wrapped his arm around her. She'd done all the work for the pot pie. He'd supervised the steps, but most of the seasoning she'd done to her taste. And watching her realize that there wasn't an exact recipe—that she could just toss in extra rosemary because it tasted good to her—was one of the top five moments of his life.

And with the exception of Alessio returning home, the other moments all revolved around Breanna, too.

"What if they don't like it?" Breanna looked over at the oven, the minutes counting down.

"They will." He squeezed her shoulder and kissed her head. "They will like it."

"And if they don't, they probably won't tell me." Breanna laughed.

"Probably not." Sebastian let out a sigh. "One hardly ever tells the king and queen the truth."

His wife sat up, her eyes wide and hurt. "Sebastian, I meant that our family and friends would spare my feelings. They would ooh and ahh over the dish, as I will for theirs. Not because of their titles."

"Right." Her words made sense, of course. Even if he wasn't sure they were the complete truth. Alessio rarely spared his feelings, but in a group…in a group he'd defer until later. Beau, Annie and Hector. He doubted they'd see more than the crowns that were metaphorically always attached to Breanna and his heads when critique time came around.

"No." Breanna sat up straighter. "No, this isn't a 'right,' moment."

"I like it when you use air quotes." He winked, looking over her shoulder to see if anyone was noticing the disagreement going on. Alessio and Brie now had piping bags out. Annie and Beau were studiously cutting up something at their table with Hector by their side, laughing and trying to break the clear tension between the two of them.

Breanna looked over her shoulder, too, then back at him. "Worried someone might hear us arguing? It's one of the things we do best." She crossed her arms and shook her head. "These are our friends and family. Here, you are Sebastian, not the king."

"I'm always the king, Breanna." He let out a heavy sigh,

hating how he'd soured the evening. "As you are always the queen. And arguing isn't what we do best."

Why did she keep bring up their tendency to spat?

"I said one of the things." Breanna patted his knees. "It's not a bad thing."

"Arguing is bad." It was the definition of the word. His parents had never argued. In fact, he didn't remember seeing any kind of disagreement. They'd lived separate lives, but when they were together, it was not quite peaceful but serene enough.

"No." The timer dinged on the pot pie, but Breanna didn't move. "Arguing is communicating. And when done in a healthy fashion, it's positive. We don't yell at each other. We don't scream. We discuss. We hash things out. That is healthy."

"Somehow I can't imagine the Galanis patriarch and matriarch having solid communication capabilities." The few times he'd seen her parents together, the loathing they had for the other was hardly kept at bay. In fact, he was fairly certain the only thing keeping them together was the mutual desire for more wealth, and probably spite.

"They didn't." Breanna blew out a breath. "I took a family communications class in university. Parents can get miffed when teachers give feedback that their children are less than perfect."

The timer continued sounding. "We need to get the pot pie out."

"We do. But this is more important. You are more than your crown, Sebastian. I don't know why you can't see that. And your wife pointing it out, not fighting but arguing with that belief, is healthy dialogue."

He could see Alessio looking at the oven with the time. Then his brother glanced over at the couch, his eyes widening before turning back to the brownies. "Breanna, we can discuss this at the palace."

"This is family and friends. We aren't fighting. We aren't yelling. We are talking. They aren't listening any more than you are listening to whatever argument Annie and Beau are having right now."

Annie and Beau were working on their own. Neither appeared to be saying anything, and her back was towards them. "They aren't arguing."

"Yes. They are. I can read Annie like Alessio can read you." Breanna stood up. "The people that matter see you. Just you. But if you can't see past your crown, then that is one you." She moved towards the oven.

"Oh. It bubbled over. It will probably still taste good, but it looks a fright."

"So do the brownies!" Brie called, her laugher echoing in the room.

"My cheese dip will *actually* be spicy, but it looks a little like yellow mud," Annie responded, her eyes cutting to Beau.

Alessio held up a brownie that could only be described as a mess. "I don't know. I think this is gorgeous. It could fetch a nice price at the farmer's market."

"Only because you are the heir to the throne." Brie kissed her husband.

It was funny…because it was true.

And forgetting it wasn't an option.

CHAPTER FIFTEEN

"YOU SURE YOU'RE okay with Alessio and me going up to the ski slopes today?" Sebastian looked at his calendar.

He wasn't surprised that Breanna had wedged a day off into it, but he was a little shocked at how much he wanted to go.

"Why wouldn't I be?" She kissed his nose as she looked at her calendar. "I have more than enough meetings to keep me busy." She stuck out her tongue and laughed. "Go. You deserve a day on the slopes. And you will have more fun with Alessio than you will with me."

A knock echoed on the chamber door. "That will be your brother."

Alessio stepped in a moment later. "Hey, um, Brie is a little under the weather. We think it's because…" Alessio pulled at the back of his neck, color traveling up his neck.

"Because?" Breanna clapped; she'd seen Brie make a face after smelling Annie's cheese dip the other night. She probably should have warned people that Annie could put fire on her tongue and think it needed a bit more kick. She didn't want to assume, but she thought she knew what Alessio was getting ready to tell them.

"What?" Sebastian looked from Breanna to his brother. "I feel like I am missing something."

"Brie's pregnant."

"Yes!" Breanna danced over to Alessio, gave him a hug,

and then stepped back to let Sebastian have the time with his brother.

"Congratulations. Did you want to stay off the slopes today?"

"No, but since we aren't certain that the illness is pregnancy-related, she wanted me to give you a choice about coming. I think she wants me out of the house. I am a worrier, according to my wife."

"That makes sense. I still want to hit the slopes, if you do. And now we can talk baby things." Sebastian slapped his brother on the back, then came over to her.

He kissed her deeply, "Thank you for setting this up. I—"

For a second, she thought he might say the words she craved hearing. But instead, he pushed a curl behind her ear and kissed her cheek.

"I will see you when I get back."

"I don't think the flu that captured Brie and Alessio is going to spare me." Sebastian let out a sigh as he lay in bed. His wife was snuggled next to him.

"You are burning up." She pressed her lips to his cheek.

"I don't feel hot." It was kind of true. The chills wracking his body refused to take any of the heat pouring over his head. He felt cold...and then hot...and then freezing.

"I think you should accept that you need a sick day." She kissed his forehead, then pulled back. Breanna climbed out of bed and grabbed her phone. She typed something out quickly. "Any chance there is a thermometer in your bathroom?"

Fog coated his brain, trapping words. Plucking them out of the mental ether was exhausting. "Why would I have a thermometer?"

Breanna clucked her tongue and muttered something under her breath.

"All right. I've canceled your engagements for the next two days. Do not argue with me."

Even if he wanted to, there was no charge in his battery. Maybe he could still manage some correspondence from bed.

A knock sounded at the door, and Breanna stepped to it. "Raul, is that you?"

"Yes, Your Highness."

"Did you bring the thermometer?" She still hadn't opened the door.

"Yes. And the other things you requested."

He wanted to ask what else she'd requested, but his eyes were so heavy. A short nap and then he'd text Raul to bring any papers he needed.

"Thank you. Please leave them at the door and back away. I've already been exposed, but no sense having the staff take more risk than necessary." She waited a moment, then opened the door.

He heard her say something about schedules and thought he heard his mother's voice. But then the nap won.

Breanna kissed her husband's forehead, thankful that he was cool. Day three of their lock-in and he was finally turning a corner. Sebastian's fever had broken last night. But he was still exhausted.

He was rounding the cusp, as she tried to ignore the tickle in the back of her throat and the sweat at her temple that she knew meant the virus was on her heels now.

Smoothing the dress she'd asked Raul to bring her, she stepped into the king's suite. Which now had her sewing machine and her latest project to help her pass the time.

She checked herself in the small mirror and smiled. It was a silly alphabet dress that she'd made when she was student teaching. The ABCs were splayed in no real pattern. A few pencils and apples were sprinkled in for good measure.

One did not put it on unless you were a teacher. The kids she'd taught as a student teacher had loved this dress. And the others she'd made. It was cliché, but she enjoyed dressing up for her class. At least as queen she could reuse the outfits when she did outings for small children.

She'd been scheduled to attend a primary school today. The students were putting on a poetry reading they'd worked for weeks on. Seven-and eight-year-olds took their writing as seriously as any national poet. She was to be the exalted guest. The kids were excited to read to a queen.

But there was no way she was risking little bodies with what the doctor had confirmed was influenza. Particularly since she was fighting her own battle with it now.

Still, she'd asked Raul to check with the teacher to see if there was a way for her to attend virtually. The woman was apparently very open to it, but as soon as the virtual call was over, Breanna was crawling into bed.

"Good morning, class." The teacher's voice echoed over the computer.

She'd been instructed to keep her computer screen off until she was announced since the kids thought she'd had to cancel. A good plan in case she'd been too busy taking care of Sebastian. Or too sick herself.

"Today we are reading our poems, and I have a special surprise." The teacher clapped, and the squeals her students let out on the word *silence* stopped. A well-run classroom.

"Remember how the queen was supposed to come?"

A chorus of yeses echoed through the speaker. Little voices that brought an immediate smile to Breanna's face. She'd have enjoyed the life of teaching.

"Well, she is taking care of the king, who has the flu, but…" The teacher did a little drumroll on her desk, and the students followed.

At the top of the roll, Breanna started her camera and then

waved to the room full of excited kids. A cough built in her throat, but she smiled through it.

Was this what Sebastian always did? Probably.

"So, we are going to read our poems for the queen after all." The teacher looked at the camera, bowed her head. "Who wants to go first?"

Most of the room's hands shot up. The teacher laughed, walked to her desk, and picked up what looked to be a decorated tin can with popsicle sticks. "You know the rules. If I call your name, you can pass, but you don't get another chance to go until everyone else has gone."

She drew the first name, and a little girl with pigtails and a blue dress stood up. She read a devotion to her cat—Pickles.

After that was a funny poem about a little brother that the boy didn't want but was learning to love. And then another poem about a pet, a rabbit this time.

The afternoon wore on. It was fun and great, but the throbbing in her head, the pain in her throat, the aches in her bones grew with each passing second. But her smile never dropped.

When the final child rose to give her reading, Breanna was taking strategic breaths through her nose to keep the coughing fit at bay.

A few more minutes. A few more minutes. Hang on. Do not interrupt this child's experience. She gets the same as her classmates. A few more minutes.

The mantra repeated in her mind as she kept the smile on her face. When it was finally over, she waved one last time, knowing that if she said anything, it would be covered by coughs.

Shutting off the camera, she let out a shudder, and then the coughs erupted. Her body rocked as she tried to gain any semblance of control, but the coughs refused to abate.

"Honey." Sebastian's arms wrapped around her shoulders, gently lifting her up.

All of a sudden, there was no way to ignore the ache in her bones. She let out a little cry, but Breanna was pretty sure the coughs covered it.

"Into bed. I'll get you some lemon tea, but rest is what you need." Sebastian guided her to his room.

"Do you want me to go back to my room?" The words were garbled. The brain fog her husband had talked about seemed to leap from his brain to hers. She honestly wasn't certain she'd make it down the hall.

"You are in your room. Our room." He kissed the top of her cheek as her head traced the pillow. "You really pushed yourself for those kids."

"I needed to." They'd worked so hard. They'd been promised a royal, and… Words evaporated, and she wasn't even sure she'd gotten them all out.

"Uh-huh. I get it." His voice was far away. Dreamlike words. "And now you do, too."

Sebastian's lips were cool on her burning forehead. There were words she needed to say. A thought she wanted to get out. But no matter how hard she tried to grasp at it, the darkness pushed it farther away.

CHAPTER SIXTEEN

SHE WASN'T SURE how long she'd lain in this bed, but Breanna did know that she had no desire to spend another moment in it. Pulling off the coverings, she gave herself a shake. There were three things she wanted to do. Find her husband. Take a shower. And put on new clothes.

Preferably in that order, but at this moment, she didn't particularly care.

Stepping into the study, she wasn't surprised to find Sebastian at the desk she'd pushed out of the way for her sewing machine and fabrics back in its rightful spot. The mountain of paperwork was disheartening but not unexpected, either. "Did you take any time for yourself while I've been under the weather?"

Sebastian's head popped up. His hand moved too quickly, and the bottle of ink he was using to sign documents tipped.

"And that is why you need to put the lid back on if you insist on using a fountain pen dipped in ink." Breanna didn't laugh—her chuckle was too likely to bring on a cough—but she smiled so her husband knew she meant it as a joke.

Sebastian was at her side, ignoring the spill and the other documents it would wreck.

"Your desk will get stained." Breanna looked over his shoulder, but he just raised his hand to her forehead and let out a sigh.

"No fever." Laying his head against hers, he pulled her

close. "And the desk has a hundred years' worth of stains on it." He kissed her head. "Want a shower?"

"Do I stink that bad?" She laughed, and a small cough followed, but at least it no longer wracked her body.

"You are gorgeous, even minutes past your sickbed, but the first thing I wanted when I got up was to see you and then to shower."

To see you.

She'd felt the exact same thing.

I love you.

The words were on the tip of her tongue, waiting to drop. Still, she held back.

Why?

Maybe because she didn't want to say it while she still looked a fright from her own flu battle. Maybe...

Sebastian gazed at her, like he, too, had words that wouldn't fall.

Shower—then—then it was time to tell her husband how she felt.

Sebastian stood in what until yesterday was his reading room and desperately tried to control the anxious wobbles in his soul. This had seemed like such a good idea after the headlines regarding Breanna's "choice of outfit" for the poetry reading. The fashion columns had critiqued the ABC dress no end. The reviews online were mostly positive. But the main headlines discussed the reviews that weren't. Plastered them up front before pointing out that even the fashion icons who claimed to hate the dress admitted that it was a good option for a children's poetry event.

The cut. The tailoring. Everything she'd worked on had been pulled apart.

Because he'd fallen ill, she was sitting in the palace rather than in the classroom. Maybe if she'd attended in person, she'd have been spared most of the comments regarding her attire.

But that wasn't the only thing they'd discussed. A few podcast interviews had dissected her look on the camera. How she'd seemed focused elsewhere. Things that should have stopped the moment the palace announced she was under the weather.

Instead, the news had buzzed that the palace was crafting that narrative to give her peace after she'd looked "bored" with the children.

The thing she loved most, along with her love for children, tarnished because he'd taken a day off at the ski slopes.

He'd had to do something.

The buzz around the dress, and the fact that no one knew his wife's talent, spurred this room. She could use it to create and maybe…just maybe to teach, too. At least online. A little piece of the dream she'd once wanted, even if she hadn't put it into words for herself.

He'd put out a statement regarding the dress and the fact that the queen had made it. That most of her garments, even her wedding dress, were crafted on machines with love by her own hands.

That had sent the news cycle into a spiral. And stopped the news about her appearance at the school. Glowing articles about a queen making her own wardrobe. Creating her own custom pieces. The negative statements had eased away. And now one of the articles praising her was framed and hanging on the wall, next to a ring light and recording equipment.

She was too talented to hide this. Too special to let this gift go unnoticed. This could have been her dream. If she'd just allowed herself to have one.

He couldn't undo the crown on her head. But he could give her a dream that was for her. Show her this and then tell her how much he loved her. How lucky he was that she was his queen.

"What?" Breanna's voice hit his back. "Your reading room—"

"Never got used anyway. So…" He spun, showing off the racks of fabric the staff had carefully shifted from her old rooms. "And don't worry, they all came through the outside door. No one else got the flu."

That was an impressive feat. One he never would have thought of. But his wife had jumped into action, keeping everyone away to protect them and care for him. The woman never thought of herself. So, this was for her. Something that was Breanna's.

She looked at the machines, each in a separate area. One of the staff was into fabric works and was able to help the team understand why aesthetics weren't as important as function, with each machine having a designated place and role to play.

"Wow." Breanna's hand covered her mouth. "This. This is…" Whatever she planned to say dropped away as her eyes found the framed article and ring light.

Time slowed as she stepped towards it, shaking her head. "Breanna—"

"Why is there an article about my sewing? You framed it?"

Tears coated her eyes, but he couldn't understand why. Her skill. Her creativity. Those were worthy of praise. So much more than just the crown on her head. "People were writing articles about the queen looking upset at the poetry event. Bored. And there was a lot of focus on the ABC dress. The headlines before I told them about this were rather unflattering."

"Unflattering to the crown." Her words were soft, broken.

This was not how this was supposed to go. "I'm proud of the work my queen does. I want the world to know that the queen is talented." This was Breanna.

"My queen." Breanna let out a breath. "That is all I am, isn't it?"

"We had to answer, Breanna. Make them understand the queen—"

"No, we didn't." Breanna bit her lip, shaking her head. "And *we* didn't answer. You answered. Without talking to me."

Okay. That was a fair assessment. And one he'd worried over—apparently with good cause. "You were ill. The headlines…"

"Right. The headlines. The king and queen must respond. It is our duty to be available. Always available. Everything we do belongs to the country."

"I was proud of you. Your work is so impressive, and you were ill but smiled through it." Wrong words.

"What I meant was—"

"I know what you meant. I finally stepped fully into the role, right? The all-encompassing crown, serving even when I was far too ill." His wife crossed her arms and looked down at the ring light. "Lighting for me to show off on what, the palace social media? Or do I have to run my own video streams now, so that everyone can see what *the queen* can do?"

How had this gone downhill so fast? This was a gift. A surprise.

"No. You don't have to *do* anything. But the country—"

"The country comes first. Everything is for Celiana. Even the one thing I told you was for me. Mine. The thing I didn't share."

Sebastian pointed to the article. "Do you know what they were running before this piece? They were breaking down the cut. Discussing the neckline and why you would choose such a silly design."

"Who cares?" Breanna damp curls bounced as her bottom lip quivered. "I asked—no—I told you that this was mine. Weeks ago. Before I…" She bit her lip so hard, he worried blood was coating her tongue.

"We have an image. A duty. This humanizes you. It gives…"

"I don't care. In these rooms, I told you I just wanted to be Sebastian and Breanna. Just us." Brenna wiped a tear from her eye. "This is my job. It is not who I am."

It wasn't that simple. It would be nice if it was. But they were the king and queen everywhere. Even when they didn't want to be. Everything was tinted with the golden hue of their crowns. "You are the queen. You married the king. This is your life. We are the king and queen. It is all we are."

She'd done so well the other day. Hiding her illness to make the students happy. It was what a queen did. What a royal did. She'd truly become the queen that day.

Breanna turned, looking at the image on the wall. The article he'd been so proud of now destroying the gift he'd wanted to give.

"You're right. This is my life. I am the queen." She sucked in a breath.

Words he'd ached for her to say. Words he wanted her to believe, but her tone, the resignation in it, destroyed him.

"It's a role anyone could play, if they knew the script."

"Breanna—"

"I am going back to my rooms, Your Highness." There was no emotion in her tone. No fire. No spirit.

"Because you want to?"

"What I want doesn't matter. It's all for the crown. You showed that." Breanna pressed her hand to his shoulder as she started past him. "For what it is worth, until just now, you were never just the king, in my eyes."

Her words nearly broke him. But he needed her to understand. "I still am more than the king for you. But wanting more, a life outside the crown, that only leads to heartache, Breanna. We are royal. We are—"

"The king and queen of Celiana. I know." Her words were soft, and then she was gone.

CHAPTER SEVENTEEN

"THANK YOU FOR complimenting my dress. I didn't make it. It is the work of a young man named Mathias who is apprenticing at Ophelia's. Yes, he does amazing work. One day everyone will know his name." The queen's voice carried next to him as she shook hands with another guest who was hoping she'd made the stunning purple floor-length gown.

His eyes had bounced out of his head the moment she'd stepped into the room tonight. The first time he'd seen her all day. A common occurrence over the last week. Breanna was never late to her appointments.

As queen, she sparkled. Shining far brighter than he ever did. But the sparkle was fake. The smile plastered in place. Others might not be able to tell, or maybe they could and didn't care.

Her sewing equipment, or was it tools…crafting lingo was foreign to him…whatever they were, were still in his suite. She hadn't touched them all week.

Breanna had become the ghost he'd promised she could be when she took the crown. Separate lives. And he was dying inside.

"If you'll excuse me, my dear. I need to get a drink. Do you want to come?" A soft shake of her head was all she gave him.

Barely an acknowledgment. It stung. A week ago, he'd have leaned in and kissed her. Flitted her away for a break.

Now…a wall of his construction stood between them. "I shall bring one back for you, too."

Breanna nodded, but she never turned her attention away from the guest in front of her.

"She plays the role well." His mother slipped her hand through his arm, walking in step as they headed to the refreshment stand.

Role. The thing he'd wanted Breanna for. What a fool he'd been walking into that compound. A name from a hat. The wrong name. "She shouldn't have to play a role."

"All humans play roles." His mother's voice was soft as she took the glass from the waiter and then lifted it to her lips before looking around. "The question is, do we play the role we want or the one expected of us."

Sebastian didn't bother to hide his chuckle. "We." He downed the drink. "*We* don't get a choice."

His mother tilted her head, her eyes landing on the other side of the room. Alessio and Brie were chatting with someone. Her hand was protectively over the bundle of joy they'd shared with the palace but not the world yet. And the flu that had crippled them had done no harm to the precious little prince or princess arriving in seven or so months.

"They chose." His mother squeezed his hand. "The plan for them was to have a marriage of convenience. A fake love story, just like your father and me. But they chose a different path. A better path." Sadness passed over her eyes but no tears.

"Did you want more with father?" King Cedric only cared about Celiana. It was his greatest trait. And largest failing.

The dowager queen looked at the couples on the dance floor and sighed. "I didn't know there was more to want. But there is, Sebastian. You will always be the king to the country. To the world."

"But." He wanted there to be a but so badly. Needed a but.

His mother's eyebrows lifted. "But?"

Sebastian's ears rang, and heat cascaded over his face. "But in the palace, with the people I love, I get to choose."

Such a simple statement. One his wife had told him over and over again. And then he'd stolen the thing she was keeping for herself. Given it to the country, while she was sick and unable to voice her wants.

Her wants.

Her family had refused to let her have her chosen career field. Her chosen spouse. And she'd stayed happy. Chosen happiness for her sister. Chosen happiness with the husband who'd pulled a name out of a hat.

Been something different in a world that just wanted to see her as a cookie-cutter image. She'd been different, too. Until he'd turned her into what she was now.

"I messed up. God, that doesn't even cover it. I screwed up." Castigating himself might feel good. But it didn't do any good.

He was going to make this up to her. And tell her what he should have told her a week ago. He loved her. Loved Breanna, not the queen. Just her.

"I am stealing my sister." Annie grabbed Breanna's hand as she led her from the never-ending receiving line. "Go dance!" her sister yelled to the gathered and flabbergasted crowd.

Breanna was glad for the reprieve and shocked by the deliverer. "Annie."

"Don't look so surprised. You needed saving."

"And no one else was going to do it." Breanna bit her lip as the bitter words welled up. She'd played the queen all week. The perfect attendant. The person her husband had married her to be.

She'd spent her life looking for the bright side. Grasping

at every silver lining. A week of this was killing her. What would a lifetime look like?

"Sebastian offered you a break."

Breanna shrugged. That was true. Maybe. But being in his presence hurt too much. The man was the king first. He'd made that clear. And she was the queen. Trapped in a life of her own making. She'd make the same choice again, for Annie.

But she'd guard her heart. Some way.

"The king is back in the receiving line."

Back right after I left.

That didn't hurt. It didn't.

Maybe one day it wouldn't, but right now… "That is his job. His purpose."

"And what is yours?" Annie squeezed her hand.

"What?" Her giggle was nerves, but the question landed in her heart. "What?"

"You already said that." Annie led them through the garden. "Repeating it doesn't change my question. What do *you* want? And you can't say anything about my safety or security. You can't say something about your husband. Or a friend. What do you, Breanna, want?"

"I don't understand the question."

"Yes, you do. You're scared of the answer maybe, but you know what you want. Just like I know that Mathias helped with that dress, but it is your design. Your fabric—its reclaimed from a piece you found after the high school dance season. If the young woman who'd worn the original design knew it was on the queen, she'd squeal with delight."

Breanna ran her hand over the fabric. The original gown was a ball gown with so much tulle Mathias and Ophelia had used it to create two wedding veils. "This is mine. Something that is just mine. No one can take—"

The words were out, and Annie hugged her as a sob wracked her body.

"Sebastian wasn't taking it." Breanna squeezed her eyes shut, the truth shaking her. He was trying to give her something. Something she would not have reached for for herself.

"No. He was bragging on you. A weird feeling when no one has ever done it." Annie pushed a tear away from Breanna's cheek. "It's a good thing you have waterproof mascara."

"He should have talked to me." Breanna was grasping. She knew that. She'd have told him no. Told him that he couldn't. Even if part of her wanted the world to know. To display the benefits of sustainability in a world focused on consumerism.

"Yes, but would you have listened?" Annie was always good at knowing her sister's internal thoughts.

So much so that Breanna didn't even pretend to give an answer other than sticking her tongue out.

"That is what I thought." Annie hooked her arm through Breanna's. "Another thought, if you'll allow it."

"Do I have a choice? You didn't used to be so pushy." Breanna squeezed her sister. This was a good thing.

"My sister gave me wings," Annie beamed as she guided them back to the ball room. "But that isn't my thought. It's this: If you didn't love him, would it have hurt? You don't have to answer to anyone but yourself. But our parents can snipe at each other, then push through their next big project as a team because they don't care about each other. They care about themselves and found a partner willing to go along."

"I never said I loved him." Breanna had kept that realization to herself. Even if part of her wanted to shout it to the entire world.

"It is clear to anyone who looks. You love him. He loves you. You've hurt each other. You have two choices now. Live in this role bitter and alone. The country will be fine and most probably won't notice that you two ache being near each other. You will know. Always."

Breanna shuddered. "Or we carve our own paths together."

Annie smiled and pushed her into the room. The receiving line was longer now than it had been when she left. How was that possible? How did so many people want to spend so much time in line rather than enjoying themselves at a party?

Sebastian caught her gaze before she got to her place. She saw more than a few heads turn as he walked past the line he always stood in until the last person arrived. When he'd asked if she'd wanted a drink, she'd purposefully said no to try to get through this faster.

"Breanna." Her name was soft on his lips.

The room was watching, but all she could see was the man before her. The dark circles under his eyes. Her hand went to his cheek. "You don't look like you're sleeping."

"I'm not." He placed his hand over hers. "Dance with me?"

"The line…"

"Dance with me, please?" Sebastian asked again.

"All right." She placed her hand in his.

He squeezed it tightly. "The queen and I are dancing. The receiving line is over. Come join us on the floor. Let's have a good time."

"Over?" Breanna couldn't help the laugh. "Really, Your Highness. I thought that was our duty."

"Breanna, we have roles to play, but I never want to be anyone but Sebastian to you. As for duty, we have been in that line for almost two hours. I want to dance with my wife. Hold her. Tell her how sorry I am. This isn't the right place. I know that. But I can't wait. I don't want to."

Her mouth was open. There were words she should say. But her mind was firing too fast to find any.

"I should have waited to ask about the sewing. I am just so damn proud of you. And I wanted to show you off for something that had nothing to do with the crown. And yet I made it about the crown. I—"

She laid a finger on his lips. "I know. It took me time to

see it, and one very pushy twin sister. But I know. I've hidden all my life. Worried that others just see me as an interchangeable twin. But I don't want to hide anymore. I'm the queen, but so much more."

"And I am the king and so much more."

Her lungs exploded as she cried, "Yes." Several heads turned towards them. Alessio and Brie were watching and grinning.

"In these walls and together, we play the role we want. And I want to play the role of a man who loves his wife. Crown or no crown." Sebastian ran one hand over her cheek as he pulled her closer with the other.

"I love you, too. Just you. Just Sebastian. You could throw away the crown, the palace, everything, and I would still love you."

His head lay against hers. "I love you. I love you. I will never tire of saying that."

"I certainly hope not." Breanna let him spin her around the room. "I love you, too."

EPILOGUE

"AS YOU CAN SEE, needing to rip out a stitch happens to everyone. Even those of us who have created more garments than they can count." Breanna laughed as she held up the seam ripper to the video conference she was running from the sewing room next to their suite.

She hosted one of these monthly and had worked with Ophelia and Matthias to train a few teachers on the art of upcycling. And then worked with thrift stores to ensure that they didn't drive up the cost of their clothes just because more people were thrifting now.

It was amazing to watch her emerge from the protective shell she'd kept herself in.

"Oh, Sebastian is here, do you want to say hello?" Breanna stepped aside as he moved to where the group could see him.

A few members of the class raised their heads to wave, but most kept the focus on their projects. The aura of the throne had diminished in the last year as the people came to see the king and queen more as people than fairy-tale creatures.

Now there was a deeper connection with the populace and a palace that finally felt like a home. All because of the woman beside him—who the class really wanted to see.

"All right. Work your projects, reach out to the mentors if you have questions, and I will see everyone next month." Breanna waved and then clicked off. "One woman found that she doesn't like sewing nearly as much as knitting. So she is taking apart knitted sweaters and reusing the yarn. I didn't even know that was possible. It's really cool; she was talking about it at class when she explained this would be her last one. I need to reach out to Raul and see if he can get her contact information. I bet there are other yarn workers who would be interested in learning her technique."

"I bet there would be." Breanna's drive and care for others was invigorating, "But I didn't barge into my wife's studio on our day off to talk about projects. Well, not true, I came to talk one project in particular."

"You never barge in. You are always welcome." Breanna kissed his cheek. "What project?"

"Our anniversary is coming up, one year." The best year of his life.

She glanced at him as he looked over the fabric. "Our wedding day wasn't the best." He kept his tone upbeat, but he'd always regret that she hadn't gotten the day she deserved.

"Wasn't the worst. We had a good time."

His wife, ready with the silver lining. "I thought maybe you'd like a do-over. A vow renewal, just with our family and friends. To say all the things I wish I could have said at the altar the first time. With a dress and suit made by you?"

"I already have a dress. I think wearing the same one would be a nice touch. But as for a suit…" She bounced as she grabbed her tape measure. "I have the perfect idea. Ooh!" She danced around him, wrapping his body with the tape measure, taking notes.

Sebastian grabbed for her wrists as the tape measure slid up his thigh and her fingers wandered with it. "Still taking measurements?"

Breanna's eyes lit up as she dropped the tape. "I think this would be easier with your pants off."

"My queen." He bent, capturing her lips, then lifting her off her feet. "We have all afternoon free, and I plan to spend it with you."

"In bed?"

"Your wish is my command."

* * * * *

MILLS & BOON MODERN IS
HAVING A MAKEOVER!

The same great stories you love,
a stylish new look!

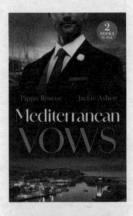

Look out for our brand new look
COMING JUNE 2024

MILLS & BOON

COMING SOON!

We really hope you enjoyed reading this book.
If you're looking for more romance
be sure to head to the shops when
new books are available on

Thursday 6th June

To see which titles are coming soon, please visit
millsandboon.co.uk/nextmonth

MILLS & BOON

MILLS & BOON®

Coming next month

THE PRINCE SHE KISSED IN PARIS
Scarlett Clarke

Awareness prickled over her skin. A sharp inhale brought about a scent of pine mixed with a masculine scent that painted a vivid image of a handsome smile and brown eyes crinkled at the corners.

'Hello.'

Squaring her shoulders, Madeline turned and laced her fingers together as she faced Prince Nicholai.

'Your Highness.'

He looked incredible. Dressed in a navy suit with a silver tie, his hair combed back from his face, he looked every inch the austere royal. His face was smoothed into an expressionless mask that made his sharp features look more like a statue than those of a living person.

Something inside her chest twisted. She missed the carefree smile he'd given her on the rooftops of Paris, the naked emotion in his eyes when they'd met in the alcove. On those occasions, she'd seen the man behind the crown.

Now, though...now he looked distant. Unreachable. Untouchable.

Continue reading
THE PRINCE SHE KISSED IN PARIS
Scarlett Clarke

Available next month
millsandboon.co.uk

afterglow BOOKS

Afterglow Books are trend-led, trope-filled books with diverse, authentic and relatable characters and a wide array of voices and representations.

Experience real world trials and tribulations, all the tropes you could possibly want (think small-town settings, fake relationships, grumpy vs sunshine, enemies to lovers).

All with a generous dose of spice in every story!

OUT NOW

Two stories published every month.
To discover more visit:
Afterglowbooks.co.uk

LET'S TALK
Romance

For exclusive extracts, competitions and special offers, find us online:

- **f** MillsandBoon
- **X** @MillsandBoon
- **O** @MillsandBoonUK
- **♪** @MillsandBoonUK

Get in touch on 01413 063 232

MILLS & BOON

THE HEART OF ROMANCE

A ROMANCE FOR EVERY READER

MODERN — Prepare to be swept off your feet by sophisticated, sexy and seductive heroes, in some of the world's most glamourous and romantic locations, where power and passion collide.

HISTORICAL — Escape with historical heroes from time gone by. Whether your passion is for wicked Regency Rakes, muscled Vikings or rugged Highlanders, awaken the romance of the past.

MEDICAL — Set your pulse racing with dedicated, delectable doctors in the high-pressure world of medicine, where emotions run high and passion, comfort and love are the best medicine.

True Love — Celebrate true love with tender stories of heartfelt romance, from the rush of falling in love to the joy a new baby can bring, and a focus on the emotional heart of a relationship.

HEROES — The excitement of a gripping thriller, with intense romance at its heart. Resourceful, true-to-life women and strong, fearless men face danger and desire - a killer combination!

 — From showing up to glowing up, these characters are on the path to leading their best lives and finding romance along the way – with plenty of sizzling spice!

To see which titles are coming soon, please visit

millsandboon.co.uk/nextmonth

GET YOUR ROMANCE FIX!

Get the latest romance news,
exclusive author interviews, story
extracts and much more!

blog.millsandboon.co.uk